FRIDAY'S
HARBOR

Also by Diane Hammond

Seeing Stars
Hannah's Dream
Homesick Creek
Going to Bend

FRIDAY'S HARBOR

A Novel

DIANE HAMMOND

WILLIAM MORROW

An Imprint of HarperCollins*Publishers*

P.S.™ is a trademark of HarperCollins Publishers.

HarperCollins books may be purchased for educational, business, or sales promotional use. For information please e-mail the Special Markets Department at SPsales@harpercollins.com.

FIRST EDITION

Designed by Diahann Sturge

Library of Congress Cataloging-in-Publication Data has been applied for.

ISBN 978-0-06-212421-0

13 14 15 16 17   OV/RRD   10 9 8 7 6 5 4 3 2 1

For Nolan

Acknowledgments

IT SEEMS APPROPRIATE to begin these acknowledgments by recognizing the place where I found a safe haven and writing space throughout the nearly two years it took to complete *Friday's Harbor:* Amore Coffee on the corner of Smith and Annapolis in St. Paul, Minnesota, my new home.

No newcomer could ever ask for more. Amore owners Cathy Hauser and Nancy Breymeier welcomed me and my husband, Nolan, into their shop, home, and hearts from the day we first arrived here with four cats, two dogs, and no friends or even acquaintances for a thousand miles in any direction. Cathy and Nancy, you gave us the best twin gifts anyone could receive: excellent coffee and unconditional acceptance. And you introduced us to a circle of new friends whom we treasure, not least because they withstood my endless whining at Amore every Saturday and Sunday morning as the early pages of *Friday* failed to take shape. To Becky and Mike Aistrup, Judy Daniel, and Kathy Ernst go my boundless gratitude. And I owe a special thank you to Kathy Farnell and her corgi, Poppy, for amazing acts of friendship through good and bad days, including throwing a ball for our dogs when it was seven degrees below zero and we were down with the flu. You two have been wonderful ambassadors for all things Minnesotan.

I'd like to extend a very special thank you to Brian Joseph, DVM, for helping with several veterinary medical issues. And my deep appreciation goes to Brenda Ambrose for her ongoing friendship and for continuing to champion my work from Bend, Oregon, including providing critical insight into *Friday* character Libertine Adagio. It would not have been the same book without you. To my sister, Laurie Coplin, and mother, Debbie Coplin, go my undying gratitude for reading and critiquing this book—yours were the first and most reassuring words I heard when *Friday*'s first draft was finally done.

My heartfelt thanks go to my greatest supporter and crutch, editor Kate Nintzel, who not only knows her editorial stuff, but also understands exactly how and when to hold the hand of this nervous writer. Kate, there are simply no words to adequately express my gratitude—you have not only kept me sane, but made me a better writer. My thanks, too, to agents Erin Malone and Anna DeRoy for having the backbone I lack, and to Jennifer Rudolph Walsh for creatively answering the question *What's next?*

Finally, I give my heart and soul to my husband, Nolan Harvey, without whom this book could not exist. You believe in me when I don't; you give me courage when mine fails me; you give me up to the voices in my head with incredible grace and fortitude. There is no way to adequately express the depth of my gratitude for sharing this crazy life with me. I love you.

FRIDAY'S HARBOR

Prologue

IN BOGOTÁ, COLOMBIA, *a twenty-one-foot-long, nineteen-year-old, North Atlantic–caught killer whale swam around and around. His small, warm, cloudy pool was the main attraction of a theme park long past its glory days. Because he always swam in a counterclockwise direction, the centrifugal force may have caused the fallen dorsal fin that curled tightly over his back. He was called Viernes—Friday—but he'd been given that name years and years ago and no one left knew why.*

Viernes hadn't lived with or even seen another killer whale in eighteen years, which was how long he'd been in captivity. He wasn't alone, though: he shared his pool with a changing cast of bottlenose dolphins that hectored him mercilessly. His skin was delicately filigreed all over with rake-marks from their teeth: while they could move fast in this small pool, he barely fit, which made him slow and awkward. Whenever he dropped his tail flukes, they rested on the bottom of the pool while his head stayed above water.

It was all too obvious that the killer whale's health was breaking down. Clusters of wartlike lesions encircled the base of both pectoral flippers and formed a black masslike bubbled tar above his tail flukes; he was two-thousand-pounds underweight. But he still performed in shows twice a day on weekdays, three times a day on weekends and in summer, producing on command a series of lumbering bows that splashed the delighted children in the front rows around his pool. Sometimes there were birthday parties, too, which he enjoyed because the children were allowed to come closer, where he could watch them. They were allowed to pet his face and head, and he liked this most of all. When they went home, they took with them cups and kites and stuffed plush toys in his likeness.

In Colombia, he was a star.

From time to time, people from other marine parks in other countries had come to assess his well-being; among the international marine mammal community he'd been considered at death's door for years. They never stayed for long, and nothing ever changed. But now, though he had no way of knowing it, a different kind of committee had arrived at the park's invitation.

The committee members included an older woman in a flowing, floor-length caftan and Nikes who held in her arms a tiny dog that interested Viernes very much. He'd never seen an animal like this before, and he hoped she'd put it down so he could take a closer look, but although they stayed at his pool for an hour or more, she kept it in her arms.

The woman reappeared off and on during the rest of the day, always with the dog and sometimes, but not always, with other people. At the end of the day she returned for the last time, accompanied by a man Viernes recognized from past visits. He and the woman talked and talked and talked, with their arms folded over their chests, considering him. This, too, had happened before.

Viernes drifted to the far side of the pool and closed his eyes.

Chapter 1

WHAT WOULD COME to be known by the Levy family and friends as the Whale Business began that day in Bogotá. The woman in the flowing Egyptian caftan and cross-trainers was Ivy Levy, a longtime board member of the Whale Museum in Friday Harbor, Washington, who had traveled to Bogotá at the very last minute, filling in for another representative stricken with food poisoning.

At sixty-two, by her own admission, Ivy was a boozy old gal with more time and money than she knew what to do with; broad in the shoulders and wide through the beam, canny and keen-eyed, plainspoken and possessed of unshakable convictions—that most people were more stupid than they thought they were; that young people squandered their elders' wisdom; that in all the world only animals were honest; that if God were truly almighty, things would be going a lot better.

Ivy had joined a blue-ribbon panel convened by the Bogotá theme park to solve Viernes's increasingly desperate housing and health problems. In addition to the Whale Museum, the committee included representatives from SeaWorld, the Vancouver Aquarium, Shedd Aquarium, and Sea Life Park—some of the world's preeminent marine parks. The committee's unqualified conclusion was that the whale had run out of time, but that saving him would require an immediate move out of Bogotá. Unfortunately, not a single zoo or marine park would take him. He was a high-profile, failing animal that might die of stress during or shortly after transport, on top of which no one had a pool that was at the same time big enough for a full-grown killer whale and unoccupied, which it had to be in case he arrived with something contagious. And then there was the problem of money—enough to underwrite the crippling costs not only of transporting a killer whale out of Central America, but also of sustaining him through a long and uncertain rehabilitation.

Ivy's last-minute involvement was, as she would put it, a game-changer. She knew what no other committee member did, namely that the tiny Max L. Biedelman Zoo in Bladenham, Washington, had just finished constructing, but not yet populating, a large saltwater pool intended to exhibit porpoises, thereby beefing up the zoo's dwindling revenue stream; that the zoo was run by Ivy's nephew Truman, a newly minted lawyer and recently appointed executive director; and that Ivy herself was exceedingly, excessively, congenitally rich.

In her eyes, the project was perfect.

ON THE SAME day that Ivy got back to her home on San Juan Island, off the northern Washington coast, Truman sat at his computer drafting a staff memo with a subject line reading *No More Fear and Trembling at the Zoo!* Though he had only been appointed zoo director six weeks earlier, he knew the Biedelman zoo very well, even intimately. He'd been its business manager until three years ago, when he'd cast aside his normally pragmatic judgment and colluded in a plot to smuggle the lone Asian elephant, Hannah, out of the zoo. After that, his career in shambles, he'd enrolled in law school. He had just gotten word that he'd passed the bar exam when the Bladenham City Council petitioned him to come back as the zoo's director. The board had just fired his predecessor and former employer, Harriet Saul, and thought he'd be an excellent replacement. Unfortunately, the zoo had also just completed construction of a porpoise pool for which Harriet had advocated tirelessly.

"Nothing brings people in the door like dolphins. Have you ever seen one? Of course not. No one in the Northwest has, except maybe on vacation at SeaWorld," she'd famously asserted during her campaign to persuade—some would say browbeat—the city's mayor and councilmen into approving the expansion. They had eventually capitulated in the face of Harriet's tireless hectoring, but from the moment ground was broken, a year and a half ago, the pool had proved to be a never-ending son-of-a-bitch. The fourteen-month timeline had been determined by Harriet's trademark impatience rather than by its inherent doability, forcing the facility's design and construction to occur more or less simultaneously. There had been issues with the ozone filtration system; with the company responsible for constructing realistic-looking underwater rock work that would make the pool look less like the cement box that it was and more like some undersea grotto; and, most recently and disastrously, with the intergovernmental permits required to move three harbor porpoises from their current rehabilitation facility in Vancouver, British Columbia, to the

Biedelman Zoo. No one seemed able to say when the animals might be transported; the pool had already been filled, making its lack of inhabitants that much more damning. The fiasco had cost Harriet her job, though *Bladenham News-Tribune* reporter Martin Choi allowed her a face-saving quote in which she stated she'd been successfully headhunted by an up-and-coming safari park in Texas.

It was Harriet's dramatic fall from grace that had motivated the skittish Bladenham City Council to woo Truman to take her place, and not only because of the extensive working knowledge of the zoo he'd gained during his tenure as business manager, but also because he had not one contentious or narcissistic bone in his body, which would be a welcome relief after Harriet's disastrous reign. Being the quiet only child of one appellate court judge and one high-profile attorney had made Truman an ideal consensus-builder, though it sometimes gave him a falsely milquetoast demeanor. Milquetoast he was not.

Truman had no illusions about his lack of passion for the law, but he'd worked hard to get where he was, and was looking forward to the relative financial security it offered him and his fourteen-year-old son, Winslow. Working at the zoo, even at the top, would mean a life of basics. Still, he'd invested a lot of himself in the place before he left, and he felt the facility could thrive under a measured hand, so before he could think better of it he'd said yes.

Harriet Saul had been a bully and a micromanager who had so relentlessly ridden her employees that the zoo personnel were paralyzed. When the head of maintenance came all the way across the zoo grounds to request Truman's permission to order toilet paper—*toilet paper!*—Truman had had enough.

I welcome any and all ideas, *he now typed with two fingers,* and hope that you will all feel welcome to bring them to my attention, either in person or in writing. I believe we can bring this zoo to greatness, but it will take the brainpower of every one of us. By the same token, do not feel you need my permission to carry out your job's day-to-day functions. I trust you and your dedication to this zoo implicitly. You were hired for your expertise. Use it.

His phone rang as he was deliberating over whether to change *I welcome* in the first sentence to *I'd love to hear.* On the other end of the line he heard his Aunt Ivy's strident voice say, "I have a proposition for you."

He moved the receiver six inches from his ear.

"There's a killer whale I need you to take in."

"What?"

"That got your attention, didn't it?"

It did.

"Here's the thing," Ivy continued. "There's this poor killer whale named Viernes in an awful place in Colombia—"

"Missouri?"

"Central America."

"Ah."

"—who's been living in a terrible little pool for *years* and now he's dying."

"Okay," said Truman. "I'm listening."

"You need to take him. The zoo needs to."

"You're kidding," Truman said flatly.

"You know me better than that."

Truman sighed. He did. "But there must be facilities much better equipped to deal with an animal like this."

"Evidently not. If you could have seen the poor thing, honey, it would have broken your heart."

"I understand that, but we're a zoo. An *inland* zoo."

"Don't patronize me, Truman," Ivy snapped. "You have a brand-new pool with no one living in it." And Ivy was in a position to know: she'd contributed nearly seventy-five thousand dollars to its construction.

"A pool, yes," Truman acknowledged. "Expertise and staff, no. Right at the moment, we can't even get permits to bring in porpoises, never mind a dying adult killer whale."

"If that pig of yours was dying you'd be more responsive," Ivy said bitterly.

"Now you're just trying to cheer me up," Truman said. Miles, his three-year-old potbellied pig, was always a tender topic.

"What do you mean?"

Truman sighed. "We're fighting over who gets the bed."

"Your bed?"

"Yes. Or, as Miles would tell you, his."

"You let him on the furniture?" Ivy sounded appalled. "Honey, he's a pig."

"I know he's a pig. I know it and you know it, but *he* thinks he's a dog, and dogs get to be on furniture. Ipso facto, he wants the bed."

"Your father told me he goes to some cockamamie doggie preschool," Ivy said.

"First of all, it's doggie day care," Truman said defensively. "*Neva's* doggie day care." Three years ago his girlfriend, Neva Wilson, a career zookeeper, had been fired for her role in the plot to relocate Hannah. In order to be close to Truman, she had stayed in Bladenham and taken a job managing *Woof!* Now

Truman told Ivy, "Second of all, it keeps him socially engaged. Otherwise he roots."

"Roots?"

"It's what pigs do," Truman said absently, mulling. "Look, I'm sorry but I don't think the zoo's in a position to help."

"Oh, that's just a bunch of hooey," Ivy said. "And you know it."

Truman sat silently for a long beat. There were certain resources he could probably tap into, charitable trusts with soft spots for marine mammal welfare projects. "If I approach the board about this—and I'm saying *if*—I have to be able to guarantee them that all the funding will come from donations," he said. "One hundred percent, and up front. There's no surplus in the budget—zero." And that, at least, was the absolute truth.

"I have a checkbook, don't I?" Ivy said irritably. "And frankly, I'm surprised you're not looking at this as a chance for the zoo to get some favorable press for a change. BIEDELMAN ZOO TAKES IN AILING ORCA. Look—I want you to talk to a fellow named Gabriel Jump. He's an expert in this kind of thing. He was down there with me, and he can answer all your questions."

Truman became aware of the vertiginous feeling he always got before he jumped off the cliff of moderation. In words he was sure he'd live to regret he said, "Have him call me."

"Hah!" Ivy crowed. "Now you're talking, baby. Come up this Saturday and I'll have Gabriel here."

It was at that exact moment, Truman would later recall, when he first should have known he was screwed, screwed, screwed.

TWO DAYS LATER Ivy waited in her car for the early afternoon ferry to bring both men to San Juan Island. She watched the ferry pull into the dock, its workers bright in yellow rain gear and safety vests as they secured the boat and signaled the first car to clatter ashore. She'd been watching this unchanging ritual all her life and she was still thrilled to hear the sound of car and truck tires *chunk-chunking* one by one off the steel ramp and onto the asphalt streets of Friday Harbor, the island's only town. She spotted Truman walking off from the upper passenger deck, and she thought what she always thought when she first saw him: that at thirty-nine years old, his pleasant appearance couldn't be more unmemorable, belying the keen and agile mind spinning within. Of all her nieces and nephews, Ivy loved him most—not that she'd ever let that on to him or anyone.

She threw open the car's passenger door and waved him over—as though he could miss her old robin's-egg-blue, four-door Mercedes. With the sort of reverse snobbery practiced by the old-moneyed and the very rich, it was cheerfully and unapologetically down-at-heel: the antenna was bent, the driver's side door was dented, the bumpers showed spots of incipient rust.

Truman put his overnight bag in the car's backseat and hopped in, moving his feet at the last minute to avoid a neat little dog turd on the floorboards.

"Oh, for god's sake," said Ivy, looking down. "Really, Julio!" She pulled a wadded-up tissue from her pocket and with practiced efficiency picked up the turd and tossed it out her window. The culprit was a Chihuahua named Julio Iglesias, with whom she'd been locked in a passive-aggressive warfare for years; he glowered at her from a booster seat clipped into one of the backseat belts. "He must have done that this morning while I was in the drugstore," Ivy said. "And then he wonders why I make him sit back there."

The dog shot Ivy a look of pure contempt.

"Gabriel was on the ferry, too," she told Truman. "He's one of the pioneers of marine mammal husbandry and rehabilitation. People talk about him with a certain degree of reverence." She spotted a weathered pickup matching the description Gabriel had given her, and waved. He waved back, and once she was sure he was following her, she pulled out of the ferry parking lot. By her reckoning, she had six minutes alone with Truman to cogently review the killer whale's plight. Once they got to the house the show would belong to Gabriel.

"Let me tell you what I know," she said, making sure Truman's passenger-side window was fully raised so it didn't dribble.

"Fire away," said Truman, giving her a quick kiss on the cheek. "Hello, by the way."

She waved this away impatiently. "Now, listen. His name is Viernes, which means Friday, and he's in this tiny pool he shares with Satan's dolphins—"

"Is that a species?" Truman said.

"Of course not."

"Oh."

"—and they make him do these shows even though he's thin as a rail and weak. *Cheesy* shows with beautiful girls standing on his head giving parade waves to the crowd while he swims around the pool, and they have him jump out of the water and splash people in the front rows of the bleachers, that kind of thing. Tacky."

"I didn't know animals could die of poor taste," Truman said.

"Don't you mock me," Ivy said, giving him a dangerous look.

Truman subsided. "Sorry. Go ahead."

"His food is crap—whatever they can get cheap at the local fish market, which means it's spoiled a lot of the time, plus there's never enough of it. They're inland like your zoo, so they make seawater with this stuff called Instant Ocean—"

"As will we," Truman pointed out.

"With polluted water?" Ivy said archly. "I think not."

"No," Truman said. "Of course not."

"Well then. The water system's also antiquated, so they can't chill the pool adequately, which means the water's hot all the time. And he's from the North Atlantic, so you can only imagine. He's also got this nasty skin condition, like big patches of warts, which means his immune system's probably shot."

"My god," Truman groaned, "the only thing you haven't mentioned is that he has some inoperable tumor somewhere."

"No, no tumor." Ivy frowned thoughtfully. "At least not that I know of."

She pulled into her driveway, looking in the rearview mirror to be sure Gabriel had made the turn, which he had. She turned off the car but made no move to get out. She sensed that Truman was unconvinced.

"Come on—think about what it could do for the zoo," she said. "You'd be heroes for taking him in. And people would come out of the woodwork to see him. Think of the revenue stream. Anyway, you don't have to take my word for anything," she said. "That's why I want you and Gabriel to talk. This could be the perfect marriage of need and opportunity."

With that she got out of the car, released Julio Iglesias from the detested booster seat, and came around to Gabriel's truck, rapping it smartly on the flank. "Watch out for the dog," she called. "He bites."

But Julio Iglesias had already disappeared under a scraggly rhododendron from which emanated a delicate but unmistakable odor of rot.

THE LEVY ANCESTRAL home was one of the biggest and oldest on the island, shingled and squat above a notch in the shoreline too tiny to have a name. Three generations of Levys had grown up there, including Ivy and Truman's father, Matthew; Ivy had never left. Inside, it was as fusty and worn as a soft paper bag. Braided rugs covered the original fir floors; pine cabinets lined the kitchen walls, and the old upholstered furniture was as enveloping as an embrace. Ivy shooed Truman and Gabriel into the living room. "Get the pleasantries over with," she called over her shoulder, "while I scare us up some coffee."

Truman, being naturally bookish and inclined toward indoor activities, had always loved coming here with his parents. From his favorite sprung old club chair in the living room he'd done a hundred jigsaw puzzles, watched killer whales stitch through Haro Strait, followed seals and sea lions, cormorants and pelicans as they worked the gray water. Nearly everything he valued came from here in one way or another: his love of books and art and living things; his deep sense of family and its commitment to upholding the highest moral standard.

Now, in the light, Truman regarded Gabriel Jump, who had picked up a pair of high-powered binoculars from the coffee table and was peering at something on the water. Though he guessed Gabriel was eight or ten years older than he was, Gabriel was big and powerfully built—the sort of man Truman would instinctively steer clear of on a dimly lighted street; the sort of man to whom Truman, to his deep and lasting shame, had once surrendered his wallet without protest. But now Truman could see that Gabriel's size, strength, and air of easy athleticism would be excellent qualities in a profession that required hefting big, slippery animals in and out of the water. And there was something incongruously gentle about him, too, as he put down the binoculars and held out his hand to Julio Iglesias, who had come mincing in from the kitchen still munching on some rank and festering tidbit he'd dug up under the rhododendron. Ivy followed close behind him, commanding in a deep and no-nonsense voice, "Drop it, Julio. *Drop!*"

Over his skinny shoulder the dog shot her a look of mild amusement, swallowed, and jumped onto her favorite, newly upholstered chair to buff his foul-smelling coat against the seat and armrests.

"Oh, you get down from there *right now!*" Ivy shrieked, flapping her arms at him as though to launch a flight of birds. He gave a leisurely yawn and hopped down.

"Do you see what I have to deal with?" she demanded of Truman and Gabriel.

"You can always give him up," Truman said, just as he'd been saying off and on for the last nine years.

"Never," Ivy said grimly, setting down a tray of thick mugs of coffee. "I'd never give him the satisfaction."

"Here, sit down." Truman offered her his chair and took her soiled one. Once she was settled in, he turned to Gabriel. "I think the best thing will be if you take it from the top—pretend I know nothing."

Gabriel stirred sugar and cream—a surprising amount of both, Truman thought—into his coffee and licked the spoon before putting it down. "I've been looking in on this whale off and on since he got there," Gabriel said. "And for the last few visits I've assumed he'd be dead within a year or two. Every time, he's surprised me."

"And now? Why don't you think he'll rally now?"

"Call it professional intuition. Call it a worsening trifecta of insupportable realities." Gabriel ticked them off on his fingers. "His food sucks. His water quality sucks. And his pool sucks. Nothing new there. But his immune system's beginning to fail, and that *is* new. At some point he's going to reach a tipping point, and when that happens—when, not if—even God won't be able to save him."

"And you think he's at that tipping point now?"

"No—if I thought that, I wouldn't be here talking to you. But I do think he's close. Really close."

"Then why hasn't anyone tried to save him before now?"

Gabriel shrugged, swishing coffee around in his mouth reflectively. "Easy. No market."

"What does that mean?" Truman said.

"It means no one would buy an animal like him, and until recently the Colombians wanted to sell him, not give him away. There isn't a facility out there that would fork out a million dollars or whatever for an animal that's been socially isolated, is out of condition, and let's face it, probably wasn't the brightest bulb to begin with."

"What makes you say that?" Ivy asked.

Gabriel pressed his thumb and forefinger into the inside corners of his eyes as though he felt a headache coming on. "When you collect them in the wild, the smart ones don't end up in the nets."

"Poor thing," Ivy said.

"Plus the market for wild-caught whales in general has dried up. SeaWorld, Loro Parque in Spain, Kamogawa SeaWorld, and

Nagoya Aquarium in Japan—the big facilities have captive-breeding programs that spit out healthy, well-adjusted calves like clockwork. They're in their third and fourth generations of captive-born whales, and they supply the second-tier facilities. There are almost no wild-caught animals left."

"And are captive-bred animals better?" Truman asked.

"You tell me. Captive-born animals never know anything other than a big pool and a buffet of the finest seafood. They have no diseases, no injuries from tangling with boats or fishing gear, and are given the best veterinary care in the world. Then, on top of that, there's the cost of collecting animals, plus getting through the politics and permits—government regulations make it almost impossible to bring in captured marine mammals, particularly killer whales. Most institutions just don't think the headache's worth it. There are diverse enough bloodlines that the captive-breeding population is genetically viable."

"But Ivy tells me he's been in captivity since he was one. Isn't that almost as good as captive-born?"

Gabriel shrugged. "Sure, if he'd been living at a top-of-the-line place like SeaWorld his whole life. He's not—he's living in a third-world slum."

Truman put his head in his hands. "Did you know all this?" he asked Ivy.

"For the most part," she admitted.

"For god's sake, why didn't you tell me?"

"Because if I had, you wouldn't have considered taking him."

"For good reason!"

"That," said Ivy, "is where you'd have been wrong."

The three of them talked well into the night, circling around and around the one point on which Truman wanted assurance that Gabriel was unable to give him: whether the killer whale would arrive in Bladenham alive. Truman rightly pointed out that selling his board of directors on rehabilitating a high-visibility, desperately sick animal would be hard enough. He didn't feel he could recommend taking on an animal that might die on their doorstep.

"Look," Gabriel finally said. "I'd be an idiot or a liar if I guaranteed the transport would go off without a hitch. You have to understand there's a risk anytime you move *any* animal, no matter what shape it's in. But what I can tell you is that this killer whale should have died years ago—*years* ago—and yet he's still alive. He's two thousand pounds underweight, his living conditions are deplorable, his diet is worse, and he's lived like that for *eighteen years*. He's a survivor. My professional instincts are that he'll not only make it to your zoo alive, he'll recover once he gets there. Can I guarantee that? No. Would I tell your board this animal's worthy of a second chance? Absolutely. The bottom line is, you've got a state-of-the-art pool with no animals, and I've got an animal needing a pool."

Truman sighed, considering Ivy, considering Gabriel. "Say I'm convinced that it's a win-win for the whale and for the zoo. We still haven't talked about money. I have no idea what we're talking about here. Tens of thousands?"

Gabriel and Ivy exchanged a quick glance. "More like a hundred thousand," Gabriel said.

"For a year?"

"For the transport. More, depending on what equipment we can borrow."

"There's no way we can come up with that," Truman said.

"Of course there is," said Ivy. Julio Iglesias hopped into her lap, circled, and settled. "*I* have it. You know that. What the hell else am I going to do with it?"

"Let's say the zoo accepts your donation. What about once he's there?"

"You must have budgeted something for the porpoise program," Ivy pointed out.

"Yes," Truman said. "A minimal amount. We knew we weren't ready to open it yet."

"Then I'll make up the difference," said Ivy, pulling on Julio Iglesias's ears absently. He put on his Greta Garbo eyes.

"Ivy—"

"No!" snapped Ivy. "Don't try to talk me out of spending my money on something I believe in! Honey, if you could just have seen him." She swirled her fourth whiskey and soda around and around, finally looking toward Gabriel in a mute appeal.

"I'm sorry—I don't know what more I can tell you," he said to Truman. "I'd be glad to come talk to your board if you want."

"But you honestly believe if he stays down there he'll die?"

"No question about it. I give him six months. A year, tops."

"And if you can rehabilitate him, how much more time is he likely to have?"

"We don't know how much his life expectancy has been compromised by the crappy food and environmental conditions, but it could be years—a lot of years. Ten."

Truman sat with his chin in his hand, gazing out the window into the darkness. Finally he said to Gabriel, "I have one condition if I take this to the zoo's board."

"What?"

"That you head up the project—set up the transport and rehabilitation program and run it at the zoo. Without your experience and expertise, we could never take something like this on."

"You mean would I work for you?"

"Yes."

"No."

"We'd pay!" Ivy assured him. "Whatever you'd ask for, we'd pay you."

"What if we hired you as an independent contractor?" Truman asked. "I'd recommend that the board consider a twelve-month, renewable commitment."

"Oh, honey, say yes!" Ivy spilled Julio Iglesias out of her lap to lean forward. "Please say yes."

Gabriel looked at her for a long time, considering. "I'll give you one year. If the whale isn't healthy by then, he never will be."

Ivy clapped her hands. "You won't be sorry. I know you won't."

THE DEBATABLE WISDOM of opening the zoo's doors to the sick killer whale circled around and around in Truman's head long after Ivy saw him off on the next day's midmorning ferry. The zoo was a small affair with roots in a turn-of-the-century menagerie privately owned by Maxine L. Biedelman, daughter of a Pacific Northwest timber magnate. Max, as she'd insisted on being called, had willed the property and all her exotic animals to the City of Bladenham upon her death in 1958. A wildly eccentric woman, she had lived in a hilltop mansion and housed her animals along winding pathways on the grounds in whimsical thatched and conical huts and pastoral barns, many of which still survived. By all accounts she'd been an eminently practical woman despite her penchant for swashbuckling and cross-dressing, and Truman suspected she would have advised that in the wake of Hannah's loss, the rest of the animal collection should be found new homes and the zoo closed.

Once back in Bladenham, Truman methodically worked through the steps he'd need to take in presenting the project to the zoo's executive committee, a collection of small-town businesspeople more familiar with running family-owned diners and auto-body shops than high-profile rescue projects with budgets manyfold greater than their net worth. Before he and Gabriel Jump had left Ivy's house that morning, they'd drafted a written summary of the killer whale's current living conditions, health profile, relocation requirements, and budget, including the cost of one year's rehabilitation at the zoo. At the same time, Ivy wrote a letter of commitment to send back with Truman, guaranteeing that she'd cover any or all of the expenses that exceeded the zoo's preexisting budget for completing and operating the porpoise pool. If the committee showed interest, both Gabriel and Ivy had agreed to come to Bladenham and meet with the full board.

Feeling the morning's cup of strong coffee turn to pure acid in his gut once he was back in Bladenham, Truman decided to drive straight to *Woof!* to caucus with Neva Wilson. The doggie day care business was housed in an empty Chevy dealership on Main Street, fueled by the bottomless guilt of commuters who spent twelve-plus hours each day working in and commuting to and from Seattle. As Truman walked in he saw his pot-bellied pig, Miles, mixing with the large-dog group. Three years ago, when the pig was just a piglet, Truman had given him to Winslow as an eleventh birthday gift, for reasons that had been sketchy even at the time and which he'd often come to regret. The animal snored, wheezed, and passed eye-watering gas; he scared the living daylights out of the UPS driver and the mail carrier. On the bright side, Truman no longer received unwelcome door-to-door entreaties to buy

Girl Scout cookies, candy bars, magazine subscriptions, holiday wreaths, or any other merchandise formerly inflicted on him. And the pig was utterly devoted to him and Winslow. When they ate dinner every night in the kitchen he lay on his horse-blanket bed on the other side of a baby gate and mooned over them like a middle school girl. He was not as fond of Neva, whom he apparently viewed as competition, but he adored going with her to *Woof!*, and had a well-established social circle there, composed of several pit bulls, a Rottweiler, two chocolate labs, and a mastiff. The pig was black and white, sparsely haired, and blessed with an unsinkably sunny nature. The minute Truman walked in Miles sensed his presence and, beaming with porcine delight, tip-tapped over on the absurdly small hooves that reminded Truman of the bound feet of Chinese women. Truman patted his shoulder and told him what a good pig he was, and then suggested, with no hint of irony, that he go back to playing with his friends. Miles grunted his boundless adoration and trotted off.

The noise of two dozen dogs was nearly deafening, even once Truman was in Neva's small office with the door closed. Both he and Winslow had unusually low auditory thresholds. Neva fished out a couple of noise-dampening foam earplugs from her top desk drawer, handing them to him wordlessly across her desk.

At thirty-six Geneva Wilson was small but mighty from years of hard physical work with large animals, and gingery in color, manner, and temperament. She sat across the desk from him in her messy office, wearing canvas army boots, a stained sweatshirt, and cargo pants, her thick red hair indifferently knotted and stabbed through with a chopstick. Truman thought she was the most beautiful woman he'd ever seen.

"Your aunt is reacting out of sentimentality," Neva said after he'd given her a synopsis of the situation. "And pity. You know that, right?"

Yes, Truman knew that. He remembered a number of unlikely orphans that Ivy had been sheltering when Truman came to visit—not just the usual assortment of hapless domesticated animals, but an owl, a nutria, and once, memorably, a male raccoon that washed its food in a dog dish Ivy had put on the floor expressly for that purpose, its splint tapping on the kitchen linoleum like a pirate's peg leg. The animal had long, thin, artful fingers that deftly rolled pats of butter into perfect little balls the size of BBs before dipping them in the water. "She's always had a soft spot for lost causes," he said now. "Take Julio Iglesias. But it doesn't make her wrong."

"You know that politically having a cetacean—"

"A what?"

"A cetacean. A whale or dolphin."

"Oh."

"—having cetaceans brings the nuts out of the woodwork. They don't mind so much when you have fish or lesser marine mammals—seals, sea lions, even walruses—but the anticaptivity people go absolutely nuts over whales and dolphins. You could end up being picketed day in and day out for years. I'm not saying it's going to happen, but it could."

"We're helping an animal in need—a deserving animal. Our motives are purely altruistic. It seems pretty straightforward to me."

Neva smiled at him fondly. "You're so naïve. You haven't seen it, but people lose their minds when it comes to killer whales. I'm serious. You can't bring a killer whale here without making headlines. Ask anyone at SeaWorld."

"Are you saying you don't think we should take him?"

"I'm saying you have to be prepared for whatever is slung at you. If you're okay with that, I think it's great."

Truman laced his fingers together, regarding her thoughtfully. "This man Gabriel Jump thinks the whale's only got six months to a year, at the longest, if he stays where he is. I wish I didn't know that, but I do. Ivy's promised to pay for everything, if necessary. I've got Gabriel's commitment to work with us for at least the first year. Would you be willing to come back to the zoo and work with him? It means Marla will have to find a new manager." Marla was the owner of *Woof!*

"Honey, I don't have any marine mammal experience. I'd kill to work with him, but I'll be more of a liability than an asset, at least in the beginning."

"He says if you can work with elephants, you can work with killer whales."

Neva pressed Truman's arm across the desktop. "In that case, of course I'll come back. You know there's no one I'd rather share a frying pan with than you."

FROM *WOOF!*, TRUMAN drove to the Oat Maiden, a cheerful garage sale of a café in downtown Bladenham. It had gouged and rippling old floorboards, silvering mirrors, mismatched chairs, and heavy wooden tables brightly painted with celestial, aquatic, safari, and Bicycle-playing-card motifs in primary colors. Sitting at a back table waiting for him was Samson Brown, a seventy-one-year-old black man, tall and trim, his lined face testifying to a life of hard work cheerfully undertaken, including forty-one years of caring for Hannah. Truman shook his hand before sitting down.

"So what's this all about?" said Sam. "You got yourself a whale now?"

"Maybe. Yes. And he's right up our alley," Truman said wryly. "He's sick, he's needy, he's in a terrible facility, and bringing him here might kill him. Oh, and once he's here he'll be alone, just like Hannah. On the other hand, he'll certainly die if he's left where he is now."

"I don't believe the good Lord ever meant for death to be the right choice if there's an alternative," said Sam. "You got a way to move him?"

"Yes."

"You got a place to put him once you move him?"

"Yes."

"Somebody got the know-how to take care of him once he's here?"

"Yes."

"Anybody else want to do the same thing?"

"Evidently not."

"Sounds like you got your answer."

Truman smiled. "It sure does. The reason I asked you to meet me is, I want to know whether you'd consider helping."

"Be glad to help, but I don't know a thing about killer whales. Come to that, I've never even seen one except on TV. Can't swim, either."

"I'm sure there are ways you can help that won't involve heavy physical work. Or swimming. You could be more of an observer. And you could work strictly on an as-needed basis. The main thing is, I'd feel a lot better about all this if I knew we could tap into your experience."

"You don't even need to ask that. It's yours anytime you want it."

"Thank you," Truman said. "From my heart."

A young girl approached the table wiping her hands on her apron. "I'm so sorry. We're backed up in the kitchen. Can I get you something?"

"I'll have whatever he's having," Truman said, indicating Sam's glass of iced tea and pizza slice. "And tell your boss we said hi." Johnson Johnson was another member of Hannah's band of schemers, a man of infinite shyness, few words, and great artistry, who had also recently taken over the Oat Maiden. The round table at which they were sitting was a piece of his work, painted with bright animals from the African veldt and Serengeti Plain in a never-ending circle.

"Perfect," said the girl and trotted away.

"He's doing a good job with the place," said Sam. "Who'd of thunk? Your mom and dad still helping him?"

"From time to time," said Truman. "Mostly it's Neva, though. She does the books, helps him order things if he gets too busy, generally keeps an eye on him."

"She's a good woman."

"That she is," Truman agreed. "That she is." The waitress set Truman's drink and a slice of pepperoni pizza in front of him and trotted off again. Truman absently rubbed his thumb through the condensation on the side of the glass. "You know, you said once that Max Biedelman thought the worst thing she'd ever done was to bring Hannah here. I keep thinking about that."

"She didn't feel bad about giving shug a home," Sam corrected him. "What she felt bad about was not being able to give her another elephant. She gave her me—that's the best she could do except for those couple of years right at the beginning with old Reyna."

"So was that a mistake?"

Sam shrugged, stirred his ice cubes around in his glass with a straw. "She always kept on forgetting shug would've probably died over there in Burma. Elephants have to earn their keep over there, and who'd have hired an elephant who was blind in one eye? And she was just a little bitty thing even after she was full-grown. Don't get me wrong, it would've been nice if the girl would have had another elephant or two to play with, like she does now. But it's apples and oranges—there wasn't anything like that back then. I think Miz Biedelman gave her a fine life. Girl never wanted for anything, always had the best food, never had a sick day in her life except for her foot sores."

Truman frowned. "But she was alone here. This whale will be, too. Does that make it morally wrong to bring him here?"

"Never heard anybody say the right thing is the perfect thing."

"Max Biedelman—what do you think she'd do, if it were up to her?"

Sam grinned. "Heck, that's easy. She'd have already packed her bag to go down there and get him."

ON JUNE THIRD the board of directors of the Max L. Biedelman Zoo voted unanimously to bring the killer whale to its facility as soon as arrangements could be made. Three weeks later, Truman and Gabriel departed for Bogotá to transport him home.

That evening, Ivy and her older brother, Matthew Levy, sat at their respective dining room tables, Ivy on San Juan Island and Matthew in Bladenham, connected via Skype. Matthew, a retired state appellate court judge, had drawn up a legal agreement between Ivy and the zoo, even though he had told Ivy numerous times and in no uncertain terms that she was poised on the brink of a headlong dive into a yawning black fiscal hole. His had always been the Levy family's voice of pragmatism, even when he was a boy, and over the past several weeks he had spent significant energy trying to dissuade both Ivy and Truman from undertaking such a high-risk, low-yield project. Then, when it became clear that he wouldn't prevail, he crafted as ironclad an agreement as he could between Ivy and the zoo, protecting her assets as much as possible, not only in the event of the animal's untimely demise, but also in the case of a flood of surplus revenue.

While Matthew reviewed the terms of the agreement, Ivy filled in the Os in the document's immaculate title page with a leaky ballpoint pen and drifted away, wondering if she should burn a little sage to cast out any negative energy and attract positive energy to the whale transport scheduled for first thing the next morning.

"Are you listening?" she was suddenly aware of Matthew asking her.

"Apparently not," she said. "Honey, can't we do this when I come down there tomorrow?"

"You should have done it a week ago. Until you and the zoo president sign this, you're not protected," Matthew said. "And neither is the zoo. You don't seem to realize how vulnerable you are."

Ivy sighed.

"Look, let's just get through it. It won't take long."

And so he took her, page by numbingly tedious page, through an agreement between her and the Max L. Biedelman Zoo (henceforth referred to as THE ZOO) that laid out the conditions under which she (henceforth referred to as THE DONOR) would and would not finance the ongoing care and maintenance of the killer whale Viernes. Under the agreement, she would be the sole contributor to a trust, blah blah blah.

It wasn't that Ivy didn't care; as a rule she managed her significant fortune very attentively. Her grandfather Levy, the family patriarch during her childhood years, had always stressed that it was her duty to support the Needy, including food banks, homeless shelters, and women's centers; the Greater Good, including the local police and fire departments; and Our Cultural Legacy, including the Seattle Art Museum, Portland Art Museum, and several local arts and historical organizations—all just so much bland philanthropic toast, though worthy. Ivy had dutifully supported all of them in generous, though reasonable, ways. This gesture, right now, was the one and only rash financial move she had ever made.

"And you understand that you will have a vote—not the controlling vote, but a vote—in decisions affecting the animal's ultimate disposition," Matthew was saying.

Ivy snapped to. "What does 'ultimate disposition' mean?"

"It means any decision affecting where the animal lives. In the event of his relocation to another facility, for example."

"Why on earth would he be moved to another facility?"

"I don't have the faintest idea," said Matthew. "I'm just trying to cover all possible eventualities."

"Oh." Ivy subsided, nibbling at a cuticle. "You know, if I were you I'd have opened a vein years ago."

He gave her an exasperated look. "Ivy, Truman has told me these things can become very political. We want to be sure you have a say, if and when it becomes necessary to move him."

"Can I have the controlling say?"

"I've looked into that. It would be illegal, given that the zoo is a municipal organization. Besides, giving you the controlling interest in a specific animal's welfare would set a terrible precedent."

"Well, I don't see why," Ivy said sullenly, aware that she was just being difficult. "It's not like I want to have anything to do with the sloth or the dik-diks."

"Nevertheless."

"Oh, all right."

In fifteen minutes more, Matthew directed Ivy to sign there, there, there, there, and there, and the ship of Ivy's impulsivity set sail.

Chapter 2

"ÁNDALE!" SHOUTED A beautiful young Colombian trainer as Viernes labored around his small pool one last time. Twenty thousand people had come to the park and the surrounding streets to say good-bye to their national treasure. The trainer made the sweeping gesture she had used to cue him in a thousand shows. *"Ándale, Viernes!"* Sleek and showy in a short-sleeved black and purple wet suit, her long hair flying behind her, she clapped extravagantly as a TV crew edged closer.

After the show Gabriel and Truman stood side by side watching Viernes hang inert in the water. Truman asked the Colombian trainer if, for Viernes, this torpor was normal. The trainer laughed musically and dismissed the question with a coquettish roll of her eyes. "Of course," she said. "That is because he is lazy."

Truman could feel Gabriel stiffen, but he said nothing as the trainer left the pool. Once she was gone Truman asked him, "Is she right? Is he lazy?"

"He's in an advanced state of starvation."

"Don't they realize?"

"No. In all fairness, they've never worked with a healthy killer whale, so they don't have anything to compare him with."

Truman nodded. He'd quickly come to rely on not only Gabriel's wealth of knowledge, but also the pragmatic remove he was able to maintain. Especially when compared with what Truman was coming to understand as his and Ivy's rampant anthropomorphizing, Gabriel's was a cool, dispassionate eye.

The next morning came early. Truman reported to Viernes's pool at three o'clock to find Gabriel and the beautiful young trainer already busy smearing the whale's back and dorsal fin with zinc oxide to protect them from drying out during the trip to Bladenham. Then they guided him into a custom-made canvas sling with cutouts that allowed his pectoral flippers to poke through. A construction crane lifted the whole apparatus out of the pool and lowered it into a huge fiberglass box until he was three-quarters submerged in icy freshwater. Once the box was secured on the flatbed, the truck heaved into motion, airport-bound.

Standing beside the box on the flatbed, Truman was stunned to find the streets packed with throngs of noisy well-wishers who'd come to say good-bye to their beloved whale. They cheered and wept along the entire six-mile route; what would ordinarily have been a ten-minute drive took an hour and a half.

For the next twelve hours Truman silently chanted what was fast becoming his mantra: *please don't let him die.*

ON ORCAS ISLAND, one ferry stop away from Ivy Levy's San Juan Island home, animal communicator Libertine Adagio was trying to sort out a new animal presence in her head. Animals never understood the concept of *here* or *me;* they simply *were;* so pinning down a location or even identifying the species always took time—sometimes a lot of time. Right now she sensed that the newcomer was male, captive, and ill, but that was all.

She padded around her kitchen in an old Friends of Animals of the Sea T-shirt, a pair of sweat socks flapping off the ends of her feet like clown shoes. At forty-seven she was small, frail, and mousy-headed. She loved her tiny cabin, covered as it was with rose trellises, garden art, and ferns, its seven-hundred square feet cozy and warm, furnished and decorated over the years with bright colors, gay rugs, and art in every medium. From her front window she was able to watch the ferries come and go, carrying commuters, food, dry goods, construction materials, walk-on visitors, and produce distributors. She knew most of the small island's other year-round residents, but the nature of her work and unpredictable travel schedule meant that she kept mostly to herself. This little house was the one place where she never minded her isolation.

She had only arrived home the night before from two weeks in Las Vegas. Initially she'd gone there to visit an elderly aunt, but she'd stayed on behalf of a small troupe of white tigers in an animal show that her aunt had insisted, with the single-mindedness of early-stage dementia, that Libertine take her to see. Despite a dislike of captive animal exploitation that bordered on horror, Libertine had given in, and the first tiger on stage had conveyed to her that the troupe wasn't being well cared for. With a sinking heart Libertine had taken her aunt home, tucked her into bed with a shot of neat whiskey, and gone back to the casino in time to attend the last show of the evening. The tigers had been belligerent and disorganized until Libertine had finally conveyed that if they couldn't straighten up and focus, she was going home. They had fallen into line, of course (in her experience tigers were twitchy, emotional creatures with surprisingly low self-esteem and a tendency to bully and then fold under pressure), but the casino's management hadn't been at all interested in what they—that is, she—had had to say. In the end a public protest was the only option. Knowing she was an abysmal protester—like the tigers, she tended to fold under pressure—she'd tried to convince a local, terrestrial animal offshoot of animal rights group Friends of Animals of the Sea to commit people and resources, but the few people who'd responded had milled around in a lackluster way for a week or so and then drifted off. After the eighth day Libertine had been alone on the sidewalk, brandishing a different sign each morning—STOP THE DOLPHIN EXPLOITATION NOW! and IT'S NOT ENTERTAINMENT, IT'S ENSLAVEMENT! and the satisfyingly cryptic IT'S JUST WRONG! Her face burning with every step, she'd made herself stay in Las Vegas for the entire endless week as penance, pilloried for her failure to incite zeal.

While her lack of finesse with people was well-established, her understanding of animals was effortless and keen. She'd never intended to become an animal communicator but she'd heard animals in her head for almost as long as she could remember—particularly captive animals, and especially captive marine mammals. Her earliest marine mammal memory was during a visit to a dank little aquarium in Seaside, Oregon. An old, blind harbor seal had sought her out to communicate that some of the animals were on the brink of death because of substandard living conditions, and she asked if she could do something about it. She was only six; there was, of course, nothing she could do. But the old cow, who called herself Auntie, had stayed with her off and on until her death six years

later. It had been Auntie who had taught Libertine to quiet her
own thoughts so she could hear the thoughts of others: not
only whales, dolphins, porpoises, seals, sea lions, and walruses,
but also more prosaic, terrestrial animals—cats, big and small,
dogs, cows, and the occasional rodent (though if truth be told
she'd never enjoyed the company of rats or mice very much:
they focused almost entirely on their babies—babies, babies,
babies; always too many and always too often).

While Libertine drank a cup of tea she listened to the morning news on NPR—including a spot about a sick killer whale's
journey that day from a facility in Colombia to the Max L.
Biedelman Zoo in Bladenham. As though on cue, the animal
presence from the day before stirred in her consciousness.
Though it was a long shot, Libertine thought with a sinking
heart that this animal might be the one that had come to her
last night. She pulled on jeans, the single clean shirt left in her
closet, and her warmest sweater, a beautiful Fair Isle given to
her several years ago by a grateful alpaca breeder for settling a
rebellion in the herd that had been caused by the sire, who was
a narcissist and a troublemaker.

Exhausted but resolved, she threw an armload of dirty
clothes into the suitcase she'd just unpacked the night before—
surely there were Laundromats in Bladenham. Then, before
she had time to think better of it, she fired up her Dodge Dart,
a car of significant age and mechanical infirmity, and headed
out to the accompaniment of an alarming new chatter in the
engine.

LATE THAT AFTERNOON, Truman found his prayer had been
answered: the killer whale was still very much alive. Truman
wasn't able to see him, but he could hear Viernes exhale two

or three times a minute. As they had in Bogotá, hundreds of
people lined the streets of downtown Bladenham, watching
the truck creep by. Viernes seemed to sense that the trip's end
was near and squirmed in his canvas cradle, sloshing water up
and over the side and giving a mighty exhale that blew spray
high above the box's walls. A collective cheer went up and
people waggled signs saying THANK GOD IT'S VIERNES and WE
♥ KILLER WHALES!

As the truck made its final turn through the zoo gates
Truman saw a half-dozen television trucks lined up along the
curb, their satellite dishes raised and ready to broadcast. His
head swam as momentary déjà vu took him back to Hannah's
final day, when the zoo grounds swarmed with reporters and
cameramen, and transmissions were carried unedited and live
like wartime news from the front. He recognized not only
most of the reporters and camerapeople, but the engineers and
technicians who made such live transmissions possible. As he
waved from the truck with what he hoped was a modest greeting, Harriet Saul's dismissive voice played over and over in his
head: *oh please*.

In Bogotá he and Gabriel had handled the crush of press
together at Viernes's small pool, and Truman had been relieved
to find that Gabriel handled the media very capably. He'd told
Truman in private that he didn't have much use for reporters, especially television talent, but he'd given no hint of that
this morning and, presumably, would give no hint of it now.
As during most of the trip, he was sitting above Truman on
one corner of the whale's box, listening to Viernes breathe.
Twice—before takeoff and again after landing—he'd dumped
a half-dozen blocks of ice into the water, explaining to Truman
that the icier the water, the more comfortable the whale: if the

canvas sling chafed, he'd be less likely to feel it. And despite the fact that Viernes had been parboiling in Bogotá for years, he was a North Atlantic–caught whale, and there the water ran cold.

WHILE GABRIEL AND Truman were moving the whale, Ivy Levy was driving south to Bladenham from Friday Harbor. The journey hadn't had an auspicious start: she'd missed the 9:05 ferry because she'd had to stop at the vet's office to pick up a fresh tube of steroidal cream for Julio Iglesias, whose nervous eczema was flaring up.

Long car trips, in Ivy's experience, were like sensitively wired bombs. One minute you were driving along admiring the scenery in perfect tranquility, and the next, *bam,* you were revisiting a bruising litany of failures and humiliations dating all the way back to grade school. Halfway to Bladenham she found herself juggling the unexploded mines that was her history of poorly chosen life companions, of whom Julio Iglesias was only the latest example. When she was just four she'd insisted the family take in a tough old feral tomcat named Socks Afire. He'd had one eye, six teeth, a stumpy tail, and body odor, but in her eyes he'd been perfect. In retrospect she had extracted him from what had probably been a blissful old age spent mousing and whoring, consigning him to living out his waning days in a gingham-lined laundry basket in the pantry. He'd died a year to the day after his incarceration, his spirit utterly broken by her acts of love.

Despite the fact that none of her family members shared her wide-open if misguided heart, Socks Afire was followed by a long procession of strays and indigents that had included, besides the raccoon Truman remembered, dogs, cats, bunnies, and birds. Her mother referred to these animals serially as Your Latest Victim. Even her brother Matthew, who had been a loving boy before he grew up to be a lawyer, didn't share her enthusiastic embrace of Nature's down-and-out. Unfortunately, Ivy's poor early-life choices in the animal kingdom had been later destined to repeat themselves among men, yielding an unbroken stream of sad sacks, sponges, creeps, and leeches. Matthew's wife, the cool and elegant Lavinia—she of the delicate bones, tidy hips, flawless pearls, and Yankee pedigree—occasionally hinted that Ivy herself might be at fault, which at least partially explained why Ivy had, from the minute they'd first met fifty-some-odd years ago, thoroughly and secretly disliked her sister-in-law.

But she was extraordinarily fond of her nephew Truman, in whom Ivy's genetic legacy had bloomed three years ago when he'd first acquired Miles, and secondly saved Hannah. He was an even-tempered man with the capacity to love simply, openly, honestly, and deeply. His awful ex-wife, Rhonda, whom Ivy had loathed, had had a gift for wielding criticism like a scalpel. Ivy was much fonder of Truman's girlfriend, Neva Wilson, who was practical, matter-of-fact, and clearly and fiercely loved both Truman and his son, Winslow.

In order to interrupt the downward flow of thoughts Ivy switched on the car radio, set to the local public broadcasting station. To her astonishment she caught the last of a story about Viernes's journey to Bladenham. She pushed her speed to just under eighty and sped south on the final stretch of highway like an avenging angel, reaching Bladenham forty-five minutes before Viernes did. When the whale and entourage finally pulled up to the facility, Ivy was waiting on the open pool top in a light drizzle, wearing a rain slicker, scarves, boots, hand- and foot-warmers, and holding a half-filled thermos of hot coffee and brandy. Julio Iglesias glowered from a Snugli strapped to her chest.

THE PORPOISE POOL was built on the footprint of Hannah's old elephant barn and yard, at the bottom of a gentle slope. Most of the forty-foot-deep pool was above ground, supported by a cement block casing. The public side had an underwater viewing gallery with four huge acrylic panes that looked into a deep-sea landscape of realistic rocky hills and valleys. On the opposite side were an equipment bay, food preparation area, locker room, huge shower and toilet, and an office with an oversized window looking into the pool.

As soon as the truck stopped, Gabriel sprinted up the stairs to the pool top so he could guide the crane operator from overhead. Truman was right behind him. He came over to greet Ivy, who was struggling mightily to pull herself from the depths of an old Adirondack chair she'd brought with her from San Juan Island.

"Can you help me get out of this damned thing?" she huffed at Truman. "Otherwise I'll still be here come Christmas." She took Truman's steadying arm. "It's humiliating, I'll tell you that. In your mind you're thirty-five, and then this." Once on her feet, she freed Julio Iglesias from the Snugli and watched him pick his way along the pool top stiff-legged. "He's proud," Ivy said. "But he's no spring chicken, either."

"Hardly any of us are," said Truman.

"So it went well?"

"Very well."

"And he's still breathing?"

"Still breathing. He tolerated the trip better than Gabriel thought he would. He just went to sleep for most of it. Thank god."

"Whew," said Ivy. "I'm as nervous as a cat."

"Here we go, folks!" Gabriel called out, and then a crane lifted Viernes high above the pool. He hung suspended forty feet above the street, illuminated by powerful TV lights and strobing flashes, dripping and calling out in a high, thin, eerie wail. And in the absolute quiet of the moment Truman felt a sudden, nearly overwhelming sadness: that there were orphans in the world, that there were those who deserved better than they got, that isolation could be so profound. This alien creature without hands or ears or facial muscles amplified a hundredfold the incredible hubris of enforced captivity. Maybe in their misguided kindness they had made an appalling mistake.

And then the moment passed.

Chapter 3

BY THE TIME Libertine arrived in Bladenham—a town she'd never even heard of before that morning—the zoo was closed, but brilliant lights shot into the rainy sky from that direction. The streets that were closest were barricaded, so she pulled into a side street and parked, then dug around in the backseat until she came up with a jacket that had once been waterproof, and struck out on foot. By trial and error, she found herself in front of a barricade just a block away from the huge, bunkerlike facility and pool. There she joined a small crowd trying to catch a glimpse of the whale.

At first Libertine found it hard to concentrate with so many people around, but when the crane lifted Viernes higher and higher, still in his sling, all sound ceased. As he dangled in the air, dripping, his high, keening call sliced through the air and her heart like a razor.

And then, as he was swung over the pool and out of view, a great cheer went up from the people both inside and outside the fence, indicating that he'd made it safely into the water. When she looked around, nearly all the faces were wet with tears.

As SOON AS Viernes was safely installed, Truman trotted back to Havenside, once Max Biedelman's mansion and now the zoo's administrative center, riding the crest of a clamorous wave of reporters, videographers, beta cameras, boom microphones, and sound engineers from all the local and regional media outlets, plus Reuters, the Associated Press, Northwest Cable News, and CNN.

Truman invited everyone into the ballroom, a vast space that had hitherto been used only for charitable events, the annual zoo volunteers' banquet, and the occasional wedding. He'd had the foresight to have a podium and microphone set up ahead of time, and though Gabriel hadn't arrived yet, Truman self-consciously moved to the front of the room and introduced himself. Knowing the last news deadline of the night was fast approaching, he gave what he hoped was a fast-paced but thorough review of the zoo's facility, Viernes's history, and the zoo's hopes for a total rehabilitation that would give the whale an infinitely better, never mind longer, life. He was just about to take questions from the media when the crowd parted enough to allow Gabriel through, still wearing his wet suit.

"Ah," Truman said. "Here's the man of the hour. Let me introduce Gabriel Jump, who's pulled this rescue together in record time, and who will be in charge of Viernes's rehabilitation. He'll give you a status report on the whale's condition first, and then he can answer your questions."

Over the course of the endless trip north, Truman had developed a deepening respect for Gabriel. Hour after numbingly cold hour he had radiated a profound, even shamanlike inner calm. Now, he briefed the gathering with an enviably easy informality and humor. As soon as he wrapped up his remarks the room burst into furious action: cell phones came out, laptops bloomed, TV crews and engineers scrambled to edit B-roll, and both Truman and Gabriel were assaulted by reporters eager for exclusive quotes and sound bites. But what they wanted most was access to the top of the pool so they could get close-ups of Viernes, which Gabriel had been adamant about denying for at least twelve hours, or until he felt Viernes was stable and settled in. Truman offered instead to open the underwater viewing gallery to the media. Though the pool's depths were dark, the TV lights might lure him to the enormous windows, where the photographers and videographers would have a chance to see him up close.

SATISFIED THAT THIS whale was the animal that had summoned her, Libertine checked into the town's cheapest motel, the Slumber Inn Motor Lodge. The room was damp, cheaply paneled, and poorly lit, and from its uncomfortable straight chair she looked bleakly at the bank balance on her laptop. Even at twenty-eight dollars a night, she didn't know how long she'd be able to stay. She fervently wished that the people who doubted her abilities—which was to say, nearly everyone—realized what it cost her to follow her calling. She had to forego health insurance, a working dishwasher, nice clothes, and lasting friendships, living—barely—on a miniscule amount of money from her mother's life insurance policy and the rare stipend paid her by the U.S. Fish and Wildlife Service or comparable state agencies when she was able to convince errant seals and sea lions to move on from public docks and fish ladders. She wore thrift-store clothes and offered up her hair, naturally a dull shade of brown shot with gray, to the students at a beauty college in Anacortes, which explained why she often had hair in innovative colors and styles. The students loved her because it was widely known that they could try out anything and she wouldn't bitch or cry, not even when the processing went haywire—which, given the students' lack of experience, it often did. *Libby*—they'd say, handing her from student to student like a favorite if well-worn doll—*you're the best*.

People tended to assume that Libertine had always been single, but it wasn't true. When she was just eighteen she'd married Larry Adagio, her life's love and an earnest plumber who had taken great pride in his work. Libertine thought if he'd known a heart attack would kill him at twenty-seven, he'd at least have taken comfort from the fact that it happened while he was on the job, in a client's bathroom, at the base of a new quiet-flush toilet.

In her dreams she and Larry were together again, and neither of them had aged a day. They were usually running errands, earnestly debating whether Mini Wheats would hold him until his midmorning break. He'd had the metabolism of a chipmunk; every workday she'd sent him off with a stack of sandwiches like playing cards: peanut butter and jelly, baloney and American cheese, liverwurst and Swiss, cutting little hearts into each top piece of bread with a doll-sized cookie cutter she'd found once at a garage sale. It was still one of her most precious possessions and she wore it sometimes on a chain like a necklace.

He'd been the one and only man who'd found her beautiful. When he died she'd begged to have his corneas transplanted in place of hers so for the rest of her life she would always see the world through his eyes—he'd been an organ donor, it would have been be completely legal—but the doctors had refused and the corneas had ended up going to someone else. She'd thought she would die of grief, and the thought had brought her comfort, but instead her mother had come down to Salem, packed up their apartment, and brought her and their little dachshund, Nelson, back to Libertine's childhood home, a tiny post-war house in Portland, Oregon. She'd stayed in bed for three weeks, until finally her mother had lost her temper and said, *This poor dog misses Larry, too, but you don't see him moping. Get up and take him for a walk.* She'd gotten up.

She shut her laptop and rubbed her face and eyes. It dawned on her that she hadn't eaten a real meal since yesterday. She remembered seeing a café as she came into town, so she packed up her computer, pulled on rubber boots and a rain poncho, and by backtracking found it five blocks away: the Oat Maiden.

The minute she ducked inside she was enveloped in the aromas of childhood: pizza and chocolate chip cookies. The look of the place was playful—boldly painted tables with mismatched, whimsically painted chairs. It was empty except for a young couple huddled over a computer.

A tall, thin man in his early forties with wild hair and a wistful overbite appeared with a menu. "It's just starting to get dark out," he said helpfully, "so, you know, you might want the celestial table."

Libertine followed him to a round table beneath the streaming plate-glass window and said, "Oh, it's beautiful!" And it was: a midnight-colored sky was painted with extraordinarily detailed stars and an aurora borealis spanning the whole table. The man smiled shyly. "Did you paint this?"

He nodded, nervously rolling the paper menu into a tube. "You don't have to sit here if you don't want to." He gestured vaguely around the room.

Impulsively, and because she had a quick premonition that

she'd be here often, she said, "How about I sit here this time, and then every time I come in I'll sit at a different table until I've been at all of them."

"Okay," he said, and bolted back to the kitchen, apparently having scared himself with his forwardness.

Libertine reviewed the menu, which consisted of thirty different pizza combinations and fifteen different types of chocolate chip cookies. Though she hoped the man who'd first helped her would come back—it was a rarity to meet someone even more socially awkward than she was—a young woman came to take her order instead.

"Are you here for the whale?" she asked Libertine.

"Pardon me?"

"A killer whale came here today from South America. Colombia—is that South America or Central America?"

"South America," Libertine said. "I think I just saw him arrive. Can you tell me anything about him?"

"Well, for starters they say he's dying, but how bad can he be, if they're bringing him all the way here?"

"Didn't this zoo used to have an elephant?" She remembered a flap a few years ago about a lone captive elephant at a small Washington zoo she'd never heard of before.

"Yep," the waitress said ruefully. "That's us."

By the time Libertine was finished with her meal—and it always amazed her, even after all these years, how little time it took to eat when you were by yourself—she was exhausted enough that even the prospect of her awful motel room didn't seem so bad. Without another sign from the whale that had brought her so far from home, she fell into bed and a deep, dreamless sleep.

ONCE THE LAST of the media were outside the perimeter fence and tucked into their satellite trucks for the night, and Neva and Sam had gone home to get a few hours' sleep, Gabriel brought a bucket of fish to the pool top and put Viernes through a few familiar behaviors. The physical exertion would help him shake out any lingering muscle kinks and fully exercise his lungs, both important after remaining motionless for so long during transport. It would also give Gabriel a chance to better assess his condition.

As he watched, Viernes plowed through the water, cheating on his speed-swim by shaving the corners and riding the wave he'd created with his own initial momentum. He was slower than any killer whale Gabriel had ever seen except for the very old or dying. He was winded after a single lap around the pool, and his body jiggled when he exerted himself, even as emaciated as he was; he had almost no muscle tone. When he exhaled, he blew gobs of dirty snot. After Gabriel had given him the last of the fish—nutrient-rich fresh herring of a quality he might not have tasted since his capture off the coast of Norway eighteen years ago—Viernes swam to the far end of the pool, put his head in the corner, and closed his eyes.

Gabriel folded his arms across his chest. Viernes's recovery would be a long, long road.

Chapter 4

NEVA AND SAM came back to the pool at eleven that night, so Gabriel could get some rest. As soon as he left, Viernes approached them, propping his chin on the side of the pool.

"C'mon," Neva said to Sam. "You want to get your hands on him as much as I do."

They stepped into the four-inch-deep, foot-and-a-half-wide wet walk that went all the way around the pool, and reached out tentative hands. Neva had touched a beluga once, years before, and distinctly remembered it feeling exactly like a wet hard-boiled egg, smooth and slippery. Viernes, on the other hand, felt more like a black olive, at least where he wasn't covered with warty outgrowths. He opened his mouth wide, which Gabriel had told her meant that he was inviting them to touch his tongue. Neva reached in hesitantly, patting it, which Gabriel had said he liked. His eyes went piggy with pleasure.

"No molars," said Sam, assessing the perfectly conical teeth that interlocked, top and bottom.

"They don't chew. Their teeth are meant to bite and tear."

Sam regarded him for a long beat. "Does he look dangerous to you? They're supposed to be really dangerous, but I'm not seeing it."

"Well, he's sick," Neva reasoned. "Plus he's used to people. Hannah was supposed to be dangerous, too."

"Baby girl wouldn't have hurt a fly," Sam said loyally. " 'Cept maybe that Harriet Saul."

"I'm sure it's the same with Viernes. Truman was telling me a story they told him down there, about how a toddler fell into his pool once and he picked her up on his back and saved her. No one knows if it's true or not, though."

Viernes exhaled—*poooooo-siiiiip*—making them both jump up and backward. "Aren't we a fine pair," Sam said, and Neva laughed at them both.

At 10:00 P.M., to their surprise, Ivy Levy joined them on the pool top, an outraged Julio Iglesias still pinned inside the Snugli. Sam and Neva had set up two beach chairs, and were watching Viernes nap on the far side of the pool. When Sam saw Ivy he hopped up and offered her his chair, which she waved away.

"Hey, buddy," Neva greeted Julio Iglesias. He showed her his teeth.

Ivy watched Viernes for several minutes. "He's a good-looking whale, all things considered," she said, pulling a silver flask from her coat pocket. The air was cold, and a light drizzle was falling. "Sam?"

"No, ma'am. I made it a point a long time ago not to drink while I'm working. Never was much of a drinker anyway."

"Well, I always was one for a good brandy on this kind of night. I have plenty to go around, if you change your mind."

Neva declined, too. "But can I ask you a question?"

"Fire away."

"What made you decide to help him?" Neva asked. "He's incredibly lucky."

Ivy considered this for a long beat before saying, simply, "He needed someone to."

"Clearly," said Neva. "But why you?"

Ivy shrugged, yawned. "You've met Julio Iglesias, so it should be pretty obvious that I'm a soft touch, especially when it's not in my own best interests. When they found Julio he had cigarette burns all over his body and he *still* had—has—the chutzpah to push my buttons every single chance he gets. Give me a fighter, and I'm a pushover, and the longer the shot, the better."

Neva laughed. "Well, I'd say this whale's luck has turned."

"If he lives."

"Oh, he'll live," Neva said. "When you've been a zookeeper for as long as I have, you can spot the survivors a mile away. Gabriel knew it, too, or he'd never have let you take him on."

As Ivy decided to accept the offer of Sam's chair after all, softly grunting as she settled into its tight embrace, Gabriel was standing buck naked before the mirror in the bathroom of his hotel room. He was more tired than he'd been in a long, long time, and peered at a clutch of blisters in his throat with a halogen field flashlight. Pustular tonsillitis. He'd probably had it for a couple of days already. He normally kept antibiotics with him but he'd used them all up during the just-completed consultation with a rehab facility outside Beijing, which had lasted not the planned-for four days but nearly three weeks. He'd flown directly from China to Bogotá to finalize transport arrangements, and then from Bogotá to Bladenham to accept a food delivery of a pallet of frozen herring and make sure the pool was fully equipped with dive gear, nets, cleaning hoses, brushes, and other paraphernalia. He'd conned a prescription for amoxicillin from his long-suffering physician, who'd given up insisting on seeing him every time he prescribed meds years ago, when Gabriel had come back from Tierra del Fuego with a deep-tissue infection from a dolphin bite that had nearly cost him his leg, but he hadn't had a chance to fill it yet. In the meantime he shook a small handful of expired amoxicillin tablets from a bottle Ivy had unearthed from the back of her medicine cabinet before driving down.

Physical infirmity didn't faze him. He was powerfully built and blessed with an unusually high pain threshold. His skin was filigreed with a ghostly network of past bites, punctures, cuts, and stitches, some of which he'd sewn himself while in the field. Right now his upper right chest was a lively greenish-yellow from nipple to collarbone from a blow he'd taken while maneuvering one of the dolphins into a medical pool for a checkup.

He popped ibuprofen like breath mints.

He pulled on jeans and a T-shirt and hung on to the promise of coffee to get himself out of the hotel room. He had no idea what time it was, though it appeared to be near dawn. Time and place were more abstract to him than to most people. Before his initial trip to Bogotá, where he met Ivy, he'd been in Thailand, Holland, Portugal, and Peru. The gift that was his regular bowels could not be overrated.

Now, staggering out into the early morning, he headed directly for a Dunkin' Donuts he'd seen yesterday on the way through town.

"Hey," a cheerful young black woman greeted him from the drive-through window. Beads on her million braids clicked nicely as she turned her head to smile at him. "How you doing, honey?"

"I'm breathing. Can you tell me what day of the week it is?"

"It's Friday, baby. You have a rough night last night?"

"Yeah. I'd like four cups of coffee."

"All for you?"

"You bet."

"Why don't I just get you a thermos? We're running a special."

"Even better. And I'd like a dozen mixed doughnuts, too. Your choice." Once she'd left the window, he blew his nose out the open car door, field-style.

She returned with a torpedo-shaped thermos and a doughnut box that she handed him through the window. "You just drink that coffee, hon, and it'll fix you right up."

"Promise?"

"Promise. And if I'm wrong, you just tell the good Lord Rayette sent you."

LIBERTINE AWOKE AT dawn to find the smell of cigarette smoke wafting through the motel's cheaply paneled walls and Viernes throbbing in her head. Animals were often represented by colors, and this morning his was the purple of bruised and aching things—as could be expected after such a long journey. She was exhausted, too, but resolute, especially because in daylight the motel room was even more horrible than it had been in the dark. She took a shower as quickly as she possibly could, vowing to buy flip-flops before nightfall, and then set out to find something to eat. She drove through Dunkin' Donuts, buying not only a thermos of coffee, but also half a dozen doughnuts—figuring the combined sugar and caffeine should be enough to fuel her at least through early afternoon.

"You're the second one this morning who's bought a thermos," said the young woman at the drive-through. "Must be a lot of tired people in town. You here to see that whale they just brought to the zoo last night?"

"How did you know?" Libertine asked. She briefly wondered if she should get someone at the beauty school to do her hair in a million tiny braids like the young woman's, then dismissed the idea. White people wearing black hairstyles usually just looked silly.

"I don't know you. A town like this, you usually know just about everyone. You're like the ninth stranger to come through in the last fifteen minutes," the young woman said.

"Really?"

"Uh-huh. Most of them said they drove all night to get here. You ask me, I say that's some kind of crazy."

"Well, whales do that to people sometimes."

"Yeah?" The young woman shrugged. "I guess I just don't see it."

"I wish more people felt that way," Libertine said, taking her paper bag of doughnuts and the cylinder of coffee. "If they did, there wouldn't be as many killer whales in captivity."

"Yeah, well, you can bet those people at the zoo are seeing dollar signs all over the place."

"Oh, I'm sure they are," Libertine agreed.

Provisioned, she drove back to the zoo. At the ticket booth she asked whether visitors could see Viernes yet. "No, not today," the woman said regretfully. "We hope you'll be able to see him by Friday, though."

"There's no way I can see him sooner than that?" Libertine asked. "I came all the way down from Orcas Island."

The woman looked genuinely dismayed, but stuck to her

guns. "We have lots of other wonderful animals I'm sure you'd enjoy."

"That's okay—maybe I'll come back later." Libertine went back to her car and drove along the fence line until she reached the back entrance she'd found last night. The street wasn't cordoned off anymore, so she pulled onto the gravel shoulder. If the whale wanted to communicate with her, at least she'd be nearby. Making the best of it, she set up a nylon camp chair and TV tray she kept in her trunk for just such occasions, brought out her bag of doughnuts and coffee, and filled her mouth with sugary goodness.

WHEN GABRIEL MADE his way aloft he found Ivy yawning uncontrollably and Neva and Sam sitting in flimsy webbed lawn chairs.

"So how's our boy?" Gabriel asked, setting his thermos and box of doughnuts down on a nearby cooler top.

"He's the coolest thing ever," Neva said. "Sam and I both think so." They caught him up on how much Viernes had eaten, how much he'd slept, how he'd interacted with them during their watch. While they talked, Viernes swam over and rested his chin on the side of the pool, watching.

"Here's a question for you both," Neva said to Gabriel and Ivy, exchanging a quick look with Sam. "We both feel kind of self-conscious calling him Viernes. I mean, if you speak Spanish it probably trips off the tongue, but we were wondering if we could call him Friday. Since that's what *Viernes* means."

"Run it by your boss, but it's fine with me." Gabriel looked at Ivy. "Do you care?"

"Not as long as he doesn't."

"Truman?"

"The whale. It *is* his name."

"Believe me, he won't care," said Gabriel, crossing his arms and watching the whale watch them. "So he didn't move around much overnight?"

"No, hardly at all," said Neva. "Except to eat."

Gabriel nodded. "He's probably stiff from yesterday. We'll get him moving in a little while."

Ivy clapped him on the back and said, "Unless there's more excitement coming that I'm not aware of, this old lady's going home for a nap."

"Take one for me, too," Gabriel said.

"I wish I could," Ivy said earnestly. "You look like you could use it. Here, maybe this will help." She dug around in her purse and pulled out two pill bottles, which she shook like maracas. "This one's the amoxicillin, and this one's Vicodin from my personal stash." She toasted him with the bottle of painkillers. "To your health."

"And yours," Gabriel said, toasting her back. "Sweet dreams."

Once Ivy was gone, they all stood for some minutes in the sort of ragged silence that comes from sleep deprivation and adrenaline depletion. Friday drifted away, using minimal energy, opening and closing his mouth.

"Why's he doing that?" Sam asked.

"Because he can," said Gabriel, yawning.

"They ever scare you?"

"Who?"

"Them," Sam said, nodding toward the whale.

Gabriel took a big swig of coffee before saying, "I've been working with them for a long, long time, so no, not in the way you probably mean. But you have to be on your game. Just because they're tractable doesn't mean they can't kill you. They can play with you to death. They can keep you underwater too long. They can pin you to a wall, or whack you with one good kick of the flukes. Let your guard down and you can be dead—and they may not even realize what they've done."

Sam regarded Viernes for a few minutes. "You believe animals have souls?"

"Do I believe they're just like us only in funny clothes? No, I don't believe that. I think it demeans what they are in their own right."

"That's not the way I meant it, exactly," Sam said. "When I first met shug—that's Hannah, my elephant—I thought she was just about the funniest-looking thing I'd ever seen. But only that one time. After that she was always beautiful in my eyes. I believe it was her soul I was looking at every day."

Gabriel face softened. "Then yes, by that definition I believe animals have souls."

"I loved shug with all my heart. Still do. I don't know that I'll ever feel that way about another animal."

"You'd be amazed at how much the heart can hold," Gabriel said. "Have you been down to the sanctuary to see her?"

"Nah. Me and Mama don't travel. She doesn't need me anymore. If I showed up it would only confuse her. Girl's got what she needs. They send me DVDs from time to time, and in every one of them shug's smiling. It does a heart good to see that."

Gabriel nodded. "Saying good-bye's always tough."

"I only had to do it that once. Shug was my one and only. I never meant to be a zookeeper like you and Neva. I came back here from Korea in 1955 and next thing I know, I'm working for Miz Biedelman, and then she gives me shug to take care of. Put the fear of God in me, I'll tell you that. I always did wonder what she saw in me, to trust me with the girl."

"You're a natural animal person," said Gabriel. "That's what she saw."

"Don't know about that—shug just taught me what she needed me to do, and I did it. And now she's made friends with the other elephants down there. I was sure glad to know she still could after all those years by herself. We worry about the girl, Mama especially. You worry about this whale at all?"

"What, his being alone?"

Sam nodded. "It hurts my heart to see."

"Would I rather see him with other killer whales? Sure. But don't forget that for him, it's normal to be the only one. And it's been like that nearly his whole life. At least here he won't have dolphins beating him up."

"Well, I guess that's something," said Sam.

"Yes," said Gabriel firmly. "It is." His face gentled. "Why don't you go home, you and Neva, and get some sleep? It's been a long night."

"Think I will," said Sam, at the exact moment Neva said, "Hell, no."

Gabriel shrugged. He assumed she'd been a zookeeper long enough to know about pacing herself; and if she didn't, she was about to learn it in a hurry.

TRUMAN CLIMBED TO the pool top half an hour later, clad head to foot in what he termed his Media Suit: Max L. Biedelman Zoo turtleneck, Max L. Biedelman Zoo polar fleece sweater, Max L. Biedelman Zoo jacket. He clapped Gabriel on the shoulder. "You get some rest?"

"Yes. You?"

"I absolutely passed out. I don't remember the last time I was that tired. Probably when Miles was a piglet." He stood beside

Gabriel and Neva, watching Viernes watch them, his chin resting on the wet walk at their feet.

After a few minutes Neva turned to him and said, "Let me ask you something. We've talked it over, and we want to call him Friday instead of Viernes. It feels a lot more comfortable than, you know, pronouncing a Spanish word badly. Gabriel and Ivy both say it's fine with them."

"Sure," Truman said. "Since it means the same thing. Not that anyone seems to know why they named him that in the first place. So yes, go for it."

Neva turned to the whale and said, "From now on, you're Friday. We figure it's okay with you."

Gabriel reached into the stainless steel bucket he'd brought upstairs with him and held out to Truman a herring as big as a shoe. "You want to feed him?"

Truman shuddered. "No, thanks—I'm fine watching."

"He has sensory issues," Neva explained to Gabriel. "The slime, the scales, the smell."

Gabriel tossed the fish into Friday's open mouth. "Good thing you never wanted to be a zookeeper. On a gross-out scale, I'd say it's right up there with rendering-plant operators and slaughterhouse technicians."

"Both honorable professions," said Truman loyally, but Neva was right: he could barely bring himself to make meatloaf because of the feel of raw egg and uncooked hamburger meat being squished through his fingers. To change the subject he peered down at the whale. "What's that coming out of his eyes? It looks like, I don't know, goo."

"They're viscous tears," said Gabriel. "They protect his eyes from salt."

"Clever," said Truman. The first time he'd seen Hannah he'd

found her just as unfathomable, with her thick skin, tiny eyes, and trunk as dainty as a demitasse spoon, capable of picking up a single grape. "Killer whales are pretty much the Cadillacs of cetaceans," Gabriel was saying. "Elegant, well engineered, powerful, smart, perfectly designed for their environment. If you want to work with the ocean's top predator, work with a killer whale."

"Do you still feel he'll be ready to have the gallery open by the weekend?" Truman asked. "People are already calling— lots and lots of people. I've asked Brenda to draft a press release, but we won't send it until you're sure he's ready."

"No, barring something unforeseen, I'd say he'll be ready," said Gabriel. "It'll give him some stimulation—he's never seen people from underwater. Any stimulation is good at this point."

Truman's security radio crackled, and Brenda's voice came over. "Reception for Truman."

"Go for Truman," said Truman, feeling like an idiot. He'd tried to introduce a more casual radio protocol, but it wasn't proving to be popular.

"Hey, I've got some radio talk show guy on the phone from Florida. He wants to know if he can interview the whale. Ha ha. They all think they're comedians. What should I tell him? Over."

"I'm on my way," said Truman. "Tell him he can interview me. Over."

"And out," said Brenda.

"What?"

"You're supposed to say "Over *and out*" when you're done. You were done, right?"

Truman sighed. "I was, yes. All right—over and out."

"Over and out."

"Bye," said Truman. He hooked the radio onto his waistband and saw Neva's look of barely contained amusement. "What? She's an excellent receptionist," he said.

"I didn't say a word," said Neva. "Did I? Not one word."

BY ELEVEN O'CLOCK Libertine hadn't received any communiqués from the killer whale and she was crashing from all the sugar and caffeine. Her hands shook and her heart raced as she loaded her things into the trunk and returned to the Oat Maiden.

Through the kitchen door she spotted the tall, thin man she'd met yesterday, but he didn't come out. Instead, the girl who'd waited on her last night came over to the table. "Hey! You're back! Did you find your way to the zoo?"

"I did."

"Was he there?"

Where else would he be? But Libertine said simply, "He's not on exhibit yet. They said it would be a few days."

"Oh. Well, that's too bad."

Libertine gave her order and traced the pandas, zebras, killer whales, and penguins that circled her tabletop in black-and-white formal wear. At a table nearby, Libertine noticed a middle-aged woman eating alone. She was dressed in running shoes and a floor-length Egyptian caftan, and she seemed to be taking an unusual and lively interest in Libertine. Libertine kept her eyes on the tabletop, hoping the woman would have the good manners to stop staring, but instead she stood up and came over.

"I hate eating alone, don't you?" she said cheerfully. "It's always hard to know where to look while you're waiting, and then if you bring a book you spend so much time trying to seem absorbed in it, you don't retain a thing so you read the same page over and over. How about eating together?"

Libertine could feel a hot flash coming on—she really wasn't any good at situations like this one. Fortunately, the woman didn't wait for a response, returning to her own table just long enough to retrieve her table setting and two large totes, one of which seemed to have been wobbling.

"Hot flash, huh," she said sympathetically, setting the totes between them and gesturing at the flush Libertine could feel spreading up her neck and igniting her face. "Poor you." She pulled a wine bottle out of one of her bags. "Whenever I hear about a woman who's bludgeoned someone to death or bitten off his body part or something, I'm positive a hot flash was involved. I'm not kidding. Mine were that bad."

Libertine tugged the neck of her shirt a little higher, but the woman had moved on, extracting a wine glass and corkscrew from her bag. "I keep telling Johnson Johnson that he needs to get a wine and beer license, but until then it's BYOB. Would you like some? I know where they keep the glasses."

Libertine accepted. It might take a fortifying glass or two of wine to get through this meal. The woman hopped up and fetched an empty water glass.

"So are you from here? I'm guessing no."

"No. I mean, yes, I'm not from here."

The woman looked at her with lively amusement. "So what brings you to Bladenham?"

"A client," said Libertine, hoping she'd let it go at that.

"A client? So you're, what, a lawyer?"

"Oh, no. I'm an animal communicator."

"Really! You're a psychic?"

"I'm a communicator." A tiny head popped out of the wobbling tote. The woman reached in and extracted a furious Chihuahua. "This is Julio Iglesias," the woman said. "I know he's not supposed to be here, but he pees on things if I don't take him along. Well, to be fair, he pees on things when I *do* take him along, too, but less often."

For the first time since this whole peculiar encounter had begun, Libertine smiled.

"Of course, given your line of work you probably already know all that."

"No. The animal has to choose to communicate with me."

"Well, give him time. He probably has a whole list of complaints."

At that moment Julio Iglesias started to make a run for it, but the woman snatched him back and clamped him under her arm like an old handbag. His ears went flat.

"I'm Ivy Levy, by the way."

"Libertine," said Libertine, "Adagio."

Their pizzas arrived and Ivy immediately began picking off, blowing on, and then handing over bits of sausage to the dog, who appeared to be mollified. She looked up at Libertine. "You do know that Libertine means someone who's debauched."

Libertine slumped. "My mother thought it sounded swashbuckling, like something a woman pirate might be called."

"Well, I guess you don't develop psychic powers because you've had an *easy* childhood," Ivy mused. "So what animal?"

"Pardon me?"

"You said you were here for an animal. Which one?"

"I'm not sure yet," Libertine said. "It's complicated. When an animal gets in touch with me, I'm seeing them from the inside out, so to speak. It takes some time to figure out the rest."

"Well, sure." Ivy repinned Julio Iglesias, who had been trying to edge out from under her arm. "Here's a coincidence—I'm here for an animal, myself. A killer whale."

"Oh?" Libertine straightened in her chair.

"His name is Friday and he was dying in a horrible little pool in Colombia, so we brought him up here. He just got here yesterday." Ivy must have seen something in Libertine's face, because she said, "He's your animal, isn't he?"

"I don't know," said Libertine, but of course she did.

AFTER LUNCH IVY met Truman on the pool's metal stairs as Truman was coming down and Ivy was going up. Julio Iglesias was securely lashed into the detested Snugli.

"Everything okay?" she asked.

"He's fine, according to Gabriel. By the way, I've been meaning to tell you you're welcome to stay with us. I hope you knew that without my having to say it."

"Thank you, honey, but I doubt Julio Iglesias would do well with a pig in the house."

"Miles is a very dog-friendly pig. It's one of the benefits of his spending so much time at *Woof!*"

"I'm sure your pig would be fine—he's not the one I'm worried about. Julio Iglesias can be very ugly." She lowered her voice to a meaningful whisper. "He bites." Raising her voice, she added, "I think it would be best for all of us if I just stay with your folks. We've already worked it out."

"Well, the offer stands any time you're here."

Ivy nodded, but she'd apparently moved on. "So it looks like our boy came through the trip with flying colors."

"Evidently—Gabriel says he's probably a little stiff and sore, but he's eating well. I'm actually more concerned about Gabriel than I am about the whale. I saw him taking pills, and he looks awful. I didn't want to pry, but you might ask him about it."

Ivy knew this already. "He has strep or something—he won't talk about it."

Truman was appalled. "But he spent the whole day in forty-degree water."

Ivy shrugged. "If you ask him, he'll just tell you he's better."

"Better than what—death?"

Ivy patted Truman's cheek. "Don't fuss, dear. He's a grown man."

IVY SAW SAM on the far side of the pool, sitting in her splintery old Adirondack chair. She went over, bent to give him a quick hug, and waved away his offer of the chair. "It'll do me good to be on my feet for a little while. If you sit for too long, things tend to seize up."

"Yes, ma'am, they do."

"Don't ma'am me, Sam. We've known each other for years."

Grumbling, Sam said, "I called Miz Biedelman 'sir' until the day she passed. I was brought up to be respectful."

"Well, get over it."

"Yes, ma'am."

Ivy released Julio Iglesias from the Snugli and set him down on the pool deck. She saw Neva and Gabriel come upstairs with a bucket of fish. Gabriel walked to the edge of the pool and clanked the handle of the bucket to bring Friday over. Neva came to stand by Sam and Ivy.

"What do you think of our little boy?" Ivy asked her.

"He's amazing. I'm in love. I'm totally in love."

"Well, of course you are. Is he settling in?"

"Gabriel says he is, but frankly, I haven't learned my way around this model yet."

"You have to wonder whether he's homesick," Ivy mused. "Don't you wish we could explain it to him? Honey, would you be an angel and bring that lawn chair over?"

Neva fetched the nylon-webbed chair and set it beside Sam, who had once more offered the Adirondack chair unsuccessfully. Ivy sat with a low grunt, unwinding the empty Snugli and tucking it beneath her chair. "Getting old's a bitch, isn't it?" she said to Sam.

"Ain't it just."

They watched Julio Iglesias making a minute inspection of every square inch of the pool top, peeing here and there, while across the pool Gabriel scratched Friday's tongue. Ivy said to Sam, "What do you think Max Biedelman would have made of all this?"

Sam sat with that for a minute or two. "She'd be glad we were helping an animal in trouble. That's what she did with shug when she was just a baby and an orphan. Bet she'd never have thought of bringing a whale here, though. I think she would have been pleased with the rescue part, I just don't know if she would have put money into building something this big and this ugly. Seems like an awful lot of money for one animal."

"She did that for Hannah," Ivy pointed out.

Sam reflected for a moment before saying, "You know, she told me once that having shug sent over here was the biggest mistake she ever made."

Ivy was surprised. "Why? I always thought it was the height of generosity. Wasn't she badly wounded? Hannah, that is, not Max Biedelman."

"Yeah. Shug's mama was killed and baby girl lost an eye. She was just a little bitty thing, too."

"So what part of that was a mistake?"

"Miz Biedelman had an old elephant, Reyna, when shug first got here. She took real good care of her, too. Not many people knew about old Reyna—that was before Havenside was a zoo. She died a little over a year after shug got here. Miz Biedelman knew Hannah would be alone after that, at least where elephants were concerned. Said more than once that what she'd done was irresponsible."

"So she hired you as a companion."

"Yes, ma'am, she did."

"So Hannah wasn't alone."

"Well, I guess you could say that."

Neva interrupted, touching Ivy on the arm. "Excuse me, but Gabriel's going to put Friday through a session, and I want to watch up close, so I'm going around to the other side."

"A session?"

"A workout session. Think of it as physical therapy."

"Is he up to that?" Ivy asked, surprised.

"Gabriel?"

Ivy smiled. "Him, too, but no, the whale."

"I'm sure Gabriel will go easy on him, but it's important to keep him moving so his lungs stay clear, especially since his immune system's compromised."

"Ah," said Ivy. She watched for a couple of minutes as Neva circled the pool. Then she said to Sam, "She seems like a very nice young woman."

"She is," said Sam. "Saved shug, even though it ruined her career."

They both watched as, across the pool, Gabriel gave a hand signal and Friday swam slowly away to circle the perimeter. When Friday reached him again, Gabriel blew a high tweet on a whistle and tossed a few fish into the whale's open mouth.

Ivy regarded Sam. "Do you think you'll help out here? Only occasionally, I hope. After all, you're a carefree retiree now."

Sam cut his old eyes at her shrewdly. "I'm an old man with diabetes and free time, is what I am."

"You're better now, aren't you?"

"Mama makes sure I behave myself. I'll tell you what, though. It sure would be good to have a doughnut from time to time," he said wistfully and then brightened. "We send a twenty-five-dollar Dunkin' Donuts gift card down to shug every month."

"I'm sorry I didn't meet her before she left," said Ivy. "To tell you the truth, the only thing I really know about elephants firsthand is that at a certain point in time, their feet made dandy wastebaskets. My uncle had one in his study."

Sam blanched.

"Of course, they didn't know any better. In fact, I think he shot that elephant on a safari way back around 1912 or so. But here's justice for you—he lost his own foot in World War I. No bad deeds go unpunished or whatever the hell that saying is."

"No good deed," said Gabriel, who'd finished working with Friday and come around the pool to their side.

"I like mine better," said Ivy, and then to Sam, "Anyway, this whale's going to need someone just as much as Hannah did, if he's going to be alone here for the rest of his life."

Neva had joined them, too, and now said, "You don't know that."

"Tell that to him," Ivy said, inclining her head toward Gabriel. "He seems to think so." He'd stressed that to both Truman and Ivy at their first meeting in Friday Harbor, and had been reiterating it periodically ever since.

The others looked at Gabriel expectantly. Gabriel just

shrugged. "If no other facility wanted to take him on because of possible disease transmission, they certainly won't send one of their whales here as a companion."

"What about a rehab animal?"

"How many rehabbed, wild killer whales can you name that are in captivity?"

Ivy looked at Neva, Neva looked at Ivy, and Sam looked from one to the other.

"None, is how many," said Gabriel.

"Why is that?" Neva asked.

Gabriel shrugged. "Just doesn't happen. Even if they're injured they can probably still hunt until they either recover or die. They only come up on beaches if they're going to drown, and even so no one's going to see it. Plus the cost of bringing in an injured adult whale is astronomical. No one's going to do it."

"Well," said Ivy. "So much for *that* discussion." She hauled from her tote a long, circular knitting needle and a length of completed afghan in a Fair Isle pattern. "Do you think he's okay up here?" she asked Gabriel, gesturing to Julio Iglesias, who was still picking his way prissily around the perimeter of the pool, keeping well back from the four-inch-deep wet walk.

"As long as he doesn't fall in. We might want to find a flotation vest for him, though, just in case."

"Oh, he has a very healthy respect for the water," Ivy said. "He fell off a dock once and scared the living shit out of both of us. I was thinking more along the lines of whether our little boy might eat him."

"Is he a fish?" Gabriel asked.

"No."

"Does he look or sound like a fish?"

"No."

"Then there's no reason to think Friday would eat him. *Play* with him, yes; eat him, no."

"Play with him how, exactly?" Ivy said.

"Don't know. It might be fun to find out, though." Gabriel gave her a wicked smile. Ivy whacked him on the arm with her knitting needle.

TRUMAN CAME BACK to the pool top in the afternoon, telling himself he was legitimately responsible for checking on things, but the fact was, if he could have justified it he'd have spent the whole workday watching the goings-on at the killer whale pool instead of revising budget projections for an upcoming executive committee meeting. Harriet Saul had him well-trained: during her tenure if he was gone from his desk for more than fifteen minutes she'd get on the radio, hunt him down, and insist that he come back. Once, when he'd committed the sin of talking for twenty minutes with the zoo's sloth keeper about a new animal that had just arrived, she had not only run him to ground, she'd lectured him about spending his time doing something that wasn't related to his job. "During work hours you belong here, not wandering around the zoo," she'd concluded. "From now on I want you to tell Brenda where you're going when you leave your desk so I can find you."

Now he crested the pool top in time to hear Gabriel say to Neva, "You ready?"

"Tah-dah!" Neva Supermanned her hoodie to reveal a brand-new wet suit underneath, at the same time shucking off her waterproof bib overalls. They both greeted Truman, and then Neva asked, "So what do you want me to do?"

"Just sit on the side, for starters. Let him initiate the relationship."

"Is it safe?" Truman asked.

"It's fine," said Neva.

"It's fine," said Gabriel.

"Just don't let him, you know, eat her. Okay?" Truman told Gabriel. "No eating."

"C'mon—he's a pussycat," said Gabriel.

"That sounds like someone's epitaph." Truman readily acknowledged that one of his less attractive qualities was that he was perpetually preparing for loss. Every day he imagined the biopic that would be his life, with a dolorous voice-over saying something like *What had begun as just another ordinary day would end with the terrible knowledge that the one he loved most was gone forever.* The imagined cause of the fatality was an ever-changing multiple-choice question: car accident, sudden brain hemorrhage, random gunshot, serial killer, flesh-eating bacteria, hit-and-run driver, and now a new one, killer whale. He'd never trusted anything good to last.

He turned and walked away, bravely resisting the powerful urge to look back.

NEVA LOWERED HERSELF until she was sitting on the wet walk eight feet away from Friday, who had continued to watch everything, his chin resting on the edge of the pool.

"Splash your hand in the water a little. He'll come over," Gabriel said, using his foot to nudge the steel bucket closer to her. "Then reward him when he does."

Neva did as instructed, and, sure enough, Friday swam right over to her. She tossed a fish into his open mouth and he swallowed it. "Go ahead and scratch him," Gabriel suggested. "Use your fingernails and really dig."

Friday narrowed his eyes with bliss as Neva described circles in his skin with her fingernails, leaving tracks in the remaining film of zinc oxide, getting black skin cells under her nails. His blowhole opened, he exhaled loudly, and then his blowhole clapped shut again. Little gobs of mucous fell around her like rain. "Ooh, snot. Is that normal?" she asked Gabriel.

"No. It's probably from the pollution down in Bogotá. We'll keep an eye on it. Why don't you go ahead and get in the water with him."

Neva slipped into pool, yipping involuntarily as the frigid water splashed her neck and face. Gabriel had asked the zoo's water-quality staff to keep the temperature as close to forty degrees as possible—roughly the temperature of the North Atlantic. Gabriel grinned wickedly. "Just wait until it gets inside your wet suit."

"God," said Neva. "Do you get used to it?"

"A little. Not really."

Friday, meanwhile, had taken off for the far side of the pool. Neva laughed. "Could he possibly get any farther away from me?"

"It's going to take time," Gabriel said. "But he's a pretty social guy, so I'm betting he'll be in your pocket by the end of the week." He went to a fiberglass chest lashed to the pool railing, pulled out a scrub brush, and tossed it to her. "In the meantime, you might as well be useful."

Neva began scrubbing the light growth of algae that had already started growing on the wet walk. "Is there anything in particular you want to do with him today?"

"Get a blood sample. That's it. Mostly what I want him to

do is eat and work some of the kinks out of his muscles. We're taking his food up to two hundred twenty-five pounds. Double what he was getting in Bogotá."

"Where are we taking the sample from?"

"His flukes."

"Really?" Neva said skeptically. "How does that work?"

"Piece of cake. You just ask him to roll over and put his tail on the wet walk."

Half an hour later, after Neva had been repeatedly spurned, she climbed out of the water and Gabriel called Friday to the side of the pool, fed him a couple of herring, and then asked him via a hand signal to roll over. When Friday complied, Gabriel pulled his flukes into place, laying one on the wet walk, where it was supported, then stooped down, swabbed a spot with alcohol, and inserted a hypodermic needle into the road map of veins. Friday didn't even flinch. When he was done Gabriel blew a shrill blast on his whistle to signal to Friday that he'd done what he'd been asked to do, and slapped his flukes affectionately. Friday rolled over and put his chin on the side of the pool, and Gabriel fed him half a bucket of fish.

"Get back in," he suggested to Neva. "He may be in a more playful mood now."

For the next hour—until she was shivering uncontrollably—Neva alternated between scrubbing algae and water play, floating on her back or paddling around, trying to project a safe but come-hither attitude. Friday continued to keep his distance, dozing on the far side of the pool.

"Okay, c'mon out," Gabriel finally said. "That was a good start."

Neva climbed out of the pool, her teeth chattering.

"Can you feel your hands?" Gabriel asked.

"Not for the last fifteen minutes."

"Excellent," said Gabriel, grinning. "Welcome to the world of marine mammal care. Go on down and sit in the shower until you stop shivering."

Neva thought nothing had ever felt better than sitting in the locker room's huge shower on the teak bench Gabriel had had the foresight to order, letting hot water cascade over her, and allowing her mind to wander. She had known some extraordinary zookeepers in her career, men and women who had invested their hearts as well as their backs and minds, spending day after low-paying day in all kinds of settings and the worst kinds of weather. Her ex-husband, Howard, had described what she did as slopping the hogs and shoveling shit, and in a narrow view of the profession he was right. But he'd left out the passion that elevated their work to one continuous, arduous act of love. Neva had seen that passion in Sam as plain as day when he had worked with Hannah; now, she saw the same quality in Gabriel, amplified manyfold. Gabriel was also calm to the core, focused, reassuring, wordlessly eloquent. He would be an excellent mentor.

And what he couldn't teach her, she suspected Friday would.

ON THE POOL top late that afternoon, Gabriel put on flippers, dive weights, a mask, oxygen tank, and regulator. This would be his first dive; he was going to clean feces, dropped fish, and algae from the bottom of the pool. It was slow and tedious work, like vacuuming a ballroom with a Dustbuster. And cold; very, very cold.

From the middle of the pool, Friday watched with keen interest as Gabriel slipped into the water, and when he went under, Friday went, too, following him down, staying just out of reach. Gabriel ignored him: he intended to set a precedent during this dive. People without scuba gear were in the water to interact with him, but the presence of tanks and masks meant that business was at hand.

Gabriel pulled the clumsy vacuum hose out of a sump on the bottom of the pool's south end, struggling with the heavy grate and the hose that bloomed into a huge arc overhead. Even with exertion, his breathing was easy and regular; he had been diving for twenty-two years, in all kinds of conditions and with all kinds of animals. Still, what he had told Sam was true: an animal looking for fun could be just as dangerous as one who meant you harm. He had developed a sixth sense about his animals' whereabouts whenever he was in the water. He worked steadily, slipping into a lovely Zen state. Friday watched raptly from a distance for five minutes before coming closer, until he hovered head down directly above Gabriel. Then, with exquisite politeness, he rested his chin on Gabriel's shoulder. Gabriel reached back to touch him in gentle acknowledgment, and they finished the vacuuming together, man and whale moving in companionable slo-mo along the bottom of the pool.

Chapter 5

THE DAY AFTER Friday's arrival, the zoo's executive committee began exerting increasing pressure on Truman to open the killer whale viewing gallery to the public. Adding urgency was the fact that the previous quarter's attendance figures had been even worse than they'd projected.

"Hell," the board president, Dink Schuler, declared at the executive committee meeting. "There's a ton of money to be made here. This fish is a star."

"Mammal," Truman said mildly.

"What?"

"He's a mammal, not a fish."

"I don't care if he has wings and can fly. All I know is, when I went to Rotary yesterday, people were jumping all over me about when we plan to open up. Money, money, money—the hospitality industry guys are drooling all over themselves about the out-of-town business we'll bring in, and chamber's mentioned several times that they're willing to give us the front cover of their brochure the next time they reprint it. Oh, and get this—a couple of guys were visiting from Tacoma and they said, over there, there's a rumor that the whale actually died a few hours after he got here and we're hiding it by handing out canned footage to the TV guys instead of even letting them in to shoot their own."

"That's crazy," said Truman, appalled.

"Sure, it's bullshit, but what I'm saying is, keeping the guy off-limits could turn into a PR problem."

Truman was also taking flak from visitors who knew full well that the killer whale they were hearing about on the evening news was *right there;* from the zoo grounds they could see staff working with him on the pool top. So when the executive committee meeting ended, Truman called Gabriel and explained the situation. "Do you see any downside to opening the gallery tomorrow?"

"Not as long as he's still doing well—actually, having people in the gallery will give him some stimulation. I'm assuming that we can shut the gallery down if he gets into trouble."

"What kind of trouble?"

"Oh, nothing in particular. Death, say."

"Is he still that frail?" Truman asked with some alarm.

"No, but you still have to have protocols in place for how to deal with it. I'm just saying."

"Oh," said Truman. "Whew."

Over the phone he could hear Gabriel snort with amusement. "Man, you really need to lighten up."

"I know, I know. Then let's open the gallery tomorrow. That'll give us the chance for the maximum number of visitors over the weekend."

"Fine by me," said Gabriel.

So Truman called Dink Schuler to confirm that the gallery would open tomorrow; and Dink called the mayor of Bladen-

ham and the president of the chamber of commerce and the
county commissioners and a long list of other VIPs; by which
time Truman had called Martin Choi, the reporter at the *Bladenham News-Tribune* who had been so instrumental, if unwit-
tingly, in manipulating Harriet Saul into releasing Hannah to
the Pachyderm Sanctuary in California, who called his radio
buddy, who put the information out, which was picked up
by the regional wire service; which prompted Dink to call
Truman to pull together a ribbon-cutting ceremony; at which
point Truman called Ivy, who, thanks to the vast experience
she and her money had had with this sort of event, helped
Truman plan a speech and photo opportunity with the ad-
ditional input of Lavinia and Matthew, who strongly recom-
mended that Truman not only invite Martin Choi, but include
him in the ceremony as "one of our most important community partners" because, as Matthew put it, "Son, he's an idiot,
which means we can't overestimate his strategic value if we
need him down the road."

MEANWHILE, ANIMAL COMMUNICATOR Libertine sat in her
camp chair by the side of the street next to the killer whale
pool. For the second full day Friday maintained his silence,
which perplexed her. She was certain he'd been the one to
summon her, but it was clear he'd withdrawn from her now.
Did he want her there at all, or had he solved whatever problem
he'd intended to bring to her? In that case, her work here was
done. She never forced herself on any animal, but made herself
available as its agent, leaving it to the animal to make use of her
if it chose to. Though she had no doubt that it had been Friday
who'd summoned her from Orcas Island, now she was at a loss.

At three o'clock she had just decided to take a walk—she was probably at risk for deep-vein thrombosis, with all the sitting she was doing—when a pleasant-looking man wearing zoo apparel came through a gate to her side of the chain-link fence and said, "Is there anything we can help you with?"

Libertine pushed herself out of her chair and staggered as she found that one of her feet was asleep. "Will you be putting the killer whale on exhibit anytime soon?"

"Friday."

"Yes, Friday. Do you know when you'll let people see him?"

"No, I meant *on* Friday—tomorrow. You'll able to see Friday on Friday. My god, it's like a bad Abbot and Costello routine. Who's on first?"

"What?"

"No, what's on second. Who's on first?"

They both started laughing. "I'm sorry," said the man, rubbing his face. "It's been a long couple of days."

"I'm sure."

"I noticed you were here yesterday, too."

"I came down from Orcas Island when I heard you were going to be bringing him up."

"Do you know him somehow?"

"No," said Libertine, not quite truthfully. "I've just heard a lot about him."

"Really? Such as?"

"Mainly, that he deserves a lot of breaks."

"No kidding," said the man, holding out his hand. "I'm Truman Levy."

"Libertine Adagio." For now she decided to leave it at that.

ACROSS TOWN, *BLADENHAM News-Tribune* reporter Martin Choi was scratching around for a new story angle. The killer whale's arrival was all well and good, but he'd gotten the same story as everyone else, and that wasn't good enough. If you were to know just one thing about him, Martin Choi would tell you, it should be his unwavering ambition. Firmly believing that upper-level journalism classes were unnecessary—that in fact, they stifled a young reporter's unique voice—he'd come to the *Bladenham News-Tribune* four years ago, fresh from an introductory journalism class at the community college. His current plan was to become an online feature writer for the Huffington Post. He used to dream of becoming an investigative reporter for the *Seattle Post-Intelligencer,* but he saw all too clearly now that paper-and-ink newspapers were doomed to become nothing but a headline or two, a couple of advertorials, and a bunch of grocery store ads and True Value Hardware supplements. He had more on the ball than that—a lot more. He was a hard-nosed reporter waiting for the story that would blast him out of this rat pit town and into cyberfame.

He'd been trying to reach Truman Levy all morning, unsuccessfully. Martin was pretty sure Truman was avoiding him. If Harriet Saul had still been around, he'd have been in like Flynn; she'd never said as much, but he knew she'd had a crush on him, and justifiably—he'd stood on the front steps of Havenside three years ago and declared her a hero, blowing the lid off her secret intention of relocating Hannah to a sanctuary in California. In fact, he'd parlayed that great moment into his current title, Lead Feature Writer, which now ran beside his byline. Sure, he still wrote marriage and birth announcements, but he'd drawn the line at obituaries. Everyone knew obituary writing was a dead-end job. (And he'd come up with that amazing pun *on the fly* while outlining his demands to his editor. That was the kind of nimble wit he had.)

Truman Levy, on the other hand, was a tougher nut, and now a brand-new lawyer to boot, which meant he wasn't going to go for the easy, hand-in-glove relationship that local newspapers and nonprofit organizations so often shared. No, he'd need to find another angle on this Friday business that was his own.

Then he'd gotten the phone call from none other than Truman himself about the ribbon-cutting at the whale pool the next morning. Who said good things didn't go to those who waited, or whatever the hell that saying was? His life was charmed; this was just another sign of it.

WHEN TRUMAN LOOKED out his office window the next morning he saw a line leading all the way to the main parking lot and disappearing around a corner of the gift shop—more visitors than the zoo hosted during an average peak-season weekend. And the zoo wouldn't even be open for another half hour.

Acting fast, he had his IT guy add to the zoo's Web site basic information about Friday, the hours during which the public could see him, and a link to accept donations. He asked Brenda to create a Facebook page and a Twitter account on Friday's behalf. Then he instructed security to take down the ribbon for the noon ribbon-cutting ceremony so visitors could get into the gallery immediately, and asked the two front gate employees to open early and capture guests' zip codes—which, in the first two hours, included people from as far away as San Diego and Calgary. The Web site crashed under the weight of nearly a quarter of a million hits per hour, and children showed up with jars of pennies and crumpled dollar bills from the tooth fairy. When the day's mail arrived it included an avalanche of greeting cards, hand-scrawled good wishes, and checks—lots and lots of checks.

It occurred to him that he might have underestimated the effect this animal could have on the entire zoo.

He decided to walk through the zoo grounds, joining a tidal wave of visitors who were skipping all the other exhibits in favor of Friday's pool. Halfway there he caught up with a young couple with two tow-headed boys wearing SHAMU sweatshirts and tugging at their hands to make them go faster. "They're both just crazy about killer whales," the woman told Truman ruefully. "We've already taken them to SeaWorld twice, and he's only eight." She indicated the older boy. "When I told them we were going to get to see a killer whale right here at home, I thought they'd pop they were so excited."

"Are you from Bladenham?"

"Well, Tacoma, which is a heck of a lot closer than San Diego. We promised the boys we'd buy a zoo membership so they can come as often as they want. I home school them, and I'd already planned a unit on marine mammals, so this is just perfect. You're not planning on getting any more, by any chance?"

"No," said Truman. "I think we'll have our hands full just with Friday."

The boys, who'd never stopped tugging on her hands, said in unison, "Mom, come *on*!" As soon as they got near the doors to the viewing gallery they sprinted ahead, calling over their shoulders, "Hurry up! Come on, come on, we're going to miss him," as though the animal could come and go from the pool at will.

Truman slipped into the gallery behind them, staying on an elevated walkway at the back so he could see the visitors as well as the whale. A frisson of anticipation pulsed through the gallery like an electrical charge. When at last Friday made a single sluggish pass-by, a deafening cheer rang out.

WHEN MARTIN CHOI finally got inside the viewing gallery after waiting in line for twenty freaking minutes—he could have invoked journalistic privilege, but he decided to maintain his anonymity to preserve the integrity of his story—he arrived to find four empty windows. Water, water, water; no whale. He asked a woman standing next to him what the hell. "If you look up there," she told him, pointing, "you can just barely see his tail flukes."

She was right—he could see them hanging down in the water. Once he'd pressed his way through the crowd to stand directly in front of the window and look up, he could see not only the flukes but the whale's whole undercarriage.

"Hey, is he dead?" someone called from the crowd. "Because I don't see him breathing or nothing. I heard he might die."

A murmur of concern rippled through the two hundred or so people in the gallery.

"Nah, he's been like that for an hour," someone else said. "If you watch for a while, you'll see him take a breath. Then he just lays there. He could be dying, but they're not going to tell you that. You'll just read it in the paper one day."

A child started wailing, "Don't let him die, Mommy, don't let him die!"

The cry was instantly taken up by other children throughout the gallery. Martin turned to face the crowd, both arms raised as though to invoke a benediction, and said, "Don't worry— I'm a reporter. I'll get to the bottom of this and run it in Monday's *News-Tribune*." Given that today was only Friday he knew how lame that sounded, but what else could he do?

"So *is* he dead?" a woman at the back of the gallery demanded. "Or what?"

"He's not dead," said a quiet voice at Martin Choi's elbow.

"He's not even dying. He's just tired. It was a long trip from Colombia to here."

Martin looked down upon a pink-nosed, frowsy-haired little woman standing beside him. He was lucky he'd even heard her. Feeling his whale-death exposé slipping away, he said, "How do you know?"

"I just do."

"How?"

The woman sighed. "He told me."

"He *told* you? Who told you, the whale?"

"The whale, Friday. Yes."

"No shit. You talk to whales?"

"Not all whales, no, just the ones who approach me. I don't talk to them, exactly. I communicate with them."

Martin could feel his heart rate increase and his palms get damp. Here, *just like that,* might be the story of a lifetime, his ticket out. "I thought his name was Viernes."

"*Viernes* means Friday in Spanish," said the woman.

"Oh, yeah? How come they named him that?"

"I assume he was captured on a Friday."

"And you know that how?"

"I don't. It's a guess."

Suddenly the flukes above them kicked, the whale heaved into motion, and the gallery erupted.

"Someone's feeding him," said the woman beside him.

"You can see that?" Martin said, peering up into the water. All he could see was the killer whale's belly on the far side of the pool. "How can you see that?"

"I can't."

But sure enough a few minutes later a couple of fish drifted down. When Friday swam after them and picked them off, the gallery collectively lost its mind. Martin grabbed his camera and took shot after shot through the window.

"So listen—how about I interview you?" he said when Friday had once more disappeared from view. "Since you have, you know, an inside track."

He watched the woman dig an old Starbucks napkin out of her purse and blow her nose, fold the napkin carefully, and return it to her purse.

"So, like, what else is going on with him?" Martin asked.

"I don't know. He's not actually communicating with me right now—I only know what I can sense."

"Yeah?"

"Mostly, he's tired."

"Yeah, I get that."

"There are actually some similarities between what's been happening to him in the last few days and what would happen if he were still in the wild."

"Why would he be in the wild?"

"He was born there."

"Huh."

"So either way, he'd probably have been headed north."

"Why?"

"There are annual herring runs up north."

"Yeah?"

The psychic waited a beat. "They eat herring."

"Oh. Sure, yeah, I get that. So what does he think about being here?"

The woman sighed. "As I said, he isn't communicating with me right now. But he's obviously in a much better situation now than he was at that terrible place. Of course, he is still in captivity."

"Yeah?"

"He used to live in the wild. Now he's an attraction." She gestured around the gallery at the cheering people, many of whom were knocking on the thick acrylic windows to try to entice him back.

"He told you this?"

"No. He hasn't asked me to say anything on his behalf."

"He *asks* you to speak? Jeez, what a story!" He scribbled frantically in his reporter's spiral notebook, more to keep his excitement under control than for the notes themselves. You didn't need them anymore; everything was on his digital recorder, there for the replaying. Sometimes he interviewed people and didn't write down a single thing. "So what other stuff do you think he'll want you to say?"

The psychic shook her head wearily. "There's no way of knowing that until he communicates with me again. But I imagine he wants to go home. It's what they all want."

"Yeah? Who?"

"The captive killer whales who were born in the wild."

"No kidding?"

"No kidding."

He'd finished writing and was staring into the empty water of the pool when she said, "I'm going to leave now. Is there anything else you want to ask me?"

His first thought was, if she was really a psychic, shouldn't she know that without having to ask? But it was just as well if she couldn't read his mind, because he was thinking he'd better get her photo before she started to look any worse. He'd hate to see what was at the bottom of *that* gene pool. Instead, he said, "I'm just processing what you're telling me. It's, you know, sad."

The psychic nodded silently.

"So what's your name?"

"Libertine. Libertine Adagio."

"Your parents must have been patriots, huh? Liberty and all that. Okay, so hey, thanks for this. No kidding. You planning on talking to anyone else?"

She shook her head. "No—at least not for now."

Far out—he'd gotten the scoop! "Don't talk to anyone else if they contact you, okay? We'll treat this as an exclusive. I'll have the story filed in time to run in Monday's paper." Silently he railed again at the fact that the pissant *News-Tribune* only came out twice a week, and the publisher was considering dropping that to once a week if ad revenues continued to decline. Since the HuffPost was strictly online, it was always coming out— something newsworthy came along, you filed the story, and *bam!,* the thing went live online immediately, with your byline out there for the whole world to see. God, but he couldn't wait for that day. He would definitely put this story on the Associated Press's news feed, too, because he was absolutely sure it would be picked up.

The minute the psychic was out the door Martin hotfooted it to the back of the newsroom and told his editor, O'Reilly, that he had a story as big as the one he broke when the zoo was fighting over its elephant—maybe bigger. O'Reilly was a tool, but he also must have smelled journalistic gold because he gave Martin the go-ahead to work from home, where there would be no distractions. He beat feet to his car, an old Honda Civic he'd be able to replace once he was earning a living wage at the HuffPost.

At home, he cracked open a beer—he thought more clearly with a beer or two under his belt, which he loved about himself—and tore into the story.

DESPITE TRUMAN'S JITTERS, the ribbon-cutting ceremony went off without a hitch at midday, and in record time—Dink delivered a three-minute set of comments that Truman scripted for him, the mayor gave two minutes of observations about the zoo's importance to the community, and a round of applause rang out. Despite his father's urging, he hadn't included Martin Choi in the program. Dink snipped the ribbon in two with a pair of hastily found garden shears loaned by the buildings and grounds crew, and the zoo visitors surged back into the briefly closed gallery.

At the windows Friday showed for the first time his alleged fascination with babies, a fact they'd all been told about but doubted. Now, however, Truman saw him select a little girl in her mother's arms at the front of the crowd, hover in the water right in front of her, and watch her for a long time without going up for a breath of air. The child looked back at him, smiled, offered her bottle. The whale nodded and stayed on and on in the window, watching the bottle, watching the baby, going with them as her parents finally walked away with a regretful last look to a place where the killer whale couldn't follow.

The atmosphere in the gallery was what Truman imagined it would be at Lourdes. Though they were packed in shoulder to shoulder, people talked in hushed tones; many cheeks were wet with tears. Cameras were ubiquitous. And Friday delivered. Still dingy with the last of the zinc oxide ointment, and trailing peeling skin like mourning ribbons, he gave his visitors his fullest attention. Once the baby was gone, people set their toddlers on the deep windowsills in front of them and watched excitedly as the killer whale homed in on one after another, bringing his eye to the window inches away to look them over.

For Truman there was something slightly unnerving about the intensity of both the whale's interest and the crowd's. It was as though they were beholding a superhero or saint.

He left the gallery for the back area and office. Gabriel was at the computer when Truman came in. From the office's underwater window he could still see Friday across the pool, at the gallery windows.

"It's amazing," Truman told Gabriel. "Are all killer whales treated with this kind of, I don't know, reverence?"

"Yep. Blows your mind, doesn't it?"

Truman admitted it did. "But why?" he asked. "What's the draw?"

"They're black and white," Gabriel said, consulting a handwritten slip of paper and continuing to type.

"What do you mean?"

Gabriel swiveled around to face Truman. "People just go nuts over black-and-white animals. Pandas, penguins, zebras, white tigers, snow leopards, killer whales. No one knows why."

"Really?" To Truman the statement was at once outrageous and plausible.

"Absolutely. Don't take my word for it—ask any zookeeper and they'll tell you the same thing."

In bed that night, Truman floated Gabriel's theory past Neva. "Well, sure!" she said. "I thought everyone knew that."

FIRST THING MONDAY morning, Truman picked up a copy of the *News-Tribune* and spread it on his desktop. The headline was: KILLER WHALE WANTS TO GO HOME. The sole source quoted was one Libertine Adagio, animal psychic—the woman he'd met two days ago sitting by the side of the road. There couldn't possibly be two women with that name.

After reading it, which took a surprising amount of fortitude, he paced in his office, trying to decide what to do. He'd
always known trouble would find them—god knows Neva had
hammered that home—but he hadn't imagined it would be so
soon, or come from so close by. But in Truman's mind it was
counterbalanced against Friday's rapt attention to the visitors
who now packed his gallery. Truman was already overhearing visitors describing his antics: Friday, drifting by the gallery
windows upside down and with his eyes closed; Friday, opening his mouth wide and waggling his tongue at the crowd;
Friday, nodding his head as though accepting obeisance. It
didn't take an animal behaviorist to see that this animal didn't
just enjoy human interaction, he thrived on it.

And now some animal psychic was declaring that this very
same animal was yearning to be released back to the wild.

Truman was undecided about an appropriate response to the
article when he heard a smart knock on his door frame and
then saw Ivy swirling into his office in her customary Egyptian
abaya and Nikes, with Julio Iglesias in tow on a purple leash
studded with dog-bone-shaped rivets. She threw herself into
one of Truman's visitors' chairs, plunked Julio Iglesias into the
other, and crowed, "So I gather our boy's a huge hit! There's a
line past the parking lot. How are the numbers?"

"Excellent," Truman said glumly.

"And this is a problem why?"

"It's not a problem. Our favorite reporter, Martin Choi, is
the problem."

"The idiot at the local paper?"

"The very same," said Truman. "He's dug up some animal
psychic who's claiming that Friday wants to go home."

"To Bogotá?"

"To the North Atlantic."

"Why on earth would he want to go there?"

"I'm really not sure—the story wasn't very clear."

"Honey, he's an idiot," said Ivy.

"I know he's an idiot," Truman agreed.

"You said he was quoting an animal psychic?" Ivy asked thoughtfully.

"Evidently."

"I met one the day after Friday got here," said Ivy. "Well, a *communicator*. She doesn't like to be called a psychic."

"Here? In Bladenham?"

Ivy nodded. "Her name's Libertine Adagio, and I had dinner with her at the Oat Maiden. She was eating alone, I was eating alone, so I invited myself to her table."

"And was she raving?"

"Not at all. She was actually quite articulate. And genuine."

"About channeling for animals?"

"I know," Ivy said. "It sounded far-fetched to me, too, but she was very earnest."

"Does she think she's channeling for Friday?"

"She must," Ivy said.

"Well, she's given Martin Choi the worst kind of story we could have out there. 'Zoo as prison,' that kind of thing."

"Need I remind you who wrote the article? It's entirely possible that there's not a single accurate word in that entire story. Honestly, she seemed like a very gentle soul. Maybe I'll see if she can come in and talk to you."

Truman looked at her with alarm. "Are you planning to see her again?"

"Absolutely," Ivy said. "As soon as I can track her down. I liked her. I want to introduce her to Johnson Johnson."

Truman was appalled. "Why on earth would you do that?"

"To see if she can rent his apartment, of course. She's very poor, anyone can see that, and she apparently feels obligated to stick around for a while, so she'll need a place to stay."

"Encouraging her isn't in the zoo's best interests," Truman protested. "You know that."

"Oh, hush. I didn't say I agreed with her, just that I see no point in shunning her. And it wouldn't do you any harm to meet her. In the belly of the beast and all that. If you're your father's son, you won't banish her, you'll find a way to put her to good use."

BY LATE AFTERNOON Friday was napping with his head in a corner of the pool, and Gabriel and Neva, wearing bathing suits, were sprawled on the teak benches in the shower downstairs, beneath dual, steaming showerheads. Gabriel had finished two-and-a-half hours of cleaning on the bottom of the pool; Neva had been in and out of the water three times in an ongoing courtship. During her final attempt, Friday had let her swim up to him and take hold of his dorsal fin, which she'd assumed would feel pliable but instead found to be fixed and rigid, the curl as tight as a fist.

"I don't think heat has ever felt so good," she said now. "And I mean ever."

"One of God's little mercies. I've seen grown men weep under here, it's felt so good."

"Has anyone died of hypothermia in one of these pools? Because I'd totally believe it."

"Not that I know of, but that doesn't mean we haven't come close."

"We?" Neva said.

"We Who Swim with Whales."

"It seems like the smart people would work with warm-water cetaceans," Neva said, cracking open one eye to look at him. "Bottle-nosed dolphins."

Gabriel waved this off. "Bottle-nosed dolphins are assholes. Honestly, when you're moving, it doesn't seem as bad. We spent a lot of time today just hanging around. That's when you feel it the most."

Neva closed her eyes again. "You know, you're an enigma. How come you never talk about the work you've done?"

"I don't have any reason to. I've been working with marine mammals my whole professional life, which means since you were a girl. I've had my hands on just about every killer whale in captivity. That doesn't mean I'm an enigma, it just means I'm old."

"How many do you think you've collected?" she asked, still self-conscious about using the more zoo-friendly parlance for *captured,* though she'd said it a thousand times.

Gabriel considered this. "I've never counted. Forty, maybe forty-five."

"How many were rehab animals?"

"Not many. A few."

"What about the rest?"

"Calves."

Neva opened her eyes to watch him as he went on.

"When I first got into this business, hardly anyone anywhere had even *heard* of killer whales, never mind seen one, and half the ones who had thought they were some kind of fish. That was twenty-five, thirty years ago. Now there are killer whale toys, books, posters, stuffed animals, you name it. Hell, Southwest Airlines has Shamu airplanes. Every American kid has seen *Free Willy* at least five times. And why do kids love killer whales? Because they've seen one up close—not in the wild, but at SeaWorld or Busch Gardens or one of the other theme parks."

"I know, I know, it's the whole conservation thing, making kids better stewards for tomorrow's world. I get that—we say the same thing about elephants when people say it's inhumane to keep them in captivity. People won't take care of something they don't know anything about, blah blah blah. And I have no problem at all with captive-bred animals. I'm just not sure I'd be able to grab a young animal from the wild. That's just me."

"Well, hardly any are taken from the wild anymore anyway. Hell, SeaWorld wrote the book on successful captive breeding, and their whales are on their fourth generation. Turn any of them loose in the wild and they'd be dead inside two months."

"Do you really think our guy would have died, if he'd been left there—in Bogotá?"

"I know it."

"I wonder if he was scared," she mused.

With closed eyes Gabriel said quietly, "Nature restores a state of grace at the end. By the time you die, you don't feel a thing."

"And you know this how?"

"I've been there."

Neva looked at him.

Gabriel opened one eye. "What?"

Neva whacked him with a loofah. "Tell me the story."

Gabriel shrugged. "There's not much to tell. It was my own fault. We were collecting killer whales in the North Atlantic off Iceland and I got caught in the net. I was trying to untangle one of the calves. It was a stupid mistake."

"So what saved you?"

"Not what, who. Christian. A Frenchman—we were collecting animals for an aquarium in Nice. I should have died. I was dying. And there really is a white light, because I was headed there when he dragged me up. I wasn't scared, and it didn't hurt. It was beautiful. So now I know it's nothing to be afraid of."

Neva shook her head. "I've always been afraid of drowning."

"Really?"

"Really."

"Well, if this job doesn't get you over that, nothing will," said Gabriel.

"You think?"

"Sure. And if it does happen, remember, you'll be dying among friends."

"There's a comforting thought," Neva said.

"Yup," said Gabriel, closing his eyes again. "I thought it would be."

LATE THAT AFTERNOON Ivy stopped by the pool to reassure herself that all was well. The office was empty and she was peering through the office window to see some sign of Friday when Gabriel came out of the locker room with a towel around his neck, wearing a fresh, dry wet suit folded down to his waist. Ivy turned to look at him, and took in the greenish-yellow remnants of the deep, ugly bruise on his chest. Even from across the room she could also make out the scars up and down around his arms and several longer, deeper scars on his sides and back. "Good god!"

"It looks worse than it is," he said of the bruise.

"Did you get hit by a bus?"

"Sea lion. Same thing."

"Yowza."

Gabriel shrugged with a certain degree of pride. "Goes with the territory. In this industry all us old guys look like we've been mauled by tigers. I've broken both ankles—one of them twice—both wrists, all my fingers, most of my toes, and blown out both knees and an eardrum."

"Talk about a leaky ship."

Gabriel pulled on the upper part of his wet suit and reached over his shoulder, feeling for the zipper pull.

"Here," she said, stepping over and efficiently zipping him up. "You must be taking the evening watch."

"Yep. I want to keep an eye on him for at least one more night."

"If you call the Oat Maiden, Johnson Johnson would probably send over a pizza."

"I'm fine."

"Well, you can't object to a little company, at least."

Together they climbed the metal stairs, Ivy with one of her oversized tote bags, Gabriel with a bucket of fish, a security radio, and a flashlight. Dark was moving in and one by one the automatic lights sputtered on. Friday was fast asleep in his corner.

Ivy fetched Julio Iglesias from her car, where he'd been methodically chewing through the passenger's seat belt, brought him upstairs, set him down on the pool deck, and watched him trot away on skinny tweezer-legs to pee on a coiled hose. "He's such a little martinet," she said. "You know, in one of his lives he was either a pharoah, a king, or a fascist. I'm serious."

Gabriel dragged two Adirondack chairs to Ivy, who had bought the second one to the pool yesterday, complaining that the lawn chairs were going to do them all in. Now she pulled a cushion from her bottomless tote and put it on the chair. "Sci-atica," she said, sitting down with a soft grunt. "Handiwork of the devil."

"Think sitting out in the cold and dampness could have anything to do with it?"

"Nah. My doctor—who, by the way, sits at Satan's right hand—would tell you it's my own damned fault. Lose a little weight, exercise more, turn the clock back fifteen years, and I'd be perfect." Ivy fished out her flask and took a good swig, then offered it to Gabriel. "Scotch. *Excellent* scotch. Go on—it's not going to kill you to break the rules once."

As they passed the flask back and forth, Ivy extracted a sky-blue afghan-in-progress from her bag, peered at it, consulted a dog-eared pattern, and ripped out some of the stitches. "You know, the last time I spent this much time with a man, I was engaged to him." She gave him a puckish look before setting to work, the metal knitting needles briskly clicking.

"And?"

She waved her hand dismissively. "I came to my senses."

"Any regrets?"

"None," said Ivy. "He died at forty-nine. I'd have been a grieving widow."

"Better to have loved and lost than never to have—"

"There's a crock," said Ivy. "How about you? Ever been married?"

"Once. Back before the flood. If you believe her, and you probably should, I'm not cut out for domestic life."

"What on earth is that supposed to mean?"

Gabriel shrugged. "I travel. I put my work first."

Ivy nodded, holding a cable needle loosely between her lips like a forgotten cigarette.

"The real deal-breaker, though, was kids," Gabriel said. "She started to want them, and I didn't—if you're going to have kids, you should stay home and have some sort of relationship with them, which I obviously would not be doing. It was all very amicable, though. She's married again and has two sets of twins. I see her on Vashon sometimes when I'm home. She looks happy."

Barely visible in the darkness, Friday exhaled and inhaled, clapping his blowhole closed, his warm breath steaming. Ivy put the empty flask away and Gabriel sipped coffee from a mug that said I ❤ MY WALRUS. He watched her, after a while saying, "My grandmother used to knit. Socks, mostly. She said it was an act of contrition."

"For what?"

"She'd never tell me, and I can't imagine. The woman was a saint. Married at fourteen, five kids by twenty-one. She grew up on a cattle ranch in Alberta and single-handedly fed twenty ranch hands three hot meals a day." He gazed across the pool. "She used to say she had kids so if she ever had to go back there at least she'd have help."

"Did she? Ever go back?"

"Nope. She moved to Vancouver, B.C., all by herself, taught herself typing and shorthand, and met my grandfather taking a night-school class on modern English literature. She married him a month later, when she was twenty-two, and they moved to Vashon Island. She loved it there. I remember someone once told her she was a good woman, and she said she was motivated because she'd already been to hell and she wasn't about to go back. You'd have to work her over with a crowbar to get her to talk about her growing up. She was ashamed of her family."

"Because they were poor?"

"Because they were uneducated. She brought up my dad on Vashon, but sent him off to the University of Washington in Seattle with a promise that he'd never come back except to visit. He got a PhD in English Literature, met my mother, and waited until my grandmother died to come home and be a scholar-janitor. Cleaned the church every Sunday, shops and the bank every evening. Good honest work, he called it. He always had a book in his back pocket so he could read while he waxed the floors. Shakespeare, Chaucer, Dostoyevsky, Dickens, Joyce, Vonnegut, Clancy."

Ivy smiled. "Eclectic tastes."

Gabriel nodded. "He died when he was fifty-four, had a heart attack in the nave of St. John the Divine. Father David found him with a book in his hand and a smile on his face."

"And your mother?"

"She still lives on Vashon, still does some light cleaning for my dad's old clients."

"Do you see her often?"

"Not as often as I should, but I go when I can."

They fell silent while Ivy considered her work, employed her cable needle, then tucked it back between her lips. She hadn't thought of Gabriel as coming from an educated family; to her he'd seemed more elemental, like the son of a milkman or a plumber. "Shouldn't he be breathing more?"

"Why?"

"I don't know. It just seems like an animal that big should need more oxygen."

"First, they're much more efficient at using oxygen than we are, and second, he's dozing."

"How do you know he's not cowering in fear?"

"If he were afraid, his respirations would be faster," Gabriel said.

"Do you really think he'll be okay here?"

"Absolutely. We're going to be throwing a bunch of new stuff at him that'll keep him busy and challenged."

"I hope so—I really do. I have to admit that some of what that animal psychic said shook me up a little," Ivy said.

"Such as?"

"Thinking that he might still miss the wild, even after all these years. Who are we to play God?"

"For one thing, animal psychics are frauds—there's no such thing. For another thing, Friday would be dead inside a week if he were released back to the wild. He's used to being hand-fed dead fish, not having to figure out where the schools of fish are today and tomorrow. He's immune-suppressed, so he'd pick up the first infection he came across. And the North Atlantic is a big, big place—the odds of him finding his pod, or of them finding him, are remote. Reality bites."

Ivy nodded, only slightly heartened.

LIBERTINE SAT AT the celestial table at the Oat Maiden and talked softly into her cell phone. On the other end of the call was Katrina—Trina—Beemer, a grim-faced, sour woman in her early fifties at whose hammer toes Libertine had been unable to keep herself from staring in fascination during a Sea Shepherd gathering in Seattle two summers ago; and to whom she hadn't spoken since. Trina headed an organization called Friends of Animals of the Sea and often tagged along when the big animal activist organizations like PETA and Sea Shepherd staged protests.

"I won't ask you how you infiltrated that place, but you're a hero," Trina was saying. "Everyone's saying so."

"What place?"

"What place?—you silly woman!" Trina said coyly. "The Breederman Zoo or whatever. You're all over the Internet."

Libertine's heart sank. She believed in the animal welfare groups' efforts to improve the lives of captive whales and dolphins, even to shut their programs down when the conditions warranted it, as they clearly had in Bogotá, but that wasn't her work. She merely represented those individuals who couldn't represent themselves. She'd had no intention of taking a political stand when she talked to Martin Choi. She was just telling him what she knew to be true. It wasn't the first time she'd talked before she'd thought things through, and while it probably wasn't the last time, either, she longed for a do-over.

Trina was still talking. "—reconnaisance," she was saying.

"I'm sorry?"

She heard Trina sigh and start over, using the vaguely singsong tone women used when talking to small children and the mentally challenged. "We're hoping you'll do some reconnaissance for us, since you're there. If you could make a map of the whale building, filtration plant, entrances, exits, and which ones are locked and when, that would be really great."

"I don't think I'd be comfortable doing that," Libertine said.

"Well, you're not doing anything else, are you? I assume you don't have direct access to him."

"Him?"

"Viernes or Friday or whatever his latest name is," Trina said impatiently. "The whale."

"Oh. No, not physical access." She hadn't had psychic access to him, either, since the day after his arrival. Not that she would tell that to Trina. "I guess I ought to get online and see what people are saying."

"Listen to the radio, too. Joe Minton did a whole piece on the whale's background and prospects on NPR. You can probably find it on their Web site."

"Oh."

"Look, we really, really need that information. Will you at least think it over?" The phone line went silent until Libertine finally said, "I'll think about it."

"Oh, that's great!" said Trina. "That's my little guerrilla warrior."

Chapter 6

EARLY THE NEXT morning Truman received a call over his security radio.

"Ah, sir, we seem to have someone sneaking around the whale facility. Over." Truman had been trying to get the security officers to stop calling him "sir" for three months, but so far, no luck. On the other hand, they'd been trying equally unsuccessfully to get Truman to say, "Roger" and "Over," so Truman guessed they were even.

"Is this Toby?" he asked over the radio.

"Yes, sir, this is Security One. Over."

Truman sighed. "What do you mean, 'sneaking'?"

"Well, sir, we have a woman walking the fence line. She appears to be looking for a way in. Over."

"Is she heavyset?"

"No, sir, more like an elf sort of a person. Small like that. She doesn't look dangerous, but she's walking back and forth a lot like she's maybe looking for something. Over."

Truman sighed again. "All right, why don't you introduce yourself and bring her to my office?"

"Roger that. Over and out."

Truman couldn't help smiling as he set down the radio. Most of his security employees had wanted to be in the military or the police force, but were unfit in some way: Toby was severely asthmatic; another was an aging Vietnam veteran with lingering PTSD; a third had epilepsy; and the fourth had suffered a serious head injury which, while he adhered absolutely to the zoo's security rules and procedures, made him somewhat lacking when it came to assessing complex situations. Truman believed strongly in giving people chances, and he was very proud of his motley team, which he'd originally assembled six years ago, when, as the zoo's business manager, he'd supervised the security department. They were among the zoo's most dedicated employees, tenacious in their loyalty to the zoo and to Truman himself. This year, for the first time in what he intended to make an annual practice, he'd invited them to undertake the facility-wide security audit he'd originally proposed to former director Harriet Saul way back when and which she'd flatly rejected as busywork.

He cleared his desk of sensitive papers, pulled two teacups from his credenza, and turned on the electric teapot just as a knock on his door announced that Toby and Libertine Adagio had arrived. Truman indicated to Libertine that they'd sit at a small round table by the window, and said to Toby, "Would you find Miss Levy and ask her to come see me? I'd like her to join us."

Toby self-consciously removed and reseated his Biedelman Zoo ball cap—briefly exposing hair as sparse and fine as duck down—and then hitched up his radio holster in a pair of tandem tics. "Roger that."

Once he'd left, Truman stepped to the doorway and asked Brenda to keep an eye out for Ivy. Then he joined Libertine

Adagio across the table. She smiled at him nicely. He was surprised to find her slight and messy; her small hands flew around her like birds, checking the lay of her hair and clothes. He'd remembered her being larger and more assertive. He offered her tea and she accepted.

"I've asked Ivy to join us," he said, stalling for time. "I gather you met her at the Oat Maiden."

Libertine nodded. "She's been very nice to me. I don't always get that."

"Really?"

"It's a hazard of my profession."

"Oh?"

"You think I'm crazy."

"The thought had occurred to me."

She nodded sadly. "Most people do."

From the reception area Truman heard a small yip and then Ivy swept into the room and summarily tossed Julio Iglesias into Libertine's lap. "You may turn out to be the only person on earth he really likes," Ivy told her.

"Well, he certainly doesn't like me," Truman said wryly, watching Julio Iglesias hop down, walk smartly to his desk, and pee on the leg.

"Oh, for god's sake," Ivy said. "Julio. *Really?*"

"He has puppy issues," Libertine said while Ivy cleaned up the floor and desk with a baby wipe from her enormous tote.

"You'd better be careful, or I'll send him home with you," Ivy told her.

"No, no, we can help him work through them. He's very smart, you know."

"Well, he's certainly smarter than me," said Ivy. "I'm pretty sure we can all agree on which of us is winning."

Truman gently cleared his throat.

"Sorry," Ivy said, dropping the dirty baby wipes in Truman's wastebasket, which in his eyes was only marginally better than having dog pee on his desk leg. Julio Iglesias hopped back into Libertine's lap and looked at Ivy smugly.

"So what's the deal here?" Ivy said.

"I'm not sure," said Truman, addressing himself to Libertine. "Zoo security thought you might be trying to gain access to the pool without permission. The word *skulking* comes to mind."

The woman blushed. "No, I would never skulk. I was just trying to check on him—you saw me there yourself when we met. It's so crowded on the other side it's hard to hear."

"So I gather our whale talks to you," Truman said, steepling his fingers over the tabletop.

"Something like that. I feel his feelings."

"And how is he feeling?"

"I don't know—he hasn't been communicating since he got here."

"Does that mean anything?"

"Just that he doesn't need me to advocate for him right now. That's good. Really good."

"And you?" Truman asked her, not unkindly. "How are you feeling?"

"Better, too," Libertine said, blushing. "He's safe."

"Really? I was under the impression you thought we were jailers."

"He must sense that you're good people."

"So good jailers," Truman said.

"I think that's a little harsh, don't you?" Ivy objected.

"Is it?"

"I told you this before: remember two little words," Ivy said. "Martin. Choi."

"Did he at least get the basics right?" Truman asked Libertine. "Because he doesn't always."

"More or less," said Libertine. "Not really."

"That all captivity is bad?"

"Absolutely not. I believe captivity is a blessing for animals who are captive-born, as long as they're treated well. It's animals who've come from the wild that have a harder time."

"And that includes our whale?"

"I don't know—I haven't gotten to know him that well," Libertine said, blushing deeply. "But he was wild-born."

"Has he said anything to you about wanting to go home?" Ivy asked. "You know I worry."

"No," Libertine said. "The reporter played a little fast and loose with what I told him. Again, I haven't heard anything from him since he arrived."

"Martin Choi's an idiot," Ivy told her. "Just so you know."

"I gathered," said Libertine. "But thank you for telling me."

"So what exactly *did* Friday tell you when he was still, ah, communicating?" Truman asked. "If it didn't have to do with going back to the wild."

"Stop," Ivy warned him. "You're being rude."

Truman sighed. To Libertine he said, "I apologize—I have been rude. It's just, you can probably understand our skepticism. Especially at a time like this and with an animal like this. For all we know, you're trying to get access to him to sabotage us in some way."

Libertine put her small hand on his wrist and said, "I would never do that—never ever. I probably can't prove that to you, though."

"No," said Truman. "Probably not. But if I have your word, that means something."

"You do," Libertine said fervently. "You have my word."

"Plus he's being treated like a king," Ivy told her reassuringly. "You should see his digs."

"Oh!" said Libertine. "Oh, can I? I'd so love that! You can't see anything from my car, and it's hopeless in the visitors' gallery."

Truman sent Ivy death rays from his eyes. She smiled sweetly.

"I need to run it by Gabriel first," Truman said. "I owe him that."

"Well, of course you do!" said Ivy, grabbing the security radio from Truman's desk and transmitting, "Ivy to Gabriel. Are you there?"

"Go for Gabriel," responded a crackling voice.

"Can you come over here to Truman's office?"

"Now?"

"Yes, please."

"On my way." Gabriel said. "Gabriel out."

Truman dropped his head. "I wish you hadn't done that."

"I know, dear, but we both know you have a tendency to dither when you're left to your own devices. It's one of your less attractive qualities."

"Clear and measured thought is not the same as—"

Ivy reached across the table and patted his hand. "Don't fuss—we don't choose the faults we come with."

Ivy proceeded to engage Libertine in mindless chatter until Gabriel arrived, in boots, rubber overalls, and a rain slicker. The strong smell of fish instantly filled the room.

"Ah," Ivy breathed. "*Eau de poisson.*"

Feeling that he had no choice but to press ahead, Truman

called out the door to his receptionist, "Brenda would you bring in an extra chair, please? One of the plastic ones, not the upholstered." Once a chair had been secured, he said to Gabriel, "Ms. Adagio would like to see the pool and Friday."

Gabriel looked at Truman, appalled. "Is this the animal psychic?"

"Communicator," said Libertine in a small voice.

"You've got to be kidding," said Gabriel.

Truman said, "I'm not, actually."

Gabriel shook his head, looked out the window for a minute before saying, "I've met a lot of so-called animal psychics—"

"Communicators," said Ivy.

"—communicators," Gabriel granted, "and all they've ever done was stir the pot. Things are hard enough with these animals. They're usually very sick, scared, and alone, and they have no idea that without us they'd be dead. And then you bring in the media and propaganda and emotion that has nothing to do with these guys and everything to do with you. I'm sorry to be so blunt, but if you've heard voices, I guarantee you they weren't his."

Libertine held her ground. "I didn't say anything about bringing in the media."

"No? I read a newspaper article this morning with your name all over it."

Truman, watching, saw the faintest flicker in her eyes. It could have been guilt, or it could have been something else. Gabriel had seen it, too. He said to Truman and Ivy, "You haven't been through this before, so you don't know, but that's the way it's done. The activists get an inside look and then they go straight to the media with allegations. From there, there's no way to get the toothpaste back in the tube."

"Don't you think that's a bit harsh?" said Ivy.

"It's all right," said Libertine, and then, to Gabriel, "Most of what I communicate on behalf of my animals is very straight-forward, mainly concerning food and safety."

Gabriel shook his head. "Not this time—from what I read, you scored a political bull's eye for the anticaptivity community."

"I hear you talking to that whale constantly," Ivy pointed out. "*Constantly*. How is that any different?"

"I don't claim to know his inner thoughts, or expect him to know mine."

An uncomfortable silence fell over the room.

"Do you believe in God?" Libertine finally asked Gabriel.

"What?"

"Do you believe there's such a thing as God."

"I don't know. Yes, sure."

"And yet, you haven't seen Him."

"What does that have to do with your ability to communicate with animals? You can't possibly mean you're working for God?"

"Of course not. What I'm saying is, sometimes you have to take things on faith. I *feel* Friday. I can no more explain it than you can; all I know is, he's chosen to confide in me. Maybe I can explain what you're doing. If he'll let me."

"Which I'm totally in favor of," said Ivy. "By the way."

"If he's even open to it," Libertine said. "The fact is, he hasn't been reaching out to me, which means right now he doesn't need me. That's to your credit."

Gabriel turned to Truman. "Look, the decision's obviously not mine, but we have too much work to do and too few people doing it to have someone I don't trust in the first place taking up space or time."

Truman took a long moment, looking out the window for a beat before turning back. "I appreciate your frankness," he said. "All of you. Here's what I'd like to do." To Libertine he said, "Are you planning on staying in Bladenham for long?"

She nodded. "I feel I should, at least for now."

"Are you willing to work while you're here?"

She looked at him, confused. "Of course."

"Then I'd like you to be a volunteer at Friday's pool."

Gabriel stared at him. "You've got to be kidding."

"I'm not," said Truman evenly. "If she wants to be near Friday, then she shouldn't mind working for the privilege." He turned back to Libertine. "But let's be very clear. If you get argumentative, or if you try to influence anything about our rehabilitation program as Gabriel lays it out, no matter how minor, I'll revoke your access immediately and permanently. I'm also going to ask you to sign a confidentiality agreement acknowledging that you are in no way authorized to speak to the media or to represent the zoo. No blogs, no Twitter, no Facebook, no anonymous tip-offs, no unattributed quotes, *nada*. If I so much as suspect you've been talking to the media or trying to manipulate public opinion, you're gone. Does that seem fair?"

"Yes," said Libertine.

Gabriel stood and walked out of the room without another word, emitting wave after wave of pissed-offness. Truman watched him leave and then said to Libertine and Ivy both, "Don't give me any reason to regret this."

He took down Libertine's cell phone number and told her

Gabriel would be in touch. Libertine thanked him profusely as she left. Ivy stayed on, crowing, "So you *are* your father's son!"

Truman smiled sheepishly. "It seemed like a good idea. Now I just have to convince Gabriel to see it that way."

"Let me help," Ivy said, gathering up Julio Iglesias and stuffing him, flat-eared, into her tote.

"Gladly," said Truman.

WEAVING THROUGH THE throngs of visitors heading to Friday's viewing gallery and through two security gates, Ivy found Gabriel in the walk-in freezer, slamming around boxes of frozen herring.

"He's either insane or he's an idiot," he fumed when he saw her.

"Actually, I think he's brilliant. Haven't you ever heard the old saying, 'Hold your friends close and your enemies closer'?"

"Sure, but she's a nut job. She's going to be a pipeline straight from here into the activist camp. You don't know what these people are capable of."

"You know, I don't think so. She may be misguided, but she's very earnest. What she needs is a teacher, someone to interpret what you're doing—and who's better than you?"

Gabriel just shook his head. "I have to tell you, I'm strongly considering walking away."

"What do you mean, walking away?"

Gabriel made two fingers walk along the food prep counter. "I've been in this business for a long time, longer than anyone except a handful of other old guys. We're understaffed as it is. I don't need the headache of having to babysit a lunatic who's under my feet all day."

Ivy regarded him blandly. "I assume you believe in what you're doing here."

"Absolutely."

"Then for god's sake stop pouting and take the high ground. She may be a nutcase, but she has Friday's best interests in mind. So do you. That gives you common ground. Educate her about what you're doing, and then put her to work helping to make it happen. It's a strategy called co-opting, by the way. My brother, Truman's father, does it better than anyone I've ever met."

Gabriel stacked two boxes of frozen herring in Ivy's arms. "Come on," she wheedled, putting the boxes on the food prep counter. "She's too socially awkward to be working on behalf of any group. Teach her what you know. If you can turn her around—and I know you can—think what an asset she could be later, if we need someone to run interference with the real crazies."

Gabriel stared at her. Shaking his head, he said, "My God, you're a wily old thing."

"That I am," she crowed, clapping him on the back. "That I am."

GABRIEL WAS NOT a vitriolic man. He had opinions on many things, but he didn't feel obligated to impart them. He readily accepted that other people had other viewpoints, and believed that for the most part the world was the better for it—except when it came to animal rights advocacy. On that topic he had waged and would wage war against those who believed that all captivity was bad. That was a load-of-crap opinion, held by the ignorant and anthropomorphically confused. More and more, the wild was not a safe place. Animals were regularly slaughtered in African sanctuaries, habitats were shrinking, and zoos were the last safe havens for dozens of species that would otherwise have disappeared already. The wild, in short, could be a place of wholesale peril and death.

As far as he was concerned, Libertine Adagio was embedded firmly in the traditions of wingnutism and lunacy. He'd met scores of people like her, been picketed by them, fought with them, even been threatened with bodily harm by them. In the 1970s—the Wild West of marine park development—when he'd been collecting animals for first-time exhibits, he'd traveled the world on behalf of a half-dozen marine parks, using false identities and passports because someone had put out a contract on him.

And now, thanks to Truman and Ivy tag-teaming him, one of the most objectionable weirdos he'd met in years was being welcomed into the bosom of the family. He drank through the evening, and by his fifth beer, he'd decided, for Friday's sake, to stay. Before he could change his mind he called the number Libertine had given him, connecting to what he recognized as an even worse motel than his own. He had a sudden vision of her sitting all alone on a stove-in, spring-shot bed or bad upholstered chair marinated in years of cigarette smoke. She answered the phone on the first ring.

"Hey, this is Gabriel Jump."

"Oh!"

"You know this is going to be really hard work, right? Hard physical work."

"Yes. I do."

"And you know you can't slack off and blame it on the whale, saying he's told you he's tired or whatever."

"Mr. Jump, you may not approve of what I do, but please give me some credit. I put myself through college waiting tables at a truck stop near Bellingham. I'm not afraid of hard work. Nor am I an idiot."

"Fair enough," he said, giving her that much credit. Waitresses were among the most hardworking people he knew.

The line fell silent for several beats. "Hello?" said Gabriel.

"Hello," she said.

"All right, listen. You're going to need to go to Seattle Marine and Fishing Supply and pick up commercial grade, waterproof bib overalls and a rain slicker, and a pair of XtraTufs. Get the steel-toe ones. What size shoes do you wear?"

"Five and a half. Call it six, because no one ever has five and a halfs."

"You could have trouble finding them that small, but don't get kids' ones even if they fit—they're not going to have steel toes, and you're going to want them, trust me. Get the smallest adult pair you can find and then buy a ton of socks."

"Do you know how much this will cost?" she asked, and he could hear her voice falter.

"About three hundred bucks should cover it, three-fifty."

The line went quiet.

"Is that a problem?" he said. He could be such a dick when he drank.

She answered quietly but with surprising dignity. "I don't have three hundred dollars."

He wasn't a total dick, though; not even when he was drunk. "All you have to do is pick up what you need and tell them it goes on Ivy's account. Ivy Levy."

Her relief was palpable, even over the phone.

"And let's have you start on Monday."

"What time do you get in?"

"I pretty much live there. Let's have you work eight to five, unless we have something special going on. Doable?"

"Absolutely."

"All right then. I'll see you on Monday."

"Oh, yes," she said, and in her voice he heard the full-throated emotion most people reserved for lovers. "I'll be there. You won't regret this—taking me on, I mean."

"We'll see," said Gabriel.

LIBERTINE'S FIRST ASSIGNMENT on Monday morning was to scrub every inch and tread of three used tires in graduated sizes—car, tractor, truck—that a local tire store had donated to the zoo and Gabriel intended to introduce into the pool as toys. "They need to be clean," he'd told her. "Completely. He's immune-suppressed, so we can't afford to introduce any foreign pathogens into the pool." He handed her a pack of twenty sponges, an industrial-sized can of scouring powder, and a pair of heavy-duty rubber gloves. Then he helped her haul the things to the pool top. There, three hours later, she knelt in a foul-smelling puddle of cleanser and rubber residue and re-constituted mud. She had only finished half the truck tire and thought her arms might break if her knees didn't go first. She was not and never had been a physically strong person; men and even women usually sized her up and sprang to help her lift suitcases from airplane overhead compartments and baggage carousels.

But she scrubbed on. If this was Gabriel's way of breaking her, she refused to give him the satisfaction. Nevertheless, it was a welcome distraction when, at lunchtime, a small Chihuahua muzzle inserted itself under her rubber-jacketed arm. "Julio!" she said, slipping off a rubber glove to give him gentle noogies between the ears. "How's my favorite dog?" She rose—with difficulty—and scooped him up so he wouldn't wade through the mess she was making on the concrete deck. Ivy waved as Libertine came around the pool toward her.

"I think you lost something," Libertine said, holding out Julio Iglesias.

"Wishful thinking," said Ivy. "Are you hungry? I'm starving. Come on, let's get out of here—my treat."

"I'd love to, but I can pay my way."

"By what, eating saltines and ketchup soup?" Libertine could feel herself flush. Ivy looked stricken. "I'm sorry—that was insensitive."

"That's all right." Libertine climbed out of her bumblebee-yellow slicker and bib overalls, her XtraTufs and rubber gloves, and hung them all neatly on a series of pegs on the loading dock. "Let me just clean up. Do I reek? I feel like I do."

"Dunno," said Ivy cheerfully. "I have a sinus infection and Julio Iglesias eats poop, so clearly he's no judge."

As they walked to Ivy's car, Libertine noticed that when the two of them walked together, she always let Ivy lead the way, walking a half-step behind and to her right, like a Chinese wife. In animal terms, Ivy was clearly the alpha female.

Near the parking lot they heard one of the zoo's dozen free-roaming peacocks scream. "God," said Ivy, shuddering. "It's like hearing someone's death."

Ivy unlocked Libertine's car door and then went around to her own. Julio Iglesias hopped in as soon as Ivy opened her door, springing into Libertine's lap.

"He's a suck-up," said Ivy, miffed. "I give him the best of the best for nine years, and he's thrown me over without a second look, the little bastard."

"He's just trying his wings," Libertine soothed. "It's good for him."

"Did he tell you that?"

"No, basic animal behavior told me that."

"I guess," Ivy said grudgingly, pulling out of the zoo. "So listen, now that you're going to stick around down here, you can't commute from Orcas Island, so do you have any ideas about where you might live?"

"Actually," said Libertine in a rare moment of frankness, "I may stay in my car. I'll manage."

"No, listen," Ivy said. "I have an idea."

As Libertine had learned from her previous encounters with Ivy, she belted herself in, gave herself over, and held on for the ride.

As usual the air inside the Oat Maiden was rich with delicious smells. For a moment after they'd ducked in, Ivy closed her eyes to breathe it in, thinking that homes should smell like this, even though they almost never did, any more than they harbored perfect safety, love, and respect. Still, it was a nice thought, like praying for world peace, and it warmed her a little just to have had it.

Even on this gloomy, rainy day, most of the tables were filled. Ivy recognized several associates from Matthew's law firm, and several zoo employees. She steered Libertine to a small round table just outside the kitchen. Around the table-top trotted cats, lots of cats, each one holding the very tip of the tail of a small but unalarmed-looking mouse. There were no predators or prey here; Johnson Johnson lived in a kinder world.

The man himself approached them swaddled in several layers of flannel shirts—despite the heat in the kitchen, he was impossibly thin and always cold—and a cotton apron that tied in the back and was so blotchy with tomato sauce it looked like he'd been repeatedly stabbed.

Ivy beamed at him and said, "Johnson Johnson, meet Libertine Adagio. Libertine is an animal psychic."

"Communicator," said Libertine.

Johnson Johnson mumbled a greeting, blushing. Ivy saw Libertine's face color, too. She looked from one to the other and said with delight, "You've met before, haven't you!" To Johnson Johnson she said, "Has she told you she's going to work with our killer whale at the zoo? Well, she is, and she needs a place to stay. Do you have a tenant in your apartment right now?" Neva Wilson had lived in a converted garage behind Johnson Johnson's house for nearly a year when she first came to the zoo to work with Sam and Hannah.

"No," said Johnson Johnson. "Lots of people are allergic."

"To what, mold?"

"Cats."

"Are you allergic to cats?" Ivy asked Libertine.

"No, but—"

"Then it'll be perfect. Can we look at it?"

"Yes," said Johnson Johnson.

"Is there a key hidden someplace? We'd like to swing by today, if we can."

"It's under the mat."

"Well, that's not very original, is it," Ivy chided. "Especially from a man with your creativity."

Johnson Johnson clasped his hands together and looked at his shoes.

"Oh, honey, I'm just saying." To Libertine she said, sotto voce, "I make him nervous. He told me once I remind him of his third grade teacher, which I gather is not a compliment."

Johnson Johnson asked Libertine, "Do you like cats? Because you pretty much have to like cats."

"I do," Libertine assured him. "I communicate with them all the time."

Johnson Johnson's face lit up.

"She doesn't mean her own cats, you understand," Ivy couldn't resist saying. "*Random* cats."

"Not random," Libertine corrected her. "They've looked for me."

"I like cats," Johnson Johnson said and then, apparently believing the subject to have been thoroughly exhausted, he walked away. The kitchen door swung open and shut behind him like a fit of indecision.

"One of God's gentle people," Ivy said, looking after him fondly.

"What do you know about him?"

"You mean besides the fact that he's a sexual predator?"

Libertine paled.

Ivy poked her arm. "Honey, you have just *got* to lighten up. I'm teasing you—he's a sweet man through and through. His parents had some money—not a lot, but more than enough to provide for him. He lived with them until they passed a few years ago, and they left him the house, plus some kind of a trust that my sister-in-law Lavinia administers. There was enough for him to buy the Oat Maiden when it came up for sale a couple of years ago."

"And he runs it himself?"

"Yes and no. He came up with the menu and the recipes, plus he cooks. But Neva helps him with ordering supplies and taking care of the books. You could say it's a collective effort."

Libertine nodded, then cleared her throat. "What's the monthly rent?" she finally asked.

"What do you care—I'll be paying for it. You know, for someone who claims to be psychic you certainly misread a lot of signals."

"I never claimed to be psychic when it comes to people," Libertine said, coloring. "I don't even *get* most people."

"Frankly," said Ivy, "neither one of you has the social sense God gave a goose." She nodded in the direction of the kitchen.

Libertine looked at her water glass.

"And that," Ivy declared, "is why the two of you are perfect." A moment later Johnson Johnson placed their pizza in front of them as gravely as if he were delivering a religious relic. After they'd eaten they drove straight from the Oat Maiden to Johnson Johnson's house, a beautifully maintained craftsman bungalow in Bladenham's tiny historic district.

As promised, the key was under the mat. They circled the house to a detached garage in the back, which was also immaculately kept, with seasonal plantings and recently refreshed mulch.

"He's a gardener," Libertine said.

"That I didn't know," said Ivy, unlocking the front door. "Makes sense, though. As I said, he's gentle. You don't meet many men like that. Many people," she amended. "At least not in my experience."

"Oh! How pretty!" Libertine slipped past Ivy, who was holding the apartment door open. The walls were painted a deep, sunny gold, the ceiling the lightest blue, with puffy, fair-weather clouds drifting across the ceiling.

"Pretty Spartan," Ivy said, looking critically at the room's simple convertible sofa bed, coffee table, antique washstand, and highboy.

"Do you think?"

Ivy shrugged. "I don't know—I've always been a clutter-monger. It comes from growing up in the ancestral home."

"Well, I think it's just fine," Libertine said emphatically.

IVY DROPPED HER off at the pool, where Libertine resumed her assault on the tires, scrubbing with a nylon pad, sponge, and even her fingernails when necessary. Two hours later, Gabriel came up to the pool top, dressed in his ubiquitous wet suit and steering a fiberglass cart full of dive gear. She waved at him cheerily. When he saw her hands—bleeding from a network of cracks—he hurried over and said, "Good god!"

"I'm allergic to the gloves."

"Well, for god's sake, why didn't you say something?"

Buoyed by her lunch and the prospect of getting out of her terrible motel, she leaned into him and whispered, "I'm also wearing a hair shirt."

He peered at her with alarm, until the slightest twitch in one corner of her mouth gave her away.

"So you do have a sense of humor."

"Did you think I didn't?" Before he could respond, she said, "Anyway, this one's about done," gesturing to the soapy truck tire she was working on. "I just have to hose it off one last time."

"How do you feel about thawing, measuring, and bucketing fish?" Gabriel asked, clearly impressed.

"Just fine."

"Then plan on doing fish house tomorrow morning. Five A.M."

"Fish house?"

"Zookeeper-speak for preparing marine mammal diets. Neva will start thawing fish tonight, and tomorrow you'll work with her to weigh and bucket it. But be forewarned—it's messy. And smelly."

"Sounds great," she said, and meant it.

IN ALL, IT took Libertine only until the end of the day to get the three tires nearly surgically clean, and the work was never better than backbreaking. When it was finally time to introduce them into the pool she could hardly wait to see the whale's reaction.

When they were certain Friday was watching, Libertine and Neva pushed the truck tire into the water. It immediately filled, wobbled, and sank straight to the bottom of the pool. Friday did nothing, barely even watched it go.

They pushed the tractor tire into the water next. It filled, too, and sank. Friday hurried to the opposite end of the pool.

They decided to leave the car tire sitting in the shallow water of the slide-out. Maybe the tires had been a bad idea.

Libertine straightened the things in her locker and tried to keep her disappointment in check. The tips of her fingers were raw; her arms and hands hurt. She didn't know what reaction she'd expected from Friday, but she'd expected something. She reminded herself that this was a killer whale, not a dog. She reminded herself that he had rejected the gift, not her. This wasn't personal. Still, it felt personal.

Her purse and car keys in hand, she went upstairs one last

time to make sure she'd put away all her supplies. There was an unfamiliar, dark shape in the slide-out area of the wet walk, and as she approached, her heart began to pound.

All three tires were sitting in the shallow water, one stacked on top of the other in a perfect pyramid.

"Never underestimate a killer whale," Gabriel had told her earlier that day, and she could see why.

THAT SAME NIGHT, Libertine moved into her new apartment. She loved its snugness, its bright walls and pretty little white kitchen. The furnishings were clean and cheerful, and with a few things on the wall and a plant or two, she'd be happy to come back here at the end of the day.

Chocolate was her first feline visitor, emerging almost immediately from a tube that ran from Johnson Johnson's house to her kitchen. The cat seemed perfectly at home, and strangely incurious about Libertine. His fur was fine, sleek, and ticked— she suspected an Abyssinian ancestor or two. She sensed that he was by nature a prodigious purrer with an even temper and a sunny disposition.

Next out of the cat-tube was Chip, a stout male who wore an elegant white bib and whiskers, gleaming black morning coat and trousers. He hopped up on the end table, strode over to Libertine on the sofa, switched on a purr like a chainsaw, and turned upside down beside her to buff his coat against the couch's nubby fabric.

She was just about to get up when she heard a little bell ring, signaling the arrival of the third and last cat, a battle-scarred orange tabby with one milky eye and a considerable gut. This, then, must be the fearsome Kitty, whom Ivy had described to her. He had the brio of an aging mobster, giving off an aura of latent power that bespoke a violent past stretching all the way back to kittenhood. He strode straight over to her. She smoothed the lay of his fur.

Suddenly all three cats' ears came up. Libertine heard a greeting so distant it might have been coming from the ocean floor, and then all three, led by the redoubtable Kitty, disappeared into the tube.

Johnson Johnson had come home.

NEVA ARRIVED THE next morning at five to help Libertine with her first fish-house shift. It wasn't that Neva doubted the other woman, but on principle she felt she hadn't yet proved herself enough to be left alone in the building. Neva knew plenty of anticaptivity activists who would take this opportunity to sabotage a captive program without a hint of self-doubt or remorse. Even if Libertine was trustworthy, Neva wasn't sure she could stand up to a stronger personality with nefarious intentions.

Now she handed Libertine one of two to-go cups of strong coffee and cranked up the volume on a Coldplay CD, cheerfully telling Libertine that fish houses the world over ran on strong coffee and musical assault.

"Gabriel told me about the glove allergy," she said, pulling on a pair of heavy blue industrial-quality rubber gloves with traction palms and fingers, then turning off the water that had been running all night over a frozen, solid block of herring to thaw it. "But let me tell you, you don't want to handle fish with bare hands any more often than you have to. You don't know what pain is until you get fish scales under your fingernails. Plus they can cut. There have to be gloves out there that you can tolerate, and I'm sure the zoo will reimburse you. So okay."

Neva pulled over a rolling Gorilla Rack with five empty stainless steel buckets that would hold Friday's food rations for the day. With practiced speed, she set the first bucket on the stainless steel counter beside the sink, hauled over the soggy fish box, and brought up a double handful of now-thawed fish— capelin, each the size of a lady's shoe—which she weighed before dumping it into the bucket.

"The idea is to put about forty-five pounds in each of these buckets—two hundred and twenty-five pounds a day, to start with," she explained to Libertine. "Normally an adult killer whale would eat as much as four hundred and fifty pounds a day, but he hasn't had anywhere near that much. We're in major fatten-up mode, but we'll increase the amount he eats gradually. Okay—now you." She pushed the soggy box toward Libertine, who closed her eyes momentarily before digging her bare hands into the icy, slippery, stinging mass of fish. Neva knew from past experience that all the abrasions and cuts Libertine had gotten while scouring the tires had lit up like they were on fire. She gasped but stuck with it, piling four or five fish on the scale and then adding one more.

"You're tough," Neva said, watching her.

"Not that tough," admitted Libertine. "Hand me those gloves. My allergy can't be as bad as this is."

Neva took a pair of inside-out blue gloves like her own from a Peg-Board drying rack and gave them to Libertine. "Make sure you write down the exact weight of each bucket in the log, plus the combined total. Gabriel or I will enter it into the food records on the computer when we have time. And if you find a fish that's burst or seems gushy, throw it out. We don't get bad ones that often, but it happens."

"It's all just so disgusting," Libertine marveled.

Neva considered this. "Oh, I don't know. One summer I did raptor diets at a rehab center and that was worse. You cut up thawed mice with scissors."

The color drained from Libertine's face.

Neva grinned wickedly. "Snip, snip."

FRIDAY WAS WAITING when they arrived on the pool top, his chin on the edge of the pool, mouth open and ready for breakfast.

"He's such a goofball," Neva said fondly. "Do you want to pet him? Actually we shouldn't say things like 'pet'. He's not a golden retriever. But you know what I mean. Do you want to?"

"Oh, can I?" Libertine clasped her hands.

"You mean you were here all day yesterday and you didn't touch him at least *once*?"

"No—I didn't want to presume."

"Some animal terrorist you are."

Libertine looked at her, crestfallen.

"Nah, I'm just teasing you," Neva said. "Okay, first of all take off the gloves, and then come on over. Are you, like, talking to him right now?"

"No—it doesn't really work like that. I feel him, and he feels me, but it's not all the time—and in his case, not in days. Sometimes that means they don't need me anymore, and sometimes it means they've given up."

"The time to have given up would have been all those years in that awful place."

"I'm sure you're right," said Libertine. "But even the strongest spirit can only take so much."

Libertine pitched the bulky blue rubber gloves onto the dry concrete and squatted, elbowing her too-big bib overalls and slicker out of the way, and touched Friday's cheek. She could feel her pulse racing with excitement—she'd only ever laid hands on a few of the animals she worked with. His skin was warm, smooth, and firm, and he watched her evenly while she scratched him. She suddenly felt him in her head as a lovely hum, almost catlike, and then he was gone. Black skin cells floated away and collected under her fingernails as he continued to slough off the topmost layer of skin that had come in contact with the freshwater in his transport box. She scratched what she could reach of him underwater as well as above—the cold water quickly made her hands ache—and gradually his eyes got heavy and then closed altogether.

Neva stayed nearby, beaming. "Isn't he just fabulous?"

Hoping her knees weren't beginning to lock as she continued to squat, Libertine looked closely at the clumps of warty skin above his pectoral flipper. "Do these hurt, do you think?"

"No—they look worse than they are. According to Gabriel, they're only important because they're a sign that he has a crappy immune system. Why don't you go ahead and feed him?"

Libertine staggered a little as she stood up. Neva shuffled a bucket of herring to her through the wet walk. Libertine placed fish after fish in Friday's open mouth and watched him swallow. "It's kind of like feeding a slot machine or putting dollars into a vending machine or something. He doesn't chew."

"No molars."

Once Friday had finished every fish in the bucket, the women stood side by side in the shallow water, arms folded, watching him contemplatively. The morning was upon them—another gray day with swollen clouds.

"Do you ever wish you couldn't sense them?" Neva asked—the first time she'd ever indicated to Libertine that she believed she was capable of psychically sensing any animal.

"All the time," said Libertine. "All the time."

Chapter 7

FRIDAY WAS THE most easygoing killer whale Gabriel had ever worked with. Still, he did have a temper, which he lost early one morning during his first weeks at the zoo over a handful of squid he was offered for the first time. While Gabriel and Neva watched, he spit out the squid and then swam around the perimeter of the pool slapping his tail flukes on the water in outrage. In the past weeks he'd flown thousands of miles, worked hard for strangers, accepted new routines, and given blood samples without protest. But the handful of squid was too much. He didn't know its taste, didn't like its texture, would not eat it.

They cheered for this first small act of defiance.

He returned. He ate the squid.

BY HIS THIRD week at the zoo, Friday's diet amounted to nearly twice what he'd been fed in Bogotá, and as he ate, folds in his stomach began to open that had been closed for years. He regurgitated a Colombian peso, several child's barrettes, and then a partially digested, shoulder-length latex examination glove. The warty masses also began to break up and then fall off. For hours every day Gabriel, Neva, and Libertine took turns rubbing Friday down with their hands, their fingernails, silicon oven mitts, and nylon pot scrubbers, to help him get rid of the sloughing tissue. Beneath the warts was smooth, only slightly scarred skin.

All that time Friday had shown an inexplicable fear of his medical pool gates. The med pool was a small, twelve-foot-deep, rectangular extension of the main pool, accessed by two gates set in the concrete walls. The gates were amply wide and amply deep, but once he was in the small isolation pool, he didn't seem to recognize that what lay beyond the second gate was his pool, seeing it instead as a new and terrifying frontier. Although he would readily swim into the med pool through either one of the gates, he refused to swim out the other, laboriously backing out instead. No amount of persuasion could move him.

Because the finishing touches hadn't been put on his pool before Friday's whirlwind relocation, two workmen arrived one day to install fiberglass handrails in place of the hastily constructed two-by-fours ringing the pool top. One man leaned over the railing to tighten bolts with an electric screwdriver while the other held the railing in place; both men stood in the narrow wet walk. Rapt in the presence of power tools, Friday refused to leave them all day. Believing in the wisdom of choosing one's battles, Gabriel canceled the day's exercise sessions. When the final bolt was fixed in place hours later, the men finally packed up their gear and departed. On the way out one called to Gabriel, "Hey, that's quite a whale you got there!" When Gabriel asked whether the workmen had known Friday had been watching them, he said, "Are you kidding? He had his head on my foot half the time!"

Gabriel canceled the following morning's exercise sessions,

too. They'd get no work out of Friday before noon—he'd been up all night watching a team of painters power-spray his viewing gallery walls.

THOUGH WELL ON his way to physical recovery, Friday still spent the majority of his free time sleeping—far more than Gabriel thought was either necessary or healthy. To improve his overall muscle tone he and Neva had been recycling his show behaviors—bows, breaches, speed-swims, spy hops—five and six times a day, but now Gabriel decided it was time to wake up his mind. On a glorious, clear day in early July, Gabriel took delivery of a blue plastic Boomer Ball.

Made of heavy-duty plastic, Boomer Balls were designed specifically to withstand the force of even the biggest and strongest zoo animals. As enrichment devices, zookeepers often drilled holes in them and stuffed them with treats. But instead of perceiving the ball's recreational merits, Friday regarded it with abject fear. Gabriel talked to him quietly, touching the ball, rolling it, knocking on it, demonstrating its benign qualities. Then he gently pushed the ball away from the wall toward Friday—where it bobbed in his wake as he fled to the far side of the pool and put his head in the corner. The ball stalled against the side of the pool.

The next morning, they began again. Friday followed Gabriel around the perimeter of the pool as Gabriel nudged the blue ball to keep it nearby, pointing to the whale's flukes, his pectoral flippers, his nose. "Use your beak; no, not your pec, your beak." He reached out and tapped Friday's rostrum lightly. "Your beak. That's right. Good—good boy! See? That wasn't so scary. Do it again. Touch it with your beak. No, not your pec; your beak."

He talked and talked and talked, but Friday was afraid and miserable. Gabriel ended the work session with a few easy requests—squirt water through your teeth; lift your flukes in the air—to let the whale finish with success.

Later that day, at Gabriel's request, Neva directed Friday into the medical pool and then lured him to the second, suspect medical pool gate. Friday followed the fish she held out until the only thing left in the med pool were his flukes—but he refused to go any farther. Still, they were making progress, even if it was inch by inch. Neva blew her whistle: "*Good boy!*"

Friday backed all the way out of the gate through which he entered.

GABRIEL NEXT DEVISED a signal that looked like a gunfighter's quick draw. It would come to mean, *You can do anything you want during this work session, but you won't be rewarded for the same behavior twice.* Initially the signal meant nothing, so Friday hung in the water, awaiting further instruction. None came. After ten minutes, just to do something, he opened his mouth. Gabriel blew a blast on his whistle, signaling success. He gave Friday several fish before giving him the same signal.

Friday opened his mouth again, but this time there was no whistle, no fish. He waited. In ten minutes more, when nothing had happened, he turned to go. Gabriel blew his whistle—*good boy for turning away!*—and gave him several more fish and a quick rubdown before drawing his guns once more. The killer whale opened his mouth, then turned to swim away, but there was no whistle, no fish.

Gabriel ended the session with a rubdown and a pep talk.

VISITORS CONTINUED TO pour into the zoo, not just from across the country, but around the world. Many claimed to feel some connection with Friday that they couldn't explain.

While Neva worked primarily behind the scenes, Sam kept a running log of Friday's behavior from the viewing gallery windows. One day a young man came in, pushing an old woman in a wheelchair. As Sam pieced it together later, after talking with the young man, the woman was ninety-two and dying. The young man volunteered sometimes at her nursing home, and last week had fixed her TV for her when she was frantic that she might miss the evening news. She had confided in him that she had watched every TV news spot about Friday since he'd come to the Biedelman Zoo. She had inoperable cancer and her last wish was to be in Friday's presence.

Sam watched the young man slowly push the wheelchair through the tight crowds until at last there was no one between the old woman and one of the enormous windows. She was patient, waiting for fifteen, then twenty minutes, but Friday was across the pool, napping. Though there was no telling when he'd wake up, she waved away the young man's suggestion that they go see something else at the zoo and come back later. She would stay right here.

At last there were cries from the crowd and Friday appeared in the window. He swam past the old woman but then stopped and circled back until he was only inches away from her. They regarded one another, the whale and the woman; their eyes locked and held. Tears ran down her thin cheeks in the chilly air of the gallery.

The young man dug a camera out of the flowered plastic bag hanging from the wheelchair handles and handed it to Sam, who struggled to get both the woman and the whale in the picture. He did the best he could, snapping several mediocre shots. In the end, from what he later learned in a thank-you note, it made no difference—the old woman didn't live long enough to see them. She didn't need to: on the drive home, she told the young man over and over, *He saw me. I know he saw me.* And Sam believed she was right.

ON THE POOL top, Gabriel drew his guns once more, giving Friday the signal to do anything he wanted, but not that same thing twice. This was their third try. Friday opened his mouth, as he had before, and then he turned to swim away. Both behaviors had been rewarded at the first two sessions; both were rewarded again. Then, still stumped, the killer whale just hung there, watching Gabriel and Neva for further direction.

Gabriel and Neva stood in place, arms folded, giving nothing away. Minutes dragged by. Then, hesitantly, Friday spit a mouthful of water between his teeth.

"Good boy!" Gabriel hollered, blowing his whistle to validate the behavior.

Friday lifted his tail flukes free of the water.

"*Good boy!*" Gabriel yelled.

Friday nodded his head up and down. *Pwwwweeeeeet!* Gabriel once again blew a long, excited whistle blast. "*Good boy! GOOD BOY!*"

Friday spit water like a fountain, hung his tongue out of the side of his mouth, shook a pec, squeaked through his blowhole. With each behavior, he got further from anything he'd ever been trained to do. He did a hip shimmy, rolled his tongue, blew a ring of bubbles through his blowhole—riffing, out there on his own.

By the end of the session he was moonwalking across the bottom of the pool.

THE NEXT DAY, building on Friday's success, Gabriel led Friday around the perimeter of the pool, nudging the blue ball to keep it nearby, pointing to the whale's flukes, his pectoral flippers, his nose. "Use your beak—no, not your pec; your beak." He reached out and tapped Friday's nose lightly. "Your beak. That's right. Good—good boy! See? That wasn't so scary. Do it again. Touch it with your beak. No, not your pec; your beak."

He talked and talked and talked—for fifteen minutes; half an hour. He talked with hand signals; he talked with his voice; he talked through the sheer combined force of his will and eye contact. And, flushed with yesterday's success, Friday not only touched the ball, he cupped his flukes and dragged it. He bounced it gently with his pectoral flipper, rolled it, set it in a gentle spin. He pushed it under, at first just a bit, then completely, watching it bob back to the surface. He balanced it on his nose and dove, taking it underwater.

"I'll be damned," Sam said to Neva, watching. "Looks to me like someone just woke up."

But still, there were limits to these successes. Several days later, in a problem-solving exercise, Gabriel sent Friday to get his blue ball, which was beached on the wet walk over a grate. They'd been working on manipulating the ball with Friday's various body parts to encourage body awareness and as physical therapy disguised as play. Now, Gabriel asked Friday to get the ball, which would first require that he get it into the pool.

Friday raised a pectoral flipper and gently touched the ball. It moved slightly and went right back to where it started. He did this over and over and over, rolling the ball slightly, but never enough to get it over the lip of the grate. Each time, he checked with Gabriel: *was that good enough?* Each time Gabriel sent him back with the same signal: go get the ball.

"You can do this," he assured Friday.

But in the end, he couldn't. After fifteen minutes of futile effort, he began keening a piercing cry of fury. Gabriel went to him and pushed the ball into the water, but Friday ignored it, ignored Gabriel, and went off, alone, to the medical pool, where he refused to have anything more to do with Gabriel or the ball for the rest of the day. Gabriel told Libertine, "You always want to end a session *before* the animal fails—that's training one-oh-one. I blew it. It'll probably mean a setback. *Damn* it."

But with the next week came a chance for redemption. Gabriel asked Friday to swim into the med pool and then out the second gate—the same thing they'd been working on for weeks now. This time only two inches of Friday's tail flukes remained behind him in the medical pool; the rest of his body was in the main pool. His eyes were wide, red, locked onto Gabriel's. He was nervous.

Without breaking eye contact Gabriel grabbed a handful of herring and flipped it into the water two inches beyond Friday's head.

Instinctively, the whale reached.

He was out. He had gone through the second med pool gate.

Gabriel blew a sustained, triumphal blast. "*Good boy!*"

He and Neva fed Friday four buckets of food—most of his day's allotment. Then they jumped into the water with him to play. For days afterward, Friday spent his free time swimming in one gate and out the other, in one and out the other.

Here was a conqueror of worlds.

EVEN IN MID-AUGUST the world media continued to take an unabated interest in Friday's progress. And with the extensive coverage came requests from movie stars and other VIPs for private audiences with Friday. Neva spent more and more time playing host to these visitors—who, Truman reminded her when she got cranky about it, often left the zoo sizable donations after their visits. One was the star of a hugely successful 1990s detective series who arrived in floppy shapeless pants, sneakers, a baseball cap, and no makeup, looking unabashedly like hell, which earned her Neva's grudging respect. She was very breezy and crooned softly to Friday, "Look at you, you beautiful thing!" Friday hung motionless in the water, watching her watch him. She squatted down on the wet cement and extended her hand for Friday to sniff, by which Neva knew she was a dog person. Dog people invariably held their hands out this way, a pointless courtesy in Friday's case, since he breathed through the blowhole on top of his head and had no olfactory sense at all.

Still, he came within a few inches of the movie star's outstretched hand—but every time she leaned forward, he backed up. After going through this little dance several times, the TV star asked Neva who had hit him.

"What?" Neva said, startled.

"Who hit him? Look how head-shy he is. You see that with horses when they've been beaten. Dogs, too."

Neva was impressed. She and Gabriel had often wondered the same thing—and a few days later got an unwelcome insight. Gabriel took a new cleaning implement into the pool, a scrubbing head on the end of a long aluminum pole. He had just begun using it on the pool's rock work when he heard a loud, ominous buzzing—a killer whale's unmistakable expression of rage. He looked up just in time to see Friday heading toward him fast, straight, and livid. Before he'd had a chance to react, Friday bit the pole cleanly in half.

Too startled to be afraid, Gabriel hollered at him around the regulator in his mouth and windmilled his arms. Contrite, Friday swam meekly away and took his blue ball into a corner, where he remained in a self-imposed time-out for the rest of the afternoon.

"Now we know," Gabriel told Neva. "They hit him with poles. Maybe other things, too, but definitely metal poles."

IN LATE SEPTEMBER Truman announced that one of Friday's Colombian trainers would be visiting—the one who'd called him *Gordito,* Little Fat One. She brought along a film crew that was shooting a documentary about her and her husband, a famous Colombian soap opera star. Neva dutifully accompanied her to the pool top, where she was promptly surrounded by cameras and sound gear. The trainer wore an expensive purple and black wet suit, and sat on the side of the pool with her legs dangling in. Now and then her fingers described circles in the water, a gesture she had used in Bogotá to summon him. Friday declined over and over, until the director began to get anxious, pacing, crouching occasionally, and, to show he was calm and patient, rubbing the young woman's back, or at least rubbing the unyielding wet suit.

The fact was, they were running out of time and light and they were scheduled to leave first thing in the morning. The director had indicated on their way here that the beautiful trainer should let her sorrow flow as she contemplated parting from Friday once again. On camera she'd already described Friday as her best friend, her lover. They needed a close-up, one close-up. They needed the whale.

Far below Friday hunkered down at a window. In the viewing gallery, a workman was buffing the acrylic.

AN HOUR BEFORE the zoo opened several days later, Neva escorted a noted wildlife photographer and the marketing director of a major toy company to the empty visitors' gallery, where the photographer meticulously laid out his cameras, lenses, filters, and a tripod. Then he wadded up two small pieces of duct tape, applying them to the window. With great solemnity the marketing director opened a box, gently removing the prototype of a special-issue scuba-diving doll with Baby Friday. Truman had given the toy company permission to use Friday's likeness in exchange for a sizable donation. The doll wore a stylish wet suit and pink plastic scuba gear, and the photographer gravely stuck her to the window so she appeared to be swimming. He quickly dodged behind a camera and waited.

As they'd hoped, Friday approached. He applied his nose directly to the doll's backside. The doll fell off the window.

Neva couldn't quite stifle a guffaw.

The window was cold, the gallery was damp, and the tape refused to stick. Worse, each time the photographer did manage to successfully apply the doll to the window, Friday continued to home in on her butt. As Neva watched, the photographer began to come undone in a quiet, professional, unassuming way. He twisted his cap around backward; he screwed new lenses onto his camera; he moved pointlessly from side to side; he snapped a few halfhearted shots in what he later told Neva was the blind hope that a miracle would happen and the images would come out better than what he was seeing in the viewfinder. Finally, he vowed that he would never again accept a product photography assignment, if only he could salvage one shot.

He salvaged exactly one shot.

FRIDAY HAD BECOME a full-blown international celebrity. Crews arrived from as far away as Australia and China. Television stations from Vancouver, B.C. to San Diego begged their affiliates in Portland and Seattle to file weekly stories with plenty of B-roll to pad the longer segments. Radio stations lobbied to broadcast their morning drive-time shows live from the pool top. (Truman wondered about this. After all, it was *radio*. Couldn't they just *say* they were there?)

With his newfound health, Friday gradually revealed a deep inner silliness. He hovered in the gallery windows for hours on end, sleek, black, and glossy as a patent-leather purse. He waggled his tongue at visitors and blew bubble rings from his blowhole. He swam his blue ball around the pool underwater; he glided past the gallery windows upside down with his eyes closed. He unfurled a yard-long penis from his genital slit and ejaculated, forcing parents to answer awkward questions from young children.

In early October, Christian Thereaux, the colleague who'd once saved Gabriel's life, spun through Bladenham on a lightning trip from Seattle to San Francisco. Gabriel insisted that he stop at the zoo for a few hours, at least; like Gabriel, he had often visited in Bogotá to look in on Friday.

Now, when Christian arrived in the office, Friday looked at him through the window and swam off, unimpressed.

"Man, he looks *great*," Christian told Gabriel.

"Want to do a session with him?"

"Yeah?"

"Come on." Gabriel grabbed a bucket of fish, tossed Christian a pair of XtraTufs, and they went upstairs.

It was a sunny, windless day, the first in a long time. Friday was in excellent spirits. Christian stepped into the wet walk, set down a bucket, and, like an orchestra conductor, raised an imperious hand: *attention!* Friday approached him and Christian asked him to nod his head, a nursery school behavior. For a long beat Friday regarded him through slitted eyes. Then he exhaled explosively in the Frenchman's face, turned around, and swam very, very slowly to the far end of the pool, where he sank underwater, returning to his fans in the viewing gallery. The snub was absolute.

On the pool top Gabriel and Christian collapsed in hoots of laughter. Only a healthy animal had the wiles to best you.

Chapter 8

ON THE FIRST Sunday morning in November Truman woke up at six o'clock, his favorite time of day, when the rest of the world was still asleep and no one needed him for a single thing. Beside him Neva was sprawled on her back with the covers kicked aside, her mouth slightly open and her fiery hair going every which way across the pillows. She was an energetic sleeper, giving the appearance of being on her way to someplace else—an impression she also gave him sometimes when she was awake.

Miles, a light sleeper like Truman, got up from his nest of blankets on the floor with a piggy stretch and a soft grunt and followed on his soft little hooves as Truman tiptoed out of the room and pulled the bedroom door closed with great care. Man and pig paused for a moment to listen to Winslow's gentle snoring—the boy suffered from year-round allergies—before padding downstairs to retrieve the Sunday *New York Times* from the front stoop.

Truman yawned with pleasure, knowing that for now and the next hour or two, the people he loved most were safe beneath his roof. It occurred to him, and not for the first time, that if he were to drop dead at this exact moment, he would die in a state of contentment. After the terrible drama of his marriage to Rhonda, he didn't take for granted even an instant of grace.

As always, Miles followed him to the den, where he curled up on his special blanket at Truman's feet, resting his head cozily on Truman's instep. Truman patted and scratched him a little here and there, whereupon Miles heaved a deep sigh, gave Truman one last adoring look, and fell utterly asleep. Say what you would, the pig did have an undeniably sweet and accommodating nature.

Truman shook out the business section of the *Times*. As a boy, he had spent every Sunday morning with his parents in their white-and-chintz sunroom with a carafe of excellent coffee and cinnamon rolls. Lavinia always wore a pair of white cotton archivist's gloves to keep the ink off her hands, about which she was vain; Matthew chewed the stem of a pipe he hadn't lit since 1982. They had encouraged a lively give-and-take over the news of the day, and sometimes the discussions had gone on between his parents until midafternoon. In those cases they excused Truman, who went off to his room and solitary play.

Truman realized once he'd had Winslow that Lavinia had treated him less like a child than like a very small defense attorney. There had been no mother-and-son afternoons of Let's Pretend or play with wooden blocks. Truman's earliest construction had been a set of bookshelves; his blanket-fort had been a courtroom. He rarely had friends visit—he had very few friends to begin with, which Lavinia preferred—and was hardly ever invited to the never-ending circuit of birthday parties and sleepovers he'd heard about in school. He was a solemn boy, responsible, careful, and disciplined. Family lore had it that his first words were "May I be excused?" Life was not a festival as his parents led him to believe, but a set of increasingly serious challenges to the concepts of what was right and what was wrong and why.

Giving Miles to Winslow on his eleventh birthday was arguably the first indefensible thing Truman had ever done. It had been a heady experience, fueling a faint suspicion that the older he got, the more childish he would become. Running out for ice cream in place of a meal; taking a drive to nowhere in particular and staying there overnight; falling in love with Neva, a woman who lived almost entirely in the right-now: these were all outgrowths of his hike through the unspeakable muck and stink of Miles's barnyard, and among his proudest moments.

If they had had shortcomings as parents, Matthew and Lavinia had been more successful as spouses, each finding in the other a best friend, which hadn't prepared Truman at all for Rhonda. When she left him, and despite her awful nature, he'd felt stricken. His days had been defined by her: what they ate, what movies they saw—even who they saw on holidays and weekends. At first it had been because she had cared so much more than he did, but within a year he had just found capitulation easier.

With Neva, it was all so different. They liked the same foods, hated the same movies, talked the same politics. When conversing with Rhonda—and not even deep conversations; it could be a quick exchange in the cereal aisle at Safeway—Truman had always felt she had the whole thing scripted out, only to have him blow his lines. With Neva, there were no lines or unmet expectations. She wasn't as well read as Rhonda, or as sophisticated in her tastes in art and music, but she was fiercely committed to what she believed in—which, to his everlasting amazement, included him; she was earnest and generous; she knew how to make Winslow, naturally a grave child, get silly; and she was a superb auto mechanic. His household had gone from bleak and lonely to a sunny meadow. Not a day went by that didn't find him raising his face to the heavens in thanks.

Just before ten o'clock, Winslow slap-slap-slapped into the den in his new wet suit, hood, booties, and flippers. Miles rose from Truman's feet to greet him and squeeze into his favorite spot beneath the den's piano while Winslow removed his flippers, placing them within easy reach beside the piano bench. The boy had Rhonda's dark eyes and Truman's tendencies toward gravitas and introspection. Truman loved him fiercely. From the first trimester, Rhonda had proudly declared the pregnancy difficult, saying that from the moment he'd quickened, the baby took perverse pleasure in punching and kicking her where it would inflict the most pain. When she was awake, she claimed, he slept; when she tried to sleep, he not only woke up, but he brought out weapons. *He's like Hephaestus,* she liked to say. *It's like he's in there forging armor.*

But in this as in nearly everything else, Winslow, as well as Truman, had proved to be a disappointment. He was a placid, sober, sleepy baby who, as long as there'd been music playing, could happily deliberate over his hands and feet for hours. Later, perversely, Rhonda had refused to acknowledge that the boy might in fact possess a prodigious musical talent, which Truman chalked up to her disinclination to acknowledge any talent that might burn brighter than her own. Truman had taken Winslow's musical education upon himself and quietly presented him to Mrs. Iris Leahey, a classical concert pianist who took on a student or two by audition when she wasn't on tour.

Now Truman said, "What are you going to practice, *La Mer*?"

"Ha ha."

"Come on, that was good."

Winslow failed to suppress a smile. "Yeah, it was."

"So what does it feel like in there?" Truman asked, of the wet suit.

"Hot. I bet its gets really stinky, too. All that sweat. I hope we get to go in the pool soon. Neva said the saltwater and the neoprene make it so easy to float that if you want to go to the bottom you need dive weights."

The thought of sharing a pool with one of the ocean's top predators, even a debilitated one, didn't strike Truman as nearly the great opportunity everyone else seemed to think it was. "Let's just take it one step at a time, Winnie. Let's not get ahead of ourselves."

By now beads of perspiration had begun to dot Winslow's forehead and upper lip, and his cheeks were blotchy. He turned his back on Truman and said, "Can you undo the zipper?"

Truman unzipped him from neck to waist, releasing a wave of muggy heat. Winslow shucked off the suit until he stood there in nothing but a pair of faded swim trunks—a soft-bodied, moon-pale boy of minimal athletic prowess and late-onset puberty. Truman couldn't help smiling. "Winnie, let me ask you something. What do you think of Friday, overall?"

"Are you kidding? He's awesome! The kids at school all want to come meet him. Nobody teases me or Reginald anymore, because Reginald told them we might be able to invite them over."

"You know it doesn't work like that," Truman cautioned. "He's not a pet."

"Yeah, we know, but Reginald says just because *we* know doesn't mean *they* have to. Not yet, anyhow."

Truman sighed and shook his head. "That boy's going to grow up to be either a millionaire or a con man."

"He says he might be president one day."

"Which combines them both. Anyway, no one's ever going to be allowed to come over and swim with Friday, not even you—at least not until Gabriel says it's safe."

"At least I can see him whenever I want. Do you think he likes that, having people come to watch him?"

"Apparently—especially little kids."

Winslow ruminated. "Yeah. Maybe seeing them keeps him from getting lonely, at least until Gabriel gets something else to put in with him."

Truman looked at his son sharply. "Did he say he planned to do that?"

"No. Me and Reginald think he should, though."

"Reginald and I," Truman corrected. "You know, not everyone agrees he should have come here. There are people who believe he'd be better off dead than in captivity."

"Nuh-uh. How can you let anything die if they don't have to?"

"I happen to agree with you, but there are people—lots of people, according to Gabriel—who think otherwise."

"Max Biedelman saved Hannah from dying, and she got to live for over forty more years," Winslow pointed out.

"But she was also alone here that whole time. That was the trade-off for getting to live."

"That's not true. She had Sam."

"And Friday will have us, but some people are going to say we just saved his life so we could exploit him, turn him into a lucrative attraction, a sideshow."

"Like Siamese twins in the old days?"

"Exactly."

"Actually, that would be cool to see," Winslow said. "I bet Reginald would want to, also."

Truman sighed. "That wasn't exactly my point."

Winslow wrapped his arms around himself. "Now I'm cold."

"All right—go take a hot shower. And rinse out the suit while you're at it. You can leave it hanging in the tub."

"If I promise to practice tonight instead of now, can I go over to the pool? You've had all this time over there, but I haven't." Truman had refused to let Winslow go after school, only on weekends, and then only if he had his homework done.

Truman conceded. "Call Reginald and see if he wants to go, too. Tell him if it's okay with Sam and Corinna, I can pick him up."

But before Winslow had even left the den, the phone rang and it was Gabriel. Truman raised a finger to Winslow—*don't leave yet*—and listened with a series of *uh-huh*s and *sure*s. When he hung up the phone he told Winslow there had been a change of plans: Gabriel wanted to try something new with Friday and he needed their help to do it.

"Oh boy," said Winslow. "Reginald, too?"

"Reginald, too."

Within half an hour, they'd all squeezed into the pool's small office: Neva, Gabriel, Sam, Libertine, Truman, Winslow, and Reginald. Friday hung in the window, watching them.

"Here's the deal," Gabriel told them. "We've been working with him on finding a shape or object in the pool windows.

So far it's been easy stuff." He nodded to Neva, who held up a cardboard triangle, circle, and square. "That's the problem, though: it's too easy. So I want to put a bunch of other stuff in the viewing gallery windows to throw him off, and then send him to find one of the shapes.

He distributed among them not only the triangle, circle, and square, but a ratty stuffed goat, a coffeemaker, a flat white cardboard star edged in black, a similar hexagon, a bright blue notebook, and a basketball. While everyone else scattered to the viewing windows, where they placed the objects and shapes, Gabriel fed Friday, then gave him the directive to go find the triangle.

Friday swam straight to the gallery windows, scanning all three as he approached. Gabriel had told everyone to stand well away from the objects, so they didn't accidentally broadcast the correct answer, but it was still no contest. Though he seemed to enjoy looking at the ratty stuffed goat, Friday gave it a regretful last glance and zeroed in on the triangle.

At the postsession confab with all the players, Gabriel announced that he would suspend the shape identification program. It was simply too easy.

LIBERTINE CAME TO the whale pool every morning with a glad heart, knowing the day would be full of meaningful work, intelligent company, and an increasingly healthy and fun-loving killer whale. She enjoyed even her menial duties because they meant she was right there, where the real work was being done. She didn't think of the pool as a prison; didn't even realize she'd stopped thinking of it that way. For her, as for Friday, it was simply a place of event and excitement.

And Gabriel was always nearby.

It had been a long time since Libertine had had a crush of any kind, never mind one so epically inappropriate. Her last one had been nearly eleven years ago now—Paul Fortunati, a baked-goods supplier who had serviced the ferries between Anacortes and the San Juan Islands. A cheerful, hearty soul, he'd been as meaty and solid as an old prizefighter, and she believed he was capable not only of keeping the world safely at bay, but of doing so with a smile. He'd called her Libby—*Hey, there's my Libby, talked to anyone interesting lately?*—and would periodically toss her a muffin or baguette or cookie as a treat. In fact, he was the only man who'd ever crafted a nickname for her, which she treasured. When she was alone she'd sometimes contemplated a different life, a life filled with fresh yeasty smells and warm, papa-san embraces that would envelope her and keep her from harm. She had spent a fortune on the ferries that year just to see him, though she always claimed pressing business when he asked her, which anyway he hardly ever did. In her experience, he was a man of the moment, cheerfully taking in the world around him, slapping backs and calling out hearty greetings to other favorites, none of whom were women, though she jealously watched, prepared to fight for her position.

A year—one full year of feeling cosseted and shielded from the full blast of a lonely life, and then, just like that, he'd stopped coming to the ferry—any ferry. She knew because in her desperation she'd started riding on different routes, at different times, hoping he'd simply been transferred, in which case she was prepared to adjust her own schedule accordingly. But after two weeks without a sighting she'd broken down and asked his replacement, an impossibly tall, thin, awful woman named Deirdre, who told her he'd retired and was moving to Arizona.

Libertine called the phone number the woman gave her, a lapse in judgment she deeply regretted to this day. When she'd identified herself, carefully giving her first and last names, he'd said the single most terrible word ever uttered: *Who?*

She had never seen him again.

After that she rarely stayed home for more than a few days, avoiding the ferries, driving hither and yon to consult with her clients face-to-face. Bit by bit, animal by animal, her emotional hemorrhage was sopped up with their neediness until Paul Fortunati became a memory she could regret from a safe distance.

But now there was Gabriel, a man who didn't share her beliefs and who reviled her profession. She listened for him on the stairs; she watched him from the office window; she conjured him at night as she fell asleep. He had completely stripped her of the brittle dignity she'd worked so long and so hard to create.

Libertine was in love.

SHE AND IVY had taken to eating dinner together every Thursday at the Oat Maiden, since Ivy continued to spend the majority of her time in Bladenham. Now, over a classic pepperoni pizza, Libertine described to Ivy her most off-the-wall interview yet with Martin Choi—as approved by Truman.

"He wanted to know what Friday thinks about having so many people come see him." Libertine watched Ivy pick pepperoni from her pizza slice and put it in a paper napkin. "Don't you like pepperoni? You should have told me when I ordered it."

"What? No, I'm saving them for Julio Iglesias. He loves pepperoni. It gives him gas, but it gives me gas, too, so we just pretend it isn't happening and fart away."

Dismayed, Libertine said, "If you'd said something we could have ordered something else."

"You said pepperoni was your favorite."

"It is, but if I'd known——"

"My god, will you just *stop*?" Ivy reached across the table to give Libertine's hand a stinging slap.

Libertine blanched. Ivy had once told her that she had the lowest self-esteem of anyone she'd ever met. "We have to work on that," she'd said; and Libertine had been secretly thrilled by the use of the word *we*.

"So what does the whale think of all the people?" Ivy asked, slurping at a cup of coffee.

"I assume he loves it."

"Of course he does. He's a star. Who doesn't love fame?"

"But he's still living in a box. It's a nice box, but it's still a box. He's completely cut off from everything natural."

"Is that you talking, or him?"

"Neither. It's just the truth. He was wild-caught, you know. He experienced the larger world, even if it was a long time ago. He was born into a pod and swam in the North Atlantic. That's not something you can unknow."

"And you think after all this time he still remembers?"

"Maybe not consciously, but of course he remembers. If nothing else, he'll always have a visceral sense of loss. Any sentient being would."

"Has he told you that?"

"It doesn't really work like that."

"You always say that."

"I always say it because it's always true," Libertine said evenly. "I *sense* him, and I assume he senses me——though it's been weeks and weeks now."

"Really?" Ivy sat up a little straighter, intrigued. "Do you think you're not psychic anymore?"

Libertine had long since given up trying to get Ivy to call her a communicator. Now she smiled in spite of herself. "It's not a superpower. I just have this . . . ability. For all I know, anyone can do what I do, if they learn how to listen—or sense, really."

"Huh," said Ivy, clearly losing interest. "So anyway, listen. I was thinking of driving home for the weekend. I love my brother and sister-in-law like life itself, but if I don't get away from them soon I might kill someone. I thought you might want to come along."

"To Friday Harbor?"

"Yes. We can catch the last ferry tomorrow night, then stay Saturday and come back on one of the late ferries Sunday. Or you can keep me company on the drive and go home to Orcas."

"No, I'd love to come with you."

"Great. And if you want some stuff for your apartment, I have rugs and a desk and couch I don't know what to do with, plus a bed if you like a hard mattress. I'll have whatever you want shipped down here."

And so, at five o'clock the next day—after Libertine had finished working, a commitment she took very seriously even if, as Ivy kept reminding her, it was volunteer work, and therefore flexible—Ivy pointed the nose of her old Mercedes north to the ferry in Anacortes. One windshield wiper stuck and the other smeared the rain around unhelpfully. Julio Iglesias rode on Libertine's lap, jubilant that the booster seat sat empty. Ivy squinted through the heaviest rain, and when it finally let up just south of Olympia she said to Libertine, "So tell me, what do you do when you're not channeling the animal kingdom? You never talk about anything."

Libertine shrugged, looking out her side window. She wasn't used to talking about herself. Over the years she'd found that if she didn't volunteer information, very few people solicited it, especially in her line of work. "I garden. And I paint sometimes—watercolors. I walk."

"You'd have made the perfect paid companion."

Libertine looked at Ivy blankly.

"Haven't you ever read *Rebecca*? No? Anyway, you're brave, I'll give you that."

"Not really," said Libertine.

"Sure. You do what you do in spite of three-quarters of the world thinking you're certifiable. If that's not bravery, I don't know what is."

Libertine could feel herself flush.

"Oh, for god's sake," Ivy said, seeing her. "You know I'm only stating the facts. Take it as a compliment."

"It didn't sound like a compliment," Libertine said doubtfully.

"You're probably just not used to them."

Libertine nodded: it was true. They continued in silence for several miles before Ivy said idly, "Why do you think it's so much easier to talk in the car than anyplace else?"

"Because you're not looking at each other."

"Do you think?"

"Yes, I do."

"Maybe so," Ivy said thoughtfully. "You know, my brother Dickie and I drove from home to Amherst, Massachusetts, once, while he was going to college there, and by the end we were ready to throttle each other—but in a very insightful way. Until then he'd still been the twelve-year-old kid who liked to beat me at chess and feed his peas to the dog."

Libertine closed her eyes and rested her head against the seat-back. "A road trip—I've never traveled like that. My mother used to talk about driving to California, but we never did."

"Why not?"

"She was very disorganized."

"How much organization does it take to get into a car and drive?"

"None, if you have money," said Libertine.

"Ah," said Ivy.

They drove in silence past winter-flooded pastures and ramshackle barns and mossy woods, until Ivy said, "There's something I've been wanting to ask you. If you had had a family, or at least children, do you think you'd still, you know, hear animals?"

Libertine took the question in her gut like a blow. "I've sensed them ever since I can remember," she said carefully.

"You didn't have siblings, right?"

"No."

"So couldn't it just be, I don't know—loneliness?"

"You mean could I be making it all up, like imaginary friends?"

"All I'm saying is, couldn't it just be your way of filling a void?"

"At three years old? What you really want to know is whether it's real. My sensing them."

"I just don't see how it's possible."

"Me, neither, but I do."

Ivy looked sidelong at her.

"What you really mean," Libertine said bitterly, "is, could I be schizophrenic or have some weird personality disorder?" How many people had asked her that over the years?

"You do seem lonely."

"Maybe I'm lonely because I sense animals. It sets you apart."

Ivy nodded. "Chicken and egg, then."

"What—the voices came first, and because of them I got lonely? Or I was lonely first and then the voices came?"

"Exactly."

"I don't know. I only know what I know. One day maybe I won't hear them anymore." Then she gave an uncharacteristically sly smile. "One day maybe they'll choose you, instead."

BY THE TIME they reached Ivy's house it was too dark to see much besides the fact that it was wood-sided and sprawling, as though additions had been added haphazardly over the years. Once inside, Libertine looked around avidly, finding to her surprise that the house didn't look at all like the home of a wealthy person, or at least not as she'd pictured it. The rugs, though Persian, were worn and spotted; the leather furniture was cracked in several places, and a number of dead flies lay on some of the windowsills. Still, it was cozy in its own messy way, and she breathed in the delicious smell of basil, a spice her mother had worn like a fine perfume.

She excused herself while Ivy spooned out coffee grounds for the morning and set up the pot. Julio Iglesias accompanied her into the bathroom, where he lodged a host of complaints. When they got back to the kitchen she said to Ivy, "I'm afraid Julio Iglesias has something he wants me to mention to you."

Ivy stared at her and then said bitterly, "It's the Snugli, isn't it—it's about the damned Snugli."

Libertine couldn't help smiling. "You'd think so, but no. He'd doesn't like being outdoors so much when you're at the pool."

Outraged, Ivy protested, "Are you kidding me? He's dressed

to the nines in a custom-made Gore-Tex jacket with special pockets all over it to hold those little chemical hand warmers you get at REI. Mink costs less. And if I don't take him outside with me, he bitches about being left behind, by himself, in the office. He has his own set of china dishes and he sleeps on a memory foam mattress that costs almost as much as mine did."

Libertine looked at Julio Iglesias, who looked back at her sulkily, and then she said, "Never mind."

OVER A DELICIOUS late dinner Ivy made with groceries delivered to her house that afternoon—Dungeness crab, asparagus, potatoes—Libertine sipped the last of a whiskey sour Ivy had mixed for her. "I've never had one of these before," Libertine said. "It's yummy."

Ivy smiled. "See? I told you I thought you'd like them."

"Mmmm," said Libertine.

"They're potent, though."

"You've already had three," Libertine pointed out.

"Yes, but I've been drinking them since I was eleven."

"Then I better catch up." Libertine drained her glass and held it out for another, and then one more. They talked about everything and nothing, and watched the rain run down the windows, and a couple of hours later, when she was tottering down the upstairs hall toward the guest room with Ivy's protective arm around her waist, she said dreamily, "Do you think maybe we're falling in love?"

"Oh, honey," Ivy said. "The only thing falling is you. C'mon, let's get you into bed." She opened the guest room door and led Libertine inside with some effort, tumbling her onto the bed and saying cheerfully, "You're going to feel like death warmed over in the morning."

"Mmmm," Libertine purred softly, cozying into the sheets and thick down comforter, which she pulled up to her shoulders. "Night night. Sleep tight." She giggled. "Sleep *tight,* get it? I just made that up."

IVY STRAIGHTENED THE bedding over Libertine, who'd passed out cold, and sat beside her for a while in a little slipper chair that had once belonged to her mother, keeping watch and contemplating friendship. She had never imagined that she would reach the age of sixty-two alone. There had been so many people in her life over the years, but then the falling-out came as surely as springtime, and though the details varied, the outcome was inevitable. Still, she continued to hope she would one day find someone capable of loving as fiercely as she did, who wouldn't break and run before the roaring winds of her affection.

Maybe we're falling in love. Ivy would like to be in love, to have someone fall in love with her, and she didn't even care whether the quality of the affection was platonic or flavored with a watery hint of sexuality—intimacy was the key thing, the kind of intimacy that allowed you to offer up the worst, least attractive, most shameful things about yourself; the kind of intimacy that came with the bottom line, *I know you and I love you anyway.*

Perhaps she'd find, even this late in life, that she was drawn to other women and had been all along without recognizing the fact. She'd even welcome it—on the whole, she enjoyed the company of women. Plus her sexual experiences with men over the years had been consistently disappointing: wet, nasty kisses followed by groping and fumbling, then panting and pain and a final few merciful wheezing breaths in the dark to signal it was finally over. There might be such a thing as orgasms, but if so, they were happening to someone else. Hardly the stuff blared from the covers of magazines read by young women.

She bent over the sleeping figure and kissed her lightly on the forehead. Libertine sighed and slept on.

Ivy turned off the light and went out, whispering, "G'night, little bird."

THE NEXT MORNING, once Libertine's atom bomb hangover had begun to lift and she'd been able to stomach a hearty breakfast of French toast, bacon, and jam made from wild berries harvested right there on San Juan Island, Libertine decided to go home after all. Ivy's keen attention always left her feeling flayed, plus she suddenly missed her little house, with its cheerful glass and garden art.

If Ivy was disappointed at Libertine's leaving, she didn't show it; she simply reiterated that Libertine should pick out furniture before she left so Ivy could have it sent down to Bladenham. In the end Libertine chose the bed she'd slept on in the guest bedroom. The cost to Ivy, she knew, would be considerable, but the soft mattress on the little twin bed Johnson Johnson provided gave Libertine terrible backaches which, combined with the physical nature of her work now, produced enough misery for her to buckle under Ivy's insistence. The bed was a pretty walnut piece and, granted she'd been drunk, but it had given her a blessedly comfortable night's sleep. She also capitulated to Ivy's insistence that she accept the chintz-covered slipper chair that had sat beside the bed. "Julio wants you to have it, and there's no turning him down," Ivy had said. "You know how easy it is to hurt his feelings—I'll have a pee-fest on my hands if you say no."

They agreed to meet in Anacortes the next day at noon for the return drive to Bladenham, and Libertine walked onto the interisland ferry to Orcas Island with a sense of vast relief. Once home, she petted her walls and gave the refrigerator a light kiss on its old white door. In all the world, this was the one place where she was perfectly herself. She had just put on the teakettle—hoping green tea might flush out any lingering toxic remnants of Ivy's whiskey—when her old wall phone rang. Libertine picked it up before she had time to think better, and heard the unwelcome voice of animal activist Trina Beemer.

"Oh, good! I've been trying to reach you—you've become quite the hero around here. How did you manage to infiltrate that place?"

"Pardon me?" Libertine said disingenuously. Trina would have to work for whatever she was after.

"The *zoo*! The Biedelbaum or whatever. They had that poor, sweet elephant—and now this. We've always had them on our radar, of course, what with their building that new porpoise pool, but a killer whale! It's so much worse. I can't tell you how happy we are that one of us is on the inside!"

"What do you mean, *worse*?" Libertine said, ignoring the *one of us* reference and banging around in her cupboards for some honey for her tea.

"Well, I mean, at least the elephant was a terrestrial animal. Keeping a killer whale in captivity, never mind alone, is no different than putting any one of us in lifetime solitary confinement."

"I'm pretty sure there's a difference," Libertine said, turning off the burner and pouring scalding water into her mug.

She could feel the woman hesitate. Then Trina said, in her

oddly atonal delivery, "We're hoping you'd be able to work for us from the inside. You *are* still on our side, right?"

"I'm not really on anyone's side," Libertine said. "Well, I'm on Friday's side."

"You know, a lot of people are saying the whole rehab story is just a cover-up for the fact that they're bringing in a show animal. Is that true?"

"No," said Libertine.

"No?"

Libertine sighed. "Look, he was dying, pure and simple. Go back and watch the TV footage."

"He was wild-caught, you know."

"He's nineteen years old. That was a long, long time ago." She had no intention of fueling Trina's fire.

"Not that long ago," Trina said. "Killer whales have excellent memories. And they know when they're incarcerated."

"You know, it's funny," Libertine said. "He's never once indicated that, at least not to me. Not once. *Sick,* yes. A prisoner, no."

"That just means he's given up hope. They do, you know."

"Really," said Libertine neutrally, taking her tea into her little living room and settling into a perfectly lovely chintz chair she'd found once by the side of the road.

"Really," said Trina grimly. "I'm surprised you don't know that, given that they talk to you and everything."

"It's not exactly talking," Libertine began, and then decided, *Oh, to hell with it.*

"You know, we'd love to have you as a speaker at our January meeting," said Trina, evidently deciding to try another tack. "Would you be able to do that?"

"No," said Libertine. "Probably not."

"Really?"

"Really. But listen, if you're willing to keep an open mind and want to go down there sometime and see what we're doing, I can probably arrange it." And then, just like that, she hung up and had the most seditious thought: *Wait until I tell Gabriel!*

ON THE DRIVE down to Bladenham, Libertine told Ivy about the call from Trina.

"Hah!" Ivy crowed. "I knew it would work."

"What would work?"

"Inviting you to be part of the project." When Libertine turned in her seat to face her, Ivy patted her hand. "It's nothing Machiavellian. I just thought if you could see for yourself what was involved in caring for our boy, you might feel less black-and-white about his being in captivity. So to speak."

"So it was your idea to make me a volunteer?" Libertine asked, startled. The thought had never occurred to her before. She'd always assumed it was Truman's, but Ivy must have planted it.

"It was. Of course, Truman and Gabriel had to agree."

Libertine looked out her window at the flooded pasturelands while she collected herself. As a longtime loner, she wasn't used to having other people direct her life, and though in this case she knew she should be grateful—*was* grateful—there was still something high-handed about Ivy's pulling the strings. "I don't know how I should feel about that," she finally said.

Ivy glanced over at her. "You shouldn't feel any way about it. We invited you and you accepted and now you know how much work and thought is involved in his rehabilitation. And if you happen to spread that word, it wouldn't do any harm, either."

"And what if I hadn't ended up feeling that way?"

Ivy just smiled complacently. "I had faith."

"This is making me really uncomfortable," Libertine said, looking hard out of the passenger-side window.

Ivy glanced over, surprised. "Really?"

"I feel manipulated."

"You shouldn't. If anything, it was a vote of confidence in you. You know, your profession doesn't exactly inspire confidence." Libertine's jaws clenched, but Ivy, apparently oblivious, went on. "Anyway, I wanted to give you a chance to have firsthand access to the whale. To help him, if he needed you."

"And to help you, if he didn't."

"Exactly."

"Well," said Libertine doubtfully, "I guess I can't fault your logic."

"Of course not," said Ivy.

But Libertine had moved on. "And Gabriel—what does he think of me now?"

"As far as I know, he's accepted you as a member of the team."

Is that all? Libertine thought but didn't say. She could feel Ivy looking over at her, trying to get a read on her state of mind.

"No, more than that," Ivy amended. "I know he's glad you're there. You're providing a valuable extra pair of hands, and you don't get in the way."

"He told you that?"

"He did."

At least it was better than *Who?*

THEY REACHED BLADENHAM in a driving rain. After waving good-bye to Ivy, Libertine pulled up her hood and reached into her raincoat pocket for the keys she was sure she'd put there.

No keys. She scrabbled in her purse, with the same result. Getting wetter by the second, she was relieved to see lights on in Johnson Johnson's house. He'd have an extra key. She dodged the puddles and knocked at the kitchen door. When there was no answer she gently pushed the door open and called out.

Johnson Johnson appeared in the doorway between the kitchen and living room. "Have you ever walked on the ceiling?" he asked her.

"What?"

"Walked on the ceiling."

"Metaphorically, you mean?" She tried and failed to dampen a rising sense of impatience.

Johnson Johnson offered her the little square mirror he'd been holding and she declined.

"I'm sorry—I don't know what—"

He demonstrated, holding the mirror against the bridge of his nose and looking down into it. "You have to be real careful not to step on the lights or kick them. Sometimes I trip over the door jambs, so you have to watch out for them, too."

Helplessly Libertine watched him weave and giant-step his way around the kitchen and wondered if there was someone she should call.

"Here," he said, holding out the mirror to her. "Now you."

"I don't really think—"

He held the little mirror to her face helpfully. She flinched, but he said, "Now look down."

She looked down—and instantly understood. Reflected back to her was the kitchen ceiling, giving the illusion that this, not the floor, was where her feet were firmly planted. "Now walk," Johnson Johnson said excitedly. "Go 'head."

Sure enough, Libertine found herself circling the light

fixture, which appeared to be growing vertically at her feet, its chain magically transformed into a stem, the glass shade a mushroom top. She laughed out loud. When she lowered the mirror after completing a thorough circuit of the kitchen, Johnson Johnson was beaming, his hands clasped to his chest in delight. "See?" he said, bouncing a little on the balls of his feet. "*See?*"

"I really was walking on the ceiling," she marveled, handing the mirror back. "I felt like I could sit right on the light and it would hold me."

"I like to jump from the kitchen into the living room and back. You have to jump pretty high, though, because it's a long way from the ceiling to the archway. Sometimes I don't even make it."

Libertine high-stepped over the doorway and almost immediately caught sight of the upside-down living room wall beyond. Lowering the mirror, she saw that the entire wall was covered by a fun-house array of carpeted shelves and ramps and tubes and hammocks. Several holes in the ceiling led to upstairs rooms. In the very center, Kitty was peacefully snoring in a suspended faux-fur hammock. Libertine stood motionless in the doorway, transfixed. "Oh!" she cried. "Neva described this to me, but I had no idea it was so wonderful!"

"The hammock is heated, so Kitty can sleep there in the winter," Johnson Johnson said. "He has arthritis."

"He's told me," Libertine said. "I guess on an especially damp day even the small bones in his tail hurt. So I can imagine how much he appreciates this."

"I *know,*" said Johnson Johnson.

Libertine checked her watch and saw that it was nearly six o'clock. "Hey, shouldn't you be at the Oat Maiden?"

"Truman says I have to take at least one evening off every week."

"Well, that's smart. So you don't burn out."

Johnson Johnson nodded soberly.

"Just out of curiosity, what do you do on your days off?" Libertine asked.

"I make treats for the bears."

"Bears?"

"At the zoo."

"What kind of treats?"

"They really like fruit bars."

"They do?"

"With apricots. And raisins."

"Sounds like a busman's holiday." She suddenly became aware of her rain-damp jeans and the leaking seams of her jacket, and set down on the counter the small mirror she still held in her hand. "I almost forgot why I came over," she said. "I've lost my key."

He looked grave. "But then you can't get in."

"Exactly. If you can unlock the door, I'll find my key eventually, or I can have a copy made tomorrow if I don't."

"Course."

So she followed him into the rain, pulling up her hood and concentrating on his Doc Martin–booted feet splashing ahead of her down the little path to her apartment.

"I'm so glad you were home," she said when he'd unlocked the door.

"Me, too," he said, and she wondered whether he meant he was glad to have been home because he so seldom was, or that he was glad he'd been there to help her—nuance was not his strong suit. In any event she watched him until he'd reached his back door and ducked into the warmth and light without looking back. For the merest fraction of a second, she felt his presence in her head, the first human she'd ever perceived, as sweet and light as a whisper.

THE NEXT FRIDAY, on one of Libertine's days off, the phone woke her from a sound sleep. Neva was on the other end.

"Hey, we just stopped at the Oat Maiden on the way to work to pick up a muffin and it wasn't open. No sign, no explanation, nothing. We called Delilah and she said she'd waited for half an hour and then she went back home. She tried calling Johnson Johnson, and then she tried calling you, but no one answered."

When she wasn't working late Libertine had fallen into the habit of having a mug of milk and a chocolate chip cookie at the Oat Maiden just before closing. Once the door was locked, she helped Johnson Johnson and sometimes Delilah clean up the kitchen and restock condiments, top off the soda dispenser, and wipe down and set the tables for the following morning.

"Maybe he's sick. But I saw him yesterday and he was fine," Libertine said.

"He worked a few months ago with a temperature of a hundred and four," Neva said. "So he's not sick. Can you check on him?"

That woke her up. She pulled on jeans and a Biedelman Zoo sweatshirt and ducked out into the rainy morning. When Johnson Johnson failed to answer her knock she tried the kitchen door, pushing it open when he didn't answer; and saw him sitting on the kitchen floor cradling a dying cat in his arms, his cheeks streaming with tears.

"Oh, no—oh, honey, not Kitty." Libertine squatted down beside him, her knees going off like gunshots.

Johnson Johnson looked at her, brokenhearted. "He always comes to eat. He likes tuna, which is what we have on Friday mornings, but he didn't come. I found him in his favorite basket, the one in the bathroom where all the clean towels are."

"And he was like this?" Libertine sat on the floor. "May I see?"

Johnson Johnson nodded miserably. Libertine gently lifted the old tomcat in her arms, smoothed his fur, listened to him breathe; and then, returning him to Johnson Johnson's arms, she sat down on the floor. "He's in no pain," she said softly. "And he isn't frightened."

They sat together for five, then ten more minutes before the old cat drew a few deep breaths, pressed a little more heavily into Johnson Johnson's arms, and was gone. Johnson Johnson gave an involuntary cry.

"I'm so sorry," Libertine said. "He was a wonderful cat and you gave him the best home in the world. He knew how much you loved him, and that you were with him at the end." She plucked a paper towel off the roll and gently blotted his face.

"Can you hear him?" he whispered.

"No."

"I'm going to miss him so much," Johnson Johnson said.

"I know you will," Libertine said.

"Do Chocolate and Chip know?"

"I'm sure they do. Animals can sense when death is near." Libertine was quiet for a long beat, and then said, "Neva and Truman stopped by the Oat Maiden a little while ago. They're worried about you. I want to call so they know you're all right."

Johnson Johnson barely nodded.

"And then let's bury Kitty and get some flowers for his grave. I think he'd like that."

Soberly he said, "Yes."

"May I have him?"

Johnson Johnson allowed Libertine to take the body gently from his arms. "Do you have any clean dishtowels?" He pointed mutely to a drawer and she pulled out two plain white linen cloths, shrouding the body tenderly on the kitchen counter.

"One of us needs to call Neva back," she said. "Do you want to do it?"

Johnson Johnson was still sitting on the kitchen floor. "You," he said; and so she did, telling her their sad news.

"Oh, no."

"He's devastated."

"I'm sure." Libertine could hear Neva cover the mouthpiece and say over her shoulder, presumably to Truman, "Kitty died. The old one—the tomcat." And then to Libertine she said, "I'd like to come and pay my respects. He was a good cat. I know how much Johnson Johnson loved him."

Libertine put her cell phone against her chest and said, "Neva and Truman would like to come pay Kitty their respects. Is that okay?" Johnson Johnson nodded mutely. Libertine turned the phone back and said to Neva, "How soon can you get here?"

"Half an hour, plus or minus."

"They're coming in half an hour," she told Johnson Johnson once she'd hung up. She extended a hand. "Come on—let's get you off the floor."

Johnson Johnson took her hand and she pulled as hard as she could, until they were perfectly balanced, and then he flew forward and she staggered backward right into the kitchen counter.

"Ow," said Johnson Johnson, looking at her with alarm.

Libertine rubbed her back ruefully. "I'm fine. Do you have coffee? I could make coffee. I think we could use some."

Johnson Johnson directed her to a bag of beans, a grinder, and the coffeemaker—a very good one, she was surprised to find. She wouldn't have pegged him as a coffee drinker; he seemed like more of an herbal-tea-with-sugar type. She didn't really want coffee and he probably didn't, either, but it gave her something to do, and that was the point. Once the machine was burbling and huffing, she admired the room, as she always did when she was here. Like the Oat Maiden, it was a cheerful masterpiece, with a black-and-white checkered mopboard and a compass painted on the floor.

Johnson Johnson was standing in a corner of the room with his arms abandoned at his sides. "I'd love to hear what Kitty was like when you first met him," Libertine said. She motioned Johnson Johnson to sit across from her at the kitchen table, which was painted with the kind of black-and-white spiral used in optical illusions and 1960s movies to denote a time change or entrance into a dream state.

To Libertine's surprise Johnson Johnson pulled his chair in to the table and closed his eyes. "I was taking out the garbage and I heard meowing in the bushes—those purple rhododendron by the mailbox. I looked underneath and it was Kitty. He was bleeding from his ear, and he was really brave, because I had to use a little shampoo to get the blood out of his fur. He didn't try to bite me or run away or anything. After that I gave him some milk and a can of tuna, and he ate the whole thing. Maybe he hadn't eaten in a while. So then, when he was done, I fixed him a nice bed in a box and told him he could live with me if he wanted to, and he did."

"You could tell he was very happy here."

Johnson Johnson nodded solemnly. "I know."

Then they both got quiet for a few minutes. Libertine was surprised at how comfortable the silence was, as though talk between her and Johnson Johnson was unnecessary—something she'd never felt with anyone before, not even with Larry Adagio. "Do you have any family here?" she asked after a while.

"My parents," he said.

"But I thought they were . . . gone."

He nodded. "They're in the cemetery, but that's here."

"Oh. No brothers or sisters?"

"No. After me, I don't think they wanted anybody else."

"I've heard you were a very good son. Truman said you took excellent care of them right to the end."

"Well, I mean, they were home and I was home, so. . . ." He appeared to struggle for a minute with a thought. "Do you think Friday misses his family?"

"I don't know. I'm sure he must have, at least in the beginning. He was caught when he was still very young and dependent. I've definitely had the sense that he was frightened. His mother was on the other side of the net, I think, trying to get him out, but she couldn't do it."

"I didn't know they caught him. Why did they catch him?"

Libertine could see his distress. "So people could come and see him. There's a lot of money in that."

"Oh. Who caught him?"

"I don't know."

"Maybe someone should catch *them*."

Libertine laughed, but he was deadly serious. "Then they'd know."

They sat with their thoughts until Libertine said quietly, "You know, neither one of us has family nearby—living family, I mean—and everybody needs that. So I have an idea: would it be okay if I'm your family, and you're mine?"

Johnson Johnson looked at her solemnly before nodding.

"So from now on," she said, "if you need help, if you're sad or happy, if you're unsure about something, come to me and we'll figure it out together."

Johnson Johnson nodded emphatically. "Yes," he said.

WHEN THE COFFEE was ready Libertine found thick white mugs in a cabinet over the stove and poured them each a brimming cup that neither of them touched. Outside, a freshening wind made skeletal branches tap insistently against the window over the sink and sorrow filled the room. Neither of them said another word until Neva and Truman arrived with a dozen carnations for Kitty's grave—Neva had gotten to know Kitty well during the year she'd rented the little apartment that Libertine lived in now. Ivy roared up in her emissions-belching Mercedes, and Sam and Corinna pulled in right behind her. Sam put a box of Dunkin' Donuts on the counter and Corinna hugged Johnson Johnson tightly and Libertine slipped out back during the commotion and dug a grave beneath a rhododendron.

When they were all outside, Neva asked Johnson Johnson, who carried the shrouded Kitty with the utmost care, if he would like to say any last words, and when he looked stricken Corinna placed a hand on his arm and said, "Honey, would you rather have one of us to do that?"

He nodded and they all exchanged glances—*You? No, you*—and Libertine noticed that through the telepathy of close friendships they all agreed it should be Truman. Clearing his throat and with heartfelt solemnity, he said, "We are gathered here to honor a cherished family member and comfort our good friend." He turned to Johnson Johnson and said, "Kitty found unconditional love in your heart as well as your home. Because of you, in his senior years he never went hungry, never suffered in the cold and rain, and always knew he was safe in the home you gave him. No gifts are greater." He paused a moment, and then concluded, "Here lies a good cat. He will be missed."

There was a low murmur and then Johnson Johnson lowered Kitty into the grave Libertine had prepared. She handed him the trowel, and he spaded several clods of dirt on top of the body before gulping and handing the trowel to Neva, who handed it to Truman when she was finished, and so on, until the grave was filled. Then Libertine took his elbow and led Johnson Johnson back into the kitchen—it had started to rain, a halfhearted, weepy drizzle—and the others followed.

And then Truman said to Johnson Johnson, "You know, it just occurred to me there's someone who I think would really like to meet you." Johnson Johnson looked at him through puffy eyes and Truman said, "Let's do this. Let's swing by the Oat Maiden and leave a sign on the door saying you'll open again first thing in the morning, and then we'll take you over to the zoo. It's really high time you met Friday."

WHILE JOHNSON JOHNSON and Truman placed a note on the café door, Neva called Gabriel to warn him that they were on the way to the pool, explaining about Johnson Johnson and Kitty. "I'm so sorry," Gabriel told him with the utmost gravity when they got to the pool.

Johnson Johnson nodded numbly.

"Let's take you upstairs so you can meet our boy."

They all trooped upstairs. Gabriel had already staged a bucket of fish in the wet walk, and now handed an extra pair of XtraTufs to Johnson Johnson. "Put those on and wade right out there." Friday was already at the poolside, keen to see what this new visitor might hold in store. He put his chin on the side of the pool and opened his mouth. "You can hand him a fish or two," Gabriel suggested. "And he likes to be touched. Just go slowly at first so he has a chance to look you over."

Neva waded out beside Johnson Johnson, handing him a fish to give to Friday. When Friday accepted it, Johnson Johnson reached out with exquisite care, touching the whale with just his fingertips. Neva could hear him draw in a rapt breath. She encouraged him. "Go ahead. Give him a couple more." Friday exhaled lightly, as though he didn't want to startle the fragile man before him.

Gabriel called, "He won't break, and he's already decided you're okay or he would have backed up or left by now. Go ahead and scratch him. He likes that."

Johnson Johnson fed and scratched Friday for ten minutes, then fifteen minutes, until the steel bucket was empty and he admitted that his hands were numb from the icy water. As he left the pool top, Friday followed him with his eyes until he disappeared down the stairs.

"I think he knew who I am," Johnson Johnson told Neva gravely as they brought the empty bucket downstairs.

"Yes," she said. "I think so, too."

Chapter 9

IN HIS OFFICE Truman went over the numbers again and again. Before he presented them to the zoo's executive committee he wanted to be absolutely sure they were accurate. And once he was sure the figures were correct, he called his mother, Lavinia, and asked if she'd run them herself, which she did, appearing in his office in a pair of impeccably tailored wool slacks, a cashmere twinset, and what she liked to call her "weekend pearls."

The numbers matched exactly. Seeing his face, she asked if he was all right.

"I'm fine, but I'm not looking forward to presenting this."

"It'll be fine, I'm sure. For heaven's sake, Truman, they're businesspeople. They'll understand."

"I know," Truman sighed. "Still, it'll complicate things."

"Then your job is to keep it simple. Don't let them get lost in the minutiae."

"I know, Mother. But still. The bottom line is what it is."

"Well, be strong," Lavinia said, looking faintly amused.

Half an hour later Truman reported to his committee that in

the nearly six months since Friday had arrived at the zoo, the total number of visitors had jumped by 700 percent from the same period the previous year.

"So why the voice of doom, bud?" Dink Schuler asked, clapping him on the back. "Hell, I thought somebody might have died."

Truman took a beat and then said carefully, "There are people out there who think we took this animal in strictly to make money. And they're people with loud voices."

"Show me where it says we can't make money," said Dink dismissively. "Hell, we deserve it, after the last three years we've had—there've been a few times I'd have shut the place down if it had been up to me. I'm not kidding—show me where it says we can't be successful. You can't."

"It's more of an ethical issue than a fiscal one," Truman said. "That is, it's not about the money, per se; it's more about what brought the money in, if you see what I mean."

"Look, three years ago, who got rid of the single most popular animal in the zoo? We did! Because that was the right decision for that animal. Now this animal needed someone to help him, we were that someone, zip-zop, story over." Around the conference table all the heads nodded. "We have absolutely nothing to feel ashamed of. And I'm pretty sure I speak on behalf of the entire board when I say our balance sheet could use a few more years of having this fish here."

"Mammal," Truman said.

"Whatever. Cash cow."

Truman blanched. "Please be careful who you say that around."

Dink leaned across the conference table to slap him on the shoulder. "Jesus, lighten up, buddy—don't go all bleeding heart on us. It's fine! Hell, the board will probably give you a nice fat raise."

"I'm just saying we all need to be cautious. We don't want to come across as exploitative and money-hungry."

"But we *are* money-hungry." Dink grinned. "Don't know about the exploitative part."

Truman smiled weakly. "Look, here's what I'd like to recommend to you, and, if you agree with me, you can propose it to the full board. I'd like to take a percentage of the surplus revenue Friday's bringing in and set up an endowment that will fund projects for the greater good. Say, for instance we could develop a large-animal rehab facility, or a terrific large-animal orphanage. Or we could establish a rehab facility for environmental disaster victims. We have the land—the orchard alone covers two-hundred square acres. I'm just tossing out ideas here—we'd need to do a lot of brainstorming and planning, but there are probably a ton of worthy projects. And that way, no one can say we've exploited Friday to fill our own coffers. In fact, we could call it the Greater Good Project and approach major donors for matching funds." He ended somewhat breathlessly and looked around the conference table. The executive committee members looked back at him blankly except for Dink, who was tipping his chair back on two legs and shaking his head.

"Whoa! Easy there, cowboy. The fish just got here! We could just pad the operating budget, bankroll anything left over, and call it the Great to Have Money Project." Dink was clearly getting a kick out of himself. "Just ease back, enjoy the cushion, and rake in the cash for a while." He let the chair thump down on all four legs and sprawled toward Truman across the table. "In my mind that looks an awful lot like fiscal prudence."

And loathe the man though he did, Truman had to admit

that he was right. Or, as he put it to Neva that night, "He's a Neanderthal, but I've got to admit the man is unnaturally gifted with horse sense."

"So there's been a nuclear war," Neva replied in the dark, starting one of their favorite games, "and society as we know it is gone. Your only shot at survival is to find people who can lead you to safety. Name three people."

"Easy," said Truman. "My father and Gabriel Jump." He always named Matthew first, because his father was the most gifted leader Truman had ever known, but the second and third spots were always up for grabs. Gabriel had been in the number two spot since coming to the zoo; Neva was number three. "But I have to admit that Dink Schuler might edge you out."

In the dark, Neva backhanded him smartly across the chest.

THE NEXT DAY was one of Libertine's days off, so Neva arrived at the pool at 5 A.M. to do fish house. She was paying for day after day of diving in the forty-degree water to clean the pool and play with Friday. Her energy level was at rock bottom, she had a splitting sinus headache, and every injury she'd ever sustained over her years as a zookeeper—and there were many, from a separated shoulder to a broken nose and torn meniscus—now ached. Music, wielded like a tactical weapon, was her only hope, so she put on a Black Eyed Peas CD, cranked the volume until the stainless steel counters were vibrating, and got to work.

When all the buckets were weighed and filled, she pulled up her hood, hoisted the first bucket of the day, and murmured a fervent prayer as she climbed the rain-slick steel stairs to the pool top: *please, God, don't let Friday have been sucking on a herring all night.* He sometimes did. No one knew why.

A nasty little wind was blowing east from Puget Sound fifteen miles away and it was still as black as night. The concrete looked oily in the dim fluorescent lights. Friday was already waiting expectantly as Neva zipped up the last inch of her rain gear, lowered the bucket of fish, and went to the poolside to scratch the killer whale's head.

He opened his mouth wide and there it was, despite her prayers: a foul, ruptured, sucked-upon fish. The smell could have killed a cow. Preventing herself from retching by the narrowest margin, she flung a fresh fish in with the old one so he'd swallow them both. Looking into his eyes, she was absolutely certain he was laughing.

Once she was sure he'd swallowed the mess she squatted beside him and petted his tongue, head, and jaw until his eyelids drooped with pleasure. She had never known an animal that craved interaction as much as this whale did. Even Hannah had contentedly spent hours by herself, puttering around her little yard while Neva and Sam had done their chores. Friday so desired her attention that Truman sometimes joked he was beginning to feel like he had competition, and there were times when Neva thought he might be right. The whale was in her thoughts constantly, whether she was at work or at home. During her first week at the pool, Gabriel had warned her that she would have to bring her A-game to work every single day. She had thought he was blustering a bit to shake her cage, but she could see now that he'd simply been stating a fact. No animal she'd ever worked with had been at once so hard to read and so exceptionally intelligent. Some of his inscrutability came from the fact that he had no facial muscles—he couldn't smile, raise his eyebrows, grimace, frown, or do any other of the thousand and one things terrestrial mammals did to express a state of mind: essentially, he was masked. And while Gabriel could read minute clues the killer whale expressed through his body posture and eyes, Neva guessed she was years away from having the necessary experience.

She had found out just how hard it was to interpret Friday's actions during a recent stretch of unseasonably clear weather, when sunbeams had streaked the water and dappled the whale's head. He had feinted, parried, and threatened with an open mouth something invisible to the rest of them. Gabriel had challenged them to figure out what he was doing. All of them—including even Libertine, who, as an animal communicator, should have known—were completely stumped. Gabriel let them swing in the wind for a day and a half before giving them the answer.

Friday was boxing with his shadow.

He continued to spend hours and hours in the gallery windows, watching people watch him—acting up for them by waggling his tongue and blowing bubbles from his blowhole and tracking specific visitors as they made their way through the crowd.

Today he was in a contrary mood, either refusing to do what Neva requested or doing it in the sloppiest possible way. She finally broke when he responded to her speed-swim command with a halfhearted circuit around the pool that he abandoned altogether halfway around in order to inspect a piece of Styrofoam on the wet walk. She threw her arms in the air: *what is it with you?* To her astonishment, he immediately rose straight up on his tail and pushed himself backward through the water. Dumbfounded, she called Gabriel upstairs and repeated the gesture. Once more Friday stood on his tail and labored backward.

"What the hell?" she said.

"Well, I'll be damned," Gabriel said softly.

"What?"

"Right at the beginning, when he first got to Bogotá, a friend of mine from Marineland went down to help them train him for his first show. They used that signal for a tail-walk, but he was never really good at it, so they stopped using it. I guarantee you he hasn't seen that signal in eighteen years."

When she told Truman the story that night, he said, "I think now I know how some husbands feel when their wives bring home a new baby."

"What do you mean?"

"You almost never talk or think about anything anymore besides that whale."

"Really?" She'd been dismayed.

"Luckily I've been through that, except it wasn't Rhonda who was besotted, it was me, and instead of a whale we had Winslow."

"I bet he'd love the comparison. How about we do this—I'll have half an hour every day to talk about Friday and after that you can cut me off."

"Nah," Truman said. "That's okay. I was probably like that with Miles when he was a piglet. There's no denying love when it finds you."

"And is that what this is—love?"

"If it walks like a horse and it sounds like a horse, it's probably a horse."

Neva said, "For the record, I've always hated that expression. In my business, sometimes it is a zebra."

"Or a whale," said Truman.

"Or a whale," Neva agreed.

FOUR DAYS LATER any suggestion of good weather was a distant memory and the wind on top of the pool was blowing so hard it knocked Libertine off her feet. Even Friday stayed on the surface only long enough to breathe and then returned to the visitors in the gallery, which was packed in spite of the filthy weather. A TV crew from Germany was attempting to put together a five-minute segment using indoor footage exclusively.

Looking for something new and stimulating to give Friday on such an unpromising day, Gabriel recalled an offer from Winslow's friend Reginald to bring his pet rat to the office for Friday to see. It was a Saturday, so he called Sam's house, and soon Molly, a pretty little gray and white rat, was sitting on the office windowsill. She was young, even tempered, and entirely unconcerned about the killer whale looming inches away on the other side of the glass. She turned every bit of her small back on him and groomed her fur and whiskers. Friday didn't leave the window for half an hour.

"Cool!" said Reginald, when Friday had left at last. "Let's do a snake next time."

"You got a snake I don't know about?" Sam asked him.

"Not yet," said Reginald.

"Then let's just keep it that way. A rat's bad enough, but a snake would put Mama right into an early grave." Reginald subsided, and Sam continued, "What we should do is, we should bring in a power tool or two and run 'em." He turned to Gabriel and said, "You got something you might want us to paint or drill holes in? He likes that."

"Not that I can think of," said Gabriel, "but here's a thought. Do you by any chance have an extra television, or know somebody who does?"

"There's that big one shug used to watch," Sam said. "Don't know where it is, but it stayed here at the zoo. Truman might know."

"Excellent," said Gabriel.

Later that day Truman came to the office and Gabriel asked the whereabouts of the set. "The nights alone get pretty long and killer whales don't sleep the way we do."

"No?"

"They're voluntary breathers," Gabriel explained. "If they slept in the sense that we do, they'd die. No one really knows how it works, actually. They may sleep with one half of their brain at a time; or they might only doze and not really sleep at all. In either case, the nights go on and on."

"They did for shug, too," said Sam sadly.

The television was quickly resurrected from a storage room, and two nights later Johnson Johnson pulled together a pizza and cookie dinner for everyone, to be held in the killer whale office. The TV was wheeled around so it faced into the pool from the office window. Neva set up a few folding chairs she and Truman had brought from Havenside's conference room; Ivy brought Julio Iglesias and her knitting; Sam and Corinna brought the old lamp and armchair they'd used when they watched TV with Hannah in the elephant barn; Libertine transported the Oat Maiden pizzas and cookies Johnson Johnson had prepared.

"I should have brought some wine or beer," said Ivy, smacking her forehead.

"It's just as well you didn't," said Gabriel. "I've instituted a zero-tolerance policy for alcohol here."

"At the zoo?"

"At the whale pool. Killer whales and alcohol don't mix."

"He's behind a pane of glass, for god's sake," said Ivy.

"Acrylic," said Gabriel.

"Whatever. He's not going to come flying through the window, is he?"

"Doesn't matter. You may have to go in the water with little or no notice, and believe me, booze plus whales is a bad idea."

"Well, I guess that makes sense," grumbled Ivy, "though you are a killjoy. Even Julio Iglesias appreciates a little beer from time to time." The dog was on the floor, sniffing for crumbs. Neva fed him a piece of mozzarella.

"Oh, sure," Ivy said, watching her. "Now you're going to be the golden one."

As soon as the pizza was gone they all settled into a screening of—what else—*Free Willy*.

"You think he's going to get some bad ideas from this picture?" Sam said doubtfully. "What with Willy jumping over that jetty and all?"

"You know what actually jumped that jetty?" asked Gabriel, grinning. "A life-sized, neoprene-covered model. They catapulted it. Want to know how you can tell? There's no genital slit. Censored for your family's viewing discretion."

Since Friday wasn't even in the window anymore—and hadn't been since the janitorial staff had arrived to buff the floor in the visitors' gallery—they fast-forwarded the movie to the denouement. A great whoop went up as "Willy" indeed sailed over the jetty in the movie's climactic shot, his underbelly smooth and featureless as a cue ball.

"You think Friday would recognize the ocean anymore?" Sam asked. "I always wondered with shug whether if you dropped her into that tea plantation in Burma she'd even know where she was, she'd been gone so long."

"I bet he would," said Reginald. "I bet he still gets homesick sometimes, too."

"Just because he was born there doesn't mean he can remember anything about it, son," Sam said. "He was just a little bitty thing when he was captured." He looked to Gabriel for confirmation. Gabriel nodded.

"Well, I bet he can still remember," Reginald said stubbornly. "I bet he remembers and he misses it. Bet he misses his family, too."

They all looked at Libertine. "Don't ask me," she said. "I don't have the faintest idea."

Reginald folded his arms tightly over his chest, which was when Libertine realized they probably weren't talking about the whale at all.

"I bet if you let him loose right now he could find his way back home," Reginald said.

"Honey, it was a different ocean," Ivy said gently.

"I bet he could anyways."

Winslow spoke up. "If you let him go, would he survive, do you think?"

"No," said Gabriel firmly. "I don't."

"Maybe he could, though," said Winslow. "At least for a while."

"Someone should try it," said Reginald. "You could, like, put a whale-cam or something on him and follow him."

"You'd radio-tag him," said Gabriel.

"Yeah?" Reginald said eagerly. "You'd, like, suction cup it to him or something?"

"We'd attach it to his dorsal fin. It doesn't even take that sophisticated a device. We track animals all the time."

"See?" said Reginald. "That way you could get him back if he starts starving or something."

"That's probably a little simplistic," said Truman, looking to Gabriel for confirmation.

"It is, but he's got the basics. You track where he's going, and if he stays in one place too long, you send a boat after him to see if he's okay."

"Theoretically," said Truman.

"Theoretically," Gabriel agreed.

"Could we do it?" said Reginald. "He'd probably really like that."

Sam said, "It's not that simple, son."

"Yeah," said the boy hotly. "But you could, if you wanted to."

Sam gave the boy a look that said he'd gone too far. Reginald set his jaw and then they changed the subject.

AT FOURTEEN REGINALD Poole—now Brown, since Sam and Corinna had adopted him—was large in presence if not yet in stature. Evidently his father had been a big man, so Reginald was likely to become one, too. They had never met, but his mother used to talk about him all the time when Reginald was little and there was still a chance the man might come back. By the time Reginald was five it was clear he wasn't coming, and his mother started dissing him big-time. "He's nothing but a good-for-nothing, piece-of-shit freeloader. Don't you go asking me about him 'cause he's nothing, not even a gnat in God's eye. I don't even want his name in this house—not so much as his name." But that was just pride talking.

And the truth was, if Reginald were his father, he wouldn't come home, either. His mother was a hard-drinking, wild-haired, ramshackle, slack-mouthed woman who liked to tell anyone within earshot that Reginald was her ball and chain. "He a good looker, honey, but he be draggin' me down. You wouldn't know it now, but before he come along I was a fine-looking woman, made men run into each other on the street, they was so busy staring. In those days my legs reached right up to heaven, and the Lord gave me a fine ass to go with them." She used to tell Reginald, "You got your looks from me, baby. You got your mama's pretty mouth. When you grow up, girls gonna be all over you."

A month before his eleventh birthday his Aunt Ella drove down from Bladenham to pick him up and bring him back home with her. On the ride back she told him, "You know, your mother always did have a screw loose, even when we were kids. Our mama used to say, 'Ella, you better make something of yourself, because you're going to end up taking care of your sister one day. That girl's got less sense than God gave a goose.' It used to make me mad when she'd say that, but even then I knew she was right."

It took his mother three days to even realize he was gone, and as far as he knew there'd never been any talk about his going back. It took his mother three days to even realize he was gone, and as far as he knew there'd never been any talk about his going back. If anyone had asked him—and no one ever did—he'd have gone right back home. When she was straight he could make his mother laugh until she had to run to the bathroom to keep from peeing herself; when she was on crack—which, by the end, was most of the time—she let him do whatever he wanted, like go outside at two o'clock in the morning and talk to the old man who lived in a red sleeping bag on the sidewalk a couple of blocks away. At his aunt Ella's he had a special place in his room, in the far corner behind his bed, where he liked to pretend he could time travel, go home to when home was still good. Not that he believed in that kind of kid stuff anymore, but still. He became the only black kid in his entire school, which on the one hand sucked, but on the other made him something of a celebrity.

Then he'd met Samson and Corinna Brown and Hannah, and Winslow Levy, and that's when things started turning around, especially when he and Winslow were recruited to help Hannah escape from the zoo so she could go to California. Reginald's picture had been in the paper for that, even though Martin Choi called him "Dillard" instead of Reginald. In his prior experience the only kids his age who got their pictures in the paper were kids who'd been collateral damage from gang shootings or who'd been kept locked in the basement or a closet for years and were eighteen years old and weighed forty-five pounds.

Right after Sam got back from the sanctuary in California, he and Corinna had had a long talk with Ella about letting the boy come and live with them, and once she'd been satisfied that they were good Christian people she'd said yes. "He's a good boy, but he's high-spirited," Reginald had overheard Ella saying when he was supposed to be taking out the trash. "He needs a firmer hand than I've got the strength for, plus he deserves to be raised by someone who believes in him. I finished raising my own kids a long time ago and honey, I'm tired."

After six months his grades were all As instead of Cs and Ds, and Sam asked Ella if she would help him find Reginald's mother. She agreed, and when a month later they found her, she signed away her parental rights so Sam and Corinna could adopt him. Reginald was pretty sure money had changed hands, but he was also sure he wasn't the first kid who'd been sold for crack cocaine. It didn't matter to him: once he was adopted, Sam and Corinna couldn't change their minds later on and make him leave, no matter what kind of stupid thing his reckless brain put him up to. Sam was even stricter than Ella, especially when his mouth got him into trouble, which was often; but all in all, that was okay with Reginald. Sam took him for walks in the orchard behind the zoo so they could talk about what it was to be a man, and Corinna was always hugging and loving on him, which he pretended not to like but really did because she was big, soft, and warm, and she smelled like a ton of different shampoos and other beauty products. Now, at fourteen, he had a home and a family, and he and Winslow were still best friends even though Winslow had that dopey pig that was always sniffing you in the behind and worse.

The day after the TV party, on his way home from school, Reginald had reached Bladenham's main commercial street when he saw Martin Choi, the *News-Tribune* reporter, walking toward him from the other direction. Reginald had run into the reporter several times since Hannah's departure, and the guy always said the same thing: "S'up, dude? You hear about anything interesting over there at the zoo, you let me know first, huh? You've got my number, right?"

Reginald loved being treated as though he could be in possession of confidential information, so he always said he would, but he never meant anything by it—at least not until today; in fact, not until this minute. Call it the devil, call it a wild hair, but Reginald ducked under the drugstore's sagging canvas awning and blurted out, "If I tell you something, you've got to never tell anyone it was me who told you."

The reporter looked surprised—as surprised as Reginald was at where his show-off self was taking him. "Yeah? Sure, kid, that's what reporters do—we go to jail instead of giving away our sources." He looked at Reginald with sudden excitement. "Hey, are they getting another whale?"

Reginald heard a high, whiney little buzzing in his ears, which was what always happened when his mouth outpaced his brain, but it just made him talk faster. "No, something way better."

"What?"

"They might let him go."

"What do you mean, let him go?"

"Home—back to where he came from."

"Colombia?" said Martin.

"No, man. The wild. Like that whale in *Free Willy.*"

"Holy shit! You mean they might release him?"

Suddenly this conversation seemed like a bad idea, a really bad idea, but Reginald was in too deep now to deny it. Faintly he said, "Yeah. I mean, maybe."

"Man—whoa!" Martin said eagerly. "So does anyone else know about this? You call anyone at a radio station or TV or Northwest Cable News or anything like that?"

"No." Reginald was already wishing he hadn't told Martin Choi, either.

"Keep it that way, okay, kid? I mean it."

"Man, you better not rat me out."

"Hey, take it easy. Your name's Raymond, Reynolds, Remington, something like that, right?"

"Winslow," said Reginald. "My name's Winslow."

THE FIRST HINT of trouble came in a phone call from Martin Choi. Truman was in his office working on a formal Greater Good Fund proposal to present to his full board of directors when Brenda put the call through.

"So, hey," Martin said. "I hear the whale's gonna swim home."

"I'm sorry?" Truman could feel in his stomach that wherever this conversation was going, it wouldn't be anyplace good.

"A little bird told me you're thinking about sending him back there to Iceland or Norway or wherever."

"Who told you that?"

"No can do, bud," Martin said. "We're all about protecting our sources."

"Listen to me carefully," Truman said, deepening his voice to its most forceful tonal range. "There is not one iota of truth to that, not one—it is completely and totally without merit. I can't even imagine why anyone would say it, unless they were trying to make trouble for the zoo."

"Right on, man," said the reporter. "I hear you." Truman had the sinking feeling that if Martin were in the room with him right now, he'd be winking. And with that, the reporter hung up.

Rattled, Truman searched for a reason why anyone would say something so baseless. Could it be an animal activist planting a seed that would turn into a toxic flower when debated in the press? Gabriel had warned him over and over how noxious the whale activism community could be. But why this story, and why now?

There had been a lot of people at the pool the night before last, but everyone except Gabriel, Ivy, and Libertine had been through the Hannah media blitz three years ago and had experienced firsthand the awesome power of an untruth if it was repeated enough times. He trusted them completely. That left Gabriel, Ivy, and Libertine. Why would any of them be talking to Martin Choi in the first place, let alone planting a false story?

Telling himself he was going to the three for insights, not to make accusations, he called Gabriel, who said, "The man's an idiot. Hell, no, I didn't talk to him."

"But do you have any idea who might have?"

"I've always said Libertine shouldn't be here. I'll say it again."

"All right," said Truman. "Other than Libertine."

"Nope," said Gabriel. "Sorry, bud."

Next Truman called Ivy's cell and described his conversation with Martin Choi. "For heaven's sake," Ivy said. "He's an idiot. You know that."

And of course, he did know that. It just didn't help. "Do you think this is something Libertine might have planted— maybe something she'd been planning since the day Friday got here? Gabriel warned us."

"Shame on you," Ivy said. "That woman is one of the gentlest people I've ever met. There isn't a nefarious bone in her body."

"Normally I'd agree with you, but let's face it, she's also a little, hmm, unbalanced."

"Why, because she claims to hear animals?"

"It's not exactly normal," Truman said drily.

"That's mean, is what it is. She may be a little odd, I'll grant you that, but she cares about that animal as much as any of us, maybe more. And anyway she's said he's stonewalling her, that she hasn't 'received' anything or whatever from him since right after he got here. Plus she knows if it *was* her and she got busted, she'd have to leave the project. Isn't that in her contract?"

"Yes."

"Well?"

Truman sighed. "If it wasn't her, I'm stumped."

"My advice is, let it go. The man's an idiot. You know that. Everyone knows that. Maybe he made it up all by himself— maybe he's trying to shake the trees a little and see if something falls out. Though I have to say I wouldn't credit him with enough intelligence to actually do something like that, but it's possible. No matter what, the story won't have legs. No one's going to back up whatever source he had, if there even *is* a source, which I doubt."

The only person left was Libertine.

With the greatest reluctance he picked up the phone.

LIBERTINE AND IVY had a standing pizza date at the Oat Maiden every Thursday night. Libertine tried to back out—she'd been crying for hours, ever since Truman's call—but Ivy wouldn't let her. Fortunately one of the back tables was empty, because her face was swollen and blotchy. Once Ivy had ordered their customary pepperoni and onion pizza, Libertine described Truman's careful questioning. "He was trying to be very fair, but he thinks it was me. They'll all think it was me. If I were them, *I'd* think it was me."

"Well, was it you?"

"Of course not."

"Then just say so."

"I did, but it's almost impossible to prove that you didn't do something. Plus I've never been very good at sticking up for myself."

Ivy picked a piece of pepperoni off her pizza slice and popped it in her mouth. "I know. You're worse at standing up for yourself than anyone I've ever met."

Libertine looked at her plate.

"That's all right. But what did he say—he didn't fire you, did he? Because I'll call him right now, if he did."

"No—he just told me what had happened and then he asked if it was me, and I said no, which was when I started crying, and now I can't stop."

"I can see that," Ivy said.

Libertine nodded. "I'd give a lot for a pair of sunglasses."

"That's all right, honey," Ivy soothed, patting her hand. "They'll just assume there's been a death in the family."

THE NEXT MORNING, too miserable to sleep, Libertine went out at five-thirty and drove around town until she found the *News-Tribune* in a vending box. Above the fold a huge headline blared, KILLER WHALE TO GO FREE. The story attributed the information to "an anonymous source close to the zoo." It went on to state, "The Max L. Biedelman Zoo, which made the controversial decision three years ago to let its lone elephant, Hannah, move to a sanctuary, is now considering letting Bladenham's favorite wild-caught whale go free." It got worse from there.

At the pool, a copy of the paper was spread across the office desk. Neva and Gabriel avoided her. Gabriel didn't even make eye contact.

By noon Libertine decided to go to Truman's office and get the firing over with—she was still so unhinged she was a danger around the pool anyway. She told herself it was a blessing in disguise: she'd known for weeks that she was running out of money, and this way she'd be able to go home to Orcas Island and live in her own house and seek out a job that would bring in a little money. But while all that was true, it didn't make her feel any better. She was relieved when Truman made time for her right away, indicating that she should sit in his visitors' chair.

"Have you read the story?" he asked her without preamble. A copy lay faceup on his desk, its headline exposed.

Libertine nodded miserably. "I know you're going to have to fire me. I came over here to say I won't make any kind of fuss."

To her surprise, Truman looked at her kindly. "Absolutely not. Whoever the source was, it certainly wasn't you. I know you've had experience with the media in the past, and whoever this was, was a rank amateur. "

Stunned, it took Libertine a moment to understand that Truman, at least, didn't think she was the mole. She reached across his desk impulsively to press his hand. "Oh, thank you, thank you, thank you!" Then she started to cry again. He held out a box of Kleenex.

"We do still have someone leaking information to the media, though," he said. "Someone who's trying to force an outcome. Do you have any ideas? Someone within the animal rights community?"

"No, but I'll put my ear to the ground. It's not that big a subset." Libertine pushed herself out of the chair. "And thank you so, so much. I hope you know how much being here means to me. We may have philosophical differences, but I'd never do anything to jeopardize that. Or Friday."

Truman smiled. "I know. And I think most of the other people around here know, too."

ONCE LIBERTINE WAS gone Truman asked Brenda to hold his calls for a few minutes while he collected himself for the inevitable media onslaught. He attempted to calm himself, unsuccessfully, watching the unending line of visitors snaking out to the parking lot. The more popular Friday became, the more media scrutiny the zoo would come under, even over untruths and trivialities.

Then he took a strengthening swallow of coffee and told Brenda to open the floodgates. For the rest of the day he fielded calls from every regional newspaper, both daily and weekly;

Northwest Cable News, Associated Press, Reuters, the *Seattle Times,* the *Oregonian,* Sky TV, and ITN. All the area television stations sent satellite trucks for live shots on the noon, late afternoon, and evening news. He appeared on every single one, refuting the rumor that, he quickly realized, everyone fervently wanted to be true.

WHEN HE FINALLY got home, Truman sat with Winslow at the kitchen table over a bag of potato chips and a copy of the *News-Tribune* he'd laid out. Miles snuffled around them ingratiatingly, waiting for Winslow to slip him a chip Truman pretended not to see.

"So what's this?" Winslow said, looking at the newspaper.

"I wondered if you knew anything about it."

Winslow pulled the paper closer, read the story, and then said excitedly, "Cool! We're letting him go? That would be just like *Free Willy!*"

Truman was startled—he hadn't made the connection before. "No. We never were. It would be the ultimate cruelty. He'd stand no chance in the wild."

"He could learn, though. Couldn't he?"

"He's not just lacking skills, Winnie. He isn't physically in any shape to be on his own. That's why he came here in the first place."

"So who said we were releasing him?"

"I was hoping you might have some idea," said Truman.

"You mean did *I* tell him?"

"Did you?"

"No way!" Winslow said. "He's an idiot."

Truman couldn't help a small smile. "I know, but even idiots can ask questions sometimes that are hard to avoid answering."

Winslow shook his head adamantly and handed Miles a couple of potato chips which he crunched with piggy zeal.

"Let's put him behind the gate."

"He hates that," Winslow protested.

"You do know Dr. Bly says he's too fat, right?"

Winslow sighed. "He's a *pig*. They're supposed to be fat. Hey, did you show Neva that story? Maybe she was the one."

"No."

"No, you haven't shown her the story, or no, she's not the one?"

"Both."

"You don't think it was me, do you?" Winslow said, as the gravity of the situation apparently began to sink in.

"No, but you did raise an interesting point about *Free Willy*. Has Reginald said anything about sending Friday back to the wild?"

"No, and he wouldn't talk to Martin Choi, either," Winslow said loyally. "He thinks Martin Choi's an idiot, too."

"Well, if you do hear him talking about anything to do with Friday's going back to the wild, would you let me know?"

"Yeah."

But Truman knew he wouldn't. Winslow was nobody's snitch, which was exactly the way Truman had raised him.

ACROSS TOWN SAM had just finished reading the *News-Tribune* story with a sinking heart. Reginald was sitting across the table from him, looking like butter wouldn't melt in his mouth.

"You read this story?" Sam asked him.

"What story?"

"This story about Friday."

"There's a story about Friday?" Reginald said disingenuously.

Sam sighed and pushed the newspaper across the table. Reginald didn't touch it.

"Go on and read it."

Reginald read it. When he was done, Sam asked, "Was it you who talked to him?"

"No. It could've been Winslow, though. I mean, he knows that reporter guy, Martin Choi."

Sam studied him for a while before saying, "Son, I've been around a long time and over the years I've learned some things. One of them is when people talk about something that's none of their business, it catches up to them. Could take a day, could take a year, but trouble's going to find them one way or the other. The other thing I've learned is, your word is the only thing you really own—money, houses, jobs, clothes, cars, even family can come and go, but as long as you're alive, you got your word. So you have to take good care of it, protect it from harm, and make sure people can always count on it. The day people start wondering if you're telling the truth, that's the day you squander the one thing you got that you can be proud of. Do you understand?"

Reginald nodded, avoiding meeting Sam's eyes.

"Now, are you the one who talked to this reporter?"

"Yes, sir," said Reginald faintly.

"And does it make you feel like a big man, pretending you know things no one else does?"

"Sometimes."

Sam nodded. "There was a saying back during World War II: *loose lips sink ships*. You know what that means?"

"Keep your damn mouth shut."

"Language, son," Sam said, trying not to smile.

"It means keep your mouth shut," the boy amended.

"That's right. Any idea why that might still be important?"

"Not really. I mean, we don't have any ships, and there's no war, at least not in this town."

"No, but now take family secrets. Every family has some things they don't want the world to know about. Doesn't mean those things are wrong, it just means they're nobody's business. You know how Mama does her friend Bettina Jones's hair every Tuesday?"

"Yeah."

"And every fourth Tuesday she weaves in a little extra to cover up a thin spot the poor gal has right on the top of her head, which is a shame since she wasn't much of a looker to begin with. Now, Mama knows that secret isn't hers to tell. It's not dangerous or even real important, but it's not hers to tell, just the same. You see what I'm saying to you?"

"You're saying keep your damn mouth shut."

Sam smacked Reginald lightly on the back of head.

"Ow," said Reginald, but they both smiled.

"You just remember, son, someone else's secret isn't yours to give away. You keep that in mind and people will tell you things because they know you can be trusted. Violate that trust and you might as well call that friendship over. And ending a friendship's a mighty sorry thing. Mighty sorry. You got that?"

"Yes sir."

"Fine," said Sam. "Now you're going to call Truman and tell him it was you who talked to that reporter."

Reginald protested loudly, but Sam was adamant. "When you do some wrong thing, it's up to you to make it right, and sometimes the only thing you can do is admit what you did. If you step up and be a man, then take responsibility for what you've done, that's what people will remember about you, and after a while that wrong thing you did just fades away."

Chapter 10

FOR CHRISTMAS GABRIEL bought Friday a fire truck—not just any fire truck, but one that was nearly three feet long, weighed fifteen pounds, and could produce a realistic siren and flashing lights as it sped by remote control along the smooth concrete floor of the visitors' gallery. Rapt, Friday chased it up and down the gallery for an hour, watching it raise and lower its four-foot ladder, flash its lights, sound its siren, and speed away.

"He loved it," Libertine told Gabriel once she returned from the gallery. "It was the perfect choice."

Neva had hung a wheel of Christmas lights on the office window, one hundred feet of LED lights still coiled in its packaging. It cast a piercing light all the way over to the viewing gallery from the opposite side of the pool. She had also set a small fiber-optic tree on the office windowsill, where it blinked red to green to red. Sam and Corinna brought Friday two magnificent salmon, wild-caught in Puget Sound, and Ivy, on Gabriel's advice, brought him an irregularly shaped white plastic cube the size of two hay bales placed side by side, made by the same company that made Friday's beloved blue ball. Ivy also gave Neva and Gabriel a present: a bright yellow underwater scooter, which towed them through the water fast enough for a spirited game of killer whale tag.

But it was Libertine who gave him the most unusual gift of all: a swim with Johnson Johnson.

With Gabriel's permission, she'd asked Johnson Johnson a week ago if he'd like to be Friday's Christmas gift, and he'd nearly collapsed with excitement; he hadn't been back to the pool top since the day Kitty died. So at two o'clock on Christmas Day afternoon, just as Ivy, Truman, Neva, Winslow, Matthew, and Lavinia were sitting down to Christmas dinner, Johnson Johnson pulled on a borrowed secondhand wet suit that almost fit him, and booties that did, and walked through the shallow water of the slide-out area straight into the deep water of the pool with no hesitation. He sank down until he was head-to-head with Friday, who had his mouth wide open, possibly in astonishment.

Gabriel toed a bucket of fish to the edge of the pool so Johnson Johnson could reach in. "Go ahead and offer him a few. It might take him a little while to get used to you."

Johnson Johnson placed one fish after another in Friday's wide-open mouth. "I think he's already used to me."

"Looks that way, doesn't it," said Gabriel. "Okay, hold back about half the bucket for later."

"Can I pet him?"

"You can do whatever you want. If he doesn't like something he'll just swim away from you. You're on his turf now. So to speak."

Johnson Johnson rubbed and scratched and patted and positioned himself to look Friday straight in the eye. "He sees me," he said.

"Absolutely. Pet his tongue," Gabriel suggested. "He likes that, too."

But Friday closed his mouth and sank out of sight. "Is he done?" Johnson Johnson asked, clearly disappointed.

Gabriel was grinning. "Wait."

"What?"

"Wait. . . ."

And then Friday rose up beneath him and swam away with him sprawled across his back, clutching the whale's tightly curled dorsal fin. Johnson Johnson was so overcome with delight he didn't make a sound. Gabriel shouted to him, "Stand up!"

Like a surfer, Johnson Johnson carefully rose until he was standing upright on Friday's back, wobbling a bit.

"Okay, the game is, he's going to try to make you fall off," Gabriel called. "And you try not to let him."

Friday rolled and arched and twitched and Johnson Johnson fell off again and again. Each time, Friday came back to retrieve him. After nearly an hour, tired at last, he swam Johnson Johnson to the side of the pool.

Johnson Johnson leaned down and gave him a gentle kiss just behind the blowhole.

"This was a big treat for him," Gabriel said. "We don't let him do that during the day because Truman thinks it looks too much like we're making him perform tricks, and he's retired. Personally, I don't agree, but he's the boss. Anyway, why don't you get out and feed him what's left in the bucket? Then you can get back in the pool if you aren't too cold. You'll have company."

"I'm not cold," said Johnson Johnson through chattering teeth.

A minute later, Libertine stepped onto the pool top, smiling tremulously, in Neva's wet suit and booties. "Merry Christmas," Gabriel said.

Tears stood in Libertine's eyes. "Thank you so much," she said. "Is it okay if I'm a little nervous?"

"You'd be a fool not to be. Okay, as soon as you're ready, go ahead and get in."

While Gabriel and Johnson Johnson watched, Libertine sat on the wet walk and then slipped into the pool. Friday had been watching her curiously, but as soon as she was in the water he swam away.

"Is he afraid of me?" she said, disappointed.

"It's because you're scared," Gabriel said. "He'll come back when he's ready. Well, when you're ready." To Johnson Johnson he said, "Let's get you back in, too."

Johnson Johnson jumped into the water near Neva. "Oh!" Libertine cried breathlessly as Friday, who had been in the depths of the pool, surfaced unexpectedly beneath her. Instead of carrying her on his back the way he'd done with Johnson Johnson, he slowly rolled beneath her until he was completely upside down and she was sprawled on his chest between his pectoral flippers.

"Go ahead and stand up!" Gabriel called. "Hold on to his pecs and he'll swim you around the pool like that."

"Oh!" Libertine grabbed the edges of the paddle-shaped flippers and found her footing between them. "Doesn't this hurt him?" she called a little breathlessly to Gabriel as Friday began to swim around the pool.

"If it did he wouldn't do it," Gabriel called back. "You weigh nothing, by his standards. Well, by our standards, too, but you know what I mean. When he's ready for you to get off, he'll just go underwater and you'll float away."

Libertine held on, feeling how completely their roles had been reversed—she was in Friday's environment now, clumsy and helpless. She could feel a great reserve of gentleness in him, as though he knew how fragile she was. He carried her with exquisite care.

And then he tipped her off, rolled right side up to take two deep breaths, and swam to Johnson Johnson across the pool, putting him on his back. Then he picked up Libertine, so she was riding behind Johnson Johnson, and took them for a fast circuit around the pool. "He likes this," Johnson Johnson turned to tell her.

"Me, too!" she said.

"I'm glad you gave me to him. I've never been anyone's present before."

"You're welcome," she said with a suddenly full heart. "Merry Christmas."

"Merry Christmas," said Johnson Johnson.

When an hour later Libertine and Johnson Johnson got out of the pool, both of them shivering uncontrollably, Libertine walked over to Gabriel and said quietly, "Thank you for this Christmas. It's been a wonderful day."

"You're welcome," he said.

"I hope Friday liked it as much as we did."

Gabriel raised his eyebrows. "Hasn't he told you?"

"Not in the way you mean. I still haven't sensed him since the beginning, except in the way you or anyone can."

"Any idea why not?"

"I assume he hasn't needed me," Libertine said. "He must

know he's in the best possible hands. And he knows I'm around, if something comes up."

"I thought you said he was in prison," he said, but he was smiling.

"I don't think I'll ever change my mind about that," she said. "But that doesn't mean he's unhappy. You've opened up a lot of worlds for him."

He looked down at her. "Careful—I may remind you that you said that one day."

"Go right ahead," she said. "You can remind me anytime. That will be my Christmas present to you."

BUT THERE WOULD be one more gift for Friday that holiday season, this one engineered by Gabriel: a child. Gabriel's sister in Seattle had a six-year-old daughter named Nicolle. Though she might have been the only six-year-old on earth who was not impressed with Friday—she'd rather play with the new Barbie she got for Christmas—he'd wheedled and bribed until she agreed to come and play. At about the time when most people were finally shaking off their New Year's hangovers, Nicolle was running at top speed directly at Friday through the shallow slide-out area. She didn't pause or even slow down as she approached, but the whale didn't flinch, even when she arrested her flight on his face. Gabriel could see that his eyes were wide and keen. Gabriel's sister Stella stiffened, but Gabriel held her back. "She's fine," he said very quietly, so the child wouldn't hear him. "She's safe with him."

Friday allowed Nicolle to rub and pet him for several minutes, and then he swam slowly away, hugging the side of the pool. After twenty feet, he stopped. Curious, the little girl followed, kicking water in the wet walk with her Barbie boots as she went. Each time she caught up with him he swam on, repeating the pattern over and over. Gabriel's sister Stella watched as Gabriel explained that Friday was teaching the little girl a game of Follow Me. Once Friday was satisfied that she'd learned that, he embellished: the next time they stopped, he rolled on his side and very slowly, with infinite delicacy, raised his pectoral flipper and touched Nicolle on the very top of her head, again and again, until they'd made a complete circuit around the pool. When Friday put his chin on the side of the pool, Nicolle stopped and leaned on Friday's nose.

And then, without warning, the whale sank, making it look as though Nicolle had pushed him under. Startled, the little girl kept her empty hands outstretched—and from the depths Friday surged out of the water and into them. Gabriel's sister screamed, but Gabriel restrained her, understanding that Friday was only teaching her daughter a new game: Push Me, Push You. Over and over Nicolle sank him, and over and over he rose into the tiny cup of her hands.

GABRIEL'S RESPECT FOR Friday was huge. He was easily the smartest, most tractable animal Gabriel had ever worked with. As his health continued to improve—by Gabriel's calculation he'd gained nearly a ton since arriving—Gabriel had thrown a lot of new challenges at him, and he'd caught on and mastered every one. His innovative behavior count had climbed to nearly a hundred and twenty-five, and he dreamed up new ones every day with a spirit of joyfulness. His breaches and bows were high enough for people approaching the visitors' gallery to see above the pool top; his speed-swims were now fast enough to create a breaking wave that followed him around the pool.

He was also starting to challenge them. Last week during a work session, Neva had asked him to breach. The whale took off crisply, agreeably, but instead of leaving the water in a forward jump, he leaped out of the water backward, spitting water between his teeth.

Next Neva had rolled his blue ball into the pool and asked him to touch it with his pectoral flipper. He touched it with his flukes, his nose, his head, his belly—everything but a pectoral flipper. She'd looked at Gabriel and said, "What the hell?"

"Give him a time-out," Gabriel said. "He's screwing with you." Neva removed the bucket of fish and walked off the pool top with Gabriel. When she returned five minutes later, she found Friday waiting contritely, his chin on the poolside, mouth open.

She signaled him with a raised finger: *attention!* Then she asked him for a speed-swim.

He leaped from the water in three flawless breaches.

AT THE END of January, Libertine approached Gabriel on the pool top, where he was watching Friday and Neva play grab-ass with the help of the yellow water-scooter. She said, "I want to thank you again for finding work here for me, and treating me like one of you. I know it wasn't your idea, and I understand why. But it's been a long time since I was part of something bigger than just me." She thought about this, then smiled ruefully. "Something human, anyway. I'm going to miss it."

Surprised, Gabriel asked, "Are you going somewhere?"

"I'm just about out of money. We volunteers have to eat and make house payments like everyone else."

"Have you talked to Truman about this?"

"No—I haven't even told Ivy yet. I'm trying to gather my resolve. They've both been very good to me." To her mortification, Libertine teared up.

He looked at her. "You okay?"

"I don't want to go," Libertine blurted out. "I love it here."

Gabriel gazed out across the pool, waited a beat, and then said, "Funny you should bring this up now, because I talked to Truman about you yesterday."

"Uh-oh."

He broke into a grin. "He agreed to let me hire you. Full time."

Libertine put her hands to her mouth. "*Oh!*"

"So should I tell him you want to think it over?"

She wiped her eyes and smacked him on the arm. "You," she said.

"Then how about you go buy a wet suit so you can play with the boy." Seeing her look he said, "No, on the zoo's dime. I'd also like you to take scuba lessons. If you're going to be part of the paid staff you're going to have to help keep the pool clean, which means diving. I have some ideas about training Friday on the bottom of the pool, too, but it's going to take the three of us. Anyway, the Y is giving a class in a month, so I've already signed you up. Call me crazy, but I suspected you wouldn't turn the job down."

She clasped her hands in front of her, brimful of gratitude and excitement. She'd never once considered that she might be valued in her role at the pool; she'd been grateful to be allowed there at all. "I don't know what to say."

"Don't say anything. Isn't there something you should be doing? Go!" He shooed her away. "*Go!*"

LIBERTINE SHARED HER news with Ivy that evening, at the Oat Maiden. "I feel like, I don't know—like I've been let out of the dungeon and allowed to play with the other children after being all by myself for years," she said.

"That's because people who hear what you do assume you're a wing nut," Ivy said placidly, feeding Julio Iglesias a stretchy thread of mozzarella. "Actually, you *are* a wing nut. Very nice, but still, a wing nut."

Libertine nodded matter-of-factly and reached across the table to take another slice of pizza. Julio Iglesias, who was sitting up in Ivy's tote bag on her lap, growled.

"Oh, you," Libertine said happily, rapping him smartly between the ears. Julio Iglesias lifted his lip.

"Boy, if looks could kill," said Ivy.

"Short of stabbing me in the heart," said Libertine to both of them, "nothing you can do is going to bring me down tonight, so don't bother even trying."

Ivy looked at her doubtfully. "Truman did tell you what the job pays, right?"

"Compared with zero? Yes. So you knew about this all along?"

Ivy waved this away. "It includes housing—he told you that, right?"

"It does?"

"He didn't tell you."

"I didn't actually talk to him—Gabriel was the one who told me."

"Well, the zoo will keep on paying your rent until June. After that you're on your own."

Libertine pressed her hands together in rapture. "I don't even know what to say."

"You really must be poor," Ivy said.

"I have forty-four dollars and thirty-seven cents." She gestured for Ivy to pass her Julio Iglesias across the table. In transit he sneezed over the pizza. "Talk about a class act," Libertine chided him, settling him in her lap and kissing him on the top of the head.

"I've never seen you this happy," Ivy said. "It's unnerving. Julio thinks so, too." The dog was stiff-arming Libertine, who was trying to hug him. "Here, you better give him back before he bites you in the face."

"I haven't had very many friends in my life," Libertine said matter-of-factly.

"You have me."

"I do have you. I had my husband, too."

"You were married?" Ivy said, surprised.

"I know," Libertine said ruefully. "It always surprises people. Do I look like that much of a spinster?"

Ivy thought about that for a minute. "No, you look like that much of a loner. A sad sack and a loner."

"I wasn't always." She told Ivy about Larry Adagio. "He got me. I still miss him."

"So do you, you know, hear from him or anything? From the Beyond?"

"I'm an animal communicator, not a medium."

"Did he know that?" Ivy asked.

"He knew I could talk to our cat and an old dachshund his

mom had, but I didn't start working with wild animals until he died." Libertine said. "I think he'd be proud of me, though. He always said he had more faith in me than I had in myself."

"So some things don't change," said Ivy.

"I guess. What about you—no husbands, no fiancés?"

"Nope. Oh, I went out with a fair number of men in my day. I used to spend my winters in Egypt until recently."

"Hence the dresses."

"Hence the dresses," Ivy confirmed. "There's no getting around the fact that Arabs know how to dress for comfort. Anyway, I saw a few of the men in the Egyptian ex-pat community, but nothing serious—most of them were married. I was reading a biography the other day about Wallis Simpson, and did you know she didn't really even *want* Edward? But after he abdicated the throne, what was she supposed to do, throw him over and call him a mistake? Not likely. They were apparently a phenomenally dreary couple, by the way—sponges and parasites and *boring*. After what they went through, you'd think they'd be fascinating but I guess they weren't. Bigots and fascists, yes, but fascinating, no. How on earth did I get onto that subject?"

"Beaus," Libertine prompted.

"Ah. Nothing else to say about that. It would be nice to have someone fall madly in love with me, a little less nice to fall madly in love with someone else, especially if it wasn't reciprocal, but I don't spend time thinking about it anymore. I'm sixty-two, set in my ways, and I love sleeping alone."

When dinner was over, Ivy reached for the check first, as always. Libertine tried to stop her. "No, let me. After all, I'm employed now!"

"Honey, if you paid you'd only have twenty-five dollars and

thirty-seven cents, and I can't imagine any emergency that could come that cheap. You hang on to what you've got—you can take me out another time."

Libertine gave in.

IVY HADN'T BEEN completely honest. There had been just one man in Egypt—a married man. They had met in a club frequented by U.S. State Department diplomats and functionaries; ever since, the shush of overhead fan blades turning in the heat had aroused in her a vestigial feeling of regret and longing. Ivy had been forty-nine, he'd been forty-two, and his wife had been thirty-seven—too old to be a trophy wife and not old enough for Ivy to feel sorry for. The feet touching beneath the table, the calves intertwined, the furtive hand-holding they'd succumbed to, had been agony. He had had the most beautiful forearms and hands she'd ever seen, before and since, though Gabriel's were close contenders. They had met away from the club only once during their seven-month relationship, at the Four Seasons Hotel in Cairo. But instead of the tryst they'd both been anticipating for so long, he had broken down and wept.

"What should I do?" he'd begged her. "Just tell me what I should do and I'll do it!" But the mere fact that he tried to appropriate her strength killed the passion. She would not shoulder his adultery; nor was she capable of loving someone with unclear priorities. Dutifully she'd held him, even wept with him, but she flew home the next day and never saw him again.

IN EARLY FEBRUARY Ivy invited Gabriel to her house on San Juan Island. "You need to get away," she'd told him in making her pitch. "When's the last day you had completely off?"

"I don't know. A while ago."

"When's the last time you were away from Bladenham?"

"Longer."

"I'll pick you up at the pool at two-thirty on Friday. Plan on staying overnight."

"You don't have to do that—I can find my way back."

"I know, I just assumed we'd both be drunk enough not to want to deal with ferry schedules and unlit roads."

"You do have a way of laying things out, don't you? Does anyone ever tell you no?"

"Damned few, as a matter of fact—but it's usually because I'm filthy rich. You don't seem to care about that."

"Why should I? You're the one who's rich, not me."

"You have a point."

"Almost always."

Ivy put together a grocery list and faxed it to the market in Friday Harbor, asking them to put everything in a box, charge it to her account, and have it ready for her to pick up on the way home from the ferry. Included: Dungeness crab, butter clams, fresh mussels, asparagus, romaine lettuce, various bell peppers, mushrooms, radishes and any other available vegetables that would work up nicely in a salad, freshly baked artisan bread, and a whole bakery cheesecake. They stopped at the liquor store to pick up several bottles of a superb Chilean Pinot Grigio kept chilled and in stock especially for her, and arrived home with enough time for Ivy to assemble and serve an excellent dinner, which she followed up with a very nice port.

By the end of dessert they were blotto, sprawled in the deep, comfortable club chairs in Ivy's living room. "I wish I were younger," Ivy said earnestly, picking through Julio Iglesias's fur for nonexistent fleas. When the dog bared his teeth she smacked him lightly on the nose and went back to rummaging through his coat.

"Doesn't everyone?" asked Gabriel.

"No—I mean I wish I were younger but you were your age."

"Ah."

"Is it tragic or just maudlin when old women lust after younger men?"

"I wouldn't know. I don't think I'm the kind of man women lust after."

"Au contraire."

To his credit, Gabriel let the remark go; to hers, in an act of uncharacteristic restraint, Ivy didn't pursue it. She sipped her drink and licked the rim of the glass ruminatively. "You know, it's a terrible thing to be alone."

"What do you mean?" said Gabriel.

"What do you mean, what do I mean? Just what I said." Ivy pushed Julio Iglesias off her lap and sat up straighter. "I bet you think I'm spunky. Just a spunky ol' gal."

"Well, aren't you? Not the old part, but the other."

"Yes, but that's not the point."

"So what is the point?"

"No one chooses to be alone. Maybe that's why I relate to Friday."

"Now you're being maudlin."

"I'm not. I just love him and I hate that he's all by himself."

Gabriel stared at her. "Are you kidding? One of us is with him eighteen hours a day, most days."

"You know what I mean," Ivy said, slumping back into her chair.

"If I do, I don't want to talk about it."

Ivy subsided. "Would you say you have to love the animals

you work with?" she mused. "Because why else would you spend all day and most evenings waiting on them hand and foot? Hoof—hand and hoof? No, wait, wait—flipper and fluke."

Gabriel frowned over this. "Love? Not necessarily. Respect—you have to have a high degree of respect for them. And they have to have a high degree of respect for you. Otherwise there's a good chance they'll kill you." He closed his eyes.

"Well, *that's* no good." Ivy raised herself on one arm, squinted at him, then collapsed again. "How can you be so damned smart about animals and so clueless about people?"

He cracked one eye open in protest. "What do you mean?—I am not."

Ivy nodded vigorously. "Oh yes, you are. Take little Libertine. She's head over heels in love with you—love, not lust—and you probably don't even know."

"Now I do," Gabriel pointed out.

Ivy snickered. "That's true. Now you do."

"You know, you're a mean drunk," Gabriel said, pointing at her with his wineglass, sloshing a little port on his shirt.

"Me?"

"You. She's your friend and you just outed her."

"I did not," Ivy protested lamely.

"Yeah, you did," Gabriel was saying. "Now we just have to hope I get drunk enough not to remember, because then you'll have outed-her-not."

"He loves me, he loves me not," sang Ivy. "Are you drunk enough?"

"No."

"Then we better fix that." Ivy rose with some difficulty. "You know, I have a very, *very* good scotch. Want some? Accepting would be the gentlemanly thing."

"Then I accept."

Ivy rummaged in a liquor cabinet until she found the bottle, then soda, then two glasses. Clumsily, before putting the drink in Gabriel's hand, she slopped some of it on Julio Iglesias, who'd been dozing on Gabriel's lap. The dog gave her a bitter look before jumping down and walking slowly, *deliberately,* to the other side of the room, where he glanced back at her to make sure she was watching before depositing a small, perfectly formed turd on the carpet.

"I don't know what he holds against me," Ivy said sadly, making no move to clean it up. "I've given him everything and he treats me like crap." Her eyes filled with tears. "They say maiden ladies—does anyone use that expression anymore?— maiden ladies use dogs as surrogate children. Some child. A real child would treat me better, I'll tell you that."

Gabriel slapped his chest. "Come on, Julio. Come to Papa."

The dog trotted back and hopped up. "Want a sip?" Gabriel held his scotch-and-soda where Julio Iglesias could lap up a healthy dose, then raised it overhead. "That's enough," he said. "You're the designated driver."

Ivy thought that was a scream.

By midnight Gabriel had fallen asleep on the living room sofa with Julio Iglesias curled on top of his chest and snoring like a wino. Ivy was in a similar state of dishabille on a fainting couch across the room, her voluminous dress twisted around her, her Nikes and athletic socks kicked off to reveal a fresh and immaculate pedicure. One of her pet peeves was women who, in their senior years, neglected their nails—one of the few body parts which, when skillfully attended to, could still compete with those of women half their age.

She finally roused Gabriel long enough to lead him upstairs, putting him in the same guest room Libertine had used. "G'night, you luscious thing." She gave him a peck on the cheek and said, "Dream of beautiful virgins."

The next morning they were halfway through a hangover breakfast of hash, eggs, and Bloody Marys when the phone rang. It was Neva.

"I think you'd better come back," she said starkly. "There's something wrong with Friday."

Chapter 11

GABRIEL AND IVY made it back to Bladenham by late afternoon, which was a miracle, given the infrequent ferry runs at that time of year. They drove directly to the pool, where Neva and Libertine were waiting. Neva darted out before Gabriel had even stepped out of his truck. "Slow down," he told her. "Take a deep breath." Once they'd reached the office he said, "Okay. Now."

"He does an underwater speed-swim for maybe two or three laps, until he's really got some speed, and then he slams into the gallery windows." Neva said. "It's totally unnerving."

"Headfirst?"

"God no—broadside."

"And when she says 'slams' she really means *slams*," Libertine said. "You can hear the reverberation from across the pool. And he's doing it over and over and *over*."

"Here—watch. He's getting ready to do it again." Neva pulled Gabriel over to the window. Just as she'd described, Friday wound himself up and bodychecked the nearest acrylic pane the way a hockey player slams into the boards. "It's awful," she said.

"Is he vocalizing?"

"I don't know." She and Libertine looked at each other for consensus. "No, not that we've heard."

"And how many times has he done it?"

"Maybe forty times," Neva said. "When we've been here."

"Has the sun been out?"

"I wish."

"What's his body posture like?"

"I don't know—normal," Neva said. She looked to Libertine, who concurred. "Nothing different."

"No convulsing, no arching, no cramping?"

Both women shook their heads.

"And no vocalizing?" he asked again.

"No."

"Have you been in the water to listen?"

"I cleaned yesterday afternoon," Neva said, "when he first started doing it. I didn't hear anything."

"No bleeding, no broken teeth?"

"No."

"And he's eating?"

"Yes."

"No discharge when he blows—no flying snot?"

"No."

Suspecting that whatever was going on was behavioral rather than medical, Gabriel calmly folded his arms across his chest and said, "Okay. Let me watch him."

"We were worried he'd hurt himself," said Libertine.

"If he wanted to do that, he'd be slamming into the rock

work, not the windows. Have either of you told Truman what's going on?"

"Yes," Neva said. "I thought he should know."

"Absolutely. Why don't you call him and ask him to come over when he gets a chance?" Gabriel said to Neva; and then, to both the women, "Go to opposite ends of the windows in the gallery and see if you can see anything different from over there."

With that, Gabriel leaned his elbows on the windowsill and spent fifteen minutes watching—until Friday slammed into one of the windows across the pool again, exactly as Neva had described it. Truman arrived at the office just in time to see it. "I gather we have a problem," he said to Gabriel, looking shaken.

"I'm not sure. I wouldn't say it's a problem, necessarily, but it's certainly a new behavior."

"Frankly, I'm a little worried about the windows," Truman said. "They weren't engineered to take that kind of lateral force."

They exchanged looks. "Well, that's not good," Gabriel said dryly.

"No. I've got a call in to see if we can find out what their tolerance is. I have to tell you I'm considering closing the gallery and asking you to put him in the medical pool."

Both men paused as Friday made another pass around the pool and slammed into the windows again. Truman winced at the impact. "Can you tell me some things that might cause this?"

Gabriel frowned thoughtfully, saying, "It could be a lot of things. He could be having stomach pain or some other kind of discomfort, though I don't think that's it. He could be bored. He could like the sound the window makes when he hits it. He could be seeing his own reflection in the window and thinking it's a second killer whale challenging him. His equilibrium or eyesight could be impaired by some kind of infection or virus. I want to take a blood sample and watch him for a while before I start narrowing it down."

"All right," said Truman. "Well, keep me posted."

Once Truman was gone, Gabriel asked Libertine and Neva to bring a bucket of fish upstairs while he put on a wet suit. By the time he got there, Friday was at the slide-out area with his mouth wide open, as usual. Gabriel moved the bucket back and squatted down, scratching Friday's head and tongue and talking to him congenially.

"Hey, bud. The girls tell me you're being a dick. What's up with that? You hungry?" While he was talking he inspected and wiggled all of Friday's forty-eight teeth. Only one was damaged, an old vertical crack that would need attention at some point, though right now the whale didn't flinch or show any other pain response when Gabriel moved it, convincing him that this wasn't the source of the trouble. When he was done he stood up and said, "Come on. Let's see you do your stuff."

He put Friday through a standard set of breaches, bows, and spy hops, rewarding each one with fish and a blast on his whistle. Throughout, Friday was attentive, energetic, and in a seemingly excellent humor. When the half-hour session was over, Gabriel took a blood sample for Libertine to run to the hospital lab for a rush analysis, and then got into the water. Over the next hour, in an attempt to harness any excess nervous energy, Gabriel tried to wear him out by playing high-energy tag using the yellow scooter, by letting the whale pitch him off his back, by doing rocket rides, where Gabriel stood on Friday's nose as Friday shot out of the water in a high spy hop, and by playing games incorporating the blue ball.

After all that, Friday bodychecked the gallery window before Gabriel had even reached the bottom of the stairs.

Neva, back from the viewing gallery, told him, "He's hitting pretty hard—you can actually see the window flex, and it makes a kind of booming sound. And he's definitely doing it deliberately. I mean, he's not swimming into the walls of the pool or the rock work, which I'd think he would be if it were a vision or parasite problem. Frankly, it's a little creepy. I hope the windows hold."

The hospital lab called to report that nothing had shown up in the blood work.

Gabriel called Truman to say he was convinced that whatever was going on with Friday was behavioral, not medical; but to be sure, he suggested that Truman contact the local utility and ask if they would bring their buried line detector to the pool.

"Why?" Truman asked.

"It's possible there's something in his gut that hasn't come up or out. I called down to Bogotá and they said there'd always been a story about his swallowing a brass hose nozzle, though there isn't anyone down there anymore who actually saw him do it. I've never taken it too seriously, but we might as well rule it out."

"I'm on it," said Truman.

THE NEXT MORNING dawned mercifully clear, the third straight day after a week of rain and wind. Libertine came to work even earlier than usual so she could finish fish house in time to watch as a technician from the power company carried a sophisticated metal detector onto the pool top. He wore earphones and didn't smile: he was clearly aware of the seriousness of his mission. As she watched, along with Neva and Truman, Gabriel directed Friday to roll over on his back, stretch out along the side of the pool, and hold still. Gabriel tugged his flukes until they lay partially in the wet walk so he couldn't drift, and then he beckoned to the technician. The man approached cautiously—"He's not going to eat me, right?"—and swept his wand over Friday's exposed thirty-two-foot-long undercarriage. Up and back, up and back, up and back. Then he gave Gabriel a thumbs-up signal and removed his earphones. There was no metal in Friday's body.

At Gabriel's request, Libertine scampered down the stairs and brought back the fanny pack Gabriel kept his supplies in, and Gabriel drew a fresh blood sample. "It's hard to know what to hope for, isn't it?" she said as she took the vial from him, labeled it with the day's date and time, and handed it off to Neva so she could rush it to the hospital lab.

The body slams continued.

The lab reported that the day's blood values were as normal as yesterday's had been.

Once the zoo opened, Truman asked Gabriel, Libertine, and Neva to do everything possible to keep Friday from swimming into the windows during visitors' hours. They did innovative sessions, high-energy sessions, play sessions, scooter sessions, and put every toy they had into the pool.

By half an hour before the zoo closed, they were exhausted and Friday was once again slamming into the viewing windows. Gabriel sent Neva back to the gallery to observe him and then asked Libertine to stay behind in the office for a quick chat. Her heart began beating faster as he turned to face her, and she clasped her hands together. "Look," he said, standing beside her at the office window, "I can't believe I'm even asking this, but is there anything you can tell me about Friday's state of mind?"

She smiled. "I didn't think you believed in that sort of thing."

"I don't. But at this point any input might help."

Across the pool they could see Friday hit the windows once more, feel the concussion through the acrylic office window.

"*Crap,*" said Gabriel.

"I'm sorry," Libertine said with sincere regret. "I haven't sensed a thing. Still. There hasn't been anything since he got here."

He turned to face her. "You're kidding."

"No. I thought you knew that."

"And you've stayed anyway?" he said incredulously. "Why?"

She could feel herself blush. "At first I just wanted to be here in case he needed me. He'd found me in the first place, so I assumed he'd wanted my help. And then you let me work here, and who's going to turn that down?"

"Yeah—for free."

"Not anymore," she pointed out.

He just shook his head and turned back to the window. Friday was making a first and then a second fast underwater circuit around the pool, setting himself up, and then he slammed the window again. Libertine winced.

Gabriel pointed up. Raindrops pocked the water's surface. "Crap."

"What?"

"I really thought he was charging his reflection in the

window. It all started the day the sun came out. But he isn't seeing a reflection now."

Libertine mustered her convictions and spoke. "For what it's worth, I think he's trying to see what he can get away with."

"Okay," he said, waiting for her to go on.

"Neva's been having trouble getting him to cooperate during her sessions."

"Yeah, because he's a brat," said Gabriel.

Libertine smiled. "Exactly!"

"So okay, riddle me this," he said. "He's healthy for the first time in forever, he doesn't have any dolphins beating him up, he's got great food, plenty of room, and clean, cold water. Why act up now? Why not in Bogotá? His life there was pure crap."

"Was he ever encouraged to act independently down there?"

"Probably not."

Libertine tapped the tip of her nose with her finger. "You've given him the ability to make choices, to use his mind, to decide for himself. Innovative sessions, toys to play with, visitors to watch—for most of the day, he does exactly as he pleases. You've given him power. Well, he's using it. And here's the corollary: by and large, people—and I assume, by extension, killer whales—only act out when they know they're safe."

Gabriel regarded her for a long beat. She flushed. "For a wing nut you actually make a lot of sense," he said.

"Thank you."

And with that, he left the office. Moments later, she heard the heavy steel door to the outside open and close and she was alone.

She was surprised that Gabriel hadn't come up with her analysis himself; after all, it was basic adolescent psychology. He was shrewd, and obviously extremely seasoned and skillful, but she realized that that didn't mean he was particularly insightful. She was struck, not for the first time, by how underdeveloped he was. She'd never heard him mention aging parents or siblings or any other close family members—or even friends, outside of his colleagues. Here was a man on whom no one had ever depended, whose best life relationships had probably always been with his animals.

He was a lot like her.

And thus, she thought sadly but with a measure of relief, infatuations die.

WHEN NEVA CAME back from the gallery, Truman was with her. He looked pale.

"It's not pretty over there," she told Gabriel. "He's just *ramming* those windows. And it could be my imagination, but it seems like he's picking the window that has the most people watching. Plus there's something else." She looked at Truman. "You want to tell him?"

"No, you can go ahead."

Neva drew a breath. "Somebody's started a rumor that he's trying to commit suicide because we won't release him. They're saying it's why his dorsal fin is curled over—that it's a sign of despair."

For a beat there was silence, and then Gabriel said grimly, "Welcome to the dark side."

AFTER THE ZOO closed, Truman called Sam and Ivy, who hadn't been at the zoo that day, and asked them to come in for a meeting. Once everyone was together in the office, he asked Gabriel to bring them up to speed.

"None of the labs came back positive and there isn't any

metal in his body that might be hurting him," Gabriel reviewed. "Which tells me it's behavioral." Then he summarized Libertine's explanation for the whale's behavior, giving her the credit. "I have to say, it makes perfect sense," he concluded.

"He's certainly been giving me a hard time the last few days," Neva concurred.

"But if Libertine's right—and it feels right—that's actually good news," said Ivy. "Isn't it?"

"That depends on your point of view," said Truman carefully. "It's good news for him, but not necessarily for the zoo. It's very upsetting to the visitors, and there's still the structural problem of the windows. According to the specs, the contractors are pretty sure the windows are strong enough to withstand the impact, but obviously the sooner we get him to stop ramming them, the better." To Gabriel he said, "If I close the exhibit and give you a full day to work with him, do you think you can get this turned around?"

"I hope so. I've actually just put in a call to an old friend of mine," Gabriel said. "Monty Jergensen in San Diego. He's an ex-SeaWorld veterinarian—we visited Friday in Bogotá together a few times, so he already knows him. He's willing to fly up tomorrow and work on his tooth. I don't think that's what's causing the behavior, but it'll need to be fixed at some point anyway, so we might as well do it now, to be sure. He'll give Friday a good look-over and go through the lab work while he's here, in case we missed something."

Truman nodded; Gabriel had already run this by him. He said, "In the meantime, let's be proactive about this and prepare a statement for the media that will explain the closure. I'd like your input in drafting it."

At the end of half an hour of vigorous and sometimes

heated discussion over how forthcoming they wanted to be about Friday's health in general (not at all, as far as Gabriel was concerned; very, thought Neva), Truman decided that more disclosure was safer than less. Thus:

> *On Saturday (tomorrow), the Max L. Biedelman Zoo will close its killer whale pool to the public so that Friday can undergo a routine dental procedure. We regret any inconvenience this may cause our visitors and will gladly provide rain checks for anyone who would like to return when Friday is once again on exhibit.*

But once it was down in black-and-white Truman equivocated, thinking it was probably naïve to offer up medical information that might raise more questions than it answered. How had the tooth been broken in the first place? How long ago? Why wasn't it treated before this? How much pain had he been in, and for how long? What were the signs that he *was* in pain? Etc. After another thirty minutes of discussion, they decided that a safer tack would be to focus the statement on nonhealth issues, and how the visitors' experience would be affected.

> *On Saturday (tomorrow), the Max L. Biedelman Zoo will close its killer whale pool to visitors for twenty-four hours, in order to take care of routine pool maintenance. The exhibit will be open to the public as usual on Sunday morning. We regret any inconvenience this may cause our visitors and will gladly provide rain checks to anyone who'd like to return to the zoo when Friday is once again on exhibit.*

Truman asked Brenda to prepare the press statement before she left for the day and distribute it via an e-mail blast to media outlets within a three-hour drive, so the visitors most likely to be affected were the ones informed.

In the coming months, as Truman thought back on it—and he often thought back on it—they couldn't have fueled the fire any better if they'd poured gasoline all over it and lit a match.

THE NEXT MORNING, while Truman watched, Gabriel directed Friday into the medical pool and gave Neva the word to lower the watertight gates that separated it from the main pool. Truman could see Friday eyeing Gabriel nervously, but Gabriel stayed at his head in the water and reassured him as the water level began to drop. Neva and Monty Jergensen, an affable, plainspoken, rumpled man in his early seventies who'd pioneered many of the procedures and protocols still being used in marine mammal care and rehabilitation, waited to climb into the pool until the water was shallow enough to keep Friday floating just a foot off the bottom. Then Truman saw them raise Friday's transport sling beneath him both to suspend him and hold him in place. The vet gave Friday a reassuring pat or two just behind the blowhole.

Gabriel signaled Friday to open his mouth, and the veterinarian examined the offending tooth. "See this?" he said to Gabriel. "It's fractured all the way through—you can see the crack." Directing himself up to Truman, who was squatting on the pool deck overhead, he said, "It's too badly split to fix. Let's go ahead and take it out."

Truman looked down at Gabriel, who nodded: *let's do it.* Truman gave the go-ahead.

Gabriel fed Friday several herring and then gave the signal for the whale to open his mouth again. The vet injected a numbing agent into the gum, and though Friday shuddered momentarily as the shot was administered, he continued to hold still and open wide. Gabriel scratched his head and pectoral flipper, murmuring encouraging things Friday couldn't hear. Once the numbing agent had taken effect the veterinarian applied a dental chisel and hammer and in four deft taps broke the tooth cleanly, extracted the pieces, swabbed the socket, and packed it with an antibiotic dressing. For the next three weeks, he directed Gabriel, they'd need to irrigate the area and cleanse it with hydrogen peroxide.

From beginning to end, the procedure took less than ten minutes. Jergensen wanted Friday confined to the medical pool for the next two hours, to make sure that he'd metabolized the Novocain without any adverse reactions. Downstairs, Truman paced in the food prep area while the vet read through a sheaf of lab results, starting with the last year's records from Bogotá and working forward to the sample they'd taken just the day before. Then he called for Truman to come into the office.

"I'm not seeing any red flags in the blood work—he was in crappy shape when he got here, obviously, and probably seriously immunodeficient, which is why his skin was so bad, but I'm seeing steady improvement. There are no signs of infection or injury. I guarantee you he's in better shape today than he's been in years."

"And the body slams?" Truman asked.

"Strictly behavioral," said the vet.

Truman nodded, relieved. "Any advice on how to get him to stop?"

The vet indicated Gabriel. "Not a clue, but you've got the best guy in the world right here—he'll get it figured out. The whale isn't hurting himself, so keep that in mind. It looks worse than it is. He's probably having a field day."

Truman asked carefully, "So you don't think it's a sign of deep-seated rage, say, or depression?"

"I can't imagine why it would be."

Truman smiled apologetically. "There's a rumor going around that he's trying to commit suicide. I want to be sure we have a response if the rumor catches hold," Truman said.

"There isn't an animal on earth besides us that even *contemplates* suicide, never mind attempts it," the veterinarian said. "Animals are wired for survival, not premature death. Now, you can call me crazy if you want to, but whatever this guy is doing, you can bet it's a sign of health, not psychosis. Can I prove it? No. But I've been working in this field for a long time, and all my instincts say it's a PR problem, not a veterinary one."

"I'm hugely relieved, of course," said Truman. "If we asked you to make a statement to that effect to the media, would you be willing to do it?"

"The press isn't too fond of me," said Jergenson. "I tend to call a spade a spade, and they usually want something flashier. But sure, you can have them contact me if you want to."

"Thank you," said Truman. "Hopefully we won't need you to do that, but these two"—he indicated Neva and Gabriel—"have put the fear of God into me about how things can go sideways. I want to be prepared."

Jergenson grinned wickedly. "Oh, you can never be prepared. No matter what you think's going to happen, you'll be wrong—it'll be much worse. That's my experience, anyway."

Truman smiled unconvincingly. "Well, let's hope this is one case where all of you are wrong." He shook hands with the vet and said to the staff, "Short of catastrophic window failure, we'll open the gallery tomorrow morning, so hopefully you can get a handle on the behavior by then—assuming it wasn't the tooth that was causing the problem."

"We can always hope," said Gabriel.

Truman was hugely relieved at Jergensen's assessment. The idea of having a sick whale on his hands at all, never mind under the scrutiny of the world media, was just too awful to contemplate. Now, striding toward Max Biedelman's mansion, he could finally feel his heartbeat return to almost normal.

But just outside the tapir exhibit, he saw a familiar figure wrapped in clanking cameras, lenses, and flash attachments. Martin Choi. Truman felt his jaws involuntarily clench. He took several deep breaths and mentally apologized to Harriet Saul for having criticized her shortcomings in the face of relentless media scrutiny; and then Martin was upon him, saying in his inimitable way, *"Dude!"*

WHEN THE FIRST calls came in yesterday, Martin Choi had to admit he'd been skeptical. After all, what whale would want to off himself—especially one that might be released back to the wild, a possibility in which he still firmly believed despite the zoo's ardent denials. But phone calls kept coming in from visitors, a total of seven within two hours. Each described how the killer whale deliberately swam smack into the windows time after time after time until people started leaving the gallery in tears.

Then he got the zoo's press statement. Scheduled maintenance. Yeah, right. His journalistic instincts, which he considered to be finely honed, screamed *What the hell?* Something was definitely up. For the sake of his career he certainly hoped so—something big, like some kind of a cover-up. That would be perfect. To get a jump on the suicide angle he tried to reach the animal psychic—she should know something—but he kept going to her voice mail, so he figured he'd just hoof it down to the zoo unannounced and hopefully catch something juicy in the act. And it looked to him like his timing was perfect, as usual—he had a special gift for that.

Truman Levy looked like shit.

"Martin," he greeted the reporter levelly, turning Martin around so he was headed away from the pool. "You know we ask all our media visitors to check in at the front desk."

"That's okay—I know my way around."

"Why don't you come back to my office with me? I assume there's something you wanted to talk about."

Martin let himself be diverted but waited to ask any questions until they got to Truman's office and Martin could sit down and set up his recorder. If his career was about to take a huge leap forward—and he was sure it was—he didn't want to miss anything. Truman shut his office door behind them. This was the first time Martin had been there since Harriet Saul left, and he couldn't help noticing that it had been straightened up and cleaned to within an inch of its life—not an old nacho plate or half-eaten muffin in sight.

"Martin?" Truman said.

"What? Yeah, hey, so yesterday we got a few calls that there's something big-time wrong with the whale."

"Oh?" said Truman carefully.

"Yeah. Actually, what they said was that he was trying to kill himself by swimming into the windows. And now the exhibit's closed. What's up with that?"

"Martin, Martin, Martin," said Truman. "Does that sound likely to you?"

"Hey, that's why I'm asking you, man. Where there's smoke and all that."

"If you read the press statement we sent you, you know we had scheduled maintenance that would keep the whale off exhibit for most of the day. We'd originally planned on completing the work before we moved porpoises in, but then obviously Friday came along and we put off some of the punch list. Now we're playing catch-up."

"You had three weeks, right?"

"Pardon me?"

"Weren't there three weeks or something between when you decided to take the whale and when he actually arrived? Seems like there was a lot of time to take care of stuff, or is it just me?"

"Yes, it was about three weeks, and no, there wasn't time," said Truman. "The contractor was already committed to work someplace else."

"Oh, okay, yeah, sure, I get that. So what's being worked on?"

He saw Truman take a beat. "The watertight gates between the med pool and main pool. They need a final block and tackle mechanism installed."

"And that takes a whole day?"

"Obviously."

"Huh," said Martin. "Because I didn't see any, like, contractor trucks or gear up there or anything." He scribbled some more notes, fussed with his digital recorder. Sometimes if you give people enough silence they'd hang themselves. He just loved that. But this time nothing happened, so Martin said,

"So why do you think people are saying he's trying to kill himself?"

Truman cleared his throat, croaked out a word or two, cleared his throat again—the sure sign of a nervous interviewee—and said, "Let's look at this piece by piece. You've seen Friday lately, right? I see you here pretty often. Has he looked sick to you?"

Martin pretended to take notes. "I don't know. He looked okay to me, but he'd have to be lying on the bottom of the pool before I'd know something was up."

"I promise you he's not sick *or* lying on the bottom of the pool."

"Yeah?" Martin scribbled some bogus notes. Time dragged on. Martin scribbled some more.

And that's when Truman made his fatal mistake. He said—and from the looks of him, he knew he was screwed the minute he said it—"In fact, we have a veterinarian here just to look in on him."

Hah! It was the classic novice's error: yammering into a silence. Martin jumped on it. "Yeah? A local guy?"

"No, Southern California."

"So that's handy, huh."

"I'm sorry?"

"Well, I mean, people are saying something's wrong with the whale, and then you just happen to have a veterinarian coming up. *And* the whale's off-limits for the day. Pretty awesome, dude—I mean, what are the chances? If, you know, nothing's wrong with the whale."

"There *is* nothing wrong with the whale," said Truman grimly. "We had Dr. Jergensen scheduled for a wellness check. We'll be having visits from a number of experts from time to time."

Martin wrote, flipped back and forth in his notebook like he was looking for something, then wrote some more, stretching things out.

"Would you like to talk to him?" Truman finally said. "I believe he's still here. He had a couple of things to finish up."

"Seems like a pretty amazing coincidence to me, but hey, you guys know best."

"Look at me."

Martin looked at him. "*He's not sick,*" said Truman.

"But then there's still the suicide thing."

"Please listen to me very carefully. He is not suicidal. No wild animal is suicidal. Their primary instinct is *survival*."

"Yeah, but he's a wild animal who got caught. And now you're telling him he can't go back there. No wonder the poor guy's slamming into windows."

"Let's get you out there," said Truman. "So you can see just how unsuicidal he is."

"Cool bananas!" Martin grabbed up all his camera gear, notebook, and recorder.

"Let me just call ahead so they know we're coming," Truman said, picking up the phone. "Why don't you say hello to Brenda? I'll only be a minute."

"Hey, man, no prob—I can get there by myself," Martin said. "It's not like I don't know where it is."

"I'd prefer to go with you."

Why was the guy so determined to handle him? Martin wondered. Even ol' Harriet Saul would have let him walk over alone, and she'd been a controlling harridan. "Hey," he said to Brenda dutifully out in the reception area.

"Hey," she said without even looking away from her computer screen, cracking a tiny piece of gum. He used to think

she was kind of cute in a ratted-hair-and-twenty-pounds-
overweight kind of way, but now he could see he was above
that kind of girl.

"Okay," said Truman, closing his office door behind him.
"All set."

TRUMAN HAD NO sooner gotten to the whale pool than the security radio at his hip crackled. "Brenda for Truman. Truman,
do you copy?"

"Go for Truman," he said.

"A guy just called from KIRO in Seattle. They heard the
whale died. Over."

"I'm on my way," he said. He'd have to hand Martin off to
Gabriel with only the brief heads-up Truman had given him
over the phone, but Gabriel was a pro. Hell, he'd probably have
handled this whole mess much better than Truman had.

As soon as he got back, Brenda held her hand over the phone
receiver and said, "This is KOIN in Portland. They heard the
whale died, too. They're sending a satellite truck up. So's another of the Seattle stations I can't remember the letters of right
now. You want to talk to this guy?"

He had Brenda put the call through to his office.

"Hey there," said a man who identified himself as one of
the producers for the station's evening news. "We got a bunch
of folks saying the pool down there's closed because the whale
committed suicide by swimming into the walls. We're sending
a satellite truck up there for the six o'clock news."

"No, no, no," Truman begged. "Don't waste your time.
Friday is not only very much alive, he's in excellent health and
his spirits couldn't be better."

"So how come you closed the pool to visitors?"

"We had some construction projects to finish that we weren't able to get to before Friday arrived."

"We were told he wasn't even in the pool anymore."

Truman marveled for a few seconds and then said, "Just out of curiosity, where else could he be?"

"I don't know. I don't make up the news, bud, I just report it. So you're saying he's not dead?"

"He's definitely not dead. He's alive and he's here."

"So why'd you have a vet flown up?"

Truman's heart sank: clearly his effort to confine the story had backfired. "How did you hear about that, if I may ask?"

"Come on, don't you know we hear about everything? It's just a matter of how quickly."

Truman thought that was a bit arch, but he was in no position to pick fights. He put on his most lawyerly persona, took a big breath, and began. "A marine mammal veterinary specialist was here today, yes. His name is Monty Jergensen, and he's seen Friday in the past in Bogotá. We asked him to come review the whale's blood work and look him over. This was strictly a wellness call."

"Yeah? And did he find anything?"

"As a matter of fact, he confirmed that Friday is in excellent shape, much better shape than he'd expected so soon. He did, however, find a broken tooth, which he extracted."

"A busted tooth?"

"That's right."

"Jeez, I'd hate to see the drill," said the producer, cracking himself up. Truman wondered if Martin Choi had family members in Seattle who were also in the news business. "Pretty handy, having the guy right there."

Truman sighed—and then he realized that he'd said nothing

about the tooth to Martin. Monty or Gabriel probably would. If they did, it would make Truman look even shiftier. If they didn't, Martin would see the spot on TV and assume they'd treated him differently than they treated the big-city TV stations. Either way, Truman was screwed, and another chip would be added to the already tall stack Martin Choi carried on his shoulder.

The TV producer was talking in his ear. "I'm sorry?" said Truman.

"Let me see if I got this right, because it sounds like you guys had a busy day. There was construction stuff going on, and because of that the whale was off-exhibit, which worked out okay because it *just so happened* that a whale vet was up there and he found a busted tooth you didn't know about, but that he extracted. Am I right so far?"

"Pretty much," said Truman.

"Okay, and so you're saying the whale didn't commit suicide or fail to commit suicide, even though a bunch of folks down there yesterday saw him slamming into windows off and on all day, which no one knows why he'd do something like that when it must have hurt like a son-of-a-bitch. It seems like that's a whole lot of stuff to have happening all at the same time."

"Tell me about it," said Truman.

"So if he wasn't trying to commit suicide, why was he slamming into the windows and freaking out a bunch of folks with their kids?"

"The best answer we have is that he was seeing his reflection in the windows, assuming it was another killer whale, and exerting territoriality."

"Huh," said the producer. "Don't whales get those parasites

that make them lose their sense of direction or spatial orientation or something and swim up onto beaches or whatever?"

"I think I'm over my head," Truman said. "I'm going to get off the phone and get one of our keepers to call you right back."

"That's okay—I've got what I need." The phone went dead in Truman's hand.

Truman stared at the handset for a moment. What could the producer possibly have to make a story from but wild conjectures, rumors, and conflicting facts?

Before he could decide whether he should do something—call the TV station back, tell him god knows what—Brenda stuck an ominous stack of pink While You Were Out messages in front of him. "Some of them said they heard the whale was dead, and the rest say he's on suicide watch." She cracked her gum and walked out. "Good luck, boss."

Truman flipped quickly through the packet of messages and found three more TV stations, AP and Reuters, Sky News, and NPR. Behind those were the *Seattle Times,* the *Oregonian,* and a handful of California newspapers. The evening news was being written at that very moment, based on crazy conclusions invented by people lacking even an iota of factual information, and there was no time to set them all straight.

Spin or be spun.

LIBERTINE STOOD OUTSIDE Havenside for a good ten minutes before she could summon her resolve. When she got upstairs, she thought Truman looked like hell, pasty-faced and wilted. He gestured for her to come in and sit down. She took one of his visitors' chairs and said, "I wonder if I can offer a suggestion? It might help."

"That would be nice," he said—somewhat wistfully, she thought.

She took a deep breath and began. "Here's the thing: no one except a handful of us knows Friday has chosen not to communicate with me anymore. And I'm seeing what everyone else should: a robust, active, chipper whale. I'd gladly call anyone on your media roster who's running with the wrong story and give them the same update you have, only as though he's told me, especially, how good life has become. I can say he's slamming into the windows because even though we know it's his own reflection, he's seeing another killer whale in the window and asserting dominance. Gabriel still feels that's the most likely explanation, and it is a sign of good health—he wouldn't have had the energy to do it until recently. Anyway, let me talk at least to Martin Choi on my own. He might buy it. At least it might stop the rumor about Friday being suicidal."

Truman thought.

"You, Gabriel, Ivy, or Neva are welcome to listen in, if you're worried about my being a loose cannon," Libertine said. "And I won't even affiliate myself with the zoo—that'll have better credibility anyway."

Truman smiled at her, a nice little smile, though with sad undertones.

"You've all done so much for me—let me give something back."

Truman gave her the go-ahead to talk not only to Martin Choi, but also to any of the media speeding toward Bladenham. He sent a message back with her to Gabriel: let any media who descended upon them see the whale. And if at all possible, keep him busy enough not to slam into the windows.

TRUMAN LEFT THE ZOO after the early evening news was over. The coverage was horrible, horrible, horrible, and God alone knew what would run in the newspapers tomorrow morning. He went directly to his parents' house.

It had been a long time since he'd sought out Matthew for solace. But his father's even temper, dry sense of humor, and incisive mind were exactly what he needed—that and something alcoholic. He accepted Lavinia's proffered glass of crisp chardonnay and took it into the sunroom, where Matthew was sitting with the *New York Times,* a newspaper he'd been reading daily, cover to cover, for as long as Truman could remember.

Now, seeing Truman, Matthew meticulously folded the paper, made a pass over the crease so it would lie perfectly flat, and placed it in front of him on the white wicker coffee table. The room was brilliant, saturated with light even on a winter evening, refracting off white furniture, white window casements, white drapes, white lamps, white rug. Lavinia had chosen vivid floral upholstery and well-placed plants around the room to soften it. Ordinarily it was one of Truman's favorite places, but tonight it just felt overilluminated and jarring.

"You look wrung out. Tough day?" Matthew asked mildly. "Have you had dinner?"

"Not yet. Neva's working this evening, so I told Winslow I'd pick up something on my way home. I can't stay long."

"My dear," Matthew called into the kitchen, "do we have enough dinner to feed a growing boy?"

"I'm sure we do," Lavinia called back. "Elena cooked a roast this morning." Elena was the housekeeper who'd been with the Levy family for nearly thirty-five years. "And Ivy's gone home for a few days."

"Tell Winslow to ride his bike over," Matthew suggested. Truman lived just four blocks away. Truman got Winslow on the phone and told him to be very, very careful on the ride over, despite the fact that he'd be on residential streets with very little traffic, and to use his headlamp.

"So," Matthew said with the faintest twinkle in his eye once Truman was off the phone. "Anything you want to talk about?"

Truman rubbed his eyes, then his face, then his scalp, harder and harder until his hair stood in lively little spikes all over his head. In his most lawyerly voice he attempted a cogent summary of the day for Matthew, sticking to the facts. When he was finished, what it all amounted to was this: Martin Choi, dim though he was, had brought Truman to his knees.

"My boy, there's lying and then there's what I like to call creative truth-telling," Matthew said after listening very carefully. "From what you've told me, you weren't so much lying as you were disorganized and tentative. The cardinal rule when working with the press is to keep the story so simple that even the very stupid can't get it wrong. Identify a simple message, make sure you have facts to support it—and mind you, you can get creative in your presentation—and once you've decided you have a story that can be summarized in one simple sentence, blow every hole in it you can think of and see if it sinks or floats. If it sinks, keep working on it, even if the phone is ringing off the hook. If it floats, stick to it *no matter what*. And don't lie. Never lie. In work as in life, it rarely helps. And it'll destroy your credibility forever."

Winslow came into the room with Lavinia, who kissed Truman on the top of the head, a rare demonstrative act. She handed around flatware and napkins, to be laid on TV trays rather than the dining room table.

Then she turned on the last of the evening news.

IVY FIRST HEARD that Friday had died, an apparent suicide, as she drove home from the market in Friday Harbor. She nearly drove into a tree, and Julio Iglesias was pitched right out of his booster seat onto the floor, where he fixed her with a long and baleful look before turning his back on her and curling into a sullen ball on the floorboards.

"What the hell!" she said when she connected with Truman. "When were you planning on letting me know? *Suicide?* I leave for two days and this happens?"

"Wait," said Truman. "Wait, wait, wait. Friday is alive. He's well. It's all been a huge mistake."

"Well?" said Ivy. "Who botched it?"

"I did," he said, and proceeded to give her a quick recap.

"Whew," said Ivy. "I'm pouring myself a good stiff drink. I'm even giving Julio Iglesias a small one."

"Then bottoms up," said Truman. "And by the way, if you TiVoed the news, I'd recommend you not watch."

"Oh?"

"Yep," Truman said. "Just don't."

THE NEXT MORNING Truman waited until he'd gotten to his office to open the *News-Tribune*. The lead headline read KILLER WHALE WANTS OUT. Despite what Truman knew were Libertine's best efforts, the story was a remarkable work of fiction, claiming that Friday was trying to break the glass in the zoo's visitors' gallery as a tactic to demand his return to the wild.

Apparently bowing to the fact that a suicide attempt wasn't likely, Martin had instead seized on the fact that Friday once swam free in the North Atlantic, "at one with his podmates and limitless environment." Based on the fact of Friday's wild birth—and Truman granted that at least Martin got that part right—he went on to quote Libertine: "He's a remarkably adaptive animal. His new surroundings and life are a huge, huge improvement. Imagine if you'd been living in a cardboard box for eighteen years, and suddenly you're given the presidential suite at the Hilton. That's what this feels like to him. And he's the opposite of suicidal; he's on a round-the-clock high. His new life here at the zoo is phenomenal."

The article then quoted a person named Katrina Beemer, vice president of a group called Friends of Animals of the Sea, which Truman had never heard of, who said in rebuttal, "Sure, his accommodations there are a step up, but replacing one prison cell with another, better prison cell doesn't make up for the fact that it's still a prison. He's captive and a long way from home. It's no coincidence that he's sick. Sickness is the outward manifestation of a dying spirit. Animals from the sea should be returned to the sea. I implore the Max Biederman [sic] Zoo with all my heart to do the right thing here and let him go home."

The article then revealed that Friends of Animals of the Sea was accepting donations to launch a campaign to return Friday to the North Atlantic.

"C'MON," SAID DINK Schuler at that afternoon's emergency executive committee meeting, which Truman had convened. In front of him on the table was a copy of Martin Choi's article. "The guy's an idiot—everybody knows that."

"I disagree," said Bruce Horvitz, vice president of the zoo's board of directors. "That is, yes, the guy's an idiot, but he's still capable of stirring up a storm."

"Nah," said Dink. "No one reads that paper anyway, and the people who do don't make the decisions in this town. Besides, who the hell would turn loose an animal that hasn't smelled ocean air since he was a kid-whale? That woman is bat-crap crazy." He stabbed his finger at a photo of Trina Beemer. "And while we're at it, why do the nut jobs always turn out to be such dogs? Seriously."

"Libertine?" said Truman, who couldn't see the paper. "Actually, she's turned out to be quite an asset—"

"Nah, nah, that Tina Bender or whoever, from the Animals of the Sea Society or whatever the hell it is. ASS," Dink ranted. "What kind of an organization calls itself something that spells ASS?"

"It's actually Friends of Animals of the Sea. FAS," said Truman.

"I don't care what it is; they better keep their mitts off this whale. We're making a goddamn fortune! I mean, all those years of scratching around and now we're swimming in money."

Truman smiled weakly and said he'd keep them updated as new stories appeared in the media, but the five men and one woman on his executive committee didn't care: After some very hard times, the zoo was running in the black and its name was suddenly known to half the residents of the Pacific Northwest and a hell of a lot of others across the county, even over in the UK and Germany. It was fun to be on top, politics be damned. Let them raise their money. Legally the whale belonged to the zoo.

JUST BEFORE LUNCH Gabriel called Truman and asked if he had an hour or so to come over and help with something. Gabriel refused to say what that something was, but Neva met Truman at the door to the killer whale office with his wet suit and a broad smile.

"Thank you for the concern," Truman said, "but this is not the time—"

"We think this is exactly the time," Neva said. "C'mon, a little whale therapy would do you good. And him, too. Someone advised us to keep him busy and away from the windows. Here's your chance to do your bit."

No amount of objecting dissuaded her, and anyway the thought of his office and the inevitable stack of media calls, was suddenly too much. Truman gave in.

It took him forever to put the thing on—he'd never worn a wet suit before, or even tried it on, and he was amazed at how heavy and clumsy it was. Once he was dressed, Neva hustled him to the top of the pool before he had a chance to focus on how ridiculous he felt.

He slipped into the water beside her. Cold water immediately trickled down his neck into his suit and inside his sleeves. The sensation was unpleasant but fleeting; his body heat quickly warmed the thin layer of water. He was weirdly buoyant inside the neoprene.

Almost immediately he felt a presence below; an approaching enormity. Friday surfaced just one foot away from him, utterly silent. When he exhaled it scared Truman half to death, despite the fact that it was a sound he'd heard a million times before. He could feel the whale regarding him.

Neva greeted Friday with a pat on the surface of the water—a signal that she'd give him a scratch if he came over. The whale accepted, rolling on his side and lifting one pectoral flipper high, offering her the killer whale equivalent of an armpit. Truman horned in on the moment and gave scratches, too, thinking that Friday's skin didn't feel like skin—at least not in the human sense—and it was hard to believe that this huge animal could feel something as delicate as a light touch. Still, there was no doubt that he could. He lolled and rolled with pleasure.

"Isn't he amazing?" Neva asked, clearly delighted to share this experience with him. "He's the most fabulous animal!" She'd taken to his world quickly and capably, diving and swimming and giving him exercise sessions and silly sessions and work to do. And Truman knew that almost anyone would kill to be here in his place, in this icy water beside this enormous animal, but he couldn't shake his uneasiness. He rode Friday's back and scratched him until his fingernails were black with sloughed skin cells, but then he told Neva he was ready to get out, hitching himself up to sit on the dry concrete.

"Really?" She looked crushed. "You've only been in here for a few minutes. Don't you like him?"

"It's not that—I don't even know him. I just don't feel comfortable."

"Are you scared? Because he's really just a big pussycat—"

"It's not that—I'm not scared. Well, maybe a little, but that's not it. Don't you feel like we're, I don't know, trivializing him somehow? He *isn't* just a big pussycat. He's a wild animal, and he's smart, crazy-smart—you can just feel it."

Neva looked him right in the eye. "Yes, he is. And we've been able to give him a decent life here, for the first time in forever. How often can you say that?"

"I know that, of course I know that, but I can't help feeling, I don't know—guilty."

"Why on earth would you feel guilty?"

"He's here because of us, isn't he?"

"We got him away from that terrible place."

"I don't mean *here* here," he said, indicating the pool. "I mean, you know, *here*." He held out his arms to take in the universe. "Doesn't it bother you that we've played God?"

"You didn't. I didn't."

"You know what I mean. He doesn't belong here, he didn't do anything to deserve this. What was it that woman said in the paper this morning? 'Replacing one prison cell with another, better prison cell doesn't make up for the fact that he's still in prison.' Something like that."

Neva hitched herself up to sit beside him, her feet beside his in the wet walk. Friday had taken his blue ball across the pool and left it on the surface while he sank to look into the viewing gallery. She sucked reflectively on her wet suit sleeve. "Gabriel said that only the stupid ones get caught. The smart ones get away."

"So, what, now he's somehow to blame for his own captivity?"

"No, more like it's natural selection at work. I didn't know you felt that way about captivity. It's probably not the most helpful mind-set for a zoo director."

He looked at her earnest little face beside him. Feeling a rush of affection, he leaned over and kissed her. "Don't mind me—it's just been a bitch of a day." Then he went downstairs to change back into his real clothes.

The next day, as abruptly as the body slams had begun, they stopped.

Chapter 12

IT WAS COLD on top of the pool, and very dark, even darker than it usually was at 2 A.M. The unlit water was as black and opaque as tar. When the security guard did her regular rounds, she didn't see or hear Friday. In what changed from concern to near panic, she waited and waited and waited, stock-still, for some sign that the whale was all right, that he was breathing, that he was there at all. She looked at the moon momentarily for strength and—

WAHHHHH!

Just two feet away, Friday burst straight up through the water's surface, rising higher and higher. As she told the story later, the security guard nearly had a seizure.

"If that whale has a sense of humor," she said, "you know he was laughing like hell."

From that night on, scaring the security guards became one of Friday's favorite late-night games.

IN THE EARLY spring the zoo was approached by an IMAX movie producer who wanted, in exchange for a sizable donation, to come to the zoo when the gallery was closed to the public and capture footage of Friday. Now, half an hour before the zoo would open, Neva escorted a photographer and his assistant to the gallery. They were thrilled when Friday swam right to them, keeping himself neutrally buoyant while he inspected them and their gear. Neva had predicted as much, and they thanked her profusely, but in fact the prediction was a no-brainer: in the early morning Friday had seen no one in the gallery for hours, and anyway he was always glad to see a camera of any kind. The truth was, Friday had begun to earn a reputation around the zoo as a shameless media hog. He would swim the entire length of the pool if a commercial camera appeared, cocking his head, opening his mouth, and giving a cheesy smile. The appearance of a beta-camera could wake him from a sound sleep; he would follow one for hours. No one knew why.

Best of all, this camera was enormous and made a fine, loud ticking sound Neva suspected he could hear through the gallery windows.

The IMAX photographer rolled his film; his assistant worked inside a blackout bag to load up extra cartridges. They filmed Friday inches away through the window; they filmed him following them from one window to the next. At first they were ecstatic, but after fifteen minutes and all the close-up shots they could ever want, it became clear that Friday had no intention of leaving, even though they needed swimming footage. The minutes went by. The cameraman drummed his fingers on his tripod; the assistant went out for a smoke. Friday waited in the windows with the patience of Job.

Finally, defeated, they packed up their gear and were never heard from again.

THE MAX L. Biedelman Zoo, like most other zoos, rented its facility to groups and individuals for private events. One Saturday evening when Truman was working late, he discovered a forlorn bride and groom sitting alone at the reception's head table in Havenside's ballroom. The groom was patting the bride's hand comfortingly. There was no one else in the ballroom, though there were tables that could accommodate somewhere between seventy-five and one hundred guests. On this most special of days, the newlyweds had been upstaged by Friday—all the guests were in the viewing gallery, and had been for nearly an hour. The bride and groom would have liked to cut the cake, but in spite of three requests, no one was coming back to the ballroom.

In the end it took Truman making an announcement over the public address system to pry the guests out of the gallery.

THE PARADE OF celebrities asking to meet Friday up close continued. Truman accommodated them when he could—or rather Neva accommodated them in her ever more time-consuming role of guide and interpreter—but one VIP in particular would always stand out from the rest. He was a musician, possibly the oldest-looking sixty-year-old in the world, stringy and dissipated, a health insurance nightmare, a man easily twenty years past his prime. Once, he had been the opening act for some of the greatest rock musicians in the world. Now he was playing secondary Native American casinos in Washington State. Still, his name was recognizable. He got his promoter to set up a visit with Friday on his one free night. He wanted to see the killer whale he'd been hearing about—the one that was now almost as famous as the musician still was in his dreams.

Neva had a rare night off, so Truman escorted him to the

empty viewing gallery in the early evening. For the musician this was the worst time of day, before the bars and clubs got going, after people with families had gone home, when lonely people populated the world. Truman faded back against the wall, leaving the musician to his encounter.

Friday swam over immediately. For a long time the two regarded each other through the glass, red-rimmed eye to red-rimmed eye. The musician saw on the whale's flanks a quilting of old wounds, teeth marks, lesion scars. He pulled his jacket tight, and then, astonishingly, he closed his eyes and began to yodel. The sound reverberated in the hollow air, haunting and pure.

Friday stayed, rapt. Truman called Neva at home, and she called Gabriel and Libertine, and one by one they arrived and stayed, bearing mute witness to this homage to survival.

EVER SINCE FRIDAY had arrived at the zoo, a municipal clerk from St. Cloud, Minnesota, had called Neva once a month to check on him. She always called during her lunch hour, keeping the calls short and businesslike, and declined whenever Neva offered to call her back, to save her the money it cost to make the calls. In all, the clerk had sent Friday four checks for twenty-five dollars each—what she felt she could afford.

As she explained to Neva, she had never met Friday, or even seen a killer whale in person. She saw *Free Willy* once with her grandson, and although she liked it well enough, she hadn't been overly moved. In fact, she couldn't explain her interest in Friday at all, although she had been following his progress ever since she saw a news clip about him when he first arrived in Bladenham. As she tried to articulate it to Neva, her vigilance on his behalf had to do with her sense of citizenship, the kind that might lead her to keep an eye on a neighborhood dog that had been left outside too much. She felt no psychic pull, just this abiding sense of responsibility.

She visited Bladenham one day after having just attended a professional meeting in Portland. Neva offered to introduce her to Friday, leading her to Friday's office window first so she could meet him eye to eye. This was always a big hit, but the clerk simply smiled at him when, predictably, he appeared at the glass, nodding in a mild greeting. She watched him for several minutes and then turned to Neva: *shall we go?* Neva was surprised. No one besides his staff had ever before left Friday before he left them. She asked the clerk if she was sure. Yes, she was sure.

Neva led her upstairs to the pool top, and the clerk looked around her calmly, thoroughly, asking several questions about the toys scattered around, about the tires stacked on the concrete deck. They made small talk about Bladenham and the zoo, about the clerk's home town in Minnesota. During the conversation the clerk glanced at Friday only occasionally. When they'd exhausted these two subjects, she indicated that she'd seen enough; she would go. Her visit had lasted exactly thirty-five minutes. For this, she'd driven a total of four-and-a-half hours.

A week later, they received her usual check for twenty-five dollars.

IN BOGOTÁ FRIDAY'S lungs had been compromised for years, by either the air quality or a fungal infection or both. Gabriel had been monitoring his breathing closely ever since the whale arrived, asking Sam to record his respirations at rest, after a high-energy exercise session, and during breath-holds. Upon arrival his best breath-hold was three minutes.

At the end of February, Gabriel asked Friday to roll over on his back, submerging his blowhole, and cued Sam to start a stopwatch. Five minutes went by, then ten. The whale lay comfortably on the surface, upside down, receiving a herring from Neva between his teeth from time to time.

At eleven minutes Friday began to fidget, shifting his tail flukes restlessly. Neva clapped to signal her encouragement: *hold it just a little longer.*

Phwweeeeet! Gabriel blew his whistle, releasing Friday at last. Sam consulted his stopwatch. Friday had held his breath for over thirteen minutes.

AT FOUR O'CLOCK one morning in March, a middle-aged woman approached the Biedelman Zoo's perimeter on foot, dressed in black clothing and carrying a thermal picnic cooler. She climbed over the fence—no mean feat since she was some-what bottom-heavy and hadn't climbed a fence since she was in grade school—and with the stride of a Valkyrie arrived at Friday's pool without being seen. Her excitement grew as she reached the steel staircase to the pool top, which she'd seen so many times on the evening news. A motion sensor suddenly triggered lights on the outside of the building, but she froze for several minutes in the ragged edges of the darkness and no one responded to the security breach.

As soon as the lights timed out she hurried up the stairs, gripping the cooler handle tightly. Once on the dark pool top she heard Friday before she saw him. His breathing thrilled her—it was as though this magnificent animal were beckoning to her, as though he knew of and agreed with her plan. She wore rubber boots, knowing from the extensive TV cover-age that in order to get close enough to him she'd be standing in water. Indeed, Friday was waiting for her at the poolside, mouth wide open. He knew; he must.

She set her cooler down on the dry concrete apron, removing a huge Ziploc plastic bag full of pellets and six lovely young salmon she'd bought yesterday at Pike Street Market in Seattle. It took only a minute to stuff each fish with the pellets; she'd waited to do this until the last possible moment in case contact with the fish broke down their chemical composition. She'd worried that he might sense something, but he swallowed them one after the other without hesitation—more proof that his captivity had ruined him, turned him into a broken animal doomed to live for the rest of his life in a silent, lifeless place. But after all, that was why she was here—a warrior come to deliver him.

She resisted the strong desire to lay her hands on him in benediction. Instead, before she slipped away, she whispered, "It's going to be all right now. This hell is over. You're going home."

Chapter 13

MUSIC BLARED FROM the food prep area downstairs at Friday's pool. It was five o'clock in the morning and Gabriel was taking his turn doing fish house. When he was done, he hoisted a bucket from the Gorilla Rack and trudged up to the pool top.

The first sign of trouble was that Friday wasn't in his customary place at the slide-out area, mouth open and ready for breakfast—normally his favorite meal since it meant he had both food and company again after a long night alone. Instead, the killer whale huddled in a far corner of the pool, his nose just inches from a blind concrete wall. His blue ball was beside him and he had gathered his other toys nearby.

When he exhaled, his breath was pink.

Gabriel walked to him and said softly, "Hey, buddy. What's the deal here?"

Friday didn't respond, just breathed in quick, shallow breaths. Gabriel's heart sank. When he signaled the whale to open his mouth, Gabriel was shocked to see his palate and gums peppered with small hemorrhages. When Gabriel scratched the whale's head, the skin tore and wept blood. Friday pressed farther into the corner, his blue ball bobbing gently by his head.

Something was very, very wrong.

Gabriel went downstairs and watched the killer whale from underwater, but after fifteen minutes Friday hadn't moved, so he pulled on his wet suit, grabbed the rest of his scuba gear, and was in the pool within five minutes, ignoring his own rule that no one should ever get in the pool alone. Neva wouldn't arrive for another hour, but he suspected they didn't have any time to lose. Even up close, Gabriel couldn't find any sign of injury. Then, on a terrible hunch, he put his hand inside the killer whale's genital slit, opened it several inches—and released a dense cloud of blood.

He surfaced, grabbed his first-aid pack, and from underwater took a blood sample from the underside of Friday's flukes. Normally when he drew blood he was a stickler for alcohol swabs and antibacterial protocols, but this wasn't anything normal. He drew several vials, and when he withdrew the hypodermic needle, a thin stream of blood continued to wind through the water.

Downstairs, he labeled the vials and called Truman at home. "We have a problem," he said, quickly describing what he'd observed. "I don't have any idea what we're dealing with, so I need Neva to run some blood samples to the hospital and convince their lab to treat it as a rush."

He heard Truman relaying the information to Neva in the background; when he got back on the line he said, "She's leaving now—she says to meet her at the loading dock. She'll call ahead to the lab on her way. Is there anything I can do?"

"Just for the hell of it, would you check with your security guys and see if they've seen anything unusual during their rounds over here in the last week or two?"

"What are you thinking?"

"I just want to cover all our bases. Look, I need to get back upstairs. I'll update you when either I know what we're dealing with or the whale dies, whichever comes first." Gabriel hung up, but instead of going upstairs, he lifted the receiver again and dialed Monty Jergensen's phone number. "Hey, doc," he said when the vet picked up the line, "We've got a sick whale up here." He described Friday's symptoms, including their rapid onset. "Does that sound like anything you've come across?"

"Well, whatever it is, it's hemorrhagic."

"Yep."

"How's his breathing?"

"Bad. Shallow."

"And you haven't changed the fish you're feeding him—gotten a new delivery recently or anything like that?"

"No—same fish, same vendor."

"And it came on pretty quickly?"

"He seemed fine yesterday."

Marty paused, then said, "How's security up there—pretty good?"

"I wouldn't go that far. It's probably adequate, but it's a small zoo with a small staff."

"So if someone wanted to, they could get their hands on the whale."

"Yes. I had the same thought."

"I've never seen this in marine mammals, but in my old small-animal practice I'd see an animal every once in a while that had ingested brodifacoum."

"Bro—what?"

"Rat poison."

"You're kidding."

"I wish I were. Someone would put out pellets or bait and

their dog or cat would eat it and a few days would go by and they'd begin to bleed out. It doesn't show up right away—it takes up to two weeks to present symptoms, and there's a lot of internal bleeding before it reaches the stage you're describing. The endgame is massive bleeding into the chest—constricts the lungs—and they die. When you take the blood samples in, tell them to look at his vitamin K levels, and for the presence of prothrombin, proconvertin, and Stuart factor. If something's blocking his ability to produce vitamin K, his capillaries and blood vessels are all leaking."

"And if you're right?"

"Start him on vitamin K one right away—oral. If we've gotten to him in time, he may pull through. My guess is today's the tipping point. He's either going to turn the corner or he's going to die. We'll know one way or the other within the next twenty-four hours."

"Son of a bitch," said Gabriel.

"Look, I'm e-mailing you a script right now for the vitamin K, phytonadione—there, you should have it. Hopefully your local hospital has a lot on hand. E-mail me the lab results as soon as you get them, and make sure you tell Margie to find me."

"Okay, doc, thanks."

As soon as Neva pushed open the office door, Gabriel handed her the prescription and told her to turn around and fly.

AFTER SPEAKING WITH Gabriel, Truman called first Ivy and then Sam, briefly describing the situation and asking them to come to the zoo. By the time Neva came back with the medication and Gabriel gave Friday his first dose of phytonadione, the others had assembled, grim-faced, in the killer whale office. Across the pool Friday huddled, motionless, in his far corner with his blue ball beside him. His urine was red; his stool was red; his breath was pink. Even Gabriel's usual calm was shaken.

"For god's sake, close the gallery," Gabriel said. The zoo was set to open in fifteen minutes.

"Already done," said Truman, knowing it would mean yet another media onslaught.

"The security logs don't show anything at all?" Gabriel asked. "It could have been as long ago as two weeks."

"Nothing. Toby and Janice have been swing shift and grave-yard the last couple of weeks, and I've already talked to them. There was nothing."

"Crap," Neva muttered.

"*Rat* poison, though?" said Ivy. "Doesn't that sound just a little far-fetched? Couldn't it be some obscure Colombian virus—whale ebola or something?"

Gabriel said, "Friday has essentially been in quarantine since he got here. Even if he brought something up here with him, it's way too late to develop symptoms. If we were using real seawater, I guess it would be possible for something to come in despite the filtration, but we're not."

"Could the Instant Ocean have been tampered with?" Neva asked. "Did you ask life support?"

"I will," said Gabriel. "But if I wanted to poison him, feeding him something would be a whole lot simpler and quicker than messing with the water quality."

They subsided.

"Crap," Neva said quietly.

"I don't know what kind of person would go after an animal like that," Sam said. "Must be some kind of monster."

"Where's Libertine?" asked Neva. "She's not here."

Truman ran his hand over his face. "I didn't call her."

"No!" said Ivy. "Absolutely not."

"I'm sorry, but I think we need to consider it," said Neva. "Given her ties to the animal rights community. Even if she just enabled someone else—it wouldn't even have to have been deliberate. Maybe she described the layout of the pool and access from the outside. Or left a key out. Or talked about his diet. It might have been enough for them to make a plan."

"She'd never do any of those things," Ivy said hotly. "*Never.* She loves that animal as much as any of us, if not more. For god's sake, you don't try and kill something you love."

"The animal rights people would tell you that's exactly what you *would* do, if the animal's captive," said Neva.

"She's right," said Gabriel.

"All right, look," said Truman. "Let's not get ahead of ourselves here. I gather this is her regular day off, right? I'd appreciate it if none of you talk with her about this just yet, at least not until we know whether he was poisoned in the first place."

"The lab said they'd have results for us by noon," said Neva.

"All right," said Gabriel. "So in the meantime we'll take care of him like always. Though—and I can't believe I'm going to say this—prayer wouldn't be a bad idea, if anyone feels so inclined. If the blood work confirms he was poisoned, he's been bleeding internally for at least a day and probably two. If he's still alive by tonight, he's got a fighting chance."

"*Crap,*" said Neva. "So do we go into the pool with him?"

"Absolutely not," said Gabriel. "He's got his blue ball, and one of us will be sitting with him all the time, but in case he starts acting erratically, no one gets in the water—no one. I also want someone observing from the gallery."

"Are you going to let the media know what's going on?" Neva asked.

Truman sighed. "In light of our recent fiasco, yes. Starting, god help us, with Martin Choi. Happily, the *News-Tribune*'s not due out for another three days, so at least by then we'll know the cause and the outcome. Anyway, let me worry about all that. You've got your hands full. If media calls start coming in here, just refer them all to me. Ivy, I could use your help. Would you mind working the phones with me?"

"By all means, put me to work. I don't think I can stand just waiting."

"Crap," said Neva. "Crap crap *crap*!"

"Look, this is going to be a very tough day," Truman said. "So let's take it one step at a time, all right? Gabriel, I'd appreciate an update every hour—sooner if anything changes. And let me know as soon as the lab work comes back. Good luck."

The meeting broke up in silence. What was there to say that could possibly make a difference?

ACROSS TOWN LIBERTINE was doing laundry when she had a sudden premonition that something was terribly wrong. She dropped her laundry basket and ran. At the pool she flew up the stairs two at a time. "Something's happened," she cried to Gabriel, who was sitting in one of the lawn chairs on the side of the pool beside the killer whale.

"How do you know?" he said guardedly.

"I don't know, I just do," she said. "Oh my god, he's so *sick*. How could he have gotten this sick?"

"What do you know?" he'd gotten out of his chair and moved toward Libertine as though he meant to prevent her from reaching Friday.

"I don't know anything," she said, taking a step back. "I just felt him. I think he might be dying."

"We think he was poisoned," Gabriel said bluntly.

The radio at his hip crackled. "Neva to Gabriel."

"Go for Gabriel. Switch to channel two." Libertine knew that channel two was secure and couldn't be picked up by any but specifically designated radios. She watched, feeling increasingly uneasy, as Gabriel switched channels and said again, "Go for Gabriel."

"He just had a bowel movement. It was mostly blood. A lot of blood."

"Okay."

"He's also posturing."

"How?"

"He's sort of doubling up, like he has stomach cramps."

"Okay," Gabriel said grimly. "You're keeping a log, right?"

"Yes."

Sam came up to the pool top and caught Gabriel's eye, then indicated Libertine by the slightest inclination of his head. "You want us to go into town?" he suggested. "We could pick up a donut or two. Sometimes sugar's just the ticket at a time like this."

"No," Gabriel said. "Thank you, but she's all right."

"You sure?"

"I'm sure," said Gabriel. "Thank you."

"I'll be back downstairs, then." Sam looked again at Libertine before saying to Gabriel, "You just let me know if you need anything."

Libertine got it. "You can't possibly think it was me!" she cried to Gabriel in disbelief. "How could it be me? I work with him every day like you do. I love him as much as you do."

"We're just trying to be prudent," said Gabriel quietly. "Until we know more. We don't even know yet what's wrong with him."

Libertine marshaled all her composure and said very quietly, "May I stay?"

"I think it would be best for you and for us if you didn't, at least not for now. We should hear from the lab by noon, and then we'll know what we're dealing with."

Libertine stared at him for a long beat, and then, too devastated to speak, she turned and walked away.

IT WAS QUIET at the Oat Maiden. The only table that was occupied when Libertine got there was the celestial table, where a couple of white-haired women were laughing over a packet of snapshots. Johnson Johnson was in the run-up to lunch: Libertine could smell cookies and rising pizza dough. She went into the kitchen, where he had his back to the swinging double doors, and put a hand gently on his shoulder so she wouldn't scare him, but he was startled anyway. She'd been trying to get him to put a mirror on that wall, so he could see who was coming, but so far he hadn't done it.

"Put me to work," she said simply. "There are a couple of tables I can bus and wipe down. After that, I'll ask you for something else to do, so please find it."

"'Kay," he said, and then looked at her for the first time. "You look sad."

She thought she probably looked a whole lot worse than that, but she just said, "I'm okay. I wasn't, a little while ago, but now I am."

Johnson Johnson was evidently satisfied with that. Grateful beyond words, Libertine grabbed a spray bottle of diluted bleach and a wet rag and went out into the café, wiping down all the tabletops. She set out fresh flatware and napkins, filled the salt and pepper shakers, straightened up the shaker jars of oregano and Parmesan, and aligned the sugar and artificial sweetener packets in their baskets. Then she went back to the kitchen and Johnson Johnson said without preamble, "Let's make dough." She couldn't have asked for a more cathartic task. She'd never made it from scratch before so she had to focus, following him step by step, measuring, mixing, punching, and kneading until they'd made enough dough for seventy-five pizzas and her heart rate had finally returned to normal.

And through it all, Friday, gone for so long, now keened in her head. She implored him, like a mantra: *hang on, hang on, oh, please, just hang on.*

IT WAS AN in-service afternoon at school, so Reginald walked home at noon in the rain. He was a block from the house when a car pulled up beside him, soaking his pants to the knee.

"S'up?" called Martin Choi.

Reginald slapped at his pants. "What's wrong with you, man? Now I'm going to catch pneumonia and it'll be your fault."

"Sorry, dude. Got any interesting stories for me?"

"No. And even if I did, I wouldn't tell you. You ratted me out the last time."

Reginald kept walking and Martin crept along beside him in his car. "No way."

"Well, someone did."

"Hey, if someone tells me something, I'll take their name with me to the grave. That's what journalists do."

"Yeah, well, I got nothing to say to you anyways."

"Then let me tell you something. The whale's sick. Like, really sick. Really *really* sick."

"He is?" Reginald said with surprise.

"Yep. They closed the gallery again, and this time they admitted there's something wrong, they just won't say what. I've left, like, a dozen messages, but so far, nothing. Did Sam mention anything when he went into work this morning, maybe?"

"No, man, he's not gonna tell me secret stuff. He's the one who busted me last time."

"Okay. But hey, if you find out anything, you let me know, huh?"

"Yeah, right," said Reginald, thinking he wouldn't call Martin Choi if he saw someone grow wings and fly.

Martin's cell phone went off on the passenger seat. "Okay, guy, gotta take this call. See you."

"Hey!" Reginald called after him.

The reporter leaned out the car window. "Yeah?"

"What's my name?"

"Winston. You think I'd forget a funny name like that?"

"Just checking," said Reginald.

THE LAB RESULTS came in at eleven twenty-four: sometime in the last ten days or so, someone had given Friday rat poison. Most likely, the delivery system had been fish into which poison had been stuffed or injected. Friday's best hope was that the massive doses of vitamin K would restore the clotting agents destroyed by the poison, stopping the hemorrhaging. If that didn't work, the bleeding into his chest would suffocate him. Unfortunately the zoo only kept its security videotapes for forty-eight to seventy-two hours, and while Truman asked his team to go over what they had with a fine-tooth comb, the chances were excellent that they'd never find out who had done it.

IN A VACANT cubicle in Havenside's administrative offices, Ivy and Truman spent the afternoon sitting back-to-back like cornered gunfighters, except each wielded a telephone. As soon as the lab results came in, they had split up a master media list and e-mailed a statement confirming that Friday had been poisoned, was in critical condition, and would be off-exhibit until further notice. Once the story was on the wire services, calls streamed in from everywhere.

Both Ivy and Truman were blunt in reporting the likelihood that Friday would die. From his blood work, Monty Jergensen had told Gabriel that Friday should already be dead; how he was continuing to hang on was anybody's guess, but it wasn't likely to last. As he continued to bleed out, his blood volume was dropping below critical levels, and there was no practical way to transfuse him, even if they'd had the blood on hand, which they didn't.

Truman insisted on giving the media even the grimmest details of Friday's condition; against Gabriel's advice, he even invited the AP stringer and his cameraman to come to the pool and take two minutes of starkly graphic footage with the understanding that they would distribute it as B-roll to any television station requesting it. "I want whoever did this to know just what a poisoned animal looks like when it's dying," he'd said grimly. "We owe Friday that much." No, no one had stepped forward to claim credit for the crime, and no, neither Truman nor Ivy would speculate. They only hoped the culprit was watching the news.

More than one reporter was in tears by the time he hung up. In all his years Truman had never spoken with the force he'd discovered now, fueled by rage and helplessness.

THOUGH THE KILLER whale viewing gallery was closed, the zoo itself was not. As word spread, a steady stream of people, hundreds and then thousands of them, came to the gallery doors to leave roses, wreaths, stuffed killer whales, balloons, photographs, and homemade cards. In the late afternoon Brenda interrupted Truman's telephone marathon, forcibly pulling him from his chair and to his office window. As they looked across the zoo grounds, he saw nearly seven thousand people keeping silent vigil outside the gallery. "I overheard someone say a Native American shaman is here," said Brenda. "Can you believe all those people?"

"Yes," Truman said simply. "I can."

Once every hour he continued to get a call from either Gabriel or Neva, and every hour it was the same: not yet.

GABRIEL HAD CARED for thousands of dying animals. It went with the business. He'd learned a long time ago to guard his emotions, to appreciate the animals he worked with while keeping them at a professional distance. And yet here he was, keeping watch over a dying animal that, more than any other he'd rehabilitated, deserved better. He'd survived some of the worst living conditions Gabriel had ever seen; he'd made it through a long transport and adapted to a completely new way of life with enthusiasm, courage, and a sense of humor. He'd grown, healed, and hurt no one, and now he would die at the hands of the very people who claimed to love him most. *Better dead than captive.*

So he sat beside Friday all day, giving him massive doses of vitamin K every two hours, monitoring the rapid, shallow breathing, and sluicing him with water so his skin didn't dry out and crack.

By evening, against all odds, the killer whale was still alive.

Gabriel tried to send everyone home for some rest, but they insisted on staying, and he conceded. This animal had touched every one of them. So they stayed on, even Corinna, Reginald, and Winslow stayed, bound together by the determination that if Friday died, at least he wouldn't die alone.

At first light Gabriel startled awake. He hadn't even realized he'd dozed off, but the sun was fully up—and Friday was gone. He immediately and heavyheartedly assumed the worst: that Friday had died and his body had been dragged into the medical pool to await necropsy.

And then he heard the familiar *poooooo-siiiiip* of a killer whale breathing.

Seeing him awake, Neva came around the pool, smiling. "He swam into the med pool about ten minutes ago, and he brought his ball with him."

Gabriel chafed his face hard to wake up. "Have you tried to feed him anything?"

"I gave him half a bucket. I didn't want to give him any more without checking with you. He was hungry, though."

"Okay, bring up a bucket of fish, but we're also going to have to intubate him. He's got to be mondo dehydrated, plus we want to flush whatever's left of that crap out of his system."

While Neva was downstairs rounding up five gallons of fresh water, a funnel, flexible tubing, and lubricant, Gabriel went to the med pool and squatted beside Friday. "Hey, kiddo," he said softly. "Some day we had yesterday, huh? Can you open?" He gave the whale the signal and Friday opened wide. Gabriel winced: the inside of his mouth was florid with petechial hemorrhages.

Neva trotted over with the bucket of fish and other supplies, and Sam hauled up the freshwater, warmed to body temperature. Gabriel fed about four feet of tubing down the killer whale's throat and into his stomach. Friday jerked once as the tube went down, but that was all. Once it was in place Gabriel told Neva to insert the funnel into the other end and begin pouring in the water. When they were finished, Friday swallowed his next vitamin K dose and ate three fish, but couldn't be persuaded to eat more.

"It's okay," Gabriel told him, giving the whale's head the barest caress. "It's a start."

LIBERTINE HAD GOTTEN exactly two hours and fourteen minutes of sleep since yesterday morning. She hadn't communicated with anyone at the zoo since leaving it, not even Ivy. For now, it was just as well. She knew Friday was still alive, and that was all that mattered. By midafternoon she dug a scrap of paper and her cell phone from the bottom of her purse and punched in the numbers.

Trina Beemer answered her call on the first ring, as though on high alert. When Libertine identified herself, the activist said, "Libby! God, I was hoping you'd call. Is he gone?"

"Who?"

"Don't be coy—Friday. Has he died yet?"

"No. Not yet."

"Well, it can't be long now," Trina said. "The important thing is, he's going to be free. No more walls, no more jailers. What are they saying over there? I bet it's a real cluster-fuck."

"They're frantic, of course," Libertine said. "I'm trying to keep pretty much to myself, though. I figure I can be more help that way."

"Help?" said Trina.

"You know. *Help,*" Libertine said. "Yay, team."

She could hear Trina hesitate for a minute before she said, "Really? Because I was pretty sure you weren't on our side anymore."

"Oh, no," said Libertine quickly. "I'm definitely on your side. I just didn't want them to know."

"Well, if you're serious, here's the thing that would help us the most. Let me know when he's dead. A lot of people are waiting to hear, plus that way we can release a statement to the media. Anonymously, of course."

"So it was FAS?"

"Did I say that?" Trina said. "I don't think I said that."

"There aren't that many people courageous enough to have done what you did. I assume you know that."

"I do. Listen, honey, I've got a call coming in, so I have to go. But you'll let me know when he's gone, right?"

"Absolutely," said Libertine. "Wait for my call." As soon as she hung up she called ahead, jumped in her car, and headed to the zoo.

TRUMAN AND IVY were waiting when Libertine arrived. Truman had briefed Ivy on what Libertine had shared with him when she called: that she had news about who'd poisoned Friday. When she knocked on the door to his office he thought she looked pale and tense, but then it occurred to him that he and Ivy probably looked just as bad. At his signal, Brenda closed the door behind her.

Libertine sat in the visitors' chair, across the desk from Truman. Next to her, Ivy sat stiffly upright; in her lap Julio

Iglesias wrested himself free and climbed over the chair arms into Libertine's lap. She embraced him. "They always know." she said.

"Know what?" said Truman.

"When we're stressed out."

"Well, we certainly are that." He took in the dark circles under her eyes and said, "Are you okay?"

"Yes. Not really." Libertine cleared her throat and said formally, "Thank you for seeing me."

"Oh, for god's sake," said Ivy. "I disagreed with Truman—you should never have been exiled. But it's his zoo."

"No," Libertine said quickly. "From your perspective, I think it was the right thing to do. You didn't know what you were dealing with. Now we do. I just got off the phone with Trina Beemer—"

"Who?" Ivy said.

"Trina Beemer."

"What a terrible name."

"She's a terrible person."

Truman leaned across his desk toward Libertine. "Talk to us."

"It was definitely Friends of Animals of the Sea who poisoned him," she said. "Actually, I'm pretty sure it was Trina herself."

"But *why*?" Ivy asked.

"Better dead than in captivity," said Libertine.

"That's ridiculous," Ivy blustered. "No one would do something that horrible."

"Oh, yes, they would," said Libertine grimly. "They definitely would. They're just waiting for him to die so they can declare victory."

Truman said to Libertine, "The question is, can you prove it?"

"No."

"What if you meet her and, you know, wear a wire," Ivy proposed.

"I don't think people really do that kind of thing," said Truman.

"Sure they do," said Ivy.

"Not people in Bladenham," Truman amended.

"Well, I'd love to figure out how to set her up," said Libertine. "She's not just misguided and horrible, she's *smug*."

Truman mulled this over for a minute. "We'd need to take the right steps to make sure we get legally admissible evidence. It's not quite as simple as it looks on TV."

"You're the lawyer," said Ivy, who Truman could see was in high dudgeon. "Let's roll! Hop to it! These people deserve to *burn*."

"I'll tell you what," Truman told her. "I'll look into it if you'll put together an e-mail update saying Friday may be over the worst, but he still has a long road ahead of him. Don't send it yet, just write it." To Libertine he said, "You do know he's turned the corner, right?"

"Yes—I sensed that."

"We've been getting literally thousands of calls and e-mails," Truman told her. "Jergensen told me he thinks Friday may be over the worst of it, but it'll be a few days before he's completely out of the woods." Turning to Ivy, he said, "So you'll draft the e-mail. Deal?"

"Deal."

Then he turned to Libertine. "Someone needs to go out and let people know Friday's still alive. I'd like you to handle that. Can you?"

"Yes," she said.

From his window he watched her determined little figure cross the zoo grounds and approach the nearly ten thousand people now keeping vigil outside the gallery. As though she'd been born to it, she climbed onto one of the decorative planters so she could be seen, raised a finger—*Attention!*—and spoke.

Even in his office he could hear the crowd cheer.

HALF AN HOUR later Matthew and Truman were sitting at the elder Levy's dining room table, where Matthew had been answering his e-mail on a laptop when Truman arrived. "Look," Matthew said once Truman had brought him up to speed. "I know this has been quite an ordeal for all of you, never mind for the whale. But you know your aunt. She's a generous, passionate woman, but she's always had a tendency to go off the deep end."

Truman smiled. "And this would be one of those times. But is there any other way—and by other, I mean legal—to gather enough information to implicate these people?"

Ruminatively, Matthew chewed the stem of his unlit pipe. Truman was used to these lengthy pauses; as a boy, he'd been astounded when, at friends' houses, conversations unfolded at what seemed like warp speed. Finally Matthew said, "It's all a matter of momentum. You don't need to wire anybody—all you need is to dangle a carrot tasty enough to make them bite, and make sure there are witnesses present when they do."

"All right," said Truman carefully. "Do you have some ideas about where I might find such a carrot?"

"Here's a hint: what's black, white, and loved all over?"

"Friday?"

"Absolutely. Invite these people to come see him. And bring the media along."

"By which you mean Martin Choi."

Matthew nodded. "By which I mean Martin Choi. Though if you have anyone else, you can certainly use him or her."

"There can't possibly be two reporters like Martin."

"I wouldn't think so," said Matthew. "But I always try to keep an open mind."

"I could ask Libertine to invite them to the pool, I suppose," Truman said, thinking out loud. "That wouldn't arouse their suspicions."

"You might also show them what's happened—or failed to happen—to the poor creature."

"He's going to live."

"Exactly. Bad news, indeed." Matthew smiled a little impish smile.

Each was quiet for several minutes, thinking, until Truman said, "This has great possibilities."

"Of course it does. It's a shame you won't be doing any lawyering. You're a quick study."

"On my best day, I couldn't hold a candle to you," Truman said.

"Yes," Matthew agreed, "but I've had the benefit of a good many more years on the job."

Truman stood up and pressed Matthew's shoulder fondly. "I'm going to go to the Oat Maiden for a piece of pizza. I scheme better on a full stomach. Care to come along?"

"Thank you, but in my experience, scheming is an activity best done in solitude. Of course the value of a good cookie isn't to be sniffed at, either."

THREE O'CLOCK IN the afternoon was always a quiet time at the Oat Maiden. Truman chose the table that was his personal favorite, Johnson Johnson's creation in honor of Hannah and

Max Biedelman. High jungle grass ringed the outside of the tabletop, with Hannah walking through it, high on her feet, trunk extended in front of her, proudly reaching toward whatever lay in her future. Striding ahead of her was Max Biedelman in safari gear. Truman felt the table captured all that was good and admirable about the zoo's eccentric founder and the animal she'd loved most.

Lost in thought, he was startled to find Libertine bringing him a menu. "Do you work here, too?" he asked.

She blushed. "I've been helping out when it gets busy, so. . . ." They both looked at the one other table that was occupied, hardly the sign of a busy café. Truman saw her blush deepen. "It helps him sometimes to have me around."

"Well, I'm glad you're here," Truman said. "I want to run something by you."

"I'd be honored. Let me just check on this other table, and then I'll be right back."

Truman watched her cross the restaurant. He wasn't proud of the way he'd forced her to leave the zoo yesterday. She'd been treated as guilty until proven innocent, and he, of all people, should have upheld a higher standard. Plus he'd known she wasn't capable of such a heinous act. They all knew it, even Neva, once Friday had rallied and she'd had time to calm down.

When Libertine came back, she brought along two slices of pizza, two cookies, and a couple of cups of coffee, which she divided between them before sitting down.

"Carbs, caffeine, and sugar—life's essential stimulants," Truman said, smiling.

"I don't think any of us are sleeping well right now. I thought they might help."

"Absolutely," said Truman, taking a bite of pizza. He couldn't remember when he'd eaten last—yesterday, he thought, before he got the call about Friday. "Okay," he said with his mouth full, and then, remembering his manners, held up a finger and waited to say more until he'd chewed and swallowed. "Here's what I'm thinking." He laid out his plan. "And I'd like to do it tomorrow morning. Want to help?"

Libertine gave a small, sad smile. "Of course."

"Good," said Truman. "When you've lined it up, please let me know, and Gabriel, too. I'm going to alert the police chief, so we can have an officer on standby just in case."

"Have you talked this over with him?"

"Not yet—you're the key player."

Libertine nodded and pressed up a few cookie crumbs from the tabletop with a finger. "May I tell you something?"

"Absolutely."

"Friday trusts you—all of you. I think it's why he hasn't needed me."

"But you knew he was sick—that came to you."

She waved that away. "It was like overhearing a scream. It wasn't meant for me—I just happened to intercept it."

"Which makes all this just that much worse," said Truman. "He deserves much better than he's gotten. We'll try everything we can to compensate for what we can't give him."

"I'm sure he knows that."

Truman nodded. "Then let's make this right. If you'd make the call and then let me know what time they'll arrive, we'll get the rest worked out. And thank you again for this."

"Believe me," Libertine said firmly, "it's my pleasure."

FOR AS LONG as she could remember, Libertine had always thought one of her faults was her compulsive honesty. Hardly anyone else was honest, she'd noticed. She had asked her mother about this and her mother had said, "Oh, grow up. Of course no one's completely truthful. Can you imagine telling Mrs. Brubaker that her mole repulses everyone who sees her?" Mrs. Brubaker, Libertine's babysitter, had a mole on her left cheekbone the size of a pea. It was all Libertine—and, she assumed, nearly everyone else—could think about when they looked at her.

"But maybe if we did tell her, she'd have it taken off," Libertine had argued.

"No, she'd just rethink every single face-to-face encounter she'd ever had as far back as she could remember."

"So you don't really mean it when you say not to lie?"

Her mother had snapped at her, "For god's sake, don't be so literal. Of course I meant it—except for the little lies that spare people's feelings. Little lies make the world go round. There's a difference between lies and *lies*." But Libertine had never been able to see the difference. Until now. Now, driving away from the Oat Maiden to make her call, she would have to give the performance of a lifetime, based on the lie that she agreed philosophically with Trina Beemer and her followers that animals were better dead than captive. And yet her conscience would be crystal clear. As soon as she was inside, she rang a small bell she'd begun to use to tell Chocolate and Chip that she was home, and took a strengthening deep breath or two. Then she pulled her phone from her pocket and punched in Trina Beemer's number.

Chip popped out of the cat-tube, elegant as ever in his neat black morning coat. He wound around her legs as she paced, waiting for her to give him her lap. She sat and he jumped up, allowing her to run her fingers absently through his silky fur.

Libertine gave a silent prayer that her blood pressure would go down because of his presence. Her heart was pounding so hard she was light-headed.

When she got Trina on the line she said, "I guess you know that it didn't work—he's actually getting better. They think he wasn't given enough—either that, or he could have vomited. Anyway, he's definitely not going to die."

"I know," said Trina, whose voice sounded nasal, as though she'd been crying. "We heard. That poor, poor animal."

"But here's the thing." Libertine lowered her voice to what she hoped was a conspiratorial level. "I've asked if I can bring you in for a VIP tour."

"And?"

"They said yes!"

"Really?" Trina said excitedly. "My god, how stupid can they be? Still, that's great, Libby. Absolutely great. So when can we do this—how soon?"

"I think the sooner, the better, don't you? He's still in relatively bad shape, so it won't, ah, take as much."

They made the necessary arrangements, and as soon as they disconnected, Libertine called Truman. "Two o'clock this afternoon. Do you want me to call Martin or will you?"

"Me," said Truman. "Oh, let it be me."

MARTIN CHOI WAS beside himself with excitement. This could very easily be the story of a lifetime: militant animal rights wingding meets captive-care pioneer, with animal psychic on hand.

The wingding arrived first. She was a big, big woman with a voice that was weirdly flat while at the same time being loud enough to penetrate a concrete bunker. Her teeth were gray—he was not making this up—from, what, a vitamin deficiency when she was a kid? Scarlet fever? Poor dental hygiene? She wore a flowing skirt and rubber boots, and carried an enormous purse. He couldn't imagine what was in there—a phone book? Several extra meals? A seal pup? Not that it mattered. He subscribed to the to-each-his-own approach to life.

Libertine was the next one upstairs, hailing the wingding. They embraced—Jesus, it was like watching a walrus hug a penguin—and together they approached the pool. Neither one of them acknowledged him. He'd noticed a long time ago that if you were behind a camera, people seemed to think you were on some other astral plane.

The wingding headed for the wet walk, toting her enormous bag.

"You know, you can leave that on the deck if you want," Libertine told her.

"What's the matter with you? Isn't this what we came for?" Martin overheard her hiss to Libertine without even looking back. For a big woman, the wingding moved fast.

Gabriel Jump arrived on the pool top silently and moving fast, wet-suited and handsome in an older-guy kind of way. He reached the wingding just as she stepped into the wet walk near Friday, who was awaiting them, his chin on the edge of the pool. When he opened wide, Martin almost dropped his camera. Jesus—the whole inside of his mouth, which had always been a nice light pink like the belly of a puppy, was now dotted with thousands and thousands of little, dark red dots.

Then he caught Libertine shooting Gabriel a look. His acute reporter instincts homed in: something was about to go down. Martin had kicked on his auto-winder and started shooting, watching it all through his lens, when he saw the wingding pull from her tote a string bag holding four or five fish. *Fish.* What the hell?

From then on, at least from what he remembered later, things happened at lightning speed. The wingding leaned in to feed Friday the first fish; Gabriel vaulted forward to stop her, inadvertently throwing an elbow directly into Libertine's diaphragm; Libertine flew into the icy pool with the wind knocked out of her; Gabriel took the wingding down in the wet walk, wrestling away the fish and then the tote; and Martin snapped photo after photo after photo: *What a story!* This was the stuff Pulitzers were made of. Hello, HuffPost; hello national byline.

And then, as abruptly as it began, the whole mess was over. The wingding was sitting in the wet walk on her fat ass weeping; Gabriel was throwing her confiscated fish into a cooler and locking it with a padlock; Friday was nowhere to be seen. Martin lowered his camera, scanning the pool top. Where was Libertine? He'd seen her fall into the water, but come to think of it, he hadn't seen her since. Could she still be in the pool? *Holy crap!* There wasn't so much as a ripple on the surface, so if she'd gone down, it had been a while ago, maybe a minute, minute and a half. Enough time to drown.

But before he could even yell, he heard a chuff, loud and deep, as Friday surfaced. Libertine was sprawled across his back and one outstretched pectoral flipper like wet laundry. The whale swam to the side of the pool and gently tipped until she'd rolled onto the concrete. She retched, vomited water, coughed explosively. Gabriel ran over. Friday stayed nearby, his mouth closed, eyes inscrutable.

And Martin had gotten it all—the weeping wingding, the

gasping psychic, the weird stuff with the fish. What was the deal with those fish?

"They were poisoned," Gabriel was saying over his shoulder, though Martin hadn't been aware of speaking out loud. "Did you get pictures of all of it? Because you'll be a key witness, and the photos will be evidence." In the distance he could hear police sirens, growing closer. Silently he uttered his thanks to God for dropping this überopportunity upon him.

"How do you think he knew you were drowning?" Neva asked Libertine. Swimsuited, they sat on one of the teak benches in the shower. Neva sat behind Libertine, chafing her arms to try and warm her up.

"He must have heard me," Libertine said, her teeth chattering violently.

"But none of the rest of us did."

"Not heard me; *heard* me. In his head. I remember him swimming up to me and picking me off the bottom with his teeth. He had ahold of my sweater, the hem of it. After that there was nothing but a white light. There really is one."

"Gabriel's said the same thing."

Libertine nodded. "Next thing I knew, I was on the deck with his pectoral flipper under me. And I could feel him saying. *Don't*. That's all it was, over and over: *Don't*."

"Don't what?" Neva asked.

"I don't know. He was vocalizing like crazy, too. Did Gabriel say anything about hearing him?"

Neva shook her head. "I think he was focused on stopping her from giving him those fish."

They heard a knock on the door and Truman called, "Is she okay?"

"I'm fine," Libertine called weakly.

"She's fine," Neva hollered. "Just cold. What's going on out there? Did the police come?"

"Right on schedule. They took her with them. You'll be a witness, you know."

"Me?" Neva asked.

"Libertine."

"Go ahead and open the door so we can hear you," Neva yelled over the sound of the shower. "We're decent."

Truman looked in. Neva thought he looked grim. "So did she say anything?" she asked. "Trina Beemer?"

"Not really," said Truman. "She kept crying and babbling about how she'd ruined the whale's one real chance to escape this earthly hell. Those were her exact words—'escape this earthly hell.'"

"Some ninja warrior, huh?" said Neva.

THAT EVENING THEY all gathered for dinner at the Oat Maiden: Neva, Truman, Gabriel, Libertine, Ivy—everyone but Sam, who volunteered to take the evening watch at Friday's pool. They'd agreed that someone should be with him around the clock until the medical crisis had passed: as soon as he had deposited Libertine on the pool deck, Friday had gone back to his corner, winded and exhausted. A security guard would also be stationed at the pool all night, every night, from now on.

"So how much time do you think she'll get?" Ivy asked Truman. She was disappointed that she hadn't been on the pool top to see Trina Beemer apprehended.

"You'd have to ask my father. It should be a watertight case, though." He smiled wanly. "So to speak. We have eyewitnesses, plus Martin's photos, plus my hidden video camera. I doubt it'll even go to trial. I think she'll plea-bargain."

"Maybe she'll rat out the rest of the FAS people," Neva said.

"Doubtful," said Gabriel.

"Why?"

"They don't do that. They martyr themselves. It's part of the creed."

Libertine brought a tray of drinks to the table and joined them. Johnson Johnson followed with two pizzas.

"What creed?" Ivy asked.

"Better dead than captive," Libertine, Neva, Gabriel, and Truman all said as one.

While Neva handed around pizza slices, Ivy considered Truman for a long beat.

"What?" said Truman.

"What if there was a third alternative?" Ivy asked. "Besides dead and captive, I mean. What if we really do release him?"

That got everyone's attention. "Oh, boy," Gabriel said.

"Wait, wait, let me talk," Ivy said. "Clearly captivity's been no great shakes. He's been hit, bullied, parboiled, starved, and now poisoned, and he's hung on through it all. Obviously here it's better, but what if there's an even better choice? He was wild once."

"As a calf," Neva pointed out. "He was collected right out of the crib, so to speak."

"Why do you all say 'collected'?" Ivy said irritably. "He was *captured*. Call a spade a spade. He was separated from everything he knew—and yes, including his mother. He spent a year in a small holding pool in Norway, getting some basic training— open your mouth, swim, eat this dead fish." She turned to Gabriel. "All of which is stuff that would help you, right?"

"You're starting to sound like one of the animal activists," said Neva, staring at her. "And not in a good way."

"Look, I'm just reviewing the facts," said Ivy. "Have I gotten anything wrong yet? No." She turned to Gabriel and said, "How old was he when he was caught?"

"One. Give or take a few months."

"Do you know that?" Neva asked in surprise.

Gabriel nodded.

Ivy said to Neva, "Ask him how he knows. Go on—ask him." When Gabriel sent her a look she said, "Oh, come on—let's not be coy."

Neva said, "What are you talking about?"

"Gabriel was the one who 'collected' our little boy in the first place," Ivy said.

"Who?" Neva said.

"*Friday,*" Ivy said impatiently. "Gabriel was the one who caught him."

Gabriel stared at her.

"One of the board members at the Whale Museum put it all together last week." She turned to address the rest of the table. "They went out with a fishing boat with a bunch of nets and they separated him from his pod and brought him back to a tank in a little town on a fjord in Norway and started training him up, so he'd know a few things by the time he was bought and taken to whatever zoo or theme park was willing to pay the most. That's how Gabriel knows he's a North Atlantic whale. That's why he went to see him every few years. And that's why Friday recognized that signal Neva accidentally gave him. Gabriel was the one who taught it to him in the first place."

Stunned, they turned to Gabriel as one.

"Is that true?" Libertine finally asked.

"Yep," he said, unfazed, reaching for another piece of pizza. He looked up, saw everyone looking at him, and stopped with the pizza halfway to his mouth. "What?"

"But you've never said a word," Libertine said. "Why haven't you ever told us?"

"Would it have made any difference if I had?" he asked, taking a big bite. "No, it wouldn't. And that sort of information in the wrong hands can be dangerous."

"Oh, come on," Ivy said. "That's a little hole-and-corner, don't you think?"

"Is it? I traveled under assumed names with fake passports for years because there'd been death threats made against me. Threats, plural."

"But didn't it just rip you up to take him like that?" Libertine asked incredulously.

"No."

"*Really?*" she said. "I can't believe that."

Gabriel sighed, lowered his pizza slice, and looked at them all. "Look, for one thing you're being anthropomorphic—this is an animal, not a child. Second, I'm not a heartless bastard and I didn't do it for financial gain. It all comes down to conservation. There's a huge need for zoos and parks to educate people. You don't save animals and habitats you've never seen before and know nothing about. If there'd never been Shamu, people wouldn't give a damn about killer whales. Now they do."

"Blah blah blah," Ivy broke in. "I'm sorry, but all of that is just so much mealymouthed hokum. Let me ask you a question. What if we let him go back there, to where you caught him?"

Truman stared at her. "What?"

Gabriel put his head in his hands.

"What if we let him go?" Ivy said. "I'm serious. Tell me why we can't."

"I'm not saying we can't. I'm saying we shouldn't."

"Why?"

"You may not believe in captivity," Gabriel said, "but he's spent nearly his whole life being cared for by humans. Yes, the conditions were miserable, and yes, he's been a victim. But there's captivity and then there's *captivity*. Here, he's healthy—well, you know what I mean, except for the poisoning thing—and challenged. He has great food, people to watch, games to play, and people to swim with. He's safe. Yes, we failed him by allowing him to fall into the wrong hands, but that's over now."

Ivy shook her head.

"Look," Gabriel said. "You can't compensate for past harm by turning him loose, even if he were allowed to be, which, by the way, would never happen—partly because if it ever came down to it, I'd do everything in my power to prevent it. He doesn't have even a slim chance of surviving on his own. Do you know how long ago he last caught and ate a live fish? Eighteen years."

Libertine said to Ivy, "Is it his being alone that bothers you?"

Ivy regarded her. "Well, it does give being captive an extra layer of awful. It would be like landing on another planet and having no way to ever go home or even see another member of your species again. It gives me goose bumps. I started thinking about it a few weeks ago, and now I can't stop."

"You have to," said Gabriel. "You're reacting purely on emotions, and that's exactly when bad decisions get made."

Julio Iglesias, who had been curled up in Libertine's lap, suddenly sat up, chucking her under the chin with his hard little skull. "Ow," she said. He turned his face up and licked her chin.

"Oh, for god's sake," Ivy snapped at Libertine. "You might as well just take him—he clearly prefers you. He seems to prefer all of you. And to think of everything I've done for him over the years." Then, turning back to Gabriel, she said, "Is it possible to teach survival skills to an animal that's been in captivity as long as he has?"

Before Gabriel could answer, Johnson Johnson approached the table with a platter of cookies.

"Yum!" Truman said, trying to lighten the mood. "Sugar, the brain food of champions."

But Gabriel ignored him. "It was actually tried at a facility on the Oregon coast in the late nineties, with debatable success. That killer whale was also caught in the North Atlantic as a calf, spent twenty-three years in captivity, and then got released off Iceland."

"And?" said Ivy.

"I know this story," Neva interjected. "He swam across the ocean to a fjord in Norway—which is where he might actually have been from—and died of pneumonia. The whole project was underwritten by a billionaire, nearly ruined the institution that took him in, and in the end, at least in my opinion, it was pure folly. Everyone hoped he'd hook up with a pod, but he never did. He went where the people were. The fjord he chose had a little town on it, and people came down all the time to see him. You could argue that that was why he stayed there."

"There was a little more to it than that," said Gabriel.

"Politically and diplomatically there was a lot more to it," agreed Neva, "but the outcome was still death."

Gabriel conceded the point, but said, "Look, people, snap out of it. We've been through something heinous, but Friday's going to be fine. We'll be much more vigilant, and nothing like this will ever happen again. We'll do everything we can to make sure his life is the best we can possibly give him. Is that really so bad?"

"No," said Ivy. "It's just not what I'd have chosen for him."

"Actually, you did choose it for him," Truman pointed out.

"Well, then I wouldn't choose it now," Ivy conceded.

Gabriel leaned way over the table and spoke so quietly that some of them had to lean in, too, to hear. "Look. You want him to have all the skills of a wild whale, but he doesn't. He hasn't, in years and years and years. No matter what you might want for him, you can't change that. He's smart, funny, resilient, adaptable, and he's managed to stay alive and sane through more years than anyone would have given him credit for. Let him be what he is, not what you or anyone else out there thinks he should be."

"Then I propose a toast," Truman said firmly. "To Friday. May only good things be in his future, and may that future be long and happy."

"To Friday," they echoed.

But on the drive back to Matthew and Lavinia's house, Ivy found herself thinking something over and over: Would it have been so bad if he'd died rather than face more years of isolation? Not a horrible and protracted death, of course, but something swift and painless?

Would it really have been so bad?

Chapter 14

IT TOOK FRIDAY more than two weeks to fully recover, and the whale team was never quite the same. Ivy spent more and more time back in Friday Harbor, and talked Libertine into taking Julio Iglesias, at least on a trial basis. Her exact words were, "He may be an asshole, but he deserves to be a happy asshole."

In turn, Libertine got Truman's permission to bring him to the pool every day as, of all things, a therapy dog. Gabriel jury-rigged a set of steps so the dog could climb into the deep-silled office window looking into the pool and snooze on his very own fleece, where Friday could watch him. Whenever someone went upstairs to work with the whale, Julio Iglesias liked to noodle around the concrete deck in a little orange flotation vest, peeing on his regular stations—the two big coolers, the railing uprights, the ozone tower—and any pile of new gear he might find up there.

Libertine had watched the dog and Friday play the same game of Follow Me that the whale had first developed with six-year-old Nicolle on Christmas Day. But one day she called

Gabriel, Truman, and Neva on the radio and told them breathlessly to drop whatever they were doing and come to the pool top immediately—and bring the video camera. Gabriel and Neva were just downstairs and raced up with snorkels and swim fins as well as the camera; impressively, Truman arrived from his office in less than five minutes.

There, riding on one of Friday's pectoral flippers, was Julio Iglesias.

"I'll be damned!" hooted Gabriel. "Julio, you *dog,* you!"

Julio Iglesias looked back with his enigmatic Garbo eyes.

Libertine appointed herself videographer, saying, "Ivy would never believe me." On the camera screen she saw Julio Iglesias sit down on the smooth, shiny, six-foot-long black flipper, neatly tucking his tail over the tops of his front paws. Even when Friday set sail across the pool, the dog seemed entirely untroubled. Libertine filmed for nine full minutes before Friday swam to the side and the dog daintily disembarked. With Truman's permission, Libertine uploaded the video to YouTube, giving it the title *Friendship, Big and Small.* By the next morning it had gone viral, receiving 1,442,337 hits, and that day the zoo saw more visitors than any other single day in its history.

Thinking that Friday might like to watch more animals, Truman requested from Netflix a year's worth of *Flipper* episodes, but, disappointingly, neither Julio Iglesias nor the whale turned out to be interested.

"He probably doesn't like it because it's fake," said Johnson Johnson, who, once the Oat Maiden was closed for the night, had come back to the pool with Libertine.

"What do you mean?" Gabriel said.

"Well, it's a *movie,*" said Johnson Johnson.

Gabriel looked at Libertine for elaboration, as happened more and more often.

"The characters aren't real," Libertine explained. "So the story isn't real. Julio Iglesias is real."

"He certainly is," said Gabriel. The dog was sound asleep on the windowsill, snoring.

AS LIBERTINE AND Johnson Johnson drove home, she was newly aware of a tiny but persistent presence that had been in her head intermittently since morning. Something was in trouble. "I need to make a detour," she told Johnson Johnson. "I keep sensing something. Do you?"

"No."

She tracked the presence all the way to their block, and then coasted along slowly. Three houses down from Johnson Johnson's, she pulled over to the curb and stopped. "It's right here somewhere. Help me look." She fished a flashlight out of her glove compartment.

Together they peered into bushes and up trees. "It's right *here*," Libertine said in frustration, and then Johnson Johnson knelt down and, with infinite care, parted the lower branches of a dripping rhododendron.

"What is it?"

"Look," breathed Johnson Johnson. "Oh, *look!*" He reached for a kitten that Libertine estimated was no more than four weeks old. "Isn't it beautiful?"

It was not beautiful. It was soaking wet and filthy and one eye was stuck shut. Johnson Johnson placed it very carefully in the breast pocket of his flannel shirt. "Do you think we can take it home?"

"I'm sure we can," said Libertine. "It's been in distress all day, and clearly no one's claimed it. Though how it got stuck in a bush I can't imagine."

"Let's call it Winken," said Johnson Johnson, pulling up his shirttails and packing them around his pocket to further warm the kitten.

Libertine smiled. "That's a very good name."

"Yes," said Johnson Johnson. "That way, when we get another one we can call it Blinken. Well, or Nod."

As soon as they got home, he carried the kitten into the kitchen like a precious gem while Libertine rounded up several clean dish towels. Together they unwrapped her—the kitten turned out to be a girl—and set her on a dish towel on the counter. She was even younger than they'd guessed in the dark, no more than three weeks and quite possibly less. They buffed her dry and Johnson Johnson warmed some milk while Libertine went out to her apartment and found an eyedropper.

"Sit," she said, pouring the warm milk into a mug and bringing Johnson Johnson and the kitten into the living room, where Chocolate and Chip were out cold on a couple of wall shelves. Once he'd sat down, Libertine pulled up a little milk in the eyedropper, put the thinnest dish towel over the end, and let the milk soak it before she put the eyedropper near the kitten's mouth. The kitten latched on immediately, pulling the milk down until it was gone.

"She's hungry. I bet she was in that bush all day," Johnson Johnson said, and his voice caught. "Someone should get in trouble for doing that."

"I agree," said Libertine. "But the good thing is, she's very strong. She was in my mind for hours and hours before we found her. That means if we take good care of her, she'll be just fine."

Johnson Johnson nodded soberly: Libertine had learned that

he liked things to be just fine. Impulsively, she kissed him on the top of his head and went back to the kitchen to rewarm the milk.

BEING BACK IN Friday Harbor had been even harder than Ivy had expected it to be. She felt cut off, cranky, and unmoored, and she missed Julio Iglesias, incredible as that seemed. She also missed Friday; even more than that, she missed Gabriel. But at the same time, something in her had uncoupled during that last night they'd all been together at the Oat Maiden. It came down to this: she'd given Gabriel godlike abilities to heal the sick and bridge the seemingly unbridgeable gap between two species; but he'd turned out to be a mercenary, not a savior. She simply could not reconcile his gift for making animals well with his equal and opposite willingness to capture their babies, selling them to the highest bidder without so much as a flicker of conscience.

So she busied herself with giving the house a thorough cleaning, washing the screens that she installed in the windows every spring. She donated several thousand dollars to the Whale Museum, which reinstated her as an educational docent, who would talk to giddy tourists and groups of middle school students about the cetaceans living in the Straits of Juan de Fuca and the Puget Sound. She had over to dinner the young couple who'd recently moved into the house two doors down from hers; she played bridge. It was all shallow busywork, of course, but gradually she regained her equilibrium, going so far as to begin planning a trip to Cairo.

But in late April she got a call from Libertine, who said, "I miss you. I don't understand why you feel like you have to be in exile."

"I'm not in exile," said Ivy. "Look, that was never my life."

"We miss you—all of us do. It's hard to know what to tell Julio Iglesias. He doesn't understand."

Ivy snorted. "Of all the people who don't miss me, Julio Iglesias would top the list."

"You don't understand love," said Libertine. "You don't understand it at all. It's staring you right in the face and you can't see it."

"Oh, so Julio Iglesias loves me now?"

"I wasn't talking about Julio Iglesias."

"No?" said Ivy.

"No."

"You?"

"Yes, me," said Libertine. "You're funny and you're brave and you're not afraid to make people angry when you defend an opinion. I love that about you."

"You know you just defined the word *blabbermouth,* right?"

Sounding exasperated, Libertine said, "And you say *I* can't take a compliment."

Ivy felt a warm wave sweeping up from her toes to her noggin-top. She said, "I don't know what to say."

"Well, I do. Say you'll come back and stay sometimes."

"You all have jobs," Ivy protested. "You have a place to go, and work to do. I just write checks. I can do that from anywhere."

"Not as well as from here."

"Liar," said Ivy.

"Curmudgeon," replied Libertine. "Look, maybe this isn't the time to say it, but I have a plan."

"Here we go," said Ivy.

"I know you don't like staying with your brother and sister-in-law, so when you come down you can have my apartment."

"And where will you go?"

"I'll just stay at the house."

"With Johnson Johnson?"

"Yes."

"No kidding!" Ivy said, beginning to grin. "And you've been keeping this to yourself? I *have* stayed away too long."

"Stop," said Libertine. "He's a good man who can use a little company from time to time."

"And that company would be you?"

"Not usually, no—just every now and then."

"Well, he's a lucky man."

"Anyway, come down. Please?" A long beat went by. "You aren't going to, are you."

"Nope," said Ivy.

"Did something happen? I haven't done something, have I? Sometimes I do and I don't even know."

"Honey, you're perfect in every way. I just need to live my own life for a little while. I love being in the thick of that group, but it's not real. This is real—up here."

"We seem pretty real to me," Libertine said.

"You know what I mean."

ON JUNE 24, the zoo celebrated the first anniversary of Friday's arrival at the zoo. In celebration, Truman ordered half a dozen enormous sheet cakes with Friday's image sculpted in the frosting, and put the cakes in the zoo lobby for the visitors to share. Attendance continued to climb. One month earlier, Truman had released Ivy from any financial obligation to subsidize Friday, since the extra revenue he had brought in was more than enough to maintain him.

"So are you coming down for the black-and-white gala, at

least?" Truman asked Ivy, who'd declined to be present for a series of anniversary-related educational activities at the zoo. The gala was a fund-raiser that would benefit the board-adopted Greater Good Fund. After a long beat he said, "You're not coming, are you?"

"No," said Ivy, "but I was thinking about something else. How about the next weekend you all come up here and stay overnight? We'll have our own anniversary celebration! I've already talked to Sam about whether he and Corinna and Reginald will come, but he said Corinna doesn't travel. Coming up here isn't exactly my idea of traveling, but if they prefer to stay home anyway, I asked Sam if he'd mind feeding Friday so everyone else can come. He said he'd be happy to do it."

So at the agreed-upon time, Ivy met the ferry and picked up Gabriel, Truman, Neva, Winslow, Libertine, Johnson Johnson, and Julio Iglesias. It was a brilliantly sunny day and from Ivy's living room Haro Strait looked like hammered silver, lively and bright. A pod of killer whales had been working the water just off the island all morning. Ivy gave Winslow her grandfather's binoculars and pointed them out.

"Whoa!" Winslow said. "I wonder what Friday would say, if he could see them?"

"I can't imagine," said Ivy. "Sometimes seeing them out there makes me sad for him."

"Don't be," said Gabriel, who must have overheard her. "He wasn't even from here, and if you ever went through a North Atlantic storm, you'd think again."

"Yeah, but don't they stay underwater?" said Winslow.

"Sure, most of the time. But they need to breathe. In a force-five storm, the wind picks up water and flings it."

"Cool," said Winslow.

"Not if you're out in it. Not if you're on a boat," said Gabriel.

"Really?" Winslow said enthusiastically. "Do you get sea-sick?"

"No, but everybody else I know does."

"I bet I would," said Winslow.

"I bet you would, too," said Truman, taking up the binoculars Winslow had set down and looking out over the water.

"I threw up on the up-and-over ride at the state fair last year," Winslow admitted ruefully.

"Is it just me, or is talking about throwing up before a wonderful meal a bad idea?" asked Neva. "Come on, let's see if Ivy needs any help."

So Winslow set the table and everyone else ferried heaping bowls of fresh steamer clams, crabs, fish stew, salads, rolls, and a whole, glorious grilled salmon. Julio Iglesias, who'd been closely watching the parade of delicacies from the living room, caught Ivy's eye, and unleashed a mighty pee on the carpet.

"Oh, you little *bastard*!" she cried, going to the kitchen to get a wad of paper towels. Julio Iglesias hooded his eyes and trotted over to Libertine, hopping into her lap as soon as she sat down at the table.

"He just trying to get your attention," said Libertine.

"Oh, he's got it, all right," said Ivy grimly, brandishing a wooden mixing spoon at him. "He'll have it all the way to the laundry room." But she failed to make good on her threat, instead fixing him a plate with bits of fish, wheat roll, pasta salad, and freshly steamed asparagus with hollandaise sauce, which caused the dog to leave Libertine immediately for the spot in the kitchen formerly reserved for his supper dish. When Ivy came back alone, she said, "His bed's still in there, too. If he knows what's good for him, he'll eat himself into a stupor and take a nap."

Once all the dishes had been passed and plates were heaping, Ivy said, "So catch me up! What's the news? And speaking of that, how's dear Martin?"

"You know, he actually got an interview with the Huffington Post," Truman told her. "You'd have thought he'd won a Pulitzer. Apparently his exposé on the Friends of Animals of the Sea was picked up by the wire services and got quite a bit of play. Trina Beemer has become a persona non grata lately. I guess she didn't get the organization's go-ahead before she poisoned our boy."

"Hey, they're gone!" said Winslow, turning around in his chair and peering through the binoculars.

"Who?" said Ivy.

"The pod! The killer whales. I don't see them anymore."

"They're probably following a school of fish," Gabriel said.

"Okay, never mind the whales," said Ivy, who had had several strong whiskey and sodas by then. "I want to propose a toast."

"Go," said Gabriel.

She raised her glass. "Here's to the best people in the world. I'm honored to have you all under my roof and hope that good health, buoyancy, and wisdom follow you to the end of your days."

"Amen," said Gabriel.

"Hear, hear," said Truman.

They ate until they were groaning. The conversations around the table were lively, fueled by good food, good wine, and good company. Only Libertine seemed withdrawn. Ivy tried to engage her, but she kept lapsing into a pensive silence. When she and Ivy were alone in the kitchen, loading dishes into the dishwasher, Ivy said to her irritably, "What's with you, anyway? You're way too quiet. It's a holiday. Be festive, for god's sake."

"I'm sorry," said Libertine. "I didn't realize. I've been hearing something I can't understand. Would it be rude if I go for a walk?"

"If it'll cheer you up, by all means go. You're lousy company anyway."

"I think I'll see if Winslow wants to come along. I might need some help."

Then she walked into the living room without further explanation, and even Ivy knew enough to let it go.

THE GOOD WEATHER window had slammed shut and a light mist was falling, so the two zipped up anoraks and, at Libertine's suggestion, headed down to the little beach at the foot of Ivy's property, which fronted a pocket-sized bay. The Sound was cold and crystal clear; Libertine could see a few tiny crabs scrabbling along the rocks, and small fish flitted back and forth under cover of a few fronds of kelp. But none of this was what she'd come for. She'd been hearing an animal in great distress since arriving this morning, and from the time the killer whale pod moved out of sight, it had gotten louder and louder.

"I need you to help me," she told Winslow. "You know those whales you were watching? Something's wrong with one of them. I don't know what, but it's a young animal, and it's scared. We need to find it."

"Really?" said Winslow. "How do you know that?"

"I just do. Does Ivy have a boat or something?"

"No," said Winslow. "Dad says the whole family's afraid of drowning. Isn't that weird?"

"All right," Libertine said, ignoring the added commentary. "It's close—we should be able to see it if we look in the right place."

Winslow quickly scanned the little bay. "There's nothing here."

"I know. That's why we need to walk. I want to go around that little point. It looks like we can get there if we go up into the woods. Up and over. I think there's another little inlet on the other side."

Winslow went first, holding branches out of the way for Libertine.

"Thank you," she said. "You're just like your father—a gentleman." She was silent for a minute. "You don't feel anything, by any chance? In your head?"

"No. You do?"

"Yes," said Libertine. "I've been feeling something young and in trouble ever since we got here. I think it's in the water near here. And it's so *afraid*!"

They broke through the trees and found themselves on the shore of another tiny inlet. This beach, like Ivy's, was littered with bleached driftwood that looked, in Libertine's feverish mind, like the bones of giants. Libertine grabbed Winslow's sleeve. "Look!" she cried. "Oh, look."

A tiny killer whale, no more than ten feet long, floated just off the shore.

"Is it dead?" said Winslow. But then the calf took a small, light breath.

"What's the matter with it?" Winslow said. "Why didn't it go with the rest of them? Do you think it's lost?"

"I don't know. No, I don't think it's lost, but there's some reason why the pod abandoned it. We need to get Gabriel. I'll stay here and try to keep it calm, if you'll go back. Go! *Go!*"

Even Winslow could hear the calf's keening, high and piercing. He turned around and ran.

WHILE WINSLOW WAS gone Libertine tried to soothe the animal, but it had gone beyond her reach, just as Friday had so many months ago. She stayed at the water's edge anyway, trying to send soothing energy until Gabriel, Neva, and Winslow appeared at last, followed by Truman, Ivy, and Johnson Johnson. Gabriel climbed down out of the woods and sat on a weather-smoothed driftwood log.

"For heaven's sake," Ivy cried after a few minutes. "Aren't you going to do something?"

"I am doing something," Gabriel snapped. "I'm watching."

"It's so *small,*" Libertine said.

"You're comparing it to Friday. He's a full-grown male; this animal's probably a year old, plus or minus. So of course it's small."

"Why is it here?" Ivy asked.

"Could be lots of reasons. Maybe it's injured. Maybe it's sick. Maybe it has a parasite load that's killing it."

"It's been abandoned," Libertine said.

"Obviously," Gabriel said. "What we need to know is why. I need to take a closer look before we lose the light." He turned to Ivy. "Do you think the Whale Museum has wet suits, fins, and snorkels we can borrow?"

"I'm sure they do. I'll call the executive director."

"See if we can get three sets of everything, one for Neva,

one for Libertine, and one for me. Make sure he understands it's an emergency," Gabriel said, "because we may need people to help. And a small boat and fishing net long enough to stretch across the mouth of the inlet."

"Aye-aye, cap'n," said Ivy.

Then Libertine overheard Truman whisper to Winslow, "Go with her, okay? Make sure she doesn't slip or fall or anything."

"Is she drunk?"

"No. Well, yes, but she seems functional. Just stay with her. If she has to go into town to pick things up, come get me. I don't want her driving."

"No kidding," said Winslow.

AN HOUR LATER the three were suited up and ready to get in the water. The island was small and Ivy well-known; people came out of the woodwork to see if they could help, until a small crowd had gathered behind the band of driftwood.

With a mask, snorkel, and fins, Gabriel swam slowly and quietly toward the calf. It regarded him with darting, panicky eyes but stayed put as he circled, examining its skin and pectoral flippers and flukes—and there he found the problem. Most of its left fluke and a part of its right one were gone. The injury looked like it was a day or two old; his guess was that it had probably been caught in a boat propeller. The severity of the wound would have made it almost impossible to keep up with the pod.

He reached out and touched the animal lightly on the back, and when it flinched he whispered, "It's going to be okay," and returned to the beach to explain the problem.

"Is it a boy? Girl? How old do you think it is?" Neva asked.

"I don't know if it's male or female, but it's a year old, plus or minus."

"So what'll happen to it?" asked Ivy.

"Here? Death," said Gabriel. "Especially because it's still young and probably hasn't mastered eating on his own. Mom may still be nursing it, if she isn't pregnant again."

He and Neva locked eyes. "Could we?" she asked.

"Maybe," Gabriel said. "We'll need a permit, but I think I can get that pushed through tomorrow. And we'll need to run bloods and a blowhole swab. And fecal, if we can get it."

"What are you talking about?" said Ivy, looking from one to the other.

"That's all doable, isn't it?" said Neva.

"Will someone tell me *what the hell is going on*?" Ivy cried.

Gabriel turned to her. "If the calf's in good enough shape, we might be able to bring him to the zoo."

Ivy drew in a quick breath. "You mean to live with Friday?"

"Maybe—*maybe*. With the injury he has, he's certainly not releasable."

"Oh, man!" said Ivy. "Oh man, oh man, oh man."

"Don't get ahead of things," Gabriel cautioned. "We have to keep it alive first. Do you know anyone at the urgent care here?"

"I know everyone," said Ivy.

"Then see if they have a lab that can analyze some samples— and if they can, ask them to give you lab supplies—tonight, even if it means they have to bring someone in. You'd be willing to pay for that, right?"

"Hah!" Ivy said. "In a heartbeat." She turned to Truman and said, "Come with me. You're going to be driving. I damned near went into a ditch on the way to the museum."

"I told Winslow to make sure you didn't drive."

"I know," she said. "That's why I made him stay home."

Ivy BELIEVED THAT every now and then, and usually when you least expected it, the universe looked out for its own. In the rapidly fading light, with the help of a Boston Whaler, Gabriel and Neva stretched a fishing net so the calf was contained for the night. Once it was in place they waded out and hydrated it with tubing, lubricant, and a funnel Ivy had found for them along with lab materials and the promise that a tech would stand by to analyze the samples as soon as they were brought in the next morning. Gabriel reached the Washington State Department of Fish and Wildlife guy in charge of permitting, with whom he'd worked for decades tagging seals and sea lions. He promised he'd push the paperwork through the next day, as long as a zoo representative was available to sign off. He also promised to loan them the transport gear, provided that Gabriel would vouch for the fact that it would come back promptly.

Having done all they could until daybreak, they each took turns checking on the calf throughout the evening, listening in the darkness for his breathing. Finally Gabriel sent everyone to bed, stressing that the next day was likely to be long and punishing.

But instead of going to her room, Ivy poured freshly brewed coffee and a generous measure of Bushmills Irish Whiskey into a thermos, pulled on a heavy sweater—the nights were cold here even in the height of summer—and tugged a windproof anorak over that. Then she stuck Julio Iglesias and an inflatable cushion into a canvas bag and, sweating fiercely, emerged from the house just a few minutes shy of midnight.

The sky had cleared, and a full moon lit up the band of bleached driftwood on the beach. She struggled her way to the next-door bay, where she could make out the calf's silhouetted dorsal fin, motionless in the moonlight. She froze until she heard its pneumatic exhale and inhale. Then she blew up the inflatable cushion, set Julio Iglesias on his feet, and lowered herself onto a driftwood log. There she listened to the calf breathe, all the way until morning; if it died in the night, at least someone would have borne witness to its passing. When first light came and it was still alive, she struggled to her feet, stuffed the empty thermos, Julio Iglesias, and her deflating cushion into the canvas bag, and climbed up to the house pre-pared to fix breakfast and brew up a large pot of coffee strong enough to strip paint.

The household was already stirring when she came in. Ga-briel had found eggs, cheese, bacon, and scallions in the refrig-erator and was cooking; Winslow was manning the toaster; and Truman had found and brewed coffee and was getting glasses and orange juice out on the table. Neva was making peanut butter and jelly sandwiches in case they didn't have time to stop for lunch later, and Libertine had run Johnson Johnson to the ferry, since he had promised his wait-staff he'd be back at the Oat Maiden by three o'clock that afternoon. Ivy told Gabriel that the calf had had an uneventful night, at least from the sounds of his breathing.

"That was some dumb move, going alone," he chastised her. "You could have broken an ankle out there, and no one would have known until morning."

"Now, see?" she agreed. "That's exactly what I thought."

"So?" said Gabriel.

"I decided not to listen."

BY THE END of breakfast, they'd all agreed to name the calf, a male, San Juan—Juan, for short—to commemorate the place where they'd found him. They spent the rest of the morning preparing the stretcher and transport box that Gabriel's Department of Fish and Wildlife contact had ferried over on the back of a small flatbed truck, and loading up the calf. Truman, with Gabriel, drove the truck onto the 12:10 ferry.

As Gabriel had laid out for them on San Juan Island before they'd left, they would acclimatize the calf in an above-ground, circular fiberglass pool in the zoo's holding area, which had once been used to house waterfowl while their exhibit was being upgraded. Neva now offered to take the overnight shift, but Gabriel wanted to be there to monitor the calf through the night.

AT FOUR ON the nose the next morning, Neva, already wearing a wet suit, arrived at the pool and climbed in with two Dunkin' Donuts to-go cups of coffee held high.

"You're an angel," Gabriel said.

"If I were an angel, I'd have brought donuts, too. I ran out of money." She pushed her way through the four-foot-deep water until she'd come alongside Gabriel. Though it wasn't quite as cold as Friday's pool, she still shuddered.

Gabriel set his coffee cup on a little deck on one side of the pool, beside a length of flexible tubing, funnel, and two gallons of water. "I want to hydrate him before I go." With Neva's help, Gabriel gaped the calf's mouth with a dowel as thick as a broomstick and fed the lubricated tubing down his throat and into his stomach without difficulty. In less than five minutes they'd poured two gallons of fresh water and electrolytes down his throat.

"Good," Gabriel said. "We'll feed him in an hour or so."

"So what am I going to be doing, exactly?" Neva asked.

"Walking," Gabriel said. "You're going to be walking. This kid doesn't know about walls, so unless we protect him he'll swim right into them. I want him between you and the wall, so he can get used to its being there, but you'll be directing him."

"Won't echolocation tell him where they are?"

"Sure, but when the sound bounces back at him he's not going to have any idea what it means."

"So, the walking."

"Yep. Around and around. Okay, come all the way up to him."

The calf blew out a loud pneumatic huff. Despite all the time she'd spent with Friday, and the calf's relatively tiny size, Neva jumped and then laughed at herself. "Why is his white skin yellow? Is that bad?"

"Nope, normal for a young calf. He'll whiten up later."

"It's funny to see his dorsal fin standing straight up. Poor Friday."

"Okay, let's show you what you're going to be doing," Gabriel said.

"Can I just take a look at his flukes first? I haven't had the chance." At Gabriel's nod, she held a diving mask up to her face and looked underwater, coming up grimacing. "Oh, man," she said. "The poor guy. Do you think it still hurts?"

"I'm sure it does, but at least the young ones tend to heal quickly." Gabriel stepped away from the calf, indicating that Neva should take his place. "You'll hold him this way"—he positioned her arms so they formed parentheses around Juan just behind his pectoral flippers—"and let him move as freely as you can, but keep him from making contact with the sides. That's it—that's all there is to it. Okay?"

"Okay."

"Good," Gabriel said. "I'll be back in about an hour, and I'll bring fish with me, so we can begin getting him used to being hand-fed. Sam said he'd come down and keep you company. Have him call me on the radio if you need anything."

GABRIEL HAD A yawning fit on his way back to Friday's pool. As soon as he turned on the office lights Friday appeared in the window, and Gabriel banged on it with a flat palm, in greeting. The whale was looking for an indication that it was breakfast time, and when he saw none he swam off into the gloom. Gabriel had intended to do fish house, so Friday and Juan had food for the day, but what he did do was climb onto a desktop and roll onto his back, and rather than drift into sleep, fell into it headlong, as though from a high cliff.

He was getting old for these animal transport marathons.

Until the calf came into the picture, he'd intended to tell Truman that he'd be moving on just after the first of the year. Neva and Libertine had come along nicely, and there were any number of experienced marine mammal keepers who'd kill to join them. Gabriel wasn't interested in maintaining exhibits and animals; exhausting though it was, he'd take a good crisis any day. Emergencies brought out the best in him.

He awoke from an hour's deep and dreamless sleep abruptly, looking up to see Friday in the window, peering down at him and blowing air-bubble rings from his blowhole. Gabriel smiled. He would miss Friday; he was a one-in-a-million whale. But once the calf was settled into the pool, Gabriel suspected that Friday wouldn't need any of them as much. Bringing up an orphan would keep him busy for years—for the rest of his life, presumably, unless something unexpected happened. Gabriel was sure he'd be good at it, too.

Now, getting up stiffly, he mentally amended his departure date to Labor Day. That should give them all plenty of time. In the meantime, he'd get in touch with a few of the young keepers he'd trained and see who might be interested in a position.

SAM ARRIVED AT the holding pool at 6:00 A.M., carrying a Dunkin' Donuts box.

"Oh, yum," Neva said. "You're the best."

Sam held up a thermos. "Brought coffee, too," he said.

"Great minds think alike," Neva said. "Me, too."

Sam laid a custard-filled donut—her favorite—on the rim of the pool. The calf was awake and moving, so she took a bite whenever they came around to that spot in the pool.

"You think you'll have to keep him in this little pool much longer?" Sam asked her.

"Gabriel's hoping we can move him into the med pool tomorrow. Isn't he the most beautiful thing? I'm totally in love."

"Yes, ma'am, he is. Hard to see him as a baby, though. He's awful big."

"It's all relative. He's less than half Friday's size."

With surprising speed, Neva discovered the tedium and discomfort of walking the calf. Half an hour after she'd gotten in, he stopped moving and hung quietly in the water, pecs and flukes drooping, eyes closed, dozing. Neva scratched slow, light circles around his head and blowhole to get him used to being touched and petted. She shifted from foot to foot; she windmilled her arms, trying to stay warm. Her numb hands ached, she had started shivering, and her muscles had begun to burn.

"Sam," she said over her shoulder. "Talk to me. Distract me. I'm dying here. It's been, what, two hours since Gabriel left?"

Sam consulted his watch. "One hour, three minutes."

"Dear god."

"Time flies, huh?"

"I wish," Neva said, and then, to distract herself, she said, "You know, I've been wanting to ask how Reginald's doing."

"He's good. Boy's got a lot to learn, though."

"Such as?"

"How not to talk back, for one thing. He sasses his teachers sometimes, tells them when they're wrong about things. Boy's smart as a whip, so it turns out he's usually right and they're usually wrong, but that don't make it good manners. Plus he does love a good argument. You could say the sky is blue and he'd argue it's green, just for something to do. Must have driven his aunt crazy. He and Corinna, though, they're thick as thieves. Plus she hugs on him. He pretends it embarrasses him, but he loves it. Don't think he got too many hugs in his life. Or love, for that matter."

"Well, he's got plenty now. That's the important thing."

"Yes, ma'am," said Sam. "It is."

AT TRUMAN'S INVITATION Martin Choi arrived at the pool at seven fifteen. Truman met him in the killer whale office, as they'd agreed. As they walked from there across the back area to the holding pool, Truman said portentously, "Martin, the zoo and Friday need your help."

"Yeah?"

"We need you to tell the world this little whale's story." Truman stopped walking to turn and face Martin—who ran right into him, clanking with gear and robbing the moment of some of its intended theatricality. "Because here's the thing," Truman said, "We think chances are excellent that we're going to be accused of kidnapping this little whale so Friday can have a companion."

"Yeah? So that would be good. I mean, who wants to be alone, huh?"

"Yes, but we didn't do that." Truman felt the beginnings of a headache coming on. "This animal—this baby—was abandoned by his pod off San Juan Island because he had such severe injuries he couldn't keep up. He'd never be able to survive on his own."

"Bummer."

"Yes, it is. The point I'm trying to make is, we *rescued* him. That's key."

"Yeah, sure, I get that."

"Of course you do," said Truman. "That's why he needs you to be his voice, Martin. *His voice.* He's counting on you to tell his real story, because he can't."

"Well, yeah," said Martin. "So what do you think the big guy's going to think, having a little buddy?"

"We won't know until we've introduced them to each other."

"Yeah? Well, I think he's going to go out of his mind. The first whale he's seen in, what did you say?"

"Nineteen years."

"Nineteen years. How cool is that?"

"Very," said Truman. "Very cool." They were passing through several empty holding bays; Truman could see the small rehab pool ahead. "I should also tell you that there are some people out there"—and here Truman lowered his voice and shifted his eyes back and forth several times, as though someone might at this very moment be lurking nearby—"who

may even accuse us of maiming the animal on purpose, to jus-
tify keeping him."

Martin squinted. "Yeah? So, I mean, that would be bad."

"Very bad. And very not-true."

"Sure, yeah, I get that."

They had arrived at the pool. Libertine was in the water,
Ivy was perched on a wooden stool she'd scared up, and Julio
Iglesias sat reluctantly in her lap. She kissed the top of his head,
and his ears went flat with annoyance.

"Okay, let's introduce you two," Truman said to Martin
after greeting them. "Juan, this is Martin Choi. Martin, meet
Juan."

Libertine continued walking the calf around the perimeter
of the tank. When they came to Martin again, Truman handed
him a dive mask to hold up to his face. "If you put the mask just
under the surface, you'll see the injury clearly," said Truman,
as they'd rehearsed.

"Youch," said Martin when he saw the calf's flukes. "I bet
when he swims he just goes in a circle." Truman's headache
bloomed into full flower.

For the next forty-five minutes Martin Choi snapped photo
after photo, including some through the mask, which graphi-
cally showed the full extent of the calf's injuries. Then Gabriel
arrived and fed Juan his first dead fish—or so they told Martin,
though they'd actually primed the calf half an hour earlier with
a handful—and then a second and third and so on, until he'd
gone through a quarter of a bucket. "He was hungry," Truman
said, because with Martin Choi you could never overstate the
obvious.

"So that's good, right?" said the reporter.

"Very good," said Truman, and they all nodded as one.

Next, as they'd rehearsed, Libertine told Martin how much calmer the calf was now that he was in their care, and how frightened he'd been when he was drifting into the little bay by Ivy's house, forsaken and alone. "Here, he's safe," she concluded. "He knows that. And he has the entire zoo pulling for him. He knows that, too."

Then she lobbed the interview back to Truman for a final summation. "What you have to remember," he said, "is, this is a baby. Would you leave a badly injured human baby floating out there all alone?"

"Well, of course not," Martin said indignantly.

"And that's exactly what he needs you to tell the world. Be his hero, Martin," Truman intoned, channeling Matthew. "Be his hero."

IN THE PAPER'S Wednesday edition two days later, the *News-Tribune* led with a story about the killer whale calf. Headlined OH, BABY, BABY!, it detailed the calf's rescue, with emphasis on his otherwise hopeless plight. Incredibly, Truman found that Martin Choi had gotten most of the information right. The accompanying photos were graphic enough to make it clear that this maimed orphan wouldn't stand even a slim chance in the wild. The story was picked by the regional, national, and international wire services by noon.

Predictably, the Friends of Animals of the Sea responded that afternoon with an e-mail blast to its membership and the same media outlets that had picked up the story, titled (somewhat inscrutably, Truman thought) TWO WRONGS. The e-mail made the case that the zoo had cold-bloodedly captured a hapless calf for the sole purpose of exploitation as a companion animal for the imprisoned Friday and that the calf should have been left alone to perish naturally. The fact that that death would almost certainly have been a lonely, slow, and painful one brought on by sepsis, starvation, or both was not mentioned. Apparently such a death would be mitigated by the fact of its accomplishment in the beneficent bosom of Nature.

TWO DAYS LATER once Gabriel was sure the antibiotics they were giving Juan had taken hold, they moved the calf into Friday's medical pool. Although a watertight gate separated the two whales, Friday hovered there all day, spy-hopping again and again to see over the top. His visitors complained that they couldn't see him, and neither Neva nor Gabriel could engage Friday in a work session, not even an innovative one. He wouldn't even eat until they resorted to feeding him beside the med pool. He sang, whistled, clicked, and trilled at the calf in a long and constant song. And the calf sang back.

"Can they understand each other?" Neva asked Gabriel, who was tossing in fish every time Friday opened his mouth. "I mean, they speak different languages, don't they?"

"That's a little simplistic, but yes, something like that."

"What do you mean?" asked Ivy, who was watching Libertine feed Juan on the other side of the watertight partition. The calf was a voracious eater, opening his mouth wide anytime someone appeared, with or without a bucket. Gabriel suspected that the calf had been weak even before it was injured.

"Friday is an Atlantic whale, and Juan is from the Pacific," Gabriel said. "We know there's such a thing as killer whale dialects because even within the Pacific population, transient whales have different calls than resident ones. We don't know exactly how much they overlap, or even if there *is* any overlap between Atlantic and Pacific animals. But Friday will teach the kid what he needs to know so they can communicate. Right now, he's so excited he may not be communicating anything besides a ton of variations of 'Ooh!' "

"Can you imagine?" said Truman. "For Friday, it must feel just like Christmas."

They had decided to document the entire introduction process with a video camera. Libertine, their self-appointed videographer, popped out from behind a camera on a tripod and said, "He's like a little kid. He keeps asking, *When? When? When?* over and over."

"Tell him it'll be soon," said Gabriel. "As soon as it's safe."

That afternoon, at least one day ahead of plan, Gabriel decided to lower a metal grid between the pools in place of the solid, watertight gate. That way, Friday and Juan would have visual as well as auditory contact. With the video camera rolling, they watched Friday lay his entire body along the grid separating the two pools, his eye staring through to the calf. At first the calf was hesitant, but after a few minutes he approached Friday, laying his side against Friday's.

And then, abruptly, Friday turned around and left.

"What's he doing? Hey! Don't leave," Neva called, dismayed.

Both Gabriel and Libertine were smiling. "Just wait," said Gabriel. "Watch him."

Friday swam all the way across the pool, where he rounded up his blue ball. Then he pushed it back until it bumped up against the gate.

"Is he bringing it to Juan?" Neva asked Gabriel.

"Can't we let the little one into the main pool?" Libertine asked.

"Not yet," said Gabriel. "We have all the time in the world. I don't want to go too fast and have to net the calf to get him back into the med pool."

"Why would you have to do that?" Neva asked.

"Look, he's not a puppy. You're assuming these two will get along, but it's also plausible that Friday will look at him as a competitor for the pool's resources—for food, attention, toys, or anything else Friday values."

"But he brought him his blue ball, for god's sake!" said Ivy. "His most coveted possession!"

"You're seeing it as a generous gesture. It's equally possible that he's showing it to the calf to make sure he knows he's got dibs on it."

"So you think Friday might actually be aggressive toward him? There's no reason to think he'd hurt him, is there?" Neva asked.

"No—if there were, we wouldn't have brought him down here," said Gabriel, "but it's within the realm of possibility. Anytime you get two animals together, there's some risk, especially when it's two males. All I'm saying is, let's not hurry. Let's give them a chance to get used to each other gradually. You don't want Friday to be alone anymore, and I get that, but he's already not. They can see each other. They can hear each other."

Ivy huffed impatiently, but she didn't challenge him.

FOR TWO DAYS and nights Friday rarely left the gate that separated him from the calf. He vocalized continuously through all his waking hours. Even a screening of The Day After Tomorrow, a movie he loved, failed to tear him away. A hydrophone in the pool recorded not only Friday's vocalizations, but also the calf's. By the morning of the third day, some of the vocalizations synched up. The calf was learning Friday's calls.

It was time to remove the gate.

As Gabriel choreographed it, they would let the two whales meet right after the gallery closed for the day, so they'd have as much time as possible to interact without visitors looking on. No one expected it to go badly, but YouTube was full of animal encounters gone wrong, and Truman had expressed a certain amount of concern that the two killer whales might join their ranks. So at seven fifteen that evening, Ivy, Gabriel, Libertine, Neva, Truman, Sam, Winslow, and Reginald all gathered on the pool top. There was an air of barely controlled expectation. Gabriel brought up two full buckets of fish, sent Neva to the opposite side of the pool with one bucket, and kept the other at the gate between the two pools.

On his signal, Libertine started the hydraulics that lifted the gate.

No one spoke as the gate started to move. The only sounds were the creaking equipment and the whales' breathing. Even Julio Iglesias stayed stock still in Ivy's arms.

Friday took a deep breath and sank below the waterline.

Sam, positioned in the gallery, transmitted, "Friday's going into the med pool. I can only see half his body."

"He's just rubbed his head along the calf's side," Neva announced from her radio beside the med pool. "He's moving really slowly, like he doesn't want to hurt him or scare him or anything."

Then they all heard it, even in the gallery: a high, thin, sustained duet. Ivy, standing beside Gabriel at the near end of the pool, grasped his arm tightly and whispered, "Oh my god."

With infinite gentleness, Friday backed out of the med pool, drawing the calf out with him until they were through. Once they were in the deep water, Juan slipped below and just off of Friday's right side—what would normally be his swimming position beside an adult female. Friday swam very slowly, very deliberately, barely moving his flukes. Despite his injuries, the calf was able to keep up.

"What are they doing?" Ivy asked Gabriel.

"Watch," Gabriel said. "Friday is showing him the pool."

Once the big whale had taken the calf around the pool's perimeter, he brought him to the bottom, where they swam around the rock work and along the gallery windows. "You got to see this," Sam transmitted. "It's like they're attached. Friday's going real slow, too, so the little one can look around."

Together, the whales continued their explorations until the calf began to flag and a thin trail of blood seeped into the water from his damaged flukes. Friday brought him to his favorite corner of the pool, leaving him there while he swam to his blue ball, which had fetched up onto the broad slide-out area of the wet walk. By creating turbulence with his pectoral flipper, he coaxed the ball closer and closer until it was near enough for him to move it with his nose. As the entire staff watched, Friday swam the ball across the pool to the calf, placing it by his cheek. Then he began to sing, the notes rising into the air, sweet, joyful, and pure. "Ladies and gentlemen," said Truman over the security radio, after having to clear his throat twice, "I believe it's time to alert the media."

Epilogue

IT WOULD BE early the next fall before the zoo was clear of film crews, reporters, VIPs, and journalists. Juan became an overnight golden child, faithfully attended by Friday, his constant companion, protector, and teacher, and thrilling visitors and media around the world. Within the calf's first two months at the zoo, photographs of him and Friday were on the front page of magazines and newspapers around the world, and went viral on the Internet. Visitors came back time after time, many from considerable distances. In elaborate games of Simon Says, Friday taught Juan not only his repertoire of behaviors, but how to play and pose in front of the gallery windows, to the mutual delight of whales and visitors.

Gabriel backed off Friday's training schedule; each whale had the other for companionship, and Gabriel told Truman he didn't see the need for training anymore, beyond keeping basic medical and husbandry behaviors sharp so the keepers could draw blood and weigh and examine them as needed. The staff continued to conduct innovative sessions—you can do anything you want, but you can't do the same behavior twice—because the whales seemed to enjoy them so much. Friday and Juan often played the game as a team, each riffing on what the other dreamed up, sillier and sillier and sillier.

Truman often visited the pool. One day, Gabriel called him on the radio and asked him to come over, meeting him with a pair of XtraTufs, a dog whistle, and a bucket of fish.

"Go ahead," he told Truman, clanking the handle on the bucket of fish to summon the whales.

"What?"

"Go ahead—take the session," Gabriel said. "Ask them to do something." When Truman hesitated, he said, "Come on, you've watched, what, about a thousand of these sessions by now. Ask him something—you know all the signals."

And so Truman drew his guns, feeling ridiculous until the whales responded to the command for innovative behavior, Friday with a tongue loll, the calf with a vertical spin. They came up with new behaviors for ten minutes straight.

"Feed them the whole bucket," Gabriel instructed him. "You want to reward them for working for you, especially since it's your first time."

Truman fed them fish after fish. When the bucket was empty, Gabriel said, "Okay. There's something I want to talk to you about."

"Uh-oh," said Truman. "Here it comes."

Gabriel nodded. "It's time. I'd planned to leave months ago, but then Juan came along."

"I assume I can't talk you out of it," said Truman.

"No—it's time for me to move on."

Truman felt his stomach tighten, though he'd known for months that this day would come. "What will you do?"

"I haven't decided yet. There are a couple of projects I'm interested in, in the wild," Gabriel said.

"Had enough of the zoo life?"

"I've never been the go-to-the-office-every-morning kind of guy. This is the longest I've ever worked anywhere."

Truman regarded this man, whom he'd come to deeply respect, and who had kept them from running up on the shoals of their own inexperience and naïveté time after time. "We'll miss you. You know you have a place here anytime. What's your time frame?"

"I'd like to be gone in a couple of weeks. The staff's ready—they don't need me anymore. You'll want to hire one more person, and for what it's worth, I'd promote Neva to senior killer whale keeper. She's got all the right skills, and I trust her intuition."

"And Libertine?"

Gabriel grinned. "She's great, especially for a kookaboo. Keep her as long as you can."

"She'd be very proud to know you said that," said Truman.

He gave Neva the news that night. "I have to admit it makes me nervous," he said. "I don't know how we'd have gotten to this point without him."

"We wouldn't have," said Neva. "But we'll be fine. And if we're not, we know his phone number."

IN LATE OCTOBER Ivy made one last trip to Bladenham on her way to Cairo. She took Libertine to the Oat Maiden for lunch. "How's that kitten—what's his name again?"

"Winken," said Libertine. "We bring him in sometimes. We're just hoping that the health inspector doesn't make a surprise visit. If he does, our plan is to pop him into the dirty-linen hamper."

"Does Julio Iglesias torment him?" The dog lived with Libertine full time now, after one last stay with Ivy, during which he peed on her new down sofa and ottoman, turned a small hole in the vinyl kitchen floor into a much bigger hole, and bit the Achilles tendon of a gardener who'd come to take care of Ivy's yard.

"Oh, no, not at all," Libertine said. "The two of them are thick as thieves. They sleep together almost every night. Plus naps. We got them a bed big enough for them both to curl up in. Who would have guessed it'd take a cat to gentle him? He's a different dog now."

"You're kidding," Ivy said flatly.

"He even goes through the cat-tube to the house if I give him a boost onto the counter first. Johnson Johnson's going to build him some stairs."

Ivy looked hard at Libertine until she blushed. "What?"

"You like him a lot, don't you?"

"Winken?"

"Johnson Johnson."

Libertine pinked up. "He's a very good man."

"To say nothing of unusual," Ivy said, grinning.

Libertine smiled, too. "He is. But then I'm not exactly main-stream." She stirred her cold coffee for a long beat. "Are you looking forward to this trip?"

"Yes and no. It's time to get away."

"And you do have friends there?"

Ivy reached across the table to pat Libertine's hand. "You worry too much. I'll be fine. Egypt is like a second home to me; I'm not going into exile. Is that what you're worrying about?"

"Yes."

"Well, don't."

Libertine nodded and then said softly, "Do you think we'll ever see Gabriel again?"

"I have to say, you're in a peculiar state of mind."

"I don't do well with change," Libertine admitted. "Or loss."

"Who are you losing?"

Libertine pointed across the table at Ivy. "I'll miss you," she said. "So much."

"Find me in your head."

Libertine smiled tearily. "I think we'll have to rely on Skype."

Ivy patted her hand. "Then we'll Skype. Maybe you can come over sometime."

"Maybe." They both knew she wouldn't. Libertine's life and work were here in Bladenham now, and tickets overseas were expensive.

And then it was time to go.

They parted at Ivy's car with one last, hard hug. Just as she pulled away from the curb, Ivy opened the passenger side window and called, "Hey!"

Libertine turned back.

"We did fall in love, you know. In case you missed it."

And then she was gone.

As LIBERTINE WENT back inside the Oat Maiden, she fervently wished for Ivy a life as rich and filled with purpose as her own had become. She couldn't imagine going back to her old life before Friday. In the past few months she'd begun diving regularly to help keep Friday's pool clean. She'd gotten a raise. Neva was teaching her signals and how to run Friday's workout sessions—she was inordinately proud that she had her own whistle now, which she used to signal Friday or Juan that they'd followed an instruction correctly. She worked alongside Johnson Johnson at the café in the evenings as well as on her days off, and often stayed in his house overnight. Now she paused in the café's kitchen doorway for a moment, taking in Winken curled up beneath the pizza oven where the bricks were warm; taking in Johnson Johnson, whose back was to the door, spooning freshly made cookie dough onto industrial-sized cookie sheets. And standing there, surrounded by aromas, flavors, and things she loved, she contemplated the meaning of blessings—the gifts that come to us when we have given up expecting them; the elasticity and courage of the soul. Friday had not found her because he needed her. He had found her because she needed him.

And somehow, though she hadn't made a sound, Johnson Johnson must have sensed that she was there because he came to her, cupping his warm hands over her ears until the only thing she could hear was the sound of her own heart.

About the author

About the book

Insights,
Interviews
& More...

Read on

Meet Diane Hammond

Delaney Andrews

DIANE HAMMOND is the author of four published novels: *Hannah's Dream, Seeing Stars, Going to Bend,* and *Homesick Creek,* all set primarily in the Pacific Northwest. A recipient of an Oregon Arts Commission literary grant, she made Oregon her home from 1984 to 2011, except for brief stints in Tacoma, Washington, and Los Angeles. She worked in public relations for twenty-five years, most recently acting as media liaison and spokesperson for Keiko, the killer whale star of the hit movie *Free Willy*. Then, after owning her own website design company for a dozen years, she shut down her business in spring 2011 and moved to St. Paul, Minnesota, where she and her husband share their home with three Pembroke Welsh corgis and a cat. ᔕ

A Killer Whale
Love Story

IF YOU WERE ALIVE between 1996 and
1998, and especially if you spent any
of those years in the Pacific Northwest,
you may remember Keiko, the wild-
caught killer whale star of the hit
movie *Free Willy*. In failing health
after eighteen years in a small, hot pool
at an amusement park in Mexico City,
Keiko was transported to a facility built
exclusively for him at the Oregon Coast
Aquarium. From the minute he arrived
to the moment he left two years later,
the international press reported almost
daily on some achievement, antic, or
controversy coming out of the project
to rehabilitate and then release him back
to the wild. He was a media sensation.

As the killer whale's full-time press
secretary, I witnessed his amazing
recovery at the hands of a small group
of men and women who spent hours
each day swimming with him in a pool
so cold that hypothermia was always a
danger. Day in and day out, in all kinds
of weather—most of it bad—these
dedicated people kept him company
for up to eighteen hours a day, inventing
regimens, games, and toys to challenge
his mind and body. By the time he
left Oregon for Iceland, Keiko was a
masterpiece of buff muscle and fierce
vitality. He departed as he had arrived,
in a cloud of controversy over the
morality of keeping whales and
dolphins in captivity.

As it turned out, Keiko would be ▶

my only killer whale, or at least my only real one—I took down my PR shingle for good a few months after his departure. Exhausted from the intensity of the previous two years, I tried to sort out the experience by doing what I always do—I wrote about it, creating scores of vignettes loosely based on the project's defining moments, and especially on Keiko as I'd come to know him—sly, silly, charismatic, winsome, affectionate, and, most of all, resilient.

Fast-forward to summer 2010, after the release of my fourth book, *Seeing Stars,* a novel about child actors in Hollywood. My editor and agent proposed that I next write a sequel to my third and most successful novel, *Hannah's Dream.* Always one for a challenge, I cast around for a meaningful story that would take me back to Bladenham, Washington, its tiny Max L. Biedelman Zoo, and the characters I and my readers had come to love.

After lots of false starts I decided to retool those rough vignettes I'd written so long ago, giving the fictional Max L. Biedelman Zoo and killer whale Friday some of Keiko's real-world qualities and dilemmas. I also decided to enlarge the circle of characters I'd introduced in *Hannah's Dream* with brand-new characters who would do much of this book's heavy lifting: Ivy Levy, Truman Levy's aunt and eccentric heiress; Julio Iglesias, Ivy's passive-aggressive Chihuahua; Libertine Adagio, a gentle little animal psychic; and Gabriel Jump, maverick and marine mammal rehabber.

As I once again started from scratch, I finally felt I was headed in the right direction—in fact, I was surprised at the ease with which I was able to move between the fictional and the actual. In my fictional world, as in the actual one, the morality of keeping whales and dolphins captive was polarizing; in my fictional world, as in the actual one, both sides believed absolutely in the rightness of their convictions and in the actions by which they expressed them. In the fictional world, as in the actual one, supremely dedicated people worked tirelessly to enrich the life of an animal unable to do so on his own behalf.

As with *Hannah's Dream*, it is my hope that readers will recognize that *Friday's Harbor* is, at its core, a love story. ✃

Reading Group Guide

1. As the story goes, nobody in Bogotá knows or remembers how Friday got his name—Viernes. According to the oft-quoted nursery rhyme, "Friday's child is loving and giving." What does Friday end up giving to the other characters in the novel?

2. Can Libertine really exchange thoughts with animals? It's been said that animals can sense storms and other natural disasters before they happen, and can even tell when we humans are sick. Do you think humans and animals can communicate? On what level?

3. What do you think is the difference between the sixth sense Gabriel has for animals, the psychic bond that Libertine shares with animals, and the deep friendship that Sam develops with animals? With whom do you relate most closely?

4. Neva says it best: Gabriel is an enigma. To some he may even seem to be a contradiction. He has such a deep, abiding love for marine mammals, and yet he has captured more than forty whales, including calves. How do you think he reconciles his love of animals with his aiding in their captivity?

5. When Neva asks Libertine if she ever wishes she couldn't sense animals, Libertine replies, "All the time." Why do you think this is? What

would cause her to want to give up her gift?

6. Libertine and Ivy could not be more different in their temperaments, backgrounds, and beliefs. And yet they form a very important friendship. How is it that they can find common ground?

7. Friday has a happy life in Bladenham—much better than it was before—but he is alone in the sense that there are no other killer whales around him. How does the theme of loneliness pervade the other characters' personal narratives?

8. Neva is known as the easygoing free spirit, and Truman is the sensible (sometimes uptight) one in their relationship. In what ways do you think having Friday around—and eventually swimming with him—has been good for Truman? Taking Friday in was a big risk. Was it the right choice?

9. One of the VIPs who visit Friday is an aging musician who is well past his prime. Could this be a metaphor? Why is this moment so emotional for all of those who bear witness?

10. Juan's rescue was a total surprise that brought many unexpected lessons. What did each of the characters learn from Juan's plight and eventual adoption? ⌒

Excerpt from
Hannah's Dream

IN THE FALL OF 1995, the elephant
barn was a shabby place despite a fresh
interior coat of yellow paint. A lack of
insulation made the damp a perpetual
intruder, and the high, uninsulated
ceiling and soaring hay loft gave the
place a hollow feel. It was also outfitted
with a small kitchen; a tiny office; an
open space furnished like a living room
with a couple of inexpensive armchairs,
end tables, stacked TV trays, and a
big-screen television; and Hannah's
confinement area at the back. "Hey, baby
girl," Sam said softly when he reached
the back of the barn. "How's my sugar?"

Hannah lifted her trunk and rumbled
a greeting, the same greeting she'd given
him almost every day for the last forty-
one years.

"How was your night? You hear
that thunderstorm come through?
God almighty, Mama nearly jumped
out of bed it scared her so bad. Big
woman like her scared of thunder,
that's a sorry thing. Here, look what
Papa brought you."

Sam took the donuts from the
Dunkin' Donuts bag and lined them
up lovingly on the sill of the one tiny
window in Hannah's barn. Hannah
investigated each one, inhaling delicately,
exhaling small puffs of powdered sugar.
"Go ahead, sugar. They're those custards
you like. Plus a strawberry jelly. I swear,
it was all I could do to keep my fingers
out of that bag. I'd have done it, too, if

I didn't think Mama would catch me."
Sam chuckled. "But she always does
catch me, I don't know how. When the
Lord made that woman he must have
given her supernatural powers."

While Hannah ate her donuts, Sam
eased down beside her left front foot
and unhooked the heavy chain from its
shackle. The anklet had worn away the
skin underneath and sometimes there
were open sores. Not today.

"Let Papa have a look at that foot,
sugar." Hannah lifted her foot. Max
Biedelman had told him an elephant's
toenails should be smooth and the
cuticle soft and close-fitting, but two
of Hannah's bulged, foul-smelling from
sores underneath; another had a split
that Sam had been watching for signs
of trouble. His girl had started getting
arthritic ten years ago or more, from
never having anything soft to stand on,
and the more arthritic she got, the more
she walked funny, and the funnier she
walked, the more unevenly she wore
down her foot pads, which put uneven
pressure on her toenails, which busted.
Sam spent so much time caring for
Hannah's feet that he told Corinna
sometimes he might hire himself
out as a pedicurist at the Beauty
Spot, Corinna's beauty salon.

Now he dug in his pocket and pulled
out a small plastic jar of salve. "Let's
try this, sugar. Mama made this one
up specially for you last night." Sam
had a bad foot, too, with a diabetic
ulcer the size of a chicken wing along
one side of his heel, so Corinna was
always whipping up some new healing ▶

concoction in the kitchen. If it yielded any improvement, no matter how slight, Sam would bring it in the next day and slather some on Hannah's poor feet. Nothing ever really worked, but it made him and Corinna feel better, having something to try. Sam fished out a tongue depressor from a box he'd bought with his own money from a medical supply store in Tacoma, and used it like a paddle to apply the ointment. Hannah flinched but stayed put, like she always did. It nearly broke his heart. He patted her on the shoulder.

"Okay, shug, that's done—you can put your foot down. You ready to go outside on this fine sunny day?" It was early September, when Bladenham smelled of apple orchards and harvested fields. "You bringing your tire with you?" Hannah picked up an old, bald car tire she liked to keep nearby, especially when she was alone. Corinna said it was no different than those shreds of baby blankets that some kids kept with them for comfort, and Sam guessed she was right. He watched Hannah amble outside, blinking in the sudden sunshine after the barn's dim interior, before he climbed up into the hayloft. He loved the smell of clean fresh hay in the fall, always had. It reminded him of Yakima when growing season was over and new crops were still a season away. Quiet time; healing time. Every year his father's hands had bled from early spring clear through November— working hands like Sam's now, only his didn't ever heal, especially now, what with the diabetes. He knew what his daddy would say about that. *Sick or well, you take care of what you got to take care of. Ain't no such thing as a day off when it comes to living things.* He'd meant crops, not elephants, but it was just the same. Eustace Brown had worked right up until the day he'd dropped; died in his bib overalls, the way he'd have liked it.

Sam pitchforked some fresh hay down into the yard. Hannah shambled over, propping her tire against the barn wall in the exact same spot she always did, and began to eat. He loved to watch the way she pinched up a switch of hay with her trunk, tucked it inside her mouth, and chewed as slow and deliberate as if her thoughts were a million miles away. In Burma maybe, in those teak forests Max Biedelman had used to tell him about; the place where shug was born. ∿

More from
Diane Hammond

For forty-one years, Samson Brown has been caring for Hannah, the lone elephant at the down-at-the-heels Max L. Biedelman Zoo. Having vowed not to retire until an equally loving and devoted caretaker is found to replace him, Sam rejoices when he meets the smart, compassionate Neva Wilson— the new elephant keeper. But the two soon realize that Hannah's health is deteriorating and she is lonely, and they must band together to do whatever they can to save their beloved baby girl.

"Featuring a cast of endearingly quirky characters . . . this charming story enchants and provides . . . lighthearted and poignant moments."

—*Library Journal*

More from Diane Hammond *(continued)*

SEEING STARS

Ruth believes that her daughter, Bethany, is a terrific little actress. And if Bethany wants to leave the Pacific Northwest for Los Angeles and a merry-go-round of auditions, classes, and callbacks—well, Ruth will lead the way. Hollywood, of course, eats people like Ruth and Bethany for breakfast. Surrounded by other aspiring child stars, stage mothers, managers, and talent agents, Ruth and Bethany will discover just how far they can go, and maybe just how far they want to.

Don't miss the next book by your favorite author. Sign up now for AuthorTracker by visiting www.AuthorTracker.com.